Raven plunged forward an
He fell heavily, his right le ... him. The other two
youths were onto him like dogs. One hit him on the neck
below his right ear. Dazed, he fell back on the ground.

Elena raised a hand to hit out and the youth smacked the side of
her face. As she reeled back, he grabbed her dress. It ripped
down the back and came away from her body, together with her
flimsy satin bra, leaving her naked to the waist.

The faces above Raven were blurred in the darkness. He smelt
their sweat and breath that stank of alcohol. In one last effort, he
twisted, turned and kicked. Then he was hit again, with a bottle.
Before he blacked out, he felt the boots on his head and neck and
groin.

Sharp stones pierced Elena's naked back as she lay on the
ground, legs splayed. Blood filled her mouth from the blow to
her face. Pinioned, unable to fight any more, she welcomed the
pain, because it distracted at least part of her mind from what
was happening to her . . .

HIDALGO

Kate Denver

CORGI BOOKS

HIDALGO
A CORGI BOOK 0 552 13291 8

First publication in Great Britain

PRINTING HISTORY

Corgi edition published 1988

This book is set in 10/11 Plantin

Corgi Books are published by Transworld Publishers Ltd., 61-63 Uxbridge Road, Ealing, London W5 5SA, in Australia by Transworld Publishers (Australia) Pty. Ltd., 15-23 Helles Avenue, Moorebank, NSW 2170, and in New Zealand by Transworld Publishers (N.Z.) Ltd., Cnr. Moselle and Waipareira Avenues, Henderson, Auckland.

Printed and bound in Great Britain by
Cox & Wyman Ltd., Reading, Berks.

To Alan, Nicola, Lynn and Katy

Part 1

The Present

[illegible] the daily [illegible]

[illegible] understood the [illegible]

[illegible] on a trolley [illegible]

1

Passengers who had arrived on the daily champagne shuttle from Paris passed through the small Spanish airport without pausing even to collect their Vuitton trunks and Lark suiters from the carousel. It was understood that the irritating formalities endured by ordinary travellers could be ignored by members of the San Felipe Club, whose uniformed minions were already carrying the luggage to a Mercedes van which stood outside. Its owners had only to tuck themselves into a fleet of air-conditioned, chauffeur-driven Cadillacs, one to each individual or couple travelling together. Cocooned by wealth, they were moved, like spoiled babies, to the next stop in their search for pleasure.

Two overalled porters leant on trolleys, watching them sourly. The Club's servants made their own pickings poor. They would have done better from the package-deal tourists who poured into the village off the bus from Malaga Airport.

The last passenger had slid into his limousine, most of the luggage had been stowed into the van, when a young woman came into the terminal from the apron. A lingering Club employee glanced at her questioningly, but she shook her head. The younger porter, new to San Felipe, brightened.

She was as elegant as any other woman from the shuttle, wearing a sleeveless yellow silk dress which clung around her full breasts and slim legs; high-heeled yellow sandals; a Gucci overnight bag slung over her shoulder. But there was something subtly different about her: the varnish was missing. She wore no make-up, apart from a touch of green eye-shadow, and needed none. Her shoulder-length dark hair was wind-ruffled, her bare arms and legs were tanned. And, in contrast with the Americans, Germans, Scandinavians and British who had preceded her, she was unmistakably Spanish: shorter than average, her figure curved, her skin olive-tinted, her eyes brown and lustrous.

As she paused, the younger porter started forward. At least, she would want a taxi. He was stopped by a warning gesture from his companion.

A man had parked a white Porsche in a 'No Parking' bay directly outside the entrance. He came through the swing doors towards the girl. He appeared to be in his early fifties, above medium height, with the broad-shouldered, tapering body of an athlete. Blue eyes were startling under dark, circumflex eyebrows. His thick hair was streaked with silver-grey, and he had a smooth, permanent sun-tan. His light grey trousers were tucked into hand-made suede boots and he carried a wide-brimmed Cordoban hat.

As they stood, a foot apart, facing each other, they were a spectacularly good-looking couple, transcending any age-difference. For a moment, it was as though time paused, and even the porters were aware of tension between them. Then they heard her say, 'I'm glad you're here.' He smiled, put a hand on her arm and guided her towards the car.

The young porter expelled his breath in a sigh. 'A woman like that . . .!'

'You know who the man is, don't you?'

He shook his head.

'It's Senor Maxwell Raven. You work for him.'

'I work for the airport.'

'If it wasn't for him, there wouldn't be an airport. He owns you, me and just about everyone else around here. He owns the Club, the apartments, the hotels, shops, casinos, maybe even Senora Zimmy's.'

The other grinned. He knew Zimmy's by repute, if not personally. The girls were too expensive for the likes of him.

'Who's the woman? His daughter?'

'As far as I know, *El Hidalgo* doesn't have any daughters. Not from his wives, anyway. She's probably his latest *putana*. They say he changes them as often as he changes his shirt.' He paused, then said thoughtfully, 'But I've seen that one before.'

They watched the Porsche disappear into the warm dusk, heading for the highway.

Raven parked near a stand of umbrella pines at the top of a hill, overlooking San Felipe del Mar. His arm rested along the back of Elena Ansaldo's seat. Below the car, a few rock-strewn hectares of land known as the Campo Negro sloped down to the outskirts of the village.

To their right were the greens and fairways of the San Felipe Club's golf-course, and between it and a curved, brown-sand beach, the Club itself. In the deepening darkness, it was already brilliantly lit and they could see the colonnaded arcade of luxury shops and restaurants reserved for Club members; the tennis courts and sports centre; the casino; the guest-villas, each with its own swimming-pool. Dominating the complex, with steps leading onto the private beach, was a U-shaped club-house, built around a court-yard where green lawns were broken by pools, fountains, palm-trees, flower-beds and tiled patios, sheltered by vines, which led off the ground-floor suites.

Elena's eyes travelled on, past Max Raven's white mansion, where few lights showed as yet, over the high stone wall and bank of trees which separated it from her own family home. Once the Ansaldo place had dominated the village, but for years it had been dwarfed by the Club and Raven's house. The wall between the two houses was topped by shards of broken glass.

The village beach was cut off from the Club's by a rocky headland. Three fishing-boats were drawn up on it and nets were stretched on the sand to dry. A few years ago there would have been five times as many boats, but now there were more profitable enterprises in San Felipe.

The village itself was brighter than she remembered. Its steep, winding alleys, converging on the Plaza San Juna, were outlined by lights. She could make out garish, winking neons, and the Plaza was a yellow pool in which small tadpole-like figures moved.

At the far end of the village beach was another sloping headland on which stood the Civil War Memorial, a square plinth bearing a tall granite pyramid. When she left San Felipe, the Memorial had terminated the built-up area. Beyond it, the coastline curved around a third beach, which had then been backed by rough, sandy grassland punctuated by wind-swept trees. Now the trees had been replaced by tall apartment blocks which stretched as far as she could see along the coast.

She gestured towards them. 'It's quite a kingdom, but they don't enhance the landscape.'

'They give hundreds of people a chance to enjoy the kind of life in the sun they couldn't otherwise afford, at least for a couple of weeks in the year.'

She raised her eyebrows. 'Don't tell me you've turned into a philanthropist, Max.'

'Not at all. They're also profitable.'

'What do you do next? Or have you completed your – improvements?'

'I have a few more ideas.' His eyes were intent on her and she was reminded of his ability to concentrate totally on the person in whose company he was, focusing his charm like a spotlight. It was a facet of his character which had led many a woman to his bed.

She left the car and walked to a flat picnic area with concrete tables and benches. Litter lay around over-flowing rubbish bins. The breeze coming off the sea was warm and it blew her dress against her body, outlining the curves. Raven followed her. 'How long can you stay?'

'I haven't decided.'

He glanced around as they heard hoarse singing coming from the highway behind them. 'Drunks,' he said.

'When I was a child there were no drunks here. No drunks, no traffic, no litter.'

'Why have you come back?'

'You haven't heard about Alex?'

'How would I? The Ravens and the Ansaldos don't make a habit of exchanging family gossip.'

The drunken singing stopped. Footsteps sounded on the tarmac.

'What about your husband?'

She hesitated, then said, 'Max, I wanted to see you first because . . .'

As she searched for the words she wanted, other sounds entered the silence. Three young men were peering into the Porsche.

They stepped back guiltily as Raven reached them. 'What the hell d'you think you're doing?' He spoke English automatically. They could have come from nowhere else, with their rainbow hair, torn jeans and collarless shirts. From the bottom of their trousers, like a cartoon drawing, protruded heavy Doc Marten boots.

'Nothing, mate. Lovely wheels.' The accent was thick and adenoidal.

'Get going!'

'We didn't mean no harm.' It was a whine. 'Only, you got any money? We've run out.'

'I don't carry money.'

'He don't carry money!' The speaker was a short, thickset youth. The others were taller. One of them raised a wine-bottle to his lips, draining the last mouthful. They were about nineteen or twenty years old. 'That's like our Queen. She never carries money, neither. Got anything to drink, then?'

'You can get what you want in the village.'

A car's headlights, coming up the hill, spotlighted Elena for a moment, before passing on.

'Jesus, look at that!' the shorter boy breathed.

She backed away as he moved towards her. Her high heels wobbled on the uneven surface and she almost fell. In two strides he had caught her and was clutching her wrist. 'Where you going, darling? We won't harm yer.'

Raven plunged forward and was tripped by an out-thrust boot. He fell heavily, his right leg twisted under him. The other two youths were onto him like dogs. One hit him on the neck below his right ear. Dazed, he fell back on the ground.

Elena raised a hand to hit out and her tormentor smacked the side of her face. 'Don't you try that with me!' She reeled back. He grabbed her dress. It ripped down the back and came away from her body, together with her flimsy satin bra, leaving her naked to the waist.

He pushed her, and as she fell, she caught a glimpse of a shadow under the trees. Another youth was standing there, watching.

The faces above Raven were blurred in the darkness. He smelt their sweat and breath that stank of alcohol. He heard one of them say, 'Get her pants off!'

Then Elena screamed.

'Leave her alone!' he shouted. 'I'll give you money! I'll . . .'

'Too late, dad!'

A picture flashed into his mind of another girl's naked, violated body. She had been little more than a child, scarcely older than himself, and the sight had recurred in his nightmares for years.

In one last effort, he twisted, turned, kicked. Then he was hit again, with a bottle. Before he blacked out, he felt the boots on his head and neck and groin.

Sharp stones pierced Elena's naked back as she lay on the ground, legs splayed. Blood filled her mouth from the blow on her face. Pinioned, unable to fight any more, she welcomed the pain, because it distracted at least part of her mind from what was happening. She heard words which, at the time, meant nothing to her.

Damp hands crawled over her body, and as he thrust into her, she was aware of his smell.

Where was Max? She tried to scream again, could manage only a bubbling moan. When she struggled she felt the edge of a stone cut into her skin and the youth's movements became more urgent. She realised that her writhing excited him, and lay still. Turning her head to the side to avoid the sight of him, she saw Max, sprawled like a fallen tree, and knew there would be no help from him. She clung to the thought that it would end, that nothing was being done to her that had not been done before.

It seemed to be hours before he raised himself, but even then there was no respite. His place was taken by a second youth, who pressed his mouth to her breasts. Later, she realised that she must have lost consciousness, because when she came to, she was straddled by the third, who was trying to kiss her lips. It sickened her even more than the act of rape, and her reaction was instinctive: she closed her teeth viciously on his mouth. The last thing she heard was a howl, then he hit her and her head cracked against the stones.

A goat-herd found the two bodies the next morning as he was driving his animals down towards the village for milking.

Seeing them gather near a stand of trees a few yards from the picnic site, he went towards them, slipping a stone into the sling-shot he used to control them.

Then he saw the man and woman, lying sprawled, side by side, where they had been dragged so they would not be visible from the highway. There was blood on their faces and bodies. The woman was naked, apart from a strip of yellow silk around her waist.

As he knelt beside them, the man groaned, and turned his head so his face could be seen. The goat-herd recognised him and set off for the village as fast as he could, driving his animals ahead of him with blows and shouts.

2

Paul Raven stood by his father's hospital bed. Max's eyes were closed. His skin was lined and slack, pale under the tan. Although his hair was more dark than grey, the forty-eight hour beard was white. He looked an exhausted man, still handsome, but vulnerable as Paul had never seen him. Then his eyelids fluttered. He blinked twice and the vivid blue eyes focused. In spite of his injuries, the power was still there. Paul was conscious of relief and a resurgence of the affection he had once felt for his father.

'How long have you been here?'

No greeting. No 'thanks for coming.' No 'welcome, my son.' Paul sighed. Same old Max.

'I've just arrived. I came straight from the airport. How are you?'

'I'll be okay. You've heard what happened?'

'Doctor Sanchez told me. Bloody dreadful. Have they got them?'

'No. And they won't. Three hundred package tourists left early yesterday. There's no way now of tracing them.'

'Sanchez said you think they were English.'

'I don't think. I know.'

'Have the police in England been told?'

'What could they do? Even if I could identify the bastards – which I can't – we'd never get them back. Anyway, I don't want any publicity. This country's image is bad enough already. ETA bombs have been planted in several resorts, and even here there's been violence. We've had fist-fights, rapes, some of the local boys have taken to carrying knives. This worries me more than an attack by a few drunken English yobs. We're going to have to do something about it, and I aim to set up a meeting with the police as soon as I can.' He paused. 'Good thing it happened to me and not one of the guests. If the story got out we'd be facing dozens of cancellations. We're only just living down that accident a couple of years ago.'

'The balcony that collapsed? I read about it in London.'

'Two men killed, due to a bloody contractor who used faulty cement. I had the place rebuilt, but the tour-operators were wary of us for months.'

'So you're going to let this go? Forget it? For a few extra pesetas? Jesus, Max! And Sanchez said you were with a girl. What about her?'

'I can assure you, she and her family will be only too happy to have it hushed up. Didn't Sanchez tell you about her?'

'I didn't give him a chance. I was concerned about you. From Loretta's telegram, I thought you were dying.'

'You probably wouldn't have bothered to come otherwise.'

'Maybe not. How is the girl?'

'Shocked. Concussed. Cuts and bruises, but on the whole, they're superficial.' He hesitated, then said, 'Go and see her before you leave. She's in a room along the corridor.'

'What are you doing about her?'

'She'll be taken care of.'

'You're buying her off, I take it.' Anger, born of anxiety, burst out. 'You're too bloody old to be screwing like a schoolboy up on the hill! And you brought it on yourself. There was never any trouble in San Felipe until you made it easy for thugs to come here and get drunk on cheap liquor. Maybe now you'll understand what you've done to this place.'

'You're still a hypocrite, son.' Raven spoke gently, but his blue eyes were icy. 'Just remember that what I've done to this place bought you everything you wanted.'

'I paid you back.'

'So you did, up to a point. But I'm not thinking of cash at the moment. I'm about to call in a moral loan.'

'What does that mean?'

'You owe me – and Raven Enterprises – something for the comfort and privileges you were ready enough to accept until your Puritan conscience caught up with you. I want you to stay here and run the place, at least until I'm on my feet again.'

Paul's mouth tightened. 'No way. I came to see my injured father on his death-bed. Since you're clearly not on your death-bed, I'm going back to London.'

Max's eyes closed and, for a moment, he was an old man. It occurred to Paul that, for all his toughness, his injuries might be more serious than he admitted. According to Sanchez, he had a broken ankle and his body was covered with contusions. There had been some internal bleeding and white plaster covered cuts on his head, where the hair had been shaved. When he had been brought in the morning after the attack, he had been unable to describe what had happened for several hours.

'My good health notwithstanding.' His voice was hard. 'You're needed here.'

'Manolo can cope until you're better.'

'I can't trust Manolo on his own. There isn't anyone who knows the business like you do.'

'Not any more. I've lost touch.'

'You won't have to deal with the day-to-day organisation. The staff's adequate for that, but they're flunkeys. They must have someone to sort out their crises – and there's always a crisis.'

Paul walked restlessly to the window. The hospital was built at the edge of the village and he looked out over the sea. A hot wind was blowing white foam towards the rocks. Clouds on the far horizon were tipped with gold. He was reminded how much he had loved this place as a child, had never imagined being able to live anywhere else.

He swung around abruptly. Max's eyes were narrowed and he fancied there was a look of triumph in them, a recognition of his moment of weakness. Max never believed he could lose a fight. For a crazy second he wondered whether this whole performance had been calculated in order to get him back; whether his father had been waiting all these years for an opportunity to win the one battle that had apparently ended in his defeat.

He shook his head. 'You're perfectly capable of running Raven Enterprises from your hospital bed. You don't need me. I'm leaving tomorrow.'

'Jesus Christ, you *owe* me!' Max's sudden anger was like a physical blow. He raised himself from the pillows and his breath was rasping.

'I owe you nothing!' Paul turned and left the room.

In the corridor, he passed a young nurse, but he was too irate to respond to her smile. His footsteps were loud on the polished linoleum floor. He had never been in the hospital before, but he knew it had been a gift from his father to San Felipe, and was staffed by excellent doctors and nuns from a nursing sisterhood. Max had endowed it after a guest at the Club had inconsiderately died on the premises because adequate medical treatment had not been available. Now anyone rich and privileged enough to stay there could be sure that his regular blood-pressure check or ECG would be performed in the manner to which he was accustomed in the London Clinic or the Texas General.

A nun came towards him, carrying an enormous bunch of red roses. She tapped on a door, and opened it. Paul glanced in. A man was standing beside a bed. He said, in Spanish: 'Who are they from?'

'From Senor Max. For your daughter, Don Rafael.'

'Take them away!'

She looked surprised, then shrugged. 'If you wish. There are other patients who will appreciate them.'

As Don Rafael's eyes followed her out, he saw Paul. Recognition was followed by a look of fury. He stepped forward and spread his arms. 'Get out of here!'

Paul brushed him aside and walked to the bed. He looked down on a girl whose face was so swollen and bruised she was hardly recognisable. One of her eyes was half shut, its lid a miniature balloon; her lips were puffy and black. Her body, under the single sheet that covered it, was deformed by bandages.

He bent over her. There was no recognition in her brown eyes, and he heard Don Rafael's voice: 'Yes, look at her! This is what your father caused!'

Paul stared at him blindly. The sickness he felt was not only at the sight of her injuries, but his realisation that the girl Max had, as he had put it himself, been screwing like a schoolboy up on the hill, was Elena Ansaldo.

An hour later, he was slumped in an arm-chair in the owner's suite at the Club.

He had no recollection of having walked back from the hospital, had not responded to greetings from passers-by. He had reached the iron gates, set into a wall that cut off the Club from the real world outside. A guard who had known him from childhood opened them. They must have spoken to each other, but he could not remember what they said.

He had crossed the lawns, where drops of water from sprinklers sparkled in the sun; had passed the tennis-courts, where three sleek, beautiful girls were under instruction from the Club professional, skirted the communal swimming-pool and stepped around supine bodies. Most of the women were oiled and slim, wearing only bikini pants; many of the men were overweight; all were the colour, and some had the skin-texture, of well-seasoned leather. Discarded, Pucci-bright robes made vivid patches of colour on the grass. Waiters circulated with trays of drinks. Several of the women glanced up, then looked again with interest at the tall young man with thick fair hair and peaked eyebrows over blue eyes that reminded them of someone they already knew. Paul didn't notice them.

As he walked through the blue and white tiled entrance-hall, with its central fountain, he ignored greetings from staff-members who recognised him, and made for Max's private suite of offices and living-quarters.

A waiter hurried after him. Paul acknowledged him curtly, and said, 'Bring me a bottle of whisky.'

'Senor Max has his own bar, sir . . .'

It was in an alcove in the sitting-room, lined with quilted yellow silk. Shelves held every conceivable variety of alcohol and Baccarat crystal glasses. There was champagne stacked in a refrigerator, French and Spanish wines in racks, bowls of Max's favourite pistachios and salted almonds which, Paul remembered, were emptied and refilled each morning. He sniffed at a waisted Georgian whisky decanter: a single malt, probably Glenmorangie, his father's favourite. He half-filled a glass and drank it down, gasping as it seared the back of his throat. Then he poured a second.

He looked around at the squashy sofas and chairs, covered in turquoise and yellow brocade, the Fortuny festoon blinds, the Regency hanging shelves holding a collection of Staffordshire figures which had been lovingly put together by a collector, and bought as a job-lot by Loretta Raven at Christie's. There were round occasional tables covered in flounced petticoats and a variety of bibelots, two inlaid Moroccan chairs, a smoked glass coffee-table on a brass pedestal. Unlike the tiled floors elsewhere in the Club, this was covered in thick turquoise carpet, surmounted by a couple of Kashgai rugs, each of which, he estimated, was worth at least eight thousand pounds. A Hockney swimming-pool dominated one wall, opposite a Jackson Pollock action painting. Loretta's choice again, having first made anxious inquiries to establish what would be likely to impress Max's guests.

No single item in the room was, in itself, vulgar, but the general effect was blatantly opulent. Momentarily, his mind was taken off Elena as he thought how his mother would have hated it.

He sat, drink in hand, trying to make sense of what he had just discovered. The last he had heard about Elena Ansaldo had been in a letter from Loretta, saying that her American husband, Alex Bellini, now had a controlling interest in the Ansaldo vineyards and that he and Elena were still living in the Napa Valley.

She had written: 'Your father says that Bellini was originally Rafael's equal partner, but he has had to take over full control. According to Max, Rafael couldn't run a successful ice-cream stall in a heat-wave. This could, of course, be an exaggeration. You know how he feels about Rafael!'

He did know, only too well. The two men had disliked each other since they were children, though Paul had never established the origin of the feud. He had always assumed that it must have developed gradually, as Raven built up his fortune by transforming San Felipe into the first major tourist resort on the Costa del Sol.

Rafael Ansaldo, the Spanish aristocrat, had made no secret of his contempt for the jumped-up foreigner, ignoring the fact that Max had lived in Spain since he was four years old and spoke Spanish as well as he did. It was Rafael who had originated the mocking nickname '*El Hidalgo*' for Max, never anticipating that the local people, delighted with the prosperity Raven Enterprises had brought, would adopt it out of admiration, unaware of irony. Nor that Max would amuse himelf by dressing up to the title of 'lord', with his *botas del campo*, his silver- studded belts from Toledo and his Cordoban hats. Other foreigners trying to dress like Spanish grandees made themselves ridiculous but Raven, with his dark good looks, suited the dress better than Ansaldo himself.

Paul knew that Elena had always liked Max and had regarded the feud as a stupid aberration. But Christ, he thought, Max is the same age as her father! How *could* she? The next instant, he recognised that she was only following the footsteps of countless other women who found Max irresistible. From childhood, he had watched them. They would arrive at the Club with a current husband or lover. Max would greet them, kiss their hands, fix them with that compelling, blue, you-are-the-woman-for-whom-I-have-been-waiting gaze. After that, he had only to make his choice.

Sometimes a male partner would create a scene, in which case, whatever his power or social position, he would return to his suite or villa to find his suitcases had been packed and a car was waiting to take him to the air-terminal, together with his tearful lady. They would never be allowed to return to the Club. Max did not like scenes, and there were plenty more women. Princesses, film-stars, millionairesses, all had been caught in his net. Why should Elena Ansaldo be any different?

Paul clenched his fists. He had disliked his father before, but never so much.

There was a knock at the door. Manolo Machado came in, his hand outstretched.

'Paul! *Como esta*?'

'*Hola*, Manolo.'

'Good to see you. It's been too long. This is a terrible thing!'

Manolo was a small, thickset, dark-skinned man with blue jowls that looked unshaven half-an-hour after he had put his razor away. His hair clung in tight black curls, close to his head, indicating his gypsy ancestry. He had worked at Max Raven's right hand since the formation of Raven Enterprises. After a miserably poor childhood, he had grown into a shrewd, ruthless man who had made it his business to know everyone in San Felipe who might be useful. He knew who was bribable and who was not; if Max Raven wanted to buy a piece of land, and the owner was unwilling to sell, Manolo knew how to 'persuade' him; if Raven needed permission to put up an apartment block in a beauty spot protected by building restrictions, Manolo could fix it; if builders, already employed elsewhere, were needed in a hurry, he knew just how much it would cost to make them desert to Raven Enterprises.

Paul disengaged his hand. He had never liked Manolo, and as he looked into the narrow, sly eyes, his antagonism revived. Money and association with the San Felipe Club had given the man a veneer of sophistication, but he had not learnt to disguise the peasant cunning and greed which dictated his every move.

Paul had never been able to understand his father's close relationship with him. Years ago he had queried Max, wondering whether Manolo's usefulness was not outweighed by his general unpopularity with the Club's patrons and the San Felipans. Max had said, 'Forget it. He has a job with me for as long as he wants it,'and had refused further discussion. Neither had he offered any explanation.

Now Manolo said, 'You've talked to your father? How is he?'

'He says he's okay.'

'When will he be taking up the reins again?'

'I doubt that he's let them go. Being in hospital won't stop him from running things.'

'When I heard the Senora had sent for you, I wondered if he'd want you to take over.'

'I'm going back to London tomorrow.' He thought he detected satisfaction in Manolo's smile.

'A short visit. Too bad. We have a big new project in mind. Did he tell you about it?'

'No. I wasn't with him for long.'

It seemed that Manolo had found out what he wanted to know, for he backed towards the door. 'You won't be concerning yourself with us then. I'll just go ahead . . .'

In spite of his determination to dissociate himself from his father's organisation, Paul said sharply, 'You'd better not make any decisions without consulting Max.'

'Max and I are partners.'

'I wasn't aware that he'd taken a partner.'

Manolo made no attempt to disguise his hostility. 'You didn't want Raven Enterprises. When your father isn't here, I'm in charge!' He marched out.

Jesus, Paul thought, I've been in the country a couple of hours and I've quarrelled with two people already. Three, if you count Rafael.

The memory of Rafael turned his thoughts back to Elena. Into his mind came a picture of Max making love to her. How far had they progressed? At what point had the attackers interrupted them? He thought of Max whispering to her, caressing her, looking at her with those remarkable eyes. He thought of her responding, and he seemed to feel again the shape of her body, which once he had thought belonged to him. It was almost worse to imagine her with his father than being raped by strangers.

He swung around as the door opened and, before he saw who it was, he exploded: 'For Christ's sake, leave me alone!'

Loretta, Max's third wife, stood in the doorway. 'I have to see you, Paul.'

'I'm sorry! I thought it was Manolo again.'

She kissed him on both cheeks. 'Thanks for coming so quickly. You've seen Max?' He nodded. 'And her?'

'Yes.'

'I hoped you'd come here first and I could warn you. I'm sorry, Paul.'

'Did you know about them?'

'No. It could have started last time she was here, a year ago. They'd have kept it secret because of her family.' She paused.

'Max usually doesn't care who knows what's going on.'

'It would be different with Elena.'

She nodded. 'She's not like the others. You should have married her, Paul.'

'They took her away before I had a chance.'

'You know her husband died a few months ago?'

He stared at her. 'No. I didn't know.'

'I thought she might have . . . well, never mind. How long are you staying?'

Again he said, 'Only until tomorrow. I'll fly out in the morning.'

'I'll probably come with you.' She wandered over to a big, ornately-framed gilt mirror which hung on a wall. Peering into it, she was suddenly absorbed in her appearance. She smoothed the make-up in the crevices at the side of her nose with the tip of a finger, twisted a stray lock of hair in place, sleeked her left eyebrow. Like all Maxwell Raven's women, she was strikingly beautiful, with shoulder-length brown hair, a heart-shaped face, huge, long-lashed grey eyes and a creamy skin. Her mouth was wide, the lower lip full and sensuous. She was heavily, but expertly made up, and there was a childlike innocence in her expression which did not always match her behaviour, as Paul knew from experience. Her body was perfect, kept that way by hours spent on the squash court, in the swimming-pool and the gym.

'Did I hear you right?' he said. 'What do you mean, you'll probably come with me?'

'I'm leaving him.'

'Now? When he's in hospital?'

'Sanchez says he'll be back on his feet in a few weeks. I've had enough. I haven't even been to see him, in case I feel sorry for him and change my mind. This business with Elena was the last straw. I can't compete any more, Paul.'

'Compete?'

'With girls in their twenties, without a line on their faces, who think Max is Paul Newman and Robert Redford rolled into one, packaged up just for them. They're all over the place in this damn club.' Her eyes were fixed on her reflection. 'Every time I pass a mirror, I see the difference between them and me. I'm getting tramlines on my upper lip. My neck's sagging. I have to defuzz my chin now.' She shuddered.

'Don't be silly! You're better-looking than any twenty-year-old chick I've ever seen.'

She shook her head. 'I used to be. Sometimes I think I can still make it, but it takes hours with the paint-pots every day. I'm forty-five, dammit.'

'No one would guess.' In the past, Loretta's self-absorption had amused him and he had made a game of the ritual responses, enjoying the artless way she would fish for compliments and preen herself when they were forthcoming. But this time he heard desperation in her voice as she said, 'All I've ever had is my appearance. You think I didn't realise that Max only married me because I decorated this place? He never pretended it was for my great intellect. And my first husband told me once that I'd better hang onto my looks because I didn't have anything else that would keep a man interested.'

'That's nonsense! You look gorgeous, sure, but you're . . .' He hesitated, then said sincerely, 'You're *nice*, too. Warm, affectionate, honest . . .'

'Thanks, but don't bother to go on. Whatever I have, it's never been enough for Max.'

'Why pick now to leave him? You've known about his other women for years.'

'And you thought, like everyone else, that I didn't care. Well, I've always cared. The trouble is, I love that shit. Or I did. Now, I don't know. Anyhow, if he wants Elena Ansaldo, it's the end of me. So I'm getting out before I'm sent.'

'Where will you go? Back to Los Angeles?'

'I don't know where. Not to LA.' Her voice was bleak. 'Maybe Palm Beach, Florida.'

'Why there, for God's sake?'

'I'd be ahead of the competition. I'm told that most of the women there are older than I am, and it's full of rich old men. I might have a chance to grab one while I've still got the equipment.'

'You serious?'

'You bet I am. I need a man, but not another Max. Peace,

comfort, early widowhood and a large inheritance, that's what I'm going to look for this time.'

He was almost convinced that she meant it. 'This must have been a hell of a shock, but don't rush your fences,' he said. 'Stay until he's on his feet. Talk to him.'

'I've made up my mind. I wish *you'd* stay, though, Paulie. I hate the idea of Manolo taking over, even for a few weeks.'

'He's already working on it. But I saw Max earlier and he's not looking too bad. I don't think for a moment Manolo will be able to put anything over on him, even while he's in hospital.'

'I've never understood why Max puts up with that creepy bastard.'

'I haven't, either. He's a useful trouble-shooter, I suppose.'

'Have you heard about their latest project?'

'Another high-rise?'

'Worse. The biggest supermarket in the south of Spain.'

'Surely there isn't the population to sustain it?'

'There is in summer, and he's just started a new scheme to keep the apartments full out of season. Holidays for older folk at cut prices. Max says a supermarket would relieve them of the danger that they might find a Spaniard who doesn't speak English when they want a can of baked beans or a Mars Bar.'

'I still don't see it working.'

'He brought out a couple of experts from England to do a market survey and they said that if the apartments were full twelve months of the year, a supermarket would show a profit. There'll be a camp-site next to it, too, if there's room.'

'Where does he propose to build it?'

'Hold onto your hat: on the Campo Negro, right under Rafael's nose.'

'But Victoria Ansaldo owns the Campo Negro.'

'He thinks she'll sell it to him.'

'Rafael would never let her. Christ, it's next door to their house! And isn't there a kind of shrine on it? I seem to remember a lot of old women used to go there to pray.'

'They still do. And once a year there's a memorial service. Something to do with the Civil War. But Max says they could easily find somewhere else and, anyhow, the Civil War was fifty years ago. Most of them aren't even sure what they're remembering. I've heard the locals are pretty upset about it, though.'

'He won't get permission to build.'

'Don't you believe it. Manolo will organise it. He hasn't missed yet.'

Five minutes later she left, saying she wanted to start packing. As she kissed him good-bye, she put her hands on either side of his face and said, 'You're better-looking even than Max, Paulie. It's that fair hair, dark eyebrows and blue eyes. And those eyelashes – it's not bloody fair! Men shouldn't have them so long.'

'Come off it, Retta! You're embarrassing me.'

'It's true. I've always thought so. I used to envy Elena.' She shrugged. 'And now she's had both of you.'

Alone, the luxurious suite seemed to smother him. He walked to a window which overlooked the beach. It was early evening and the sands were almost deserted. Most of the Club's guests were preparing for the evening's activities: gambling; several hours of drinking in one of the bars or on the terraces that surrounded the swimming-pool, followed by a late dinner which would extend well after midnight. There were three restaurants, from which they could choose to eat Spanish, French or American. Everything from the suckling-pig to the hamburgers would be perfectly cooked from ingredients flown in from Madrid or Paris that morning, or bought fresh from the market. A couple of local fishermen had a contract to provide daily supplies of sardines, baby eels, swordfish and lobsters. In the Sala Americana, even Texans had been heard to admit that Dallas could not better the quality nor the size of the hunks of beef that overhung the edges of their wooden platters.

In Max's bedroom, he found swimming-trunks, and took a thick white towel from the bathroom.

He had reached the glass doors which led onto the terrace when the telephone rang.

'Senor Raven?'

'This is Paul Raven.'

'Doctor Sanchez. I have some not very good news for you.

Your father has had a stroke. Not a bad one, he will recover, but it has affected the left side of his body. It happened not long after you left this afternoon.'

'My God! I'll come and see him at once.'

'Better not. He is sedated. I will call you early tomorrow and let you know how he is.'

'Does his wife know?'

'I have just spoken to her.'

After Sanchez had hung up, Paul stood by the telephone, frowning. It was almost inconceivable that his father should have suffered a stroke: not Max Raven, who always kept himself at the peak of fitness, who looked years younger than his age, who neither ate, smoked nor drank to excess and despised those who did. Even in his hospital bed he had appeared indomitable, undefeated. What could have caused it? As the question came into his mind, he remembered the sudden surge of anger that had overcome Max when he had refused to stay on in San Felipe.

Despite what Sanchez had said, he went back to the hospital, and found Loretta already there.

Together, they cross-questioned the nursing sister who was sitting beside Max's bed, head bowed over her rosary.

Paul noticed that as they talked in the doorway, Loretta resolutely kept her head turned away from the bed.

The nun was reassuring, echoing Sanchez. Senor Raven would need nursing for some time and they could expect that it would be difficult for him to talk at first, but his speech should gradually return to normal. The stroke had caused the left side of his face to drop but that, too, should be only temporary.

Bluntly, Loretta asked: 'Sister, is there any danger that he will be permanently disabled?'

'Almost none, Senora. Of course, one cannot be one hundred per cent certain, but this is a strong, healthy man. The doctor believes that he should make a full recovery, as long as he is protected from stress.' She glanced at Paul, and he wondered whether she had overheard their quarrel.

As they walked outside, towards Loretta's car, she said,

'This changes things, doesn't it? Come back to the house with me.'

It was the first time in ten years he had set foot in his family home, and he had forgotten how large it was. Built by Max on the pattern of a Spanish *finca*, it sprawled, double-storeyed, over half an acre, with the big, airy ground-floor rooms leading one into another through arches. There was a swimming pool which was divided by a sliding glass wall so half of it was inside the house and could be used in any weather. The other half was set into a terrace. Most of the floors were marble-tiled. The living-room into which the pool reached was an extension of the garden, with trees and plants in tubs and great urns of strelitzias and agapanthus. The colour-scheme was predominantly cream, spiked with vivid blue and apricot silk cushions on the sofas and arm-chairs, which had cream linen loose covers.

A few colourful oils which had been painted by Max's father hung on the roughly-plastered walls. They were all of San Felipe as it had been in the early thirties. In splashy primary colours, they evoked a life which had changed before Paul was born, and he wondered whether any visitor these days would see an umbrella-mender perched on a step, in his beret, shabby velvet trousers, bright green socks and *alpagatas*, patching worn black umbrellas. Or an old woman such as Andrew Raven had painted outside her house, weaving a basket, with a pile of her wares on the pavement beside her. Or a fisherman sitting cross-legged on an empty beach, mending his nets.

The room had a comfortable familiarity, and he realised it was exactly as his own mother had designed it nearly thirty years earlier.

Momentarily forgetting Loretta, he moved to the copper-canopied chimney-piece, where logs were permanently laid on the fire-bricks. His mother's photograph, which he expected would have been removed, was still hanging in its niche to the left of the canopy. He stood, looking at the vivacious, smiling face with its high cheek-bones and wide, generous mouth, the brown eyes and blonde hair drawn back in a chignon. He had a copy of the same picture in his house in London, but here, where she had belonged, it evoked her personality more strongly.

Loretta's voice was an interruption. 'You're like her, except for your eyes. They're from Max.'

'Don't you mind keeping it here?' he said.

'She's dead. It's the living ones I mind. Let's go to my room. It's more homelike than this. We'll have a drink.'

She led the way through a heavy, carved oak door, into a smaller room which was instantly recognisable as her creation, in the same uncertain taste as the suite at the Club.

'Drink?'

'Whisky, please.' He sank into an over-stuffed chair.

She handed him a decanter and glass. 'Help yourself. Anything with it?'

'Ice.'

She poured herself a gin and tonic and they sat in silence for a moment.

'What are you going to do now, Paul?'

'Christ, I don't know! *Could* Manolo take over?'

'It would be disastrous. He could never run this place, even with Marian.'

'Who's Marian?'

'Marian Lewis. Max's secretary. She's A Treasure.'

He could see the capital letters. 'But you don't like her?'

'I don't *dis*like her, but she's too damn efficient. And she patronises me.'

'Is she another of Max's . . .' He stopped.

'Hardly. She's good-looking enough, but she's almost the same age as he is. He likes them younger. She came to the Club six years ago with Jonas Carson. You know?'

He shook his head.

'Texan. Made a million from oil-drilling machinery. Marian was his new PA and coming here with him was her first perk. Only it apparently hadn't occurred to her that the job entailed anything more than being a super-secretary. Equally, it hadn't occurred to Jonas that his personal assistant wouldn't realise what the word 'personal' meant. He tried to get her into bed the first night. There was a terrible row. They must have heard it in the village. Finally she fought him off and left him lying on the floor of their villa, out cold. She came to Max and apologised for having created a scene. He told Jonas to get the hell out – after he'd been coming here for five years or more – and offered Marian a job. She's been here ever since.'

'Don't tell me: she's now his devoted slave.'

'Of course. She knows everything about the organisation, but she's no good with people, and that's important in a place like this. She's too starchy and stand-offish. Also, she and Manolo hate each other. They'd never work as a team.'

'Didn't it ever occur to Max that there might be a time when someone else would have to take over?'

'Never. He believes he's immortal, and I'm sure he didn't think he'd ever darken the doors of the hospital.'

Paul finished his drink and stood up. 'It looks as though I'm stuck, doesn't it?' he said bitterly. 'I'll stay until he's well enough to discuss the situation, then, if I have to, I'll help him to find someone to take over. How about you?'

'I'm still leaving. As long as you're staying, he won't need me. I don't suppose *she'll* desert him.' She hesitated. 'Is that the main reason you want to get away, so you won't have to see them together?'

He didn't want to talk about Elena. 'I'll see you tomorrow, Retta. What time will you be leaving?'

'The aircraft takes off at eleven. I'll be on it.'

'I'll come and see you off.'

'Paul . . .' She put a hand on his arm and looked up at him. 'You don't have to go back to the Club tonight. Stay here with me.'

The invitation was so unexpected that for a moment he did not take it in. As he looked down at her heart-shaped face, she came closer, thrust forward her hips so their bodies were touching, then moved gently against him. 'It's my last night here. The end of an era. I don't want to go to bed by myself.'

Why not? She was beautiful and sexy. He had always been fond of her. Add to that, it was the second time she had offered herself to him. On the previous occasion, he had rejected her. A repetition would be cruel, wouldn't it? Then a memory of

Max's words came to him: 'You're still a hypocrite, son.' So never mind the rationalisation, he told himself, just take her because in the present circumstances having a woman would be a comfort. Any woman.

Later he was to wonder, with secret shame, whether retaliation had not been the real reason for his compliance: Loretta was Max's wife; Max had taken Elena; Paul would take Loretta.

He put his arm around her and they turned towards her bedroom. Sitting on the bed, he watched her undress: first the pale blue silk shirt, then the designer jeans, under which she was wearing only brief blue satin pants. Her breasts were small and high, but some analytical part of his brain, operating independently of his body, noted the creases under them, the first signs of sagging. Her hip-bones were sharp, her rib-cage visible beneath the creamy skin. She removed the combs which held back her dark hair and came towards him. As she pressed his head into her flat stomach, his physical need became urgent. He fumbled at his trousers, but she stopped him. 'I'll do it.'

Then they were together on the bed. She was above him, her hair falling forward. Elena's hair had felt the same, like feathers brushing his face. He closed his eyes and moved his hands over her body. But this was not Elena. Elena had been soft, her breasts full and curved, fitting his hands. The rest of her body was firm and supple, but the bones were cushioned by smooth flesh. Loretta was hard and almost fleshless.

If he kept his eyes shut, perhaps she would become Elena.

He moved so he was on top of her, and it was over in a few minutes, a violent, unloving coupling which, he guessed, had left her unsatisfied.

As he relaxed, he opened his eyes and saw that hers, too, had been closed. This was no victory over his father: Max had been right there in the bed.

He lay on his back, looking up at the ceiling. Although the climax had released his physical tension, he found himself, if anything, more depressed than before at the prospect of having to stay on in San Felipe. He sat up abruptly, and heard her sigh.

'It didn't work, did it?' she said. 'The bed was overcrowded.'

This time she did not protest when he told her he would return to the Club.

When he was dressed he found, somewhat to his surprise, that his casual fondness for her remained intact. The love-making had been so emotionless that it might never have taken place. Neither was there any self-consciousness in their farewell.

Still sitting, naked, on the bed, she smiled up at him. 'That's the second fiasco, Paulie. Maybe we'll be third time lucky. Only there might not be a third time.'

'It'll be my loss.'

She hugged him. 'You always were my favourite stepson.'

Instead of going straight back to the Club, he walked around the house, skirting the terrace, and along the paved path which led to a rear gate. Every step brought back a memory. In the blue light of a full moon he could see the high wall that separated the Ravens and the Ansaldos. A couple of hundred yards on stood the willow-tree which he had climbed as a child, to whisper greetings to Elena, on the other side of the wall.

Then, eerie in the semi-darkness, there loomed the burned-out pile of his grandparents' original house. As he reached it, he saw that its outlines had been softened over the years by an exuberant growth of weeds and vines which had crept over the smoke-blackened stone walls, reaching like inquiring fingers through all the apertures. He wondered, idly, why his father had never had it pulled down.

He let himself out through the gate and walked along the highway towards the picnic area where Max and Elena had been attacked. Thinking of her pain and humiliation, he wanted desperately to be with her, to be allowed to help her back to health so she would forget what had happened. But she belonged to Max now, and he would be the one to whom she would turn.

Suddenly, he wanted a drink, and company. The black rocks and dry grass of the Campo Negro stretched down to his right. He decided to cut across it and go to the Plaza for a brandy.

Even as he concentrated on negotiating the rough ground, its stones and ridges sharpened by the moonlight, there were reminders of Elena, for this was where they had met secretly, having been forbidden to do so by her father. They had found a small, rocky cave which bit into the hillside, its entrance protected by bushes. As children they had played there; when they were older, they had kissed and explored each other's bodies on a bed of dried grass.

And this was where Max wanted to build a supermarket! He told himself again that Rafael's sister, Victoria, would never sell the land. Even if she did, Loretta had said the village was against it.

But when had anyone, Ansaldo or villager, been able to stand out against Max's determination?

He paused when he reached a grove of cypresses which had been planted around a small shrine by the village women, who believed that the tapering trees would assist a soul's flight to heaven. Here, for years, they had come to pray for their men who had been killed in the Civil War.

As he was about to go on, he became aware of the insistent brrm-brrm of a motor-cycle, coming nearer. Remembering his father's attackers, he stiffened.

A dwarfish figure, shadowy in the moonlight, ran towards him. Its hands were clenched on imaginary handle-bars. The motor-bike noises issued from its mouth as it weaved around the trees. Paul's mind eased.

'Hey, Titi!' he called. '*Que tal*!'

The imaginary motor-cycle pulled up; its engine stopped. A little man paused warily a few feet from him.

'It's me, Titi. Paul Raven.' There was no response, so Paul started up his own motor-bike, pretending to lean his body into the curves around a racing-circuit.

'Paul?' Titi ran forward and grasped both his hands, pumping them up and down, pouring out a stream of excited words. Paul thought wryly that this was the first genuine welcome he had received.

No one in San Felipe seemed to know exactly how old Titi was, no one remembered his surname. Paul believed he was much the same age as Max, though his face was almost unlined and the bright brown eyes under heavy eyebrows had remained unchanged in the years since they had last met. Under five feet tall, he was shy, gentle and unfailingly good-tempered, but his brain was that of an eight-year-old. Paul knew little about his background, being one of generations of children brought up in the village who had accepted him as part of the landscape and treated him as one of themselves. Until Paul grew old enough to be self-conscious, they had often raced around the countryside together, making motor-cycle noises, running races.

For as long as anyone could remember, Titi had lived in a kind of cupboard set into a thick stone wall which was all that remained of ancient Moorish fortifications which had once surrounded the village. A rough door had been added to the front of the alcove, and it was about two metres high, by the same wide, and a metre deep. It was furnished with a narrow canvas camp-bed and a stool. In fine weather, when he was not wandering around the village, greeting his friends, he would sit outside on the stool. If it rained, he moved the stool inside. When he slept, he pulled the wooden doors closed and secured them with an inner bolt.

The village women kept him provided with food. Each morning, supplies would be left outside the cupboard: milk, *churros*, Manchego cheese, an iron dish of *paella*, a casserole of chick-pea soup. Frequently, there was more than Titi could possibly eat, and he would share it with passing children.

Over the years, he had become the village's messenger-boy. Any shop-keeper with a small order to deliver, would call Titi, and he would happily run off with it, pretending he was riding a motor-cycle. For those without telephones, he delivered notes and messages.

Occasionally reaching out to shake hands, he chattered on, jumbled sentences in which names recurred that Paul had almost forgotten, mixed up with the old peasant names for areas in and around the village, in a local accent so heavy that Paul, his ear not yet fully tuned back into his second language, found it difficult to follow.

Suddenly, the talk ended. Without looking back, Titi raced off into the darkness. In London, trapped by a bore at a party,

Paul had sometimes recalled enviously his ability to terminate a conversation by simply walking away when he decided it had reached a natural conclusion.

Alone, the sound of the motor-bike fading, he found himself warmed by the contact. Titi was a link with a less chaotic age, the San Felipe to which his grandparents had come more than half a century earlier.

Five minutes walk brought him to the Plaza San Juan just above the beach. It was pulsating with life, with strings of lights among the tree-branches. People were sitting at tables outside every restaurant and bar, glasses of wine or brandy in front of them. Canned flamenco music from a loudspeaker forced them to shout in order to be heard. Paul leant against a tree and looked around. These were not the sleek jet-setters who patronised the Club, but package-deal tourists from the apartments and hotels. He heard North Country accents, American, Australian, German and Swedish. Their ages ranged from teens to sixties, with a scattering of children, all seeking a good time in what passed for an exotic atmosphere. Many were already drunk on the cheap liquor, and two tables of young people, one German, the other British, were raising their voices in opposition to the flamenco. The Germans were lifting their glasses to a Bavarian drinking song, the British defiantly roaring 'Rule Britannia'. He wondered how long it would be before aggression could no longer be contained.

He saw young girls, obviously recent arrivals, still with milk-white skin, in their floral cotton sun-dresses. They glanced, shyly or boldly, at groups of Spanish youths who were lurking in the background, assessing the new talent. At the end of a fortnight, he knew, liaisons would have been formed and the girls would have been taken for every peseta the youths could persuade them to spend. There would be tears as they boarded the buses for Malaga Airport, but before they were out of sight, the boys would be back in the plaza, waiting for the next contingent. There did not seem to be any Spanish families sitting at the tables. Instead, every available local resident was occupied serving the visitors. The place was jumping, noisy, and bore no resemblance to the San Felipe of his grandfather's paintings.

As he made his way back to the Club, having given up any idea of competing with the tourists for a drink from the crowded bars, he wondered what Andrew and Moira Raven would think of the place now. There was no doubt that development had brought prosperity to many San Felipans, but at a cost, for with it had come corruption, greed and vandalism. The deterioration had started before he had fled to London ten years earlier. Now, judging by the attack on Max and Elena, and by what he had just seen, it was accelerating. And for the foreseeable future, he was stuck in the centre of it.

Part 2

1929–1936

1

Andrew and Moira Raven arrived in San Felipe in June, 1929, with their four-year-old son, Maxwell.

The journey from Edinburgh had been long and tedious, by boat and trains. The last section, from Madrid to Malaga, was the worst. They shared third-class accommodation with local farmers and their wives, many accompanied by live chickens which clucked miserably in their baskets. It seemed to Moira, already exhausted and dizzy from travel-motion, that they never stopped eating. The women produced endless supplies of bread, thick omelettes and pungent goat's cheese from capacious leather satchels, the men drank from wine-skins. The combined smells were overwhelming.

There was only one lavatory for their carriage and it rapidly became a reeking cess-pit.

But their fellow-passengers were kind. Discovering that the Ravens spoke no Spanish and had long since eaten their own supplies, they pressed food and wine on them, were concerned and hurt if it was refused.

On his inadequate share of a wooden bench Andrew, a bulky six feet two, felt his legs growing numb and did not dare to stretch them because, when he did, he collided with the knees of the woman sitting opposite him. But, like Moira, he kept smiling, because the Ravens were planning to live in Spain for as long as their money lasted and had vowed to each other that they were going to become part of the country, which meant accepting cheerfully any situation which the natives regarded as the norm.

Max was the only member of the family who enjoyed the journey. He had grizzled for the first fifty miles or so, but cheered up when a large woman, wearing black from her headscarf to the thick stockings and heavy boots which were set solidly on the train's wooden floor, presented him with a piece of her omelette. Moira put out an involuntary hand to prevent him taking it, but weakly withdrew when he protested loudly.

'*Tortilla de patata*,' the woman said reassuringly. She plucked Max from Moira's knee and sat him on her own. After that, he was passed among the Spaniards like a blue-eyed doll, fed by most of them. He had his first taste of wine, diluted with water brought from a tap somewhere on the train, and swallowed it with obvious pleasure. Too insecure to protest, Moira and Andrew could only pray that the wine would neutralise whatever poisons there were in the water. 'Never, never drink the water in Spain unless you have boiled it,' Dr Campbell had told them. But neither then nor at any future time did Maxwell Raven suffer ill-effects from eating or drinking. His second wife was to liken his digestion to that of a camel.

After a seemingly endless journey, stopping at every local station, they climbed out of the train at Malaga. After Max had been emotionally farewelled by his friends, they found themselves alone, with little idea how to undertake the last miles, which were to end in San Felipe del Mar. Even the dreadful locomotive seemed a haven.

Until now, other people had taken the responsibility for transporting them from Edinburgh's grey, rain-washed streets into this hot, southern Spanish town. Their tickets had been bought in Scotland, their itinerary had been planned by a travel agent. But in Malaga, the itinerary ran out. They were not even sure how far away San Felipe was.

They stood forlornly outside the station, watching yellow dust swirled by a hot wind. Around them, dark, unshaven men wearing loose blue trousers, collarless shirts and berets, stood in groups, talking. Moira noticed that many of the passing women wore black, their skirts covering their ankles. Even young girls were soberly dressed and nearly all were accompanied by an older woman. The jazz age, with its bobbed hair, waistless dresses and short skirts, had not arrived in this part of Spain. There was not a bare arm or leg to be seen. And where was the colour and excitement she had expected? The flounced dresses, the high combs and mantillas, the toreadors, the sound of the flamenco? Uncle Henry's description of the Spain he had loved all his life seemed far from the reality.

A few motors were parked in the station's forecourt. A man emerged from one and came towards them. In beret and dungarees, he was obviously addressing them, and they heard a familiar word: 'Taxi, Senor? Taxi?'

Moira was shaking her head when she heard Andrew say, 'Taxi! Si!'

'No!' she said. 'It'll cost the earth.'

'I don't care. We've had enough discomfort. We're going to arrive in San Felipe like civilised beings. Anyhow, I don't know any other way to get there.'

'There'll be a train . . .'

'No more trains!'

Already assuming their custom, the taxi-driver had picked up the two largest suitcases, tucked Andrew's easel under his arm and scurried towards a dark blue saloon with polished brass headlamps and a tool-box set into the running-board.

'It's a Morris Oxford! I'll be damned! That should get us there.' Andrew felt suddenly happier now that the foreignness around him was relieved by something from home.

The driver was stowing the smaller items of luggage inside. He heaved the last suitcases onto the roof and secured them with rope. Then he wiped an infinitesimal speck of dust off one of the doors, climbed behind the wheel and looked at them with an inquiring smile.

'San Felipe del Mar,' Andrew told him.

The smile disappeared. 'San Felipe del Mar? No, No, Senor. Impossible!'

A stream of Spanish protest followed, but the iron had entered Andrew's soul. Moira was already tucked securely into the back of the car, with Max on her knee. He opened the front passenger seat and settled beside the driver. Whenever there was a pause, he blandly used the one Spanish phrase he had learned: '*Non comprendo!*'

'We must get out,' Moira said.

'I'm not getting out. It's his own fault. He *invited* us. Don't you move.'

'Even if he does take us, it'll cost so much . . .'

'We've travelled all this way like bloody paupers in order to save money. We are going to San Felipe in this car.'

They sat, looking straight ahead, until the driver stopped talking. Andrew smiled at him and repeated pleasantly: 'San Felipe del Mar.'

Realising he was up against a brick wall, he shrugged, muttering disgustedly as the car moved off.

Moira, jammed in by luggage and a restless small boy, saw little of the scenery. The glimpses she had were of multi-coloured fields of red poppies, grass that had yellowed in the heat, dandelions, olive groves and farm-houses, many fronted with Moorish arches, and small, square cottages, some dazzlingly white-washed, others terra cotta, with red-tiled roofs. Everything was etched sharply by the clear light.

The road out of Malaga was reasonably smooth, but after ten miles they turned onto a narrow, unpaved stretch of packed yellow earth, studded with stones. It ran parallel with the coastline and became increasingly rough. The taxi-driver, unhappier by the minute, kept up a constant litany of complaint.

An hour after leaving the city, they ran down a steep hill which consisted almost entirely of hairpin bends, and saw San Felipe below them, an irregular roofscape capping square, white houses, two and three storeys high, separated by flights of steps and narrow streets. It reached down to a wide beach shaped like a new moon. Headlands alternated with other beaches and out on the water they could see fishing-boats with black triangular sails. Andrew's fingers began to itch with the urge to hold a paint-brush and get the scene down on canvas. But how to create that extraordinary white light? He was used to grey skies and sunshine which was soft and yellow, blurring outlines, and granite buildings and black roads shining like patent-leather under the rain.

They passed a peasant sleeping on a cart piled high with hay and drawn by a donkey, which apparently knew exactly where it was going, and a group of men, trudging by the side of the road with hay-forks over their shoulders. Just outside the village there was a stone wall, behind which they could see the top floor and roof of a large white villa. A wrought-iron gate was set into the wall, giving a glimpse of a garden studded with terracotta pots of red and pink geraniums.

Without speaking, each of the Ravens knew that the other's depression had lifted. Uncle Henry's Spain had not been Malaga railway station, it had been San Felipe.

The taxi-driver blew his horn. An old woman walking ahead of them, leapt for the shelter of a doorway and cursed them shrilly. The village streets, like the country roads, were earth and stones, and there were no footpaths. Doors of most of the houses were open and women sat on the steps, knitting, sewing and weaving baskets. A herd of baby goats peered around a corner.

They came to a large, unpaved square, raised a few inches above the encircling street. It was sheltered by a spreading plane tree, under which the driver pulled up. Feeling like a vigorously-shaken cocktail, Moira tipped Max from her knee and joined Andrew beside the car. The sun blazed from a cloudless sky.

The square was surrounded by narrow houses, some of whose ground floors were shops. There was a bar with a few tables and chairs outside it, at which men sat with brandy glasses in front of them.

To one side was a well, where three women stood gossipping, their water jugs on the ground beside them. Other women scrubbed clothes with bars of yellow soap in an open-air laundry trough in the centre of the open space. An elderly man with a brown, wrinkled face sat on the ground, mending a black umbrella. There was a glimpse of the beach and the sea beyond it through a road which led off to their right.

Grim-faced, the driver was already unloading their luggage.

'Hotel?' Andrew said.

The driver ignored him. He set their brown paper packages, baskets, Andrew's portfolios, mounted canvases, Gladstone bags and suitcases in an untidy pile, spreading across the street.

'Hotel?' Andrew repeated, on a rising note.

Sullenly, he shrugged, then pointed to a sign, BAR JIMINEZ, behind the chairs and tables.

As they gathered their courage to confront a hotelier who would almost certainly not speak English, they realised they had become the centre of attention. Several small children had gathered nearby. Women had put down their work and men had stopped talking. All were staring at them.

It was not until later that they understood what an exotic sight they were in San Felipe, where foreign tourists were rare. Andrew stood half a head taller than most of the local men. His green corduroy suit, its jacket buttoned across his deep chest, his green felt snap-brim hat and polished leather shoes were, to the San Felipans, as unusual as a matador's suit-of-lights would be in Prince's Street. Moira was equally eye-catching. Nearly as tall as her husband, blonde, with thick, creamy skin and dark eyelashes and brows over light blue eyes, she was a different being from the short, olive-skinned Spanish women. Always an individualist, she had not adopted current fashion, saying she was too big for flapper styles. Her flowing, floral skirt reached almost to her ankles, her blouse was bright yellow, her waist was cinched in with a scarlet belt. Several long strings of wooden beads swung around her neck. Her hair was drawn back into a straggling bun and various embroidered canvas bags were slung over her shoulders. Suddenly overcome by shyness when she realised that she was being watched, she swept Max up in her arms, an earth-mother.

Before Andrew could move towards the bar, a girl appeared in its doorway. Unlike the rest of their audience, who were gazing at them expressionlessly, she smiled.

She was small and square and, as she approached, they saw that she was younger than an overblown figure indicated, probably not much more than twenty. Instead of the ubiquitous black, she was wearing a short red dress in a shiny rayon material with a multi- coloured, fringed shawl around her shoulders.

The stream of Spanish with which she was greeting them came to an abrupt halt as she realised they were not understanding. Then she said carefully, '*Inglese*? English?'

Andrew nodded. 'Do you speak English?'

'I speak very well,' she said proudly. She swooped on Max and picked him up, making small crooning noises. 'So pretty!'

'We are looking for a hotel,' Andrew said.

'No hotel here.'

The Ravens stared at her.

'There must be!' Andrew said. 'My uncle stayed in a hotel here.'

'Uncle?'

'Perhaps you knew him. Henry Raven. Senor Henry Raven. He came to San Felipe many times.' He was speaking slowly and clearly.

'Henry? Rah-ven? Enrique!' She put Max down and seized Andrew's hands. 'Our Enrique! Come! Come! You stay here with me! Like Enrique!' Her English was heavily accented, but fluent.

They were about to follow her into the bar when a disturbance attracted their attention: shouting, and a blare from the brass horn of a huge, gleaming Hispano-Suiza which had pulled up behind their taxi, unable to pass because of the luggage which was blocking the roadway. A chauffeur sat at the wheel and from the passenger seat behind him a woman, her hair concealed under a lace mantilla, glared at them.

An interested crowd had closed around the two vehicles and their driver was attempting to untie the suitcases from his roof, balancing on a chair which he had removed from one of the tables.

There was another long, peremptory hoot. Andrew went to help the taxi-driver, but before he could reach for the larger suitcase, it slipped off the roof, bursting open as it fell. Clothes scattered everywhere. A gust of wind picked up a pair of Moira's lace-trimmed French knickers – her best pair, reserved for occasions when she put them on especially to give Andrew the pleasure of removing them – swirled them into the air and onto the bonnet of the Hispano-Suiza, where they lay provocatively. Later Andrew was to remark that he'd have liked photographs of the minds of the male onlookers as their eyes swivelled from the knickers to Moira, and back again. For a moment, the Ravens were paralysed then, as they looked at the outraged face of the car's passenger, they began to laugh. They removed the knickers and gathered up armfuls of their dusty belongings. As they did so, still laughing, the solemn faces of the crowd began to break up and they joined in. Gales of laughter swept the square; formality was forgotten.

A few minutes later, the road was clear, the Ravens' luggage disposed in a small hall behind the bar, from which a staircase rose to the upper floors.

Andrew went towards the Hispano-Suiza to apologise to the woman for having held her up, but it swept away and she looked neither to left nor right.

'Who is she?' Moira asked their new friend.

'La Doña Maria de Ansaldo y Montesino.' The syllables rolled impressively. 'She live up . . .' She gestured towards the hill behind the village. 'Bi-ig house.'

'Must have been the one we passed,' Andrew said. 'We seem to have started on the wrong foot with her.' He pulled a handful of pesetas from his pocket and asked the taxi-driver what he owed. A sum was named, which brought a shriek of protest from the girl. After a brisk argument, she took a small number of coins and handed them to the driver, who drove off with an angry crash of gears.

Having informed them that her name was Carmen Jiminez and she owned the bar, she led them up the stairs. A little boy, aged about eleven, staggered up after them with the luggage. 'My brother, Esteban. He is my very good helper,' she said.

As they reached the first floor, a door along the passage opened and two young women peered out at them. They were heavily made up and were wearing dresses with bodices cut so low that the cleavages between their breasts were clearly visible. Carmen gestured them back into the room. They giggled and disappeared. She threw open another door and they saw a huge bed with a red satin cover on it. There were red velvet curtains at the windows, garish red and gold wallpaper and a heavily-patterned rug on the floor. Blinking, Moira parked Max in the centre of the bed as Carmen disappeared, saying she would find a cot for him.

Alone, they absorbed details of the room. A large mirror

was attached to the ceiling directly over the bed. Above the carved wooden bed-head there was an oil-painting of a lusciously overweight, nude woman, reclining on a chaise-longue, her knees bent, as a naked man, whose intention was obvious, loomed over her.

After a moment, Moira said thoughtfully, 'The sign didn't actually say that this was a hotel, did it?'

'I think we might be discovering things about Uncle Henry that we never suspected.' Andrew paused. 'You realise what this place probably is?'

'I do. But we've nowhere else to go. That girl is kind, it looks clean, and she knew Henry. It'll do until we find somewhere more permanent.'

After a moment, he said, 'I wonder if she was Henry's mistress?'

'She can't be much more than twenty. She would have been a child when he was alive.

'With what we're finding out, I wouldn't be surprised . . . does anything strike you about that painting?'

She pointed to the male figure. 'That bears a distinct resemblance to . . .'

'Himself? I thought so, too, even if he is in a state we never actually saw.'

'And isn't that his signature in the bottom left-hand corner? H.R. It's a self-potrait! But who's the woman? It isn't Carmen.'

From the doorway, the girl spoke proudly: 'Is my Mamma.'

'Good heavens! I mean . . . she's very attractive,' Moira said. 'Clearly a good friend of Henry's. I look forward to meeting her.'

'She is dead. When we heard from England that Enrique died, Mamma was so sad, and she died soon after. They were very, very good friends.'

'I'm sorry.'

'No need. Better for Mamma to join Enrique. The bar is mine now, and my little brother's. We work together. People in San Felipe like to drink – and other things.' She glanced sideways at Moira, saw her lips twitch, and winked. 'How long do you stay in San Felipe?'

'We're going to try and find a house. We'll stay . . . maybe two years,' Andrew said.

'No other English people ever come for so long!'

Moira explained: 'Uncle Henry left us some money and we plan to stay here as long as it lasts.'

'Then I will find a house for you. Now you must rest. I take the little boy.'

She picked Max up and went out, cuddling him against her shoulder. It was the beginning of an enduring friendship.

Two weeks later, they had their house. It overlooked San Felipe, on a barren hillside that stretched down to the sea west of the village. A disused *finca*, or farm-house, it had four rooms, stone walls nearly two feet thick, a terrace shaded by bougainvillea, and four hectares of land, studded with olive trees. There were low stone walls around three sides of the property, but the fourth was bounded by a seven-foot wall dividing it from the big house which they had noticed on the way in, and was owned by Don Luis de Ansaldo y Montesino. He and Doña Maria lived there, they were told, with their daughter, Christina, who was seven, and their son, Rafael, who was the same age as Max.

Thanks to Carmen, who found workmen to renovate the house and craftsmen to make furniture, they were able to move in less than two months after they arrived. They were paying what seemed to them a ridiculously low rent.

During the intervening weeks, they had learned more about an Uncle Henry whom, it seemed, they had never really known.

Moira remembered him as a tall, upright man, who had been a Guards officer during the Great War, with a parchment skin and humorous, pale blue eyes. He lived alone in a studio apartment in Edinburgh, and was a painter of large enthusiasm, but small talent. Nevertheless, he managed to sell almost everything he produced, due to the fact that he simply painted variations of the same picture, with which he'd had an early success, over and over again. It was a Highland snow-scene, predominantly white, of rolling moors and dark pine trees, with Highland cattle in the foreground.

Sometimes he replaced the cattle with a tumbledown croft. These were exhibited in a gallery in Fulham, London, and were popular with foreign visitors.

He had started visiting Spain after his discharge from the Army, and the style of his Spanish paintings varied little from those of Scotland. Yellow dust replaced white snow, but the composition of the landscape remained much the same, with goats instead of cattle and the Scottish crofts turned into *fincas* by the addition of arched doorways.

Andrew and Moira saw him often, regarded him with amused affection and openly envied him his ability to spend two or three months in Spain every year without counting the cost. They both longed to travel, but could not afford it.

It was a matter of some distress to Andrew, who was a genuinely talented painter, that Henry was financially more successful than he was, but it had not spoiled their relationship.

They were frequent guests at the parties which had earned him a modest reputation as a leader of Edinburgh's Bohemian set. These were attended by ladies of artistic bent, who wore short dresses, headbands and frilly garters just above their knees. Henry was gallant to them all, but as far as Andrew and Moira knew, had indulged in no emotional liaisons. Now they realised that Carmen's Mamma was probably the reason.

'You and Moira must go to Spain,' he had often told Andrew. 'It'll open up new worlds. Suit your style more than mine, come to think of it. Nice, hard lines, clear colours, extraordinary light.'

The opportunity finally arose after his death, when Andrew found himself the heir to two thousand pounds and his uncle's flat. In his will, Henry had written: 'The money to be used to widen Andrew and Moira Raven's horizons by enabling them to travel in Spain, and especially to visit my beloved village of San Felipe del Mar in Andalusia.'

Since Max was then only a few weeks old, they had decided to postpone their departure until he was beyond the baby stage. During that time, their urge to travel in Spain had expanded into a determination to live there for as long as their money lasted. Andrew would paint, and hope to sell his work in London and Edinburgh. If he was not successful, they would have the apartment to return to.

They'd had no inkling of the other Uncle Henry they would discover in San Felipe, whose mistress had been the madam of a brothel, whom he had painted in all her erotic nudity.

According to Carmen, he and her mother had been a devoted couple, and his visits had been the high spots of her year. He had even lent her money to buy the bar.

'Did he know about the – the other side of the business?' Andrew said.

'Of course. He told my Mamma there was nothing wrong in providing a necessary service. She had started it when my Papa died. You know, Enrique became *my* uncle, too, and I loved him. He taught me English and showed me how to keep accounts and organise the bar, and said we must have clean girls who went regularly to the doctor. So when my Mamma died, I knew how to manage by myself. One day,' she said proudly, 'I will have the best house in Andalusia.'

As they were preparing to move out of the red room into their own home, Moira said, 'I wish we'd known this Uncle Henry. He must have been fun. Our Henry always looked as though he was on the parade-ground, even at his parties.'

'The old devil, I bet he's laughing his head off now, wherever he is,' Andrew said. 'We've been just as surprised as he meant us to be. He must have known we'd find out about his double life. Well, good luck to him. He never did anyone any harm.'

'If someone had told me I'd spend my first two months in Spain living in a brothel, I'd never have believed it. But it's been fun. And the girls are so nice. I mean, you couldn't hope to meet anyone friendlier than Angelina and Pepita and Sonia.'

Recalling friendly offers he had received from the girls during the past weeks, Andrew agreed. Then he looked at her sharply, wondering how much she knew – or guessed. Despite her upbringing in a small Inverness-shire village, she was not naive. Her ebullience and breathless manner of speech, her eagerness to make friends with everyone, hid a sharp native intelligence.

But her face was innocent as she locked the last suitcase,

and he felt a wave of affection for her. She was a better wife than an impoverished painter deserved, he thought. She didn't mind their financially precarious existence, saying it was more exciting than a weekly wage-packet; she admired his work extravagantly; she appeared to enjoy their sexual encounters as much as he did. He was pleased that he had resisted Pepita's last invitation, which had been offered a couple of days earlier.

Moira had taken Max down to the beach and he had been working up a sketch in their room. He had turned to see Pepita leaning against the door. Carmen's girls wore a kind of modified Andalusian costume on duty, with short flounced skirts and tight bodices. This time Pepita had left off the bodice. The temptation was great, but he had waved her away. She had pouted, but departed obediently. As it turned out, his decision had been fortuitous, for a fierce wind, blowing the sand, caused Moira and Max to return sooner than he expected.

The one disadvantage of living above the Bar Jiminez was that anyone going to the other bedrooms had to pass their door.

One hot night, when Max was restless, Moira had risen to comfort him. To try and cool the air with a through draught, she opened the door just as one of Angelina's clients was on his way downstairs.

A gas-lamp on the landing had illuminated the round face of a short man with a moustache and hair slicked down on either side of a centre parting. He looked about thirty, had small eyes, full red lips and a high-bridged nose. For a moment, he and Moira stared at each other, and his eyes travelled appreciatively over her body, ill-concealed by a thin cotton night-gown. Then he smiled and bowed, murmured, 'Buenas noches, Senorita,' and went on his way.

'I bet he thought I was one of Carmen's girls,' she told Andrew, and he saw that the notion did not entirely displease her.

A few weeks later, as they sat on the vine-covered terrace outside their house, looking down towards the roof-tops of the village, they knew that their decision to stay in San Felipe had been the right one. Already they were beginning to understand and speak Spanish, and had made many new acquaintances, though Carmen remained their closest friend and the oracle to whom they turned with any problem. Because of her profession, she was something of an outcast among the local women, and Moira guessed that she was touched and grateful for their affection.

She was now known to them all as 'Zimmy,' which had been Max's version of 'Jiminez.' The nickname was gradually to spread throughout the village.

Much of their time during their first weeks in the *finca* was spent adjusting to Spanish ways, many of which were strange to them.

On their first day, Moira had noticed a curious omission in the kitchen: there was no cooking range.

She was looking around, puzzled, when Zimmy arrived bearing two brown paper sacks and a fan made of plaited palm leaves.

'Zimmy, where do I cook?' Moira said.

'There.' She indicated a tiled work-top, in which were set three basin-shaped, cast-iron containers. Openings in the side of the work-top gave access to their bases. She opened her paper bags. 'Here's charcoal, and pine-wood.'

She filled a basin with the fuel, set it alight and fanned vigorously at the opening. Within a few moments, the charcoal was burning. 'You cook on top. When you want more heat, you fan harder. Easy.' The fan made a slapping sound as it hit the stove. It was a sound Moira was to hear day in and day out as the village housewives cooked.

She looked at it dubiously. 'I hope I'll be able to manage it.'

'No need. Aquilina cooks for you.'

'Aquilina?'

Zimmy pointed out of the window. A small figure, almost as wide as it was tall, was rolling up the path. 'She is your maid. She comes to you every day except Sunday. Arrives half-past seven. Gives breakfast and lunch, cleans, goes home five o'clock. Leaves everything ready for your dinner.'

'But we can't afford a maid.'

'She's very cheap.' She named a sum equivalent to about

fifteen shillings a week in English money.

'I couldn't pay anyone as little as that!'

'It's more than she's been getting from Don Luis Ansaldo.'

'She's been working next door?'

'I told her she'd like you better. Doña Maria is not nice to servants.'

'But we can't possibly steal her away!'

'Too late to say no,' Zimmy said calmly. 'She's already here. She told Doña Maria yesterday.'

'Was she angry?'

Zimmy shrugged. 'No matter if she was. Aquilina is *your* maid now.'

And so she remained, throughout their life in San Felipe. A round little woman with a smiling face and black hair pulled back into a tight bun, she was, at forty-five, already three times a grandmother. Andrew likened her to a mechanical toy which, when wound up, never stopped moving until, presumably, the motor ran down each evening when she went to bed. She cooked and cleaned and washed their clothes and looked after Max. She ate her own lunch on the run at about three o'clock each afternoon, and scurried home at five. Then, Moira discovered, she cooked supper for her extended family of nine, which ranged from a baby – her youngest grandchild – to her own 88-year-old grandmother. Within a week, the Ravens felt that life without Aquilina would be unthinkable. Moira had the occasional qualm about having deprived Doña Maria, but managed to quash it.

The *finca* gradually took shape as furniture they had ordered from local craftsmen was delivered: solid pine bed-frames, rush- seated chairs, chests of drawers and wardrobes.

One day their carpenter arrived with a curious table which had a kind of frame under it, into which fitted a big, shallow metal pan. Since he spoke no English, he simply set it in the centre of their living-room, and departed.

When Zimmy arrived that evening, Andrew said: 'All we wanted was a dining-table. What on earth is this?'

She shook her head at their ignorance. 'For keeping warm,' she explained patiently.

Moira was suddenly enlightened: 'So that's what those pans

are for!' She had begun to see them as the weather had grown cooler: shallow pans outside almost every house, filled with fuel, over which *petroleo* was poured. Late each afternoon, almost as though a signal had been given, women emerged from their front doors and lit the fuel. As the *petroleo* caught, a layer of smoke spread over the village, which dissipated as the charcoal began to burn. When the pans contained a bed of glowing coals, they were taken inside.

Zimmy pointed to the framework under the table. 'Pan goes there, you spread a big cloth over the table, sit around with feet under the cloth, and keep warm. Good idea, no?'

Moira and Andrew adapted quickly to their new life, and he began to work with a feverish energy, as though he could not bear to miss recording a single aspect of his surroundings. He felt that he was painting better than ever before and his vivid, impressionistic pictures of the landscape and people vibrated with warmth and sunlight.

'God, I hope this place never changes,' he said as he poured red wine into their glasses.

'I don't see how it can,' Moira said. 'It's too isolated. Tourists won't come along that road. Anyway, there's no entertainment when they get here.'

'There's always Zimmy's.'

'And how would the wives occupy themselves? Talking of Zimmy's, isn't it time we fetched Max? He's been there for hours.'

Zimmy adored Max, and almost every day she arrived at the *finca* to carry him off to the beach or her house.

'We can leave him for a while,' Andrew said. 'Let's enjoy the peace.'

They sat in friendly silence, sipping their wine, then Moira said, 'I'm thinking of calling on the Ansaldos. What do you think?'

'They should call on us. We're the newcomers.'

'They won't, according to Zimmy. She says they're rich and proud and unfriendly and they exploit the people who work for them. Everyone's a bit afraid of them. But I hate being at odds with our neighbours. I feel guilty about taking Aquilina and about what happened the day we arrived.

Doña Maria must have thought we were laughing at her.'

'Then visit her. But don't be surprised if she snubs you. That type of Spaniard is very formal.'

'I don't care. At least I'll have made the effort. And their little boy is the same age as Max. It'd be nice if he had a friend next door.'

The following afternoon, sedately dressed in a dark skirt and neat white blouse, holding Max's hand, she tugged an iron bell-pull beside the Ansaldos' front door.

It was answered by an elderly maid in a black dress, with a white apron.

In slow, awkward Spanish Moira asked if she could see the Senora, and gave her own name.

Saying something she interpreted as 'Wait here,' the maid disappeared. When she returned, she shook her head, said curtly, '*La Senora esta ocupada*,' and started to close the door.

Moira heard footsteps behind her. She turned, to find herself looking into the eyes of the man she had last seen on his way down Zimmy's stairs in the early hours of the morning. His face froze and she was so astonished that she gaped at him. It was a moment of total embarrassment.

He recovered first, and said, in Spanish, 'May I help you?'

Too flustered to summon up the Spanish words, she said in English: 'I have come to call on Senora Ansaldo. I am Moira Raven, and this is my son, Maxwell.'

He, too, switched to English: 'I am Luis Ansaldo. May I ask why you want to see my wife?'

She kept her face blank. 'We are your new neighbours, Senor.'

His eyebrows shot up, then he said stiffly: 'We had heard of your arrival.'

'Since *we have never met*, I thought it would be nice to introduce myself to your wife, but I understand she is busy.'

Her emphasis was unmistakable and after a moment a flash of amusement crossed his face. 'She is usually busy, Senora, but I think I can persuade her to greet you. You will come in, please.'

They followed him into a dark, vaulted hall, its walls

dominated by gilt-framed portraits and a large crucifix. The furniture was heavy and ornate; an iron-branched chandelier hung from the ceiling.

'If you will wait for a moment . . .'

He returned, followed by the woman from the Hispano-Suiza and two children: a sulky-looking little boy and a girl a couple of years older.

'My wife, Doña Maria, my son, Rafael, my daughter, Christina,' Don Luis said. The woman bowed, and shook hands limply. 'She understands English a little, but she does not like to speak it. We both welcome you to San Felipe. Are you staying here long?'

'For ever,' Moira said. 'I am pleased to meet you, Senora. I was hoping that our little boys might be able to play together, since they live so close. Perhaps Rafael will come and have tea with Maxwell one day? And Christina, of course, if she would like to.'

Doña Maria glanced at her husband, and spoke sharply. It was clear to Moira that she had understood the invitation, and did not welcome it. But Don Luis said smoothly: 'Christina has lessons during the day, but that would be good for Rafael. Your son could perhaps help him to learn English.'

Later she told Andrew, 'I don't believe Doña Maria wants to have anything to do with us. Neither of us mentioned Aquilina, but that could be the reason. Still, she seems to have plenty of other servants. Don Luis is determined that Rafael must learn English, because one day he'll be taking over the family properties. She didn't like it when he accepted my invitation, but I don't think she dared to argue.'

'Did you like him?'

'After the first moment, he was very friendly.'

'He's probably afraid that you'll tell his wife about seeing him at Zimmy's if they're not agreeable.'

'Of course I wouldn't.' She laughed. 'But I'll never forget his face when he recognised me! Apparently he's been away on business, so he had no way of knowing who we were.'

'What is his business?'

'According to Zimmy, he's into everything. The Ansaldos

own property all over Andalusia: olive groves, sugar-cane fields, orchards, vineyards. They produce wine and make olive oil and export oranges. He runs the whole concern, so he's often away from home.'

'And sometimes away when he's *at* home.'

'I must ask Zimmy about him.'

'You'll do nothing of the kind! How Don Luis conducts his private life is none of our business.'

'Pity,' she said regretfully. 'It's interesting. I've never lived in such intimate contact with a brothel before.'

'I'm glad to hear it. I wonder if you'll be quite so enthusiastic when Max gets old enough to understand what it's all about. It's crossed my mind that a madam might not be the most suitable honorary aunt for a growing boy.'

She waved a hand airily. 'We'll worry about that when the time comes. It might be no bad thing that he's instructed by professionals.'

Andrew blinked. 'You constantly surprise me. Seriously, though, I wonder what Zimmy's future is? She seems to love kids, but she doesn't show any desire to get married.'

'She says, what respectable man would want to marry a woman in her profession? And she isn't interested in the other kind. She sees too many of them.'

In years to come, Max Raven would recognise that his childhood years in San Felipe were, by any standards, idyllic.

By the time he was six his parents were permitting him to wander freely about the village, secure in the knowledge that no harm would come to him.

He knew everyone, and everyone knew him. Each day he would trot down to the bakery in the plaza and carry home a round, crusty loaf of bread, exchanging greetings with his friends on the way. At lunchtime, the bread would be torn into pieces and dunked in the *gazpacho* or *paella*, thick with fresh shellfish, chicken and rice, that Aquilina had made. She would turn the remains of the stale loaves into *migas*, tiny croutons which she would fry in garlic-flavoured olive oil. Max loved them, and ate them as a snack with everything from chopped ham to grapes.

During the afternoon, he was usually to be seen perched on a chair outside the Bar Jiminez, drinking hot chocolate made with goat's milk, and chatting with Zimmy. If she wasn't too busy, a special treat was a ride on her small grey donkey, known simply as 'Burro', along the beach. Max spoke Spanish and English impartially, depending on his company.

During the years before the events which were to change the course of his life, his mother left San Felipe only for an occasional bus-trip into Gibraltar, to drink a cup of English tea or buy groceries from Lipton's shop. Andrew went back to Scotland once, to dispose of Uncle Henry's Edinburgh apartment, for they had decided to make Spain their home for the foreseeable future.

That visit coincided with his one-man show of fifty Spanish paintings in London. All but half-a-dozen of them sold immediately and he returned to San Felipe with the comforting knowledge that, for the next few years at least, their financial future was secure. He spent the proceeds of the flat buying the *finca*. With money left over, they added two more rooms and a large, light studio.

Theirs was a tranquil life, and both were content. Occasionally friends would come from Britain to stay with them. At first they seemed to enjoy the peace, but after a couple of weeks many would become restless, and the phrase, 'What shall we do now?' would be heard. Even fellow-artists, dazzled by the beauty of the surroundings, would find themselves unable to come to terms with the unfamiliar light during the short time they had. Andrew, who had worked for months on his palette before he had mastered it, was sympathetic, but not displeased when the visitors left. For the moment, at least, he had this part of Spain to himself and he was happy to keep it that way for as long as possible.

As the thirties progressed, they learned little of what was happening in the outside world. In their world, it was of more interest to follow the career of Spain's famous fighting bull, Civilon, so gentle that he would allow children to pet him and take hay from their hands, but so courageous in the ring that the crowd would shout for the *indulto* and his life would be spared.

Even Spanish politics hardly impinged on them at first. When Andrew thought about them, which was rarely, he found himself more sympathetic to the theory, though not the practise, of Communism, rather than to Fascism. This was due to his conviction that achievement, not birthright, should be the criterion for advancement. His other strong belief was that violence was no way to bring about change.

Apart from this, he was bored by politics and uninterested in pressing his views on other people. He took no part in the increasingly impassioned political discussions among the male habitués of the Bar Jiminez. His acquaintances there soon learned that a sure way to drive him away was the mention of CEDA, CNT, JONS, POUM or any other set of initials used to identify the political parties and trades union organisations which were already dividing Spain.

When the Second Republic was proclaimed in 1931 and King Alfonso XIII went into exile, their daily lives remained unchanged. They weren't sure what 'Falange' meant and had barely heard of a General Franco.

The one flaw in Moira's domestic contentment was Doña Maria Ansaldo's impenetrable reserve. If they met in the village, when Doña Maria would be sitting upright, like a young Queen Victoria, in the back of her limousine, she would acknowledge Moira with the barest nod, and clearly wished to avoid conversation.

'Why won't she be more friendly?' Moira asked Zimmy.

'She's jealous of you.'

'Don't be ridiculous!'

'You only have to look at her: she's small and square and she has a face like a monkey. You're fair-haired and beautiful. She adores Don Luis and she's afraid of losing him. She's scared of other women.'

'How can you know this?'

'I hear from . . .' She stopped. 'It's gossip.'

You hear from Angelina, who hears from Don Luis himself, Moira thought. And since that's the situation, we'll give up on Doña Maria.

Now assured that no mention would ever be made of the meeting at Zimmy's, Don Luis remained friendly. It appeared that he'd had some acquaintance with Uncle Henry and had even bought one of his paintings. When he was home from his business trips, he took to dropping in to the *finca*. Sometimes he would choose to talk with Moira, cross-questioning her about her life before coming to San Felipe, which had been so alien to his own as the scion of an aristocratic Spanish family that she might have lived on a different planet. Andrew teased her about her conquest, but on other occasions Don Luis would sit quietly for half-an-hour or so in the studio, watch him paint and drink a glass of wine. The two men had little in common but, as Andrew told Moira, 'I think he likes to escape his women. I don't mind. He watches me work and he doesn't impinge.'

'What do you talk about?'

'It's mostly superficial chat, about the village, his orange-groves, the sale of his olive-oil. The one time he started on politics I changed the subject fairly briskly. He's a natural Fascist. If I'd let him go on telling me about his contempt for the peasants, I'd have ended up disliking him, and I don't want to do that.'

They rarely saw Christina, but Don Luis usually brought Rafael with him and would shoo him out to play with Max.

The two little boys did not care for each other. Max, as outgoing as his mother, had made friends with other village children, regardless of their social position. Rafael, on the other hand, was not often allowed off the Ansaldo property unless he was accompanied by one or other of his parents or a servant. He had a private tutor, while Max attended the little village school; he was destined for the Military Academy in Aranjuez, whereas Andrew had decided that when Max was eleven, assuming their bank balance was still healthy, he would be sent to school in Britain, so he would not lose touch with his roots. With a clear idea of his own status, Rafael tended to treat Max with arrogant superiority. Once he said, 'You have not got a motor. Only peasants do not have motors.' On another, 'If we did not live next door to each other, my mother said we would not speak to you.'

Max rapidly acquired a healthy dislike for him, but as it seemed inevitable that they would be thrown together, he tried – usually – not to show it.

The advantage he had over Rafael was physical; he was

much the stronger of the two. Every now and then, fed up with being baited, he would start a fight, which would invariably end with Rafael in tears on the ground.

Max played soccer in the village, was a good swimmer, ran faster and climbed higher into the tree-branches than most of his contemporaries. The only sport at which Rafael excelled was riding. He loved to dress up in his miniature boots, made of the softest leather, his skin-tight grey trousers, frilled shirt and short black jacket, and ride through the village, then gallop along the beach at the water's edge on his chestnut pony, which was stabled at the back of his house.

One afternoon they were on the terrace while Don Luis was drinking tea with Moira. To break the silence, Max boasted, 'I'm going to buy a bicycle.'

'*You* are going to buy it?' Rafael said. 'I don't believe it. You have not got enough money.'

'I'm saving my allowance. I've saved quite a lot already.'

'I would not want a bicycle. They are for peasants. I am going to get a new belt to wear when I go riding. A black leather one with silver decorations from Toledo.'

'Have you got the money?'

'Not yet.' Then he said thoughtfully, 'I would have enough if you would lend me yours. I would pay it back.'

'I don't want to lend it.'

'I would give you interest.'

'What's that?'

'It is what banks get when they lend money. My father told me about it. You have to pay back more than you borrow, because if they had not lent it to you, you would not have been able to buy what you wanted. You could be my *Caja de Ahorros*. I would give you back more than you lent me.'

Seduced by the prospect of adding to his hoard, Max went to his bedroom, took his precious pesetas from his money-box, and handed them over.

One Sunday afternoon a little later, Moira was in the kitchen, struggling to light the charcoal, which for some reason would not catch. It was Aquilina's day off and she had decided to make a cock-a-leekie as a change from *gazpacho*. A movement outside caught her eye and she went to the window. The

Ansaldos' Hispano-Suiza had pulled up outside the front door. Rafael and his mother emerged. It was the first time that Doña Maria had come to their house.

'And she had to be chauffeur-driven a hundred yards to show us who she was!' Moira told Andrew later.

Wiping blackened hands on her apron, aware that her hair was slipping down from its roll on the crown of her head, she went to the door.

'This is a pleasant surprise, Doña Maria. Please come in.'

Doña Maria's dark eyes were angry, and there were traces of tears on Rafael's face. 'We are here to return your son's money. He is a usurer, Senora! We are not accustomed to such dealings.'

'I haven't the slightest idea what you're talking about!'

'Your son persuaded Rafael to borrow money from him, but then he demanded a great deal of interest. He threatened to hurt Rafael if the money was not repaid.'

'I cannot believe that!'

'I assure you, Senora! Rafael has told me. He has been very upset. I am forbidding him to have anything more to do with your son.'

Wordlessly, Rafael held out a handful of pesetas. As Moira took them, he and Doña Maria marched back to their car and drove off.

When Max returned from an afternoon in the village, he found his mother angrier than he had ever seen her, and his father stone-faced.

'How could you do such a thing?' Moira said. 'To persuade that little boy to borrow money, and to ask for interest! And to threaten him! I'm thoroughly ashamed of you. We've tried so hard to keep on good terms with our neighbours, and now you've spoilt it.'

'I didn't!' Max said. 'He said about the interest. I didn't even know what it was. And I didn't threaten him.'

'That's not what Doña Maria told me. I can't imagine that she was lying. And you must have frightened Rafael. I could see he'd been crying.'

'That's because he was scared of *her*!' Max's eyes were wide and furious. 'He told lies. It wasn't like that . . .'

Andrew, who was standing by the window, interrupted: 'Hell! Here's Don Luis. Now Maxwell, I don't want any more argument, and you're to apologise to him.'

'Why should I? Rafael *asked* me for the money.'

But the apologies were to come from Don Luis, not Max. It appeared that Doña Maria had questioned Rafael about his new belt and, on hearing the story he told, had taken it upon herself to rush to the Ravens without consulting her husband. Less gullible than she, he had cross-questioned Rafael.

'There has been a misunderstanding,' he said carefully. 'Rafael has wanted the belt for a long time, and I had told him he could not have it until his birthday. When Maxwell offered to lend him money to buy it he, of course, accepted, which was wrong, but he himself insisted that he would repay with interest. Only recently I explained that system to him. His mother did not understand the situation.'

'He said I could be his *Caja de Ahorros*,' Max said.

Don Luis laughed. 'Your son is a financier, not an extortionist! May we not forget all about this unfortunate episode? I understand my wife has repaid the loan. That's the end of it.'

After he had gone, Max said indignantly, 'That wasn't right, either. I never offered to lend Rafael my money, he asked for it.'

'There are times when absolute honesty has to be sacrificed to tact,' Andrew said. 'Spaniards are a proud people and Don Luis was saving face.'

'What does that mean?'

'It means finding a way to get yourself out of a humiliating situation. We've chosen to live in the same small community as the Ansaldos. Let's forget this, son. It wouldn't do to be on bad terms with them.'

'Senora Ansaldo said Rafael couldn't come here again. I don't mind, because I don't like him much.'

'I wouldn't count on it,' Andrew said. 'I reckon everything will go on as usual, including Rafael's visits with his father.'

It was so. Rafael continued to come to the *finca*, but there was a new strain between him and Max. He preferred to spend his time, whenever possible, sitting alone on the terrace, reading a book. This soon became the accepted form, and Max went about his own business, more or less ignoring him.

There was one other boy in the village who was left very much to his own devices, but the cause of his isolation was different from Rafael's.

His name was Manolo Machado. A little older than Max, he was a dark-faced urchin with a violent temper. He was constantly in trouble for minor thefts and other misdemeanours and his entry into a shop instantly put the staff on alert. He was often stopped on his way out, and the baker or the grocer, whoever it might be, would pat his pockets, run hands over his shirt to make sure he had not stolen anything. Frequently, he had, but such indignities had caused him to develop a carapace of toughness that made him generally unpopular.

Max had learnt something of his background by overhearing a conversation between his mother and father after Moira had returned from a visit to Zimmy.

'It's the first time she's ever talked about a "client," ' she said. 'Would you believe it, that young Manolo Machado went to the bar this afternoon and asked for Pepita's services. Calm as you like! Said he could afford her, and he had a right. He was furious when Zimmy sent him away with a flea in his ear. Ten years old!'

Andrew roared with laughter. 'God help the girls when he's grown up!'

'He's no better than his mother, it seems. Her name is Luisa and Zimmy remembers the day she arrived in the village with a group of gypsies. There were five of them, three men and two women, with a donkey and a camel. They'd crossed from Tangier. I wish I'd seen them. They walked down the hill just before dusk and the women were wearing long, bright skirts and scarves around their heads and lots of jewellery. Luisa was leading the camel, and she was pregnant. They slept on the beach and the next day she went to Zimmy's mother and said that the baby was coming. They put her in one of the rooms and Manolo was born that night. The following morning, the other gypsies had gone. They'd just disappeared after dark, leaving Luisa behind.'

'Who was the baby's father?'

'One of the men. Luisa didn't know which. She hung around the village for a while, sleeping on the beach with the baby, begging for food. Then she moved into a cave up in the hills and set up in business.'

'Business?'

'Catering for the men who couldn't afford Zimmy's girls. She still does, but she doesn't get many customers these days. Apparently she wasn't bad-looking, but she's deteriorated. No one knows how she and Manolo manage to live.'

Sitting outside the open window in the sun, his back to the wall, Max was deeply interested. He knew Manolo's mother by sight and found it difficult to believe she had ever been good-looking. He had seen her shambling around the narrow streets, hand held out for alms, a skinny, ragged, dark-skinned woman with dirty bare feet, who always looked cold. Any money she received was spent on rough red wine.

He thought it must be rather fun to live in a cave and be as strong and self-confident as Manolo, but none of his friends shared his admiration; they had suffered too often from the gypsy boy's explosive temper. Now they made sure they were well out of reach before they shouted abuse at him or, sometimes, threw small pebbles. Running with the crowd, Max didn't dare to protest, but he remained silent during the catcalls, and never threw stones.

His first meeting with Manolo was to have repercussions throughout his life.

Though he was a sociable boy, who enjoyed the company of his peers, he also loved to explore the country behind the village alone, and would wander in the hills, sometimes climbing trees, at others lying peacefully on his stomach, looking towards the sea over olive groves and fields of sugarcane. After the first few anxious searches, when he had been away for hours, his parents became accustomed to his expeditions, and no longer worried.

One hot July afternoon he strolled along the road which wound out of the village, then climbed one of the hills that folded into the back country. At the top, just off the track, there was a flat, grassy area surrounded by a forest of trees where he could sit in the shade and watch the scurrying ants.

Normally he saw no one, and only bird-song, chirruping insects and the wind among the branches broke the silence. But this afternoon, when he reached the outer circle of trees, human sounds made him stop, frozen. First, there was a long drawn-out moan, which was cut off suddenly, then a piercing scream, and scuffling and grunting, like a pig in its wallow. Several seconds silence, during which he remained immobile, were followed by a man's agonised cry: 'No! No!' and footsteps running away from the place down the hill.

He waited, but there was no further sound, so he moved cautiously through the trees towards the open space. There was a heap of fabric on the far side which, as he drew closer, he recognised as women's clothing. And in the shadows, dappled by sunlight striking through the branches, a girl lay on the grass. Nakedness had never embarrassed Max, because his parents had no inhibitions about their bodies, so he said tentatively, '*Hola*!'

She did not move.

He went towards her, wondering if she was asleep, and looked down. His breath choked in his throat. He had never seen a dead person before, but he knew this girl was dead. She was lying on her back with blood staining her thighs and the bush of pubic hair. Her head was twisted unnaturally, her tongue protruded from her mouth. There were dark patches on her throat and her eyes were open, wide and staring.

He recognised her. Her name was Clara and she was about fourteen, the daughter of a peasant-farmer who was one of the Ansaldos' tenants on a small-holding just outside the village. He had seen her often in the Plaza, a plump, coarse-featured girl who seemed to prefer older male company to boys her own age.

He stumbled back, turned his head and was sick. He wanted to run away, but his feet seemed to have taken root, and his legs felt like rubber hose-pipe.

Footsteps scuffled through the undergrowth towards him. Careless of the noise he made, he began to run down the far slope of the hill. He went through groves of trees, over stony ground. Panic-stricken, he lost all sense of direction, running wherever the path was easiest, until his heart was thumping and his breath wheezing. His only coherent thought was that he must not be found near Clara's body.

He ran until he could run no longer. He was further from the village than he had ever been, half way up the side of a new fold of hills. The slope ahead was steep and rocky, but to his left a lone cork oak reached towards the sky. It was old, with a thick trunk, heavy with foliage. He hobbled towards it, and began to climb the lower branches, scrabbling for holds in the seamed layer of cork.

The shock when he felt a hand grab his lower foot almost made him faint. He lost his grip, and crashed to the ground. Was it the murderer? He lay there, his eyes closed, waiting for the attack.

When it came, it was not what he expected. A bare foot nudged him in the side and his shoulder was shaken roughly. A voice said, 'What's the matter with you? Why did you run away?'

He opened his eyes and saw Manolo Machado's dirty face a few inches from his own. He opened his mouth to cry out, but it emerged as a choked cough. Tears of fright began to pour down his cheeks.

'Sit up! Stop howling!' Grasping a handful of his shirt, Manolo hauled him into a sitting position. 'What's happened?'

'She's dead! You killed her!'

'What the hell are you talking about? Who's dead? I never killed anyone. Don't be stupid!'

As Max's panic subsided, he began to think more clearly. The voice he had heard had been a man's, the thudding footsteps made by shod feet. Manolo's voice was shrill, unmistakably a boy's, and he was not wearing shoes.

'It's Clara, from the village. She's in the clearing. She hasn't got any clothes on and she's dead.' He shuddered. 'I saw an ant . . . crawling into her mouth.'

Manolo stared at him. 'You're making it up!'

'I'm not! There was a man. He ran away.'

'Who was it?'

'I don't know. I didn't see him. I thought I heard him coming back, and I ran.'

'That was me. I saw you. I thought we'd . . . oh, talk, or something.' Manolo stood up. His face was filthy, his long black hair matted. He wore no shirt; his ragged trousers had been torn off below the knees and were pulled in around the waist with string. But Max had never been so pleased to have anyone's company.

'Come on, we'll go to the clearing and look,' Manolo said.

'I don't want to go back there.'

'I'm going back, and you're coming!' He paused, then said cynically, 'There won't be anything. It was Clara, fooling about. I know her.'

But the body was still there, and now a steady procession of ants crawled over the face. Even Manolo looked sick. 'Look at her neck,' he whispered. 'Someone strangled her!'

Max's eyes were averted. 'It was the man I heard. We have to tell the police.'

'Not me! I'm not going near the police. She'll be found soon enough.'

'We can't just leave her . . .'

'We're going to!' Manolo turned from the body, then Max saw him bend down and pick something up from the ground.

'What's that?'

'Nothing. A pebble.' His eyes slid away and he looked suddenly furtive. 'I'm going home.'

Max realised that he was going to be left to make his own way to the *finca*. He didn't want to be alone with the memory of Clara, and a murderer on the loose.

'Please come with me. I don't want to go back by myself,' he said.

Manolo looked at him speculatively. When Max knew him better, he was to recognise that look. It meant that Manolo was considering the options, and which would bring him the greater advantage.

In this case, he decided for magnanimity. 'I'll come to your house with you. Only you've got to promise me you won't let on to anyone that we found her.'

'Why not? The police have to catch that man.'

'You don't know them! They won't believe anything you say. They never believe boys. They'll think *you* did it.'

'They wouldn't!' He was appalled at the suggestion.

'Of course they will! They know Clara, she'd let anyone screw her. Old men, boys like us. Why not you?'

'But I never have!'

'Not with anyone? What a baby. Won't stop them from thinking you have, though. Then they'll say you killed her to stop her from telling. They'll put you in prison, for sure. They might even sentence you to death. You know what they do? They garrotte you with a brass collar by tightening a screw until it goes right into the back of your neck.'

Max took a deep, sobbing breath. 'I won't tell. I won't tell anyone! Not even my mother and father.'

'Right. Then I'll see you home.'

They hurried down towards the village, instinctively avoiding the open path, threading their way through the trees and undergrowth. As they walked, Manolo made Max tell him in detail what he had heard when he reached the clearing. Then he said slowly, 'I reckon that man's someone we'd know, someone from hereabouts. He was hot for Clara and took her up there. Then he got rough with her and she started to scream and he wanted to shut her up, so he put his hands around her throat . . .' He made a graphic gesture and Max began to tremble again. 'Maybe he didn't mean to strangle her and when he saw what he'd done, he was so frightened that he shouted out, then ran away.'

When they reached the *finca* Max expected Manolo to turn back. Instead, he made it clear that he was coming up to the house.

Moira and Andrew were sitting on the terrace. They were momentarily taken aback to see him, then Moira, her heart touched by the ragged child, welcomed him and called Aquilina to bring lemonade. Trying to put him at ease, she did not notice Max's silence.

From that day, Manolo became a regular visitor. He soon

learnt that the grubbier and more neglected he looked, the more food and drink Moira would press on him, so although he did own one pair of cracked shoes, he never wore them. One day Max caught him outside the gate picking at the legs of his trousers to fray them more than they already were.

Clara's body was found a few days after the murder, by two young men who had been shooting birds in the hills. Suspicion instantly fell on them, but even the old doctor, who had cataracts on both eyes and was hovering on the edge of senility, was able to assure the police that she had not been shot and, indeed, a blind man could tell that she had been dead for days.

There was an inquiry, of a sort. Hunters, goat-herds, workers on the sugar-cane fields, anyone known to frequent the hills, were questioned. Nothing was discovered to connect any of them with the murder.

Several factors militated against an enthusiastic investigation: the lethargy and lack of experience in such crimes of San Felipe's two policemen; the villagers' stubborn oppostion to calling in experienced officers from Malaga who might meddle in their affairs; Clara's dubious reputation, and the fact that she was a member of a family of no importance, too poor and too ignorant to press for justice; and the current energy-sapping spell of hot, humid weather.

The village was briefly shocked, but the body was hastily buried and the tragedy was soon forgotten by everyone except, presumably, Clara's family – and Max Raven.

Moira was never able to understand why he started having nightmares which would waken him, screaming and sweating, every few weeks. As time passed, it became impossible for him ever to tell her. Manolo was the only person with whom he could discuss it.

'Don't you ever wake up, thinking about her?' he said one day.

'No.'

'Don't you wonder who the man was?'

'I know who it was.'

Max looked disbelieving. 'You can't know. Who was it?'

There was a half-sly, half-triumphant expression on

Manolo's face. 'I'm not telling. I'm keeping it for myself. It might be – useful.'

'Useful how?'

'If I want something.'

'Does he know you know?'

'Of course not.'

'Aren't you frightened of him?'

'No. I bet he's the one who's frightened, in case he's found out.'

'I don't believe you do know.'

Manolo grinned. 'Maybe I do, maybe I don't. Come on, let's go to the beach.'

Thinking about the conversation later, Max convinced himself that Manolo's claim was a fabrication. His gratitude to the gypsy boy for having, as he imagined, rescued him from the threat of execution, remained steadfast,and the two boys became friends. Max enjoyed his company, for Manolo knew the beaches and the countryside even better than he did, and liked to explore the hills and the caves, the cliffs and rocks. As the months passed, the memory of Clara faded but his nightmares returned intermittently for years.

For Manolo, there were many rewards in the friendship. Although nearly two years older, he was no taller than Max. After he had been coming to the *finca* for a few weeks, Moira gave him several of Max's shirts, trousers and jerseys. He put them on, and his gratitude touched her. Some time later, she was distressed when he turned up wearing his old rags.

'What happened to your other clothes?' she said.

There were tears in his eyes. 'My mother sold them. She didn't have any money and she hadn't had anything to eat for two days.'

So Moira not only gave him some more clothes, but presented him with half of the dish of *arroz con pollo* that Aquilina had made for their own supper, telling him it was to be shared with his poor mamma.

Later Max, who had already learnt something about his character, challenged him: 'Did your mother really sell the clothes?'

'No, I did,' Manolo said calmly.

'You told my mother a lie!'

Manolo shrugged. 'She would have sold them if she'd had the chance, so I did it first. They were mine.'

'What did you do with the money?'

'Bought myself a knife.'

Max didn't like the idea of Manolo lying to Moira, but he was acutely aware of the difference between his circumstances and that of the gypsy boy, and was self-conscious about the comfort he enjoyed. If Manolo wanted to make a little extra money, he had a right. His main source of income, Max had discovered, came from begging, and he rarely made more than a few pesetas a day. Some instinct seemed to tell him when visitors were about to arrive in San Felipe. He would wait at the bus-stop and if there were strangers from Malaga on board, would pluck at their clothing until frequently, to get rid of him, they gave him a coin. Occasionally, he managed to pick their pockets. At other times, he would wait on the outskirts of the village and as a car wound slowly around the hairpin bends, would leap onto the running-board, his hand outstretched. He was a sad little figure, with his unattractive, dirty face. If there were women in the car, they would usually respond generously. But visitors were few and far between, his mother spent anything she made on wine, and between his calls at the *finca* he often went hungry.

Shocked to discover that he was almost illiterate, Moira began to teach him to read and write with the aid of a Spanish dictionary. She found him quick and responsive, and at the same time, he picked up some English. She insisted that he should attend the village school with Max, and it was not long before he had almost caught up with other boys his own age.

Max always made sure that Manolo's path and Rafael's did not cross, because he knew instinctively that any contact between them was potentially dangerous. Rafael's arrogance would certainly touch off Manolo's fire-cracker temper.

Max's third friend at that period of his life was Titi. At eight years old, he was a round-faced, gentle little boy whose mother had died giving birth to him. He lived with his father, Jaime, who was Zimmy's handyman, in a tumble-down, one-room cottage on the edge of the village.

Jaime was simple, childlike, popular with everyone. Nearly six feet tall and built like an ox, he was immensely powerful, but his brain moved sluggishly and his reasoning powers were almost non-existent. He and Titi adored each other.

The Ravens encountered him first when they consulted Zimmy about the possibility of employing someone to clear the land around their house.

The next day, she arrived with Jaime. He stood, silent and smiling, while she explained him to Andrew: 'He will do anything you want, and come whenever he is not helping Esteban. Give him an order, he will obey. He is an honest, good man, but you must say everything to him slowly and two times, or he doesn't understand.'

At first, they found the repetition of orders tedious, but he was so gentle and good-humoured, so anxious to please, that they soon became as fond of him as they were of Aquilina.

After working for a few weeks, he asked if he might bring his son, Titi, with him. Most days after that, they would arrive together, hand in hand, and Titi would work beside his father.

Timid and under-sized, he was inevitably taken under Moira's wing. She bandaged his cut fingers and scraped knees, gave him food and clothing, whisked him away to play with Max when she thought he had worked long enough.

Titi made no secret of his admiration for Max's cleverness and strength. Max was flattered, and as their friendship flourished, became his protector. At school, he shielded him from teasing – he was a natural butt – and helped him with his work for, like his father, Titi was backward. At first Manolo was among those who treated him with contempt, but a brisk rebuke from Max made him realise that tormenting Titi would only diminish himself in the Ravens' eyes.

The three boys spent much of their time together, but although Rafael was often at the *finca* he never joined them. On one occasion Max had felt a pang of guilt about his isolation and suggested that he might come down to the beach with himself and Titi. He refused scornfully, saying, 'His father is a servant.'

2

The knowledge that their dissociation from Spanish politics was being threatened crept gradually into the Ravens' consciousness.

Andrew first became aware of it one day towards the end of 1934, when he realised, on his way home from the Bar Jiminez, that his comfortable conversations over drinks with his friends were becoming shorter. No day seemed to pass without the interference of political discussion, which frequently escalated into argument – at which point he would leave.

Despairingly, he said to Moira, 'Apart from the general boredom, there are so many damn factions in this country now, I can't keep up with them. There have been workers' risings in Madrid and Barcelona, and the talk today was that the miners in Asturias virtually took over the province before that chap Franco put them down.'

'I know,' she said. 'I was talking to old Marcos, the Ansaldos' gardener. His son's in the Foreign Legion and Franco brought the Legion over from Morocco. According to Marcos, hundreds of miners were killed and now hundreds more are in prison. It's horrible!'

He pursued his own thought: 'The trouble is, it isn't just a straightforward quarrel between Right and Left. Each side has half-a-dozen factions. I mean, on the Left, there's the official Communist party, and there's POUM, which is Communist, too, but anti-Stalinist. And there are the Right-wing Army officers who either belong to the Falange, or JONS, which is Fascist, or CEDA, the Catholic party. And they all seem to hate each other.'

'I'm glad we're so isolated here,' she said. 'We'll never have to get involved.'

'I hope not, but the workers all through Spain are on the verge of revolution and there's a lot of local bitterness against the land-owners, particularly Ansaldo, from what I hear. He's the biggest employer and he's never been popular. The chaps who work for him barely get a living wage. Esteban's been speaking out against him. You know Esteban's a dedicated Communist?'

'Zimmy told me. She says he'll get over it.'

'I don't think so. He's an intelligent lad, and he's an idealist. I've an idea that he's been recruiting for the Party. He was holding forth in the bar the other night. He's a bloody good speaker. Almost persuaded me to join.'

'I hope you'll do nothing of the kind,' she said sharply. 'It's not our quarrel. We're foreigners. We mustn't take sides.'

'I know that. But talking of Esteban . . . something I wanted to mention. When we were having coffee on the terrace the other day, after he'd delivered our wine, he was sitting in direct sunlight and I noticed for the first time how much fairer he is than Zimmy. He doesn't look Spanish at all.'

Her eyes narrowed as she brought the boy's image into her mind, the long, serious face, balanced on a thin neck, the mobile mouth, high cheek-bones. 'You're right. His hair's light brown and his eyes are grey. He's grown so much lately that he's nearly a head taller than she is.'

'I've been wondering if possibly . . .'

'Uncle Henry?'

'It could be. Zimmy's father was ill for years, and Henry had been coming here since the twenties.'

'Now I come to think of it, Esteban actually said to me once, "After my Papa died, Enrique became my father!" I'll be damned! That makes him my cousin.'

'That *could* make him your cousin. We don't know. Zimmy's never hinted at such a thing.'

'Maybe she's not sure herself. After all, it's hard to pick a resemblance between a little boy and an elderly man whom you can only see in memory. Even now he's older, I noticed the indications more or less by accident.'

'She's no fool. She knew her Mamma, and even if it was never admitted, she must suspect. It could partly explain why she's adopted us. I heard her telling Max one day that she looked on us as her family. But if Henry knew Esteban was his son, I'm surprised that he didn't mention him in his will.'

'I thought of that, too. Haven't you ever wondered why it was that Henry's estate was so small? His pictures had been selling well for years, but he only left a couple of thousand pounds. My guess is that he'd been funnelling his spare money out to Senora Jiminez. He willed me what was left in Edinburgh, with the apartment, because he knew Esteban was already taken care of.'

'Should we say anything to Zimmy?'

He shook his head. 'We don't *know*. Maybe we never will. We don't have any right to bring it up. Let's leave that to her.'

After that, they watched Esteban with new interest, and became increasingly sure that there was a basis for their suspicions.

Although he evinced no interest in painting himself, he was a sensitive boy with a deep love of the landscape and the changing patterns of sea and sky. He enjoyed looking at Andrew's pictures, and more than once his perceptive comments led to improvements. At the same time, he earned their gratitude by never attempting to press his political beliefs on them. They came to know him well, because he appeared to be almost as fond of Max as Zimmy was and frequently arrived at the *finca* to take him for a ride on his motor-cycle.

Throughout most of 1935, it seemed that Andrew's forebodings might have heen unjustified. On the surface, at least, political life in San Felipe remained tranquil.

For Max, the year was notable for a second crisis in his relations with Rafael Ansaldo.

At ten years old, he was already giving promise of the good looks that were to last throughout his life. His dark-fringed blue eyes were striking against his black hair and tanned skin and he was tall for his age. Although he was unaware of it, Pepita had already cast covetous eyes on him and decided that in a few years she would have him in her bed . . . free of charge.

On the other hand, he was well aware of the interest he had aroused in Christina Ansaldo, and was irritated and embarrassed by it. At twelve, she was a heavily-built girl with her mother's down-turned mouth and button eyes. Her body was thick with puppy-fat, and she wore her straight black hair skinned back in a plait, which made her face look like a pale pink balloon. Although she had a governess and spent all her time at home, she had only accompanied her father and Rafael to the *finca* two or three times until, one day, she was on the beach with her governess when Andrew and Max came down for a swim.

Out of politeness, they went across to greet her. She looked at Max's well-developed boy's body with new awareness. She followed them down to the water's edge and stood, watching them swim, admiring his efficient crawl. When they emerged, she was holding his towel and managed to touch his bare shoulder as she handed it to him. He backed away nervously.

After that, she pursued him relentlessly. Every time her father, either with or without Rafael, came to the *finca*, she accompanied him. Max came to dread his mother's call: 'Max! Christina's here!'

'She's just like Rafael!' he said. 'She only wants to sit on the terrace. She doesn't talk and she stares at me.'

'She's shy. Be nice to her, darling. Such a plain girl,' Moira said.

'She's not shy. She's stupid. And she keeps *banging* me. In the garden, she bumps up against me and grabs my arm and – and once she tried to give me a kiss.'

Moira laughed. 'She likes you.'

'I don't want her to like me.'

He began to feel hunted. Even when she was not visiting the *finca*, she watched him. The upper windows of the Ansaldo house overlooked the Ravens' garden and he often saw her outline behind the glass when he was with Manolo or Titi.

Then, one sunny afternoon, her head appeared over the stone wall between the two houses. She leant her elbows on the top and looked towards the terrace, where he and Manolo were making paper aeroplanes and floating them into the trees. He realised that she must have climbed the gardener's ladder and this new invasion of his privacy enraged him. He picked up a piece of gravel from the path and was about to throw it at her when Manolo stopped him. 'I've got a better way to put her off watching us,' he said. 'Do what I do.'

Max followed as he sauntered towards the wall. When Manolo was just below where Christina's round eyes were blinking down at them, he opened his threadbare trousers and began to urinate, directing the stream in an arc towards her. Her mouth dropped open in shock. Max, overcome by laughter, followed his lead. For a moment, she did not move, then she began to cry. They heard a scuffle behind the wall, and Rafael joined her. He stared at them, and his face turned scarlet.

Suddenly aware of the enormity of their action, Max did up his trousers. When he looked back, the Ansaldos had disappeared.

'Do you think they'll tell?' he said uneasily.

'Doesn't matter if they do,' Manolo said. 'Say they're telling lies. It got rid of her, anyway.'

But Max still had a vivid memory of his last brush with Rafael's family. That time he had not been in the wrong. This time, he was.

A couple of hours later, when Manolo had departed, he saw Don Luis and Rafael making their way up the path to Andrew's studio. He had been sitting under a tree, reading, and he jumped up, preparing to flee, when Don Luis raised a friendly hand in greeting.

'Here we are, then,' he called. 'Your father in?'

Max nodded, looking warily at Rafael, who did not meet his eyes.

'You boys amuse yourselves. I won't be long.' Don Luis smiled, ruffled Max's hair, and went into the studio.

They stood, looking at each other, then Rafael said, 'I haven't told my father what you and that gypsy did to my sister. Yet.'

'There's nothing to tell,' Max said defiantly.

'Oh, yes, there is. It was – It was wicked! Christina cried all the way back to the house.'

'I'm sorry. It was just that I was sick of her staring at us. She does it all the time.'

'She wasn't staring at *you*. She was just looking over the wall.'

'She was staring! And she must have climbed up your ladder specially.'

'Well, anyway, you know what'll happen to you if I tell, don't you? If your father doesn't thrash you, my father will. With his horse-whip.'

'Rafael, don't tell anyone. Please.'

'I'm going to, unless you give me your Hornby engine.' There was silence as he enjoyed the look of dismay which spread over Max's face. The green engine, trimmed with gold bands and red lettering, was his pride and joy. His father had ordered it from London and had promised to add extra carriages and signals.

'No! You can't have my engine.'

'Then I'm going to the studio to tell them now.' He stood up.

'Don't, Rafael!'

'Say you'll give me the engine, then.'

Max's mind rapidly computed the alternatives and he realised he had no choice. 'Won't Christina tell even if I do?'

'She promised she wouldn't if I get the Hornby. I said I'd give her the sugared almonds my aunt sent from Portugal.'

'What will I tell my mother and father?'

'It's my birthday next week. You can give it to me as a present.'

If his parents were surprised at Max's generosity to a boy he had never liked, they accepted it, and even expressed admiration for his sacrifice. Neither did the cessation of Christina's visits cause questions, for shortly afterwards she was sent to school at a convent in Madrid.

Max's pain at having lost his Hornby engine persisted for a long time, and matters were not helped by Rafael's account of how his mother had bought him an entire railway station, complete with guards, to go with it.

Eventually, his resentment, added to his long-standing dislike of Rafael, grew into something near to hatred.

Though the Ravens were hardly aware of them other hatreds were fermenting which were destined soon to bring violence and terror to the village.

By the beginning of 1936, regular reports were filtering through of increasing unrest among the working-classes, whose standard of living was among the lowest in Europe.

To the horror of the rich land-owners, a general election in February put the Left-wing Popular Front in power. For the labourers, the *braceros*, and tenant farmers who had been forced for generations to pay crippling rents for tiny patches of land, it was a signal for rejoicing.

One day the following month Max came home with news that a group of strangers had arrived in the village.

'Three men,' he said. 'They're all wearing red scarves and making speeches in the plaza. Everyone's shouting. Jaime's there, and so is Esteban. I'm going back.'

'No, you're not,' Andrew said. 'I don't want you getting mixed up in political meetings.'

'That's not fair! Manolo's there.'

'Don't argue with me.'

The following morning, Sunday, Max slipped out of the house without telling his parents and made his way into the village.

The plaza was even more crowded than it had been the previous day, and there was almost an atmosphere of carnival. Each of the three strangers was the centre of a circle of men, most of whom he recognised as employees of either Don Luis or one of the lesser land-owners, the *latifundistas*. Esteban Jiminez was there, too, addressing his own group, among whom was Jaime, watching the others anxiously so he would applaud and shout at the right time.

As Max moved around, he overheard phrases which, even to him, hinted of trouble to come. 'The days of slave-labour are over, brothers,' Esteban said, a clenched fist raised above his head. 'We must bring the land back to the people!' One of the strangers shouted, 'Down with the priests, the servants of capitalism!' Another cried, 'Death to the *latifundistas*!'

He saw Manolo and Titi on the outskirts of Esteban's group and was about to join them when he became aware of the sound of horses' hooves behind him.

Along the north side of the square, unheard by the villages above their own clamour, half-a-dozen horsemen had gathered.

Max began to push through the crowd, but before he had taken more than a few steps, the horsemen put their mounts to a gallop, straight into the gathering. They were flailing with whips to left and right. Screams of pain and shouts of anger added to the discord. Men fell, were trampled by the horses, others fled up the steps or down towards the beach. Max was standing, petrified, when the Ansaldos' huge Hispano-Suiza came bucketing from one of the side streets. Don Luis was behind the wheel, shouting abuse at the crowd. Max tried to leap out of the way, but his foot slipped on a loose stone. He felt himself falling into the car's path, then someone grabbed him round the waist and hauled him to safety. The motor swept past, missing him by inches. Don Luis steered it around the plaza and back the way he had come. As though this was a signal, the horsemen wheeled, and followed.

As the sound of the hooves on cobbles died away, a silence fell.

Shaking, with tears of fright pouring down his face, Max looked up at his rescuer. It was Esteban, and he was gazing, horrified, at the scene of carnage.

Men were lying on the ground, some of them moaning. Others dazed, were trying to crawl away.

Women began to arrive from Mass, and new sounds broke the silence as they ran towards the injured. Some screamed, others cried as they knelt in the dust, unable to comprehend what had happened.

They were followed by the priest, Father Miguel. He was a sleekly plump, youngish man with a strong sense of his own righteousness. A comparatively new arrival in San Felipe from Madrid, he was not generally liked, because he had not hidden his preference for the company of the well-to-do who invited him to wine and dine, rather than the peasants who could offer him nothing. He moved towards one of the three strangers, who was trying to struggle to his feet, blood running from a gash in his forehead. Ignoring the priest's helping hand, the man leant forward and spat at him.

'. . . and then Esteban took me into the bar and Zimmy gave me a glass of brandy,' Max told Moira and Andrew. In the safety of the *finca* he was enjoying their attention. 'She made me stay until everyone had gone home. She was angry with Esteban, but when I told her how he'd saved my life, she kissed him. She let me ride Burro all the way when she brought me back. She said the men on the horses were criminals.'

'Who are they?' Moira said. 'Did you know any of them?'

'I've seen most of them. Zimmy said they're all friends of Don Luis.'

'I can't believe that he would have driven straight at you!' Andrew said.

'I don't think he saw me,' Max said fairly. 'He was shouting out of the window on the other side of the car.'

'I hate to think what problems this might cause,' Moira said. 'What was Esteban's speech about?'

'He was saying the same things the others were, about giving the land back to the people, and all that. When Zimmy said about the men on horses being criminals, he said, "Don't worry, they won't be around much longer." She asked him what he meant, but he wouldn't tell her.'

That night, after Max had gone to bed, apparently none the worse for his experience, Moira said angrily: 'Even if he is – or might be – our cousin, Esteban ought to be given a good spanking! I know he saved Max, and I will be grateful to him for ever, but if the workers start fighting with the land-owners around here, he'll be partly to blame.'

Andrew shook his head. 'They'll only have themselves to blame. Esteban and his friends see the rich living on inherited money and lands, and not doing a damn thing for themselves, while the others pay exorbitant rents and barely make enough to keep alive. Did you know that Esteban gives three-quarters of his share of the profits from the bar to the cause? For an idealist like him, there isn't much alternative to Communism.'

'I know you're right, but I'm worried. They're planning something – revenge for what happened today. Don Luis is our neighbour. Shouldn't he be warned?'

'I'm sure he knows a lot more about what's going on than we do, otherwise how would he have been able to organise his friends today? Anyhow, right now I don't feel like lifting a finger for him.'

Moira shivered. If Andrew, the gentlest of human beings, felt so strongly, what effect must the incident have had on men already filled with bitterness?

For several days after that, there was an uneasy peace. It turned out that no one had suffered serious injury. One man had a broken wrist, two had cracked ribs, a fourth was concussed, several others had bruises and superficial cuts. The three strangers had disappeared, though it was rumoured that they were still in the district, hidden in one of the *braceros*' huts.

The Ansaldos kept within their stone walls. Moira knew that Doña Maria was pregnant and hoped her husband had kept news of the skirmish from her.

Then one morning Father Miguel arrived at his church to prepare for early Mass and heard a curious snuffling behind the oak doors. He lifted the latch and found a dozen pigs stabled there. A couple of buckets of swill had been dumped on the altar steps and there were droppings along the aisle and between the pews. When he went for help, he could find only a few women who were willing to clean up the mess. The Church, by now, was irrevocably associated in the Left's mind with their oppressors.

After that, the crisis in San Felipe escalated, a miniaturised mirror-image of what was happening throughout Spain.

Andrew and Moira kept their opinions to themselves, still clinging to their conviction that their friends would come to their senses and that the political conflict had nothing to do with them.

Not long after the incident in the plaza, they were taking advantage of a comparatively cool summer afternoon to paint the *finca's* window-frames when they saw Zimmy running towards them. She was wearing one of her tight-fitting, low-cut rayon dresses. In blinding primary colours, they were, she had once explained to Moira, what the girl's potential clients expected of their hostess. When she went out, she normally changed into more decorous garments. There had been a tinge of bitterness in her voice as she said, 'I don't fool anyone else, but dressing like a lady helps me to feel *ordinary* once in a while.' It was one of the rare moments when she was heard to express even the mildest disenchantment with her way of life.

Now she was panting and her shiny green dress was stained with sweat where it clung to her body. Her hair, normally neatly caught back at the nape of her neck, had escaped its tortoiseshell clip and was lying in strands against her forehead.

She ignored their greetings. 'Andrew, I must ask you to go at once to Don Luis!' Her voice was urgent.

'Whatever for?'

'There is to be an attack on his house. Already some of his lands have been seized.'

'Seized?' Andrew said stupidly.

'Haven't you heard? All over Spain the peasants are fighting the *proprietorios*, and taking the land for themselves. They are wrecking farms, killing sheep, burning barns. And the Government is behind them.'

'My God! I'd heard it might happen. I didn't know it had started.'

'Now it is coming here because of what happened in the plaza. There is a meeting. I heard Esteban talking with his friends. They have weapons, and they are led by those three outsiders, who have been hiding in the house of Jaime.'

'How did Jaime get involved? He knows nothing about politics.'

'He is easily led, and he loves Esteban. He is useful to them because he is so strong and he does everything he is told. Please, Andrew, you must warn Don Luis. I don't care about him, but there is Doña Maria, and the little ones . . .'

'You'd better come with me. You can explain better than I can.'

'No! I will not set foot on that man's land. But I cannot let this happen, and there is no one but you I can ask.'

'I'll go now. How much time do the Ansaldos have?'

'Not long. No time to call for help. They must leave as quickly as possible in their car.' She paused, and took a deep breath. 'I do not want Esteban to know I've been here, so I use the back way home. You will not tell him?'

'Of course not,' Moira said. 'Don't worry, we'll do all we can.'

Andrew heard the bell ringing in the Ansaldos' house, then he beat on the front door. Even worried as he was, he registered that this was the first time he had been here. Don Luis had drunk wine in his studio many times, but he had never been invited beyond the wall.

As he waited, Moira hurried up the drive to join him.

'Where's Max?' he said sharply.

'I made him promise to stay inside.'

'I hope he keeps his promise.'

'He will. Where can they be? Even old Marcos doesn't seem to be around.'

'Let's see if we can raise someone at the back.'

They found another door. He tried the handle. It was locked. Then they realised that all the windows were shuttered. They went to the garage. Its doors were open, and it was empty. Rafael's pony was not in its stable.

'They've gone,' Moira said. 'Don Luis must have known what was going to happen.'

'Thank God for that! Let's get home. I don't trust Max to stay put if there's anything going on.'

As they were on their way down the drive, they heard shouting. When they came within sight of the iron gates they stopped, aghast. It was as though they were looking at a Goya etching in three dimensions. Rough hands were grasping the bars, and behind them were rows of unshaven, twisted faces, the faces of men gripped by whipped-up hysteria. Some were waving pick-handles, spades, axes, iron bars. They were chanting slogans and threats.

The gates burst open and, suddenly silent, the mass of men advanced. They were led by a squat, broad-shouldered stranger. His head was thrust forward on a bull neck, a beret was pulled low over his eyebrows. He was holding a two-foot billet of firewood.

Andrew pushed Moira behind him, and raised both hands in a gesture of peace. '*Buenas tardes. Senors,*' he said, politely. '*Puedo ayudarle?*'

For a moment, they hesitated. In the centre of the group, Jaime's big frame towered half a head taller than the rest. Esteban, wild-haired, pallid, his mouth clamped in a tight line, stood to the left. Others among them were men with whom Andrew had drunk wine in the Bar Jiminez, but now they were staring at him as though he was their enemy.

Then the leader charged. The first blow of his heavy branch caught Andrew on the ridge of bone above his left eye, the second crashed against his shoulder. Pain shot through his body, and he fell. As he went down, noise broke over him like a tidal wave.

He lay on the ground. Heavily-booted feet wavered before his eyes as he struggled to his knees. He was still seeking the strength to stand when he realised that the quality of the sounds around him had altered. Instead of shouting, he could hear individual voices, one of them high-pitched. A boy's voice: Max's voice.

Moira's arms were around his shoulders and he clung to her for support, aware of a small figure standing protectively in front of him. Through a red blur of blood which was running over his eyes, dripping down his face, he could make out Esteban and Jaime, their backs to him, arms outspread, urging the mob back, herding them towards the gate.

A few moments later, they were gone.

By the time they reached the *finca* his head felt as though it was being rhythmically struck by a hammer, and he was so sick and dizzy that he could scarcely see.

Moira's hands were unsteady as she bandaged his cut and washed away the blood. When he tried to reassure her, his words were muddled incoherent. She undressed him and put him to bed, where he fell into a fitful sleep, punctuated by dreams in which he was encircled by monsters who were battering him with tree-trunks.

The grinding headache did not subside until the following afternoon, when he was able to accept a plate of soup from Aquilina. Only then did he feel well enough to hear what had happened after he was attacked.

Moira, with sunken eyes, was sitting by the bed, as she had been all night. 'When you went down, the man with the branch tried to kick you, only I was in the way.' She pulled up her skirt and he saw a bruise on the outside of her thigh, which spread down almost to her knee.

He gripped her hand. 'Sometimes I wonder whose side I should be on,' he said despairingly.

'It doesn't hurt too much. Anyhow, seeing him kick me brought Esteban to his senses. He called Jaime, who picked the man up and literally threw him back. Then Max arrived.'

'Who had promised to stay indoors.'

'We've already had that out. He stood there, screaming at them. Talk about Daniel in the lions' den! I don't think most of the men had realised what they were doing, until they saw this small boy prepared to take them all on. Esteban shouted at them, too. I heard him say that their fight was with the Fascist Ansaldo, and he'd keep.'

'I hate to think what they'd have done to him if he'd been there,' Andrew said.

'Esteban came here last night, while you were asleep. I think this has been his first experience of real violence. Up to date, it's all been theory: boot out the rich and everyone will have fair shares of the land and be happy. It didn't seem to have occurred to him that on the way he would be expected to hurt people. For a moment there, he thought you'd been killed.'

'I hope it's taught him a lesson.'

'I'm afraid not. His excuse was that the man who attacked you didn't know who we were. He assumed that as we were in the Ansaldos' place, we were on their side, so we were fair game. I told Esteban that he should get out of politics while he could, before there's more violence, but he said that he was committed now. His friends were attacked in the plaza and they're determined to fight the Fascists. Andrew, what are we going to do? Should we leave?'

'Where would we go? I still say their fight isn't our business. We won't take sides. Once they learn that, they'll leave us alone.'

'I wonder.'

'Hell, they're our friends!'

'They didn't look like friends yesterday.'

'Those outsiders have been the trouble-makers. When they leave, everything will settle down. The San Felipans aren't violent people.'

She looked at him in exasperation. 'I wish I could share your optimism. Lord knows, I don't want to leave. I love this place. But suppose the Ansaldos had still been there. We couldn't have stood by and seen them attacked without doing something, could we?'

'I can't believe Esteban and Jaime would have allowed it when the point was reached.'

'Well, anyhow, I'm glad Don Luis got Doña Maria away. From the look of her, the baby's due at any moment. Esteban told me he'd found out from old Marcos that they left before dawn yesterday morning. They must have heard that something was going to happen. The car was piled with luggage and they were driving to Malaga railway station. He thinks they're going to London, where Don Luis's younger sister lives.'

'I expect they'll stay until Doña Maria's had the baby. Surely by that time things will be back to normal.'

But soon even his optimism began to fade. The peasant land seizures continued, Right-wing opposition to the Republican Government hardened.

In and around San Felipe, there were pitched battles between land-owners and the peasants, and blood was shed on both sides. It emerged that the three men whose meetings had touched off the attack in the plaza had only been a vanguard of strangers who began to drift into the village and foment trouble. At first they came in ones and twos, then in groups, tough-looking *braceros* who flaunted their red scarves with increasing confidence. They harangued anyone who would listen, and made inflammatory speeches encouraging the workers to stand against their masters.

The local Republicans included idealists, like Esteban, who genuinely and selflessly believed in the fight for equality; poor people, seeing for the first time a chance to achieve a reasonable standard of living; opportunists, scurrying to support the side they believed would come out on top.

Broadly, the merchants, professional men, white-collar workers, shop-keepers and land-owners stood against the Government. But in both camps, the outlines were blurred. There were some workers who remained loyal to their employers, some members of the middle classes who crossed over to the Republicans.

Families began to split: father against son, brother against brother. In many cases, politics became an excuse for bringing personal hatreds into the open.

At Max's school, the children took sides more or less according to their parents' leanings. Fights became so frequent that the school was temporarily closed down.

Father Miguel's congregation diminished. Many of the women, who were the Church's mainstay, would no longer brave the jeers and stone-throwing of the anti-clerical faction as they walked to Mass.

For Max, those days were full of excitement. He watched the fights, cheering on one contestant or the other, according to whether he liked them personally. Whenever he could escape the restrictions his parents had placed on his wanderings, he attended meetings of all groups impartially.

The Ansaldo house remained deserted. To prevent any further attempt at invasion, Andrew bought a padlock and secured the gates. He let in only Marcos every few days to tidy up the lawns and trim the tubs of geraniums.

In his late seventies, Marcos had lived in San Felipe all his life, a quiet old man whose only interests were his soldier son, of whom he was immensely proud, and the garden he tended. And because he cared more for his son and his flowers than for politics, he became the first local victim of the Republican militants' blood-lust.

A few weeks after the Ansaldos' departure, two fishermen, pushing their boats into the water at dawn, saw his body floating a few yards out from the beach. He had been shot through the heart.

For a brief hour during his funeral, his friends from all parties mourned side by side.

Zimmy, who was becoming thinner and more drawn daily as she worried about Esteban's activities, told the Ravens bitterly, 'One of those animals who have invaded our village was with Angelina and he boasted that they had killed that old man because he was a bourgeois lackey!'

The second death took place three days later, when the body of one of the Red agitators was found on the beach, at almost the same spot where Marcos had been pulled ashore. Revenge killings on both sides were soon to become commonplace.

By mid-July, the whole country was in the grip of civil war. After an Army coup in Spanish Morocco, General Francisco Franco, who had been stationed in the Canary Islands, landed on the mainland at the head of an army of Spanish and Moroccan troops. Generals throughout Spain, by definition Right-wing, supported him against the Government, and the Army rising spread. Franco's men marched up through Andalusia. There were full-scale battles in major centres.

The Ravens listened with mounting horror to the radio reports of death and destruction as trained soldiers fought a rabble of ill- equipped supporters of the floundering Left-wing Government. As the tide turned in favour of the Army, the red scarves began to disappear from San Felipe's streets, and so did many of their wearers.

One morning Moira went into the village for supplies – like everyone else who could afford it, she and Andrew were laying in stocks of food against the possibility of shortages – and, as usual, dropped in to the Bar Jiminez. Zimmy was alone, washing down the tables.

'Where's Gil?' Moira asked. Gil was one of Esteban's friends, who had been working as Zimmy's barman.

'Gone.' She was unusually brisk as she squeezed out her cleaning-rag.

'Gone where?'

'How should I know? Into hiding. They're all going.'

'I don't understand . . .'

'I'll bring your coffee. As you've told me more than once, this isn't your fight, so you shouldn't ask questions.'

Moira stepped forward, a formidable figure as she glared down at the smaller woman. 'How dare you talk to me like that! I'm your friend, remember? Put away that rag – you're only making smears, anyway – and sit down. What's all this about?'

Zimmy sighed. 'I'm sorry, but losing Gil has been the last straw.' She poured two cups of coffee from an old enamel pot and joined Moira at a table.

'Tell me about it,' Moira said.

She rubbed at one of the smears on the table with her forefinger. Her face was tense and she was looking older than her twenty-six years. 'Moira, for the first time, I'm really frightened. Esteban says that the violence we've seen up to date is nothing to what's coming, and I believe him. The Left have no intention of giving in. They're – what do you call it? – regrouping. And there's a detachment of the Spanish Army of Africa on its way here to fight them.'

'Maybe they'll help to keep the peace.'

'Don't be silly! Their job is to wipe out all the Republicans. That's the order.'

'That can't be true!'

'Execute them. It's happening everywhere. That's why Esteban and his friends are taking to the hills. They're going to form their own army. It's so pathetic!' There were tears in her eyes. 'The only weapons they've got are a few ancient shot-guns and broom-handles. And they call my little brother their leader! He's such a fool! He'll be killed, like all the others.'

'I'm leaving now.'

They turned. Esteban was standing at the door. Moira had not seen him since he had called in after the confrontation at the Ansaldos' house, and she hardly recognised him. The boyishness had gone from his face. He looked hard and grim, and there was a new coldness in his grey eyes. He was wearing a tattered black shirt, black trousers and a black beret.

'Moira, can't you talk to him? You're his family, too. He should leave Spain until it's over.'

Moira glanced sharply at her, but there seemed to have been no underlying meaning in her words. She was looking up at her brother. For a moment, their eyes locked, then he turned and left the room.

Two days later, a column of soldiers marched into San Felipe and set about rounding up Republican militants. Some were betrayed by neighbours, either from conviction or personal enmity, and no one knew whom to trust. One or two men were shot trying to escape, others were arrested and taken away in trucks. Many were never to be seen again. Women no longer sang as they scrubbed their clothes in the communal laundry, and they hurried to and from the well with their water-jars, without pausing to chatter.

At least a dozen men, under Esteban's leadership, had escaped to the hills. Zimmy told Moira that she wakened every morning with a feeling of dread in case this should be the day when she would see him brought back, either dead or a prisoner.

Then the raids began. At night, a few of the Republicans, armed with primitive weapons, would make their way silently into the village. The next morning the bodies of one or two soldiers who had been stabbed or strangled, would be found in the street. One night a shop which had been taken over as Army headquarters, was set on fire. Many land-owners who, like the Ansaldos, had fled during the early peasant raids, had returned as the Army's successes were reported, but once again they found themselves under siege. No Right-wing *latifundista* could feel safe while Esteban's band was at liberty, although they avoided direct physical attacks on their own people. The hillsides were combed, caves and valleys were searched, many peasants' houses were deliberately destroyed in case they could be used as shelters. But few of the Republicans, who knew the area better than their pursuers, were caught.

One day Manolo came to the *finca* and told Max that a party of soldiers had arrived at the cave where he lived with his mother.

'She sent me down for wine, and they stayed with her.' He laughed. 'They were her first customers for weeks.'

'Are you on the Army's side, then?' Max said.

'No! When I'm a bit older, I'm going to fight the Fascists.'

'Why are you pleased about your mother and the soldiers? You should have killed them.'

'No need. She's probably given them something bad

enough. Why d'you think the men here won't visit her any longer? She never goes to the doctor like Senorita Zimmy's girls.'

As Luisa Machado profited from the lower ranks, Angelina, Pepita and Sonia did good business with their officers, who did not suspect that while they were occupied upstairs, Zimmy was handing out food parcels to messengers sent down from the hills. As the Republican raids became more frequent, the Army started reprisals. Following each raid, one family was selected to pay the price. Two *braceros* had their homes burnt to the ground. Their wives and children, left without money or shelter, had to take refuge with friends. The elderly mother and father of Gil, Zimmy's barman, were arrested and sent under guard to Algeciras. So far the connection between Zimmy and the Republican band's leader had not been made but, as Andrew told Moira, it could only be a matter of time.

The Ravens were left undisturbed. An officer had visited them during the early days, looked around the house and Andrew's studio, with its paintings stacked against the walls, then informed them that as unaligned foreigners they had nothing to fear, so long as they did not offend against the Falangist cause.

But Andrew was finding it increasingly difficult to justify to himself his determination to remain uninvolved. From all over Spain, reports were coming in of street-fighting, and atrocities and executions by the Army and its civilian supporters. It was said that in numbers and violence they already outstripped those committed by the Left.

The atmosphere of suspicion and fear was getting on Moira's nerves, and she had forbidden Max to make any more excursions to the beach or into the village. Penned up at home, with only the occasional visit from Manolo to break the monotony, he became irritable and rebellious.

Aquilina still toiled up to the *finca* every day, but one of her sons had joined the group in the hills, and she was morose and silent, often dissolving into tears.

Because Jaime was also with Esteban, the *finca's* garden became rough and overgrown. Andrew, preparing pictures for another exhibition in London, had no time to work in it himself.

Titi had accompanied his father, Jaime having refused to leave him behind. Zimmy told Andrew that the little boy was being used as a messenger. He had come to the bar several times to collect supplies, slipping in like a ghost after dark.

'They have no right to involve a child!' she said angrily. 'He's frightened, and he doesn't understand what's going on, any more than his father does. They're both weak in the head.'

Apart from Zimmy, Manolo was the Ravens' main source of news. With his eye on the main chance, as usual, he had made friends with the soldiers who visited his mother, and picked up all he could from their conversation.

One day he told Moira, 'People are angry with Esteban now. They're blaming him for what happened to Gil's parents, and they're all afraid they might be next. They think he and the others should give themselves up.'

'Who's *they*?'

'Almost everyone. Senor Lopez at the shop, and Paquito, who owns the goats, and Senora Calvino at the Post Office. Lots of others. They've had meetings with the officers. They say that when the Reds are all caught, the Army will go, and we'll be left in peace.'

That night, after Max had gone to bed, Andrew was sitting in his arm-chair as Moira sewed by the light of an oil-lamp. Suddenly he said, 'I want you and Max to leave earlier than we planned.'

They had already decided that she would take Max to Gibraltar in September and put him on a ship bound for England. There, an old family friend had agreed to take him to his school in Sussex.

'Maybe you're right,' she said. 'When do you think he should leave?'

'Not only him. You're going with him.'

'I'm doing nothing of the kind! I'm putting him onto the ship, then I'm coming straight back here.'

'I want you to go, too.' He took a deep breath. 'I'm going to join Esteban.'

She dropped her sewing and stood up. 'Andrew Raven, you shock me! This isn't our fight, we've always said so. This isn't even our country. Their civil war has nothing to do with us.'

'I know that's what we've said. But Spain *is* our country now, and I can't sit back and watch our friends die in the slaughter.'

'You want to take part in it?'

'Of course not! But if there's anything I can do to help to end it more quickly . . .'

'You're a painter, not a soldier! You don't know anything about fighting. You're not like Esteban and the others. They understand this countryside. You'd get caught and put in prison. Or executed.' There was an undertone of hysteria in her voice.

He rose, too, and faced her, a big man starting to run to fat, with steady eyes, a determined chin. 'I don't intend to be captured or killed. I have a strong sense of self-preservation, my love. Anyhow, the Nationalists can't have it their own way for much longer. The Republicans will hang on in Madrid, and they'll have time to organise . . .'

'You know very well it won't end for months, maybe years. It's gone too far for either side to give in. Andrew, I want you to come with us. We'll all go to Britain, and come back when it's over.'

'No!'

The argument raged on, with Moira sometimes furious, sometimes pleading, sometimes crying, the theme of her words always the same: 'Either we all go together, or I stay here with you.'

In the end, he gave in. Just after midnight, he nodded tiredly and said, 'I won't let you stay here, so we'll all go.'

They began to make preparations to leave. Andrew painted frantically, finishing his work-in-progress. Moira sewed dust-covers for the furniture, for she was determined that during their absence, however long, their belongings would suffer the last possible damage. 'I want it still to be *our* house when we come back,' she said.

Although they worked together, and there were no arguments, something was missing in their relationship. Andrew was quieter, Moira's cheerfulness was forced. Each, in his own way, was ridden by guilt: Andrew because he was deserting his friends, his house and the country he loved; Moira because she was forcing him to do just that.

Max's emotions were less complicated: he was only thankful that he would have their support during his entry into boarding- school. Although he had never admitted it, he had often lain awake at night, dreading the prospect of journeying to England alone, and even more, the new life and strangers he would be facing.

With only a few weeks to go before their departure, Moira realised suddenly that they had not seen Zimmy for some days. Despite the tense situation, she had never failed to drop in regularly, often leading Burro, loaded with the wine that Esteban used to deliver. 'You're my escape,' she had told them wearily. 'This is the only place where I don't have to watch what I say in case it's passed on to the wrong people.'

Aquilina gave them the explanation for her absence when she arrived for work, looking more distraught than usual.

'Is it your son?' Moira said.

She shook her head. 'It is what has happened to the Senorita Zimmy. They found out that her brother is with the men in the hills. She has been hurt, Senora.'

'Hurt? How?'

'They beat her. They came to the bar, an officer and two soldiers, and asked her questions. They did not believe her when she said she didn't know where Esteban is. They attacked her with their fists and the officer hit her with the butt of his pistol. The girls tried to help her, but they were beaten, too.'

Moira and Andrew left Max in Aquilina's care, with strict instructions to stay there, and hurried into the village. Once cheerful, bustling, the plaza was deserted and desolate. The bar was closed, its tables and chairs stacked outside the entrance. They knocked on the rear door. Angelina opened it. Normally sleek and exotic in her ruffled dress, a flower in her dark hair, she was wearing a short cotton dressing-gown that was none too clean, and felt slippers. Her face was blotchy and there was a bruise under her left eye. She led them up to the red bedroom on the first floor.

Zimmy was lying under the portrait of her Mamma and Uncle Henry, covered by the red satin quilt. She looked pale and ill, but she was able to smile at them.

'I am much better,' she said. 'Almost, it doesn't hurt now.'

'You must come away with us,' Andrew said. 'Come to Britain. They'll never let you alone now they know about Esteban.'

'Me? In Britain? I think you have enough *burdels* over there. I could not compete. No, Andrew, thank you. I was born in San Felipe, and I stay here. The soldiers will not bother me again. I don't know where Esteban is, and I don't want to know. I think that pig of an officer finally realised that I told the truth.'

'If you won't leave, at least come up and stay with us until we go. You'll be safer.'

She shook her head. 'They are not driving me from my home.'

'Is there nothing we can do?'

She stopped smiling. 'Get away from here as quickly as you can. Get Max away. And when it is all over, come back to us. I'll be here.'

Andrew leant closer to the bed. 'What do you hear of Esteban?'

She put a finger to her lips and whispered: 'I have heard that he is leaving, too.'

'Crossing the border?'

'No. All over Spain, men like him are forming themselves into a real Army, and already there are foreign volunteers arriving to help the Republican cause. It is important that he makes contact with them. His little group is like a mosquito stinging an elephant, and he does not believe that it is fair to make our people suffer any more reprisals for the sake of killing a few soldiers.'

'Is he taking all his men?'

'Some have already gone. The rest will leave soon.'

'Will you be able to see him again?' Moira said.

She sighed. 'He sent me a message that he would try to

come and say good-bye, but I wrote telling him it is too dangerous. I am being watched all the time.'

Throughout the rest of the week, either Moira or Andrew visited her daily. She recovered from her beating and reopened the bar, with one change in policy: her girls flatly refused to serve the Nationalist Army, in any capacity.

This turned out not to be the deprivation for the men that it might have been, because the detachment was suddenly withdrawn from the village. No explanation was given, they simply marched out one morning. But according to Manolo, who followed them, deliberately making them laugh as he aped their swinging strides, while keeping close enough to overhear anything that might be said, they were to rejoin their regiment near Granada. The war was still progressing in their favour: The German Chancellor, Adolf Hitler, had agreed to aid the Nationalists with aircraft, munitions and men; they had captured the city of Badajos and were about to take Toledo; they had closed the Basque-French border at the western end of the Pyrenees. It was already rumoured that by the end of September General Franco would be appointed Commander-in-Chief and Head of State.

But the Republicans were by no means beaten. Recruiting for International Brigades to support them was well under way in Britain and other countries, and Soviet aid had been promised.

Nevertheless, it was a measure of Right-wing confidence that Luis Ansaldo, his wife and their new baby daughter arrived back in San Felipe about ten days before the Ravens were due to leave. Christina and Rafael had been sent to schools in Switzerland.

Andrew and Moira saw the old Hispano-Suiza coming up the hill, and were surprised when Don Luis pushed the gates open and drove through. They still had the only key to the padlock.

Half an hour later, Andrew went to the house. The padlock, twisted open, was hanging from the gate.

The door was answered promptly, by Don Luis himself. For a moment, he stared at Andrew as though he had never seen him before.

'Don Luis, I've come . . .' He paused. From somewhere

in the house, he heard high-pitched wailing.

Don Luis did not bother to greet him. He stood aside and gestured behind him. 'Have you seen this?' His eyes were blazing, his face tight with anger.

The big entrance hall was a ruin. Heavy chests and chairs had been overturned, the legs torn off, upholstery slashed. Family portraits still hung on the walls, but the canvases had been ripped. The crucifix lay on the floor, its arms broken. There were faeces and urine stains on the rug and a pervading smell of excrement.

Don Luis was a small man, but he gripped Andrew's arm and shook him, as though his fury had to find relief in attack. 'Did you know about it?'

'Good God, no! Of course I didn't. When did it happen?'

'How would I know?' He was almost screaming. 'This – *this* is what my wife saw when we opened the door! This filth, this desecration! You hear her? Listen! She is hysterical. How can she feed the baby? Who was it? You must have seen them.' As his voice quietened, the menace intensified. 'I want to know who they were. I will see them executed.'

Andrew thought of the men who had stormed the gates weeks before. He had known most of them. Now many had left the village. Some had accompanied Esteban into the hills, others were still in their homes, apparently trying to go about their normal business, staying out of the political limelight. There was no way of guessing who had been involved in the vandalism. 'We saw nothing,' he said. 'I came here to explain that I'd had a padlock put on your gate to prevent anyone breaking in.'

'That was you? It had been broken. I find it difficult to believe that you heard nothing. There must have been noise. They have stolen my collection of antique weapons. Perhaps you just did not bother to investigate?'

'I've told you, I had no idea this had happened. In fact, my wife and I managed to prevent a mob from breaking in the very day you left. This must have occurred later, at night, when we were asleep.'

'You sleep heavily.'

Andrew had had enough. 'Yes, we do. Don Luis, you've

had a shock. Perhaps when you're calmer, you will let me know if there is any way Moira and I can help you.'

He turned to leave, but had only taken a few steps when Don Luis spoke: 'Andrew, I have lost my temper, and I was wrong. I am overwrought . . . my wife's distress . . . our long journey . . . and then this. You have my apologies.'

Andrew nodded. 'I'd probably have reacted the same way. Now, what can we do for you?'

'At the moment, nothing, thank you. Two of our servants returned with us, others will be here soon. They've already started to clear up the mess. I am most worried about my wife. I should never have brought her back, but when I heard from friends that it was safe to return and repossess my properties, thanks to the Army, she refused to stay behind. She hated England.'

Andrew said, 'We're also leaving for the UK shortly. We're sending Max to school there.'

'It will be better for you. The war won't last long now we're taking control, but it might be uncomfortable for a while longer.' He smiled. 'And now, I will walk to the gate with you. Our baby's nurse is looking after my wife, but the sounds of her distress are wearing me down.'

'The baby is well?'

'In perfect health. A beautiful little girl. We have called her Victoria.'

'My congratulations.'

At the gate, they shook hands and Andrew repeated his offer to help. Don Luis shook his head, but his face tightened. 'The only help I need is to find and punish the barbarians who destroyed my home.'

'Whatever they did, I hope he doesn't find them,' Andrew said to Moira. 'Especially, that he doesn't go after Esteban. He meant it when he said he would see them executed. I had a feeling that he'd like to do the job himself.'

'I wonder if Esteban was involved?'

He shrugged. 'It doesn't sound like him, but who knows? He's changed. According to Zimmy, nothing matters to him now but destroying the Fascists.'

Time rushed past as they finalised their preparations to leave the *finca*. The village had quietened with the soldiers' departure, but the war raging throughout the rest of the country was intensifying as the Left became more organised. There was a general fear that the protection afforded by San Felipe's isolation could only be temporary. Don Luis had taken over leadership of the local Right-wing within days of his return and had gathered around him a band of men whose hatred of the Left amounted to fanaticism.

A week before the Ravens were due to leave for Gibraltar, their trunks were nearly packed, the last dust-covers were ready for their furniture.

Max was spending a couple of nights in the village. He had returned from the beach with Zimmy that morning and said: 'Zimmy's invited me to stay at her house, only she said I had to ask you. Is it all right?'

His mother and father had looked at each other. Zimmy had never before suggested that he should spend a night at the Bar Jiminez, too tactful to face them with the embarrassment of feeling they had to refuse.

Now she said pleadingly: 'You are leaving so soon, and who knows how long it will be before I see him again? I promise you, there will be no – clients, during the time he is with me.'

There was scarcely a pause before Moira said, 'Of course he can!'

It was half-past eleven at night when Andrew stacked his last canvas against the wall, ready to be packed into the wooden crate he had made to transport his paintings to Britain. The floor was covered with wood-shavings, his oil-paints and brushes were piled neatly on the table. He stood up and stretched. 'Forty of 'em! A show in January, and if they sell, that's Max's education paid for.'

'They'll sell,' she said. 'You're painting better than ever.'

He kicked a path through the shavings and smiled at her. Suddenly, the tension between them no longer existed. 'I'll clear this stuff tomorrow,' he said. 'Before we go to bed, let's have a last look at San Felipe by moonlight.'

She was in the bedroom, draping a shawl over her fair hair,

Spanish fashion, when they heard a soft knocking at the studio door.

'Who . . .? Max!' she said. 'There's something wrong.'

'Nonsense! At worst, he might have felt homesick, so Zimmy's brought him back. He can come out for a walk with us.'

She followed as he went through the studio, where an oil-lamp still burned, and opened the door.

A dark, unrecognisable figure was slumped against the wall. In the lamplight, they saw a blood-stained hand stretched towards them.

In his room on the top floor of the Bar Jiminez, Max had his head under the sheet as he peered at the fluorescent hands of his new watch. Later, he felt that a noise must have awakened him, but he could not identify it.

At nine o'clock, Zimmy had accompanied him to his little room, with its wide bed, covered by a white candlewick quilt, its bright pottery plates on the wall, its tile-topped wash-stand with flower-painted basin and ewer. 'Your great-uncle Enrique slept in this room,' she said. Then added, with scrupulous honesty, 'Sometimes.'

'I never knew him. He died just after I was born. Was he nice?'

'Very. And because he was your uncle, I have a present for you from him. It is something that he brought from Scotland years ago. He gave it to my Mamma, and now I am giving it to you to take back. That makes a nice circle, no?'

She handed him a small cardboard box. In it was a gold wrist-watch. For a moment, he had been too overwhelmed to thank her. It was the first watch he had owned.

Having established the time, he emerged from under the sheet, thoroughly awake. He got up and went to the window, which looked out towards the hills behind the village. Someone must have lit a bonfire, for smoke was wafting down, its billows reflecting a pale glow. He thought it was pretty, and wanted to share it with Zimmy, whose room was along the corridor. He was also feeling rather lonely.

He went into the passage. As he was hesitating outside

Zimmy's room, another door opened and Pepita peered out. 'Max?'

'Hello. I was wondering if Zimmy was awake.'

'At this time? Soon it will be dawn. You should be in bed, *querido*.'

'I think there's a fire in the hills,' he said.

She followed him into his room and as they leant on the window-sill, he felt her arm go around him and a soft breast against his shoulder. He turned his head and her long hair brushed his face. Her lips settled on his forehead, her arm tightened. 'Never mind the fire,' she said softly. She stepped back and he saw her clearly in the moonlight: a pretty girl not much taller than himself, with huge dark eyes. She was wearing a long, semi- transparent night-gown through which he could see the shape of her figure. Feelings he had never experienced crept through his body. But as she held out her hand, and he moved towards her, they heard a sound from another room, a restless movement of someone turning in bed. Pepita stiffened as she suddenly imagined what Zimmy's reaction would be to finding her with Max. She pulled her hand from his and, on tip-toes, fled back along the passage.

He was half-relieved, half-disappointed. Again he contemplated summoning Zimmy, then decided that the encounter with Pepita had been sufficient excitement for one night. He wanted to settle down and think about it.

He jumped into bed and checked the bedside table to make sure his watch was in place. His interest in the view from the window had faded. There were other things on his mind.

Part 3

The Present

Guilt generated by the suspicion that he might have contributed to Max's stroke, plus anger caused by his conviction that he had been both betrayed and trapped by his father, kept Paul awake until after four o'clock on that first night in San Felipe. Even then, he was restless, drifting in and out of consciousness until early dawn, when he fell into a deep sleep.

He was awakened at nine o'clock by a waiter with a tray.

'Take it away,' he mumbled.

'Senorita Lewis ordered your breakfast, sir. She will be waiting for you at 9.30 in Senor Raven's office.' The Senorita's instructions were clearly not to be questioned.

'Oh, Christ . . .'

When he was alone, he heaved himself out of bed, feeling stiff and headachy, and padded to the window. The lawns spread out below him, startlingly green. Unlike many Andalusian villages, water was not a problem here. A constant supply, pumped down from a spring in the hills, enabled the Club's team of gardeners to keep the lawns green and the beds full of flowers even when the sun leached colour from the rest of the land.

At this hour, few of the guests were abroad, and it seemed that the place was in a state of suspended animation as it waited for the human awakening that would gradually bring it to life.

It promised to be a beautiful day, without the hot dry wind from Morocco that sometimes made the summer hard to bear. The bedroom of the duplex suite was above the sitting-room and office, reached by its own internal staircase, and high enough for him to look over the sea to the horizon.

He recalled that his plans for a swim the previous evening had been interrupted, and the bitter thoughts that had been overtaken by sleep, flooded back. As a child, he had divided his waking moments into compartments. There were the times when he would know at once that this was a good day, either because there was a promised pleasure to look forward to, or something already in train which could still be enjoyed. But there were others, as in the weeks after his mother's death and during friction with his father, when he awoke with the knowledge that there would be no joy in the hours ahead.

This day's awakening belonged to the second category.

As he ate his iced melon and drank two cups of Colombian coffee, he began to plan a programme. First, inquire about Max. Second, try and find out from what's-her-name, the secretary, what his job was likely to entail. Loretta had said that Marian Lewis was starchy and standoffish, but efficient, which would suit him. He wanted no personal involvement with the staff; if they did their jobs, he would do his for as long as it was necessary, and no longer. Third, telex Alan that he would be away indefinitely. Shit. This meant that his partner would have to carry on renovating the derelict 18th century manor near Winchester on which he himself had been working. He would have to follow the telex with a letter of instructions. Alan was inclined to be careless about details, had been known to use Victorian door- furniture in a Georgian house and settle for cheap plasterwork from inferior craftsmen. Then Loretta must be taken to the airport and later – his spirits lifted – he would visit Zimmy. Maybe she could tell him more about the situation between his father and Elena . . . only did he want to know any more? You haven't seen her for more than four years, he told himself, what's the difference whether she sleeps with Max or any other man? But there *was* a difference.

He showered and dressed and was on his way down the stairs at nine-thirty.

The office led off the sitting-room, and as he reached the bottom of the stairs, he heard voices through the half-open door. He recognised Manolo Machado's harsh, lisping Spanish. A woman was also speaking Spanish, fluently enough, but with a strong English accent. He padded silently over the thick carpet and looked through the door.

Manolo was seated at Max's desk, and two of its drawers were open. The woman was facing him. Her back was to Paul, but every stiffened bone in her body expressed outrage. He registered that she was tall, slender, with short, curling grey hair, dressed in an apricot silk shirt and yellow skirt.

'. . . no right whatsoever to go through his papers, and no right to be sitting at his desk,' she was saying.

Manolo raised his thick eyebrows. 'And who do you suppose will be running this place while Max is out of action?'

'Not you, Machado. His son arrived yesterday.'

'He's going home today. He wants no part of Raven Enterprises.'

Paul stepped into the room. 'Good morning, Manolo. And you must be Miss Lewis,' he said pleasantly. 'Paul Raven.'

There was a brief silence, then Manolo said, '*Hola*, Paul. You're off today? I was telling Miss Lewis . . .'

'I heard you. But things have changed. You know Max has had a stroke?' They nodded. 'I'm staying until he's on his feet again. Manolo, if you'll excuse us, I need to talk to Miss Lewis. I'm sure you have other things to do.'

Manolo withstood his gaze for a moment, then rose reluctantly. 'I've called the hospital,' he said. 'They say they hope for a complete recovery. There's no point in you staying, Paul. We can manage without you.'

'Maybe. But Max asked me to stay.'

'You haven't been near the place for ten years. How the hell can you expect to run things? You know nothing!'

'I'm sure you and Miss Lewis will help me.'

Manolo glared at him, and for a moment Paul thought his temper would explode, but he regained control of himself. He moved towards the door that led into the main foyer, then turned and said softly, 'Just don't try to interfere with my plans.'

As the broad-shouldered figure in its habitual, ill-fitting grey suit disappeared, Paul turned back to Marian Lewis and said wryly, 'There'll be no help from that quarter, I'm afraid.'

'He'll do what he's told, Mr Raven, as long as he thinks the order comes from your father.'

'Max won't be giving too many orders for a while. Have you been in touch with the hospital?'

She nodded. 'He had a good night and they said you can see him at any time.' She picked up a clip-board from the desk. 'I've taken the liberty of calling some of the senior staff here at ten o'clock. I thought you should meet them.'

'Won't I know some of them already?'

'I believe they've all joined us since you left. There'll be the manager, Senor Serrano, the house-keeper, Rosa Vega, our accountant, the maitre d'hotel, the chef, Monsieur Cauvigny . . .'

As she ran through the list, he studied her, seeing a good-looking woman in her late forties, with a clear, unlined complexion which she obviously protected from the sun. Clothes: neat and elegant, sufficiently informal to fit in with the Club's atmosphere, sufficiently restrained not to compete with the women guests. High cheekbones, fine features, discreet make-up. But a closed, almost expressionless face. He realised that she had not smiled once nor, even when she had been arguing with Manolo, had she looked angry. Only the stiffness of her body had expressed her emotion. He wondered why she found it so necessary to guard her feelings.

'. . . then I suggest that I show you around. Changes have been made since you lived here. You might also care to meet some of the guests. I have arranged for you to lunch with our attorney, Ramon Alvarez, who can answer any questions you might have about current projects, and this afternoon . . .'

'Hold it a minute!' he said. 'Miss Lewis, I have a few arrangements of my own. For a start, I must take my stepmother to the airport. You know she is leaving today?'

'Leaving? Why? Where's she going?'

She looked so genuinely surprised that he wondered whether she was aware of the situation between Max and Loretta. Max had never tried to hide his infidelities, so Loretta's final admission of defeat should not come as such a shock to anyone close to them.

He said carefully, 'She believes Max isn't too seriously ill. I'm staying, so she feels free to go away. She – needs a holiday.'

Her eyes slid away from his, then she said, almost to herself, 'I never thought she would . . .' She stopped, but he realised that, for a second, her face had lightened.

I'll be damned, he thought. She's delighted Loretta's going! Probably sees it as her chance. She's just like all the others.

When she spoke again, her voice was colourless, her face as calm as before. 'I'll cancel the appointments I've made. When will you be going to the airport?'

'Loretta's plane leaves at eleven. And later I want to go and see Senora Jiminez. I imagine you know her?'

'I've already phoned her, Mr Raven. She's anxious to hear from you.'

Half-amused, half-annoyed, he said, 'How on earth can you have organised everything already? I didn't know myself that I'd be staying until last night.'

'Your father told me yesterday that you'd be with us for some time. I was at the hospital most of the morning. Incidentally, I wasn't here to greet you because you hadn't let us know your arrival time.'

'I'm sorry,' he said, then added, 'Miss Lewis, do you think it's possible for a man to rearrange his health to make sure he gets what he wants?'

'I don't understand, Mr Raven.'

'Never mind. And for God's sake, stop calling me Mr Raven. I'm going to have to depend on you for assistance, advice, guidance, everything, while I'm here. I'd like to think that we could be friends.'

After a moment, when it seemed that their future relationship hung in the balance, she answered his smile. He took the hand she held out, as she said, 'I'll do all I can.'

'Friends?' he insisted.

'Friends.' She hesitated, then said, 'Did anyone ever tell you that in some ways you are very like your father?'

'A few times. Now let's get back to business. I'm sorry I'm screwing up your plans today, but I need to catch my breath. Is there anything urgent that needs attention? Max told me there's usually a crisis of some kind.'

'There are problems, but they can wait if you'd rather not hear about them until later.'

He glanced at his watch. 'That would be best. It's nearly ten and I should pick up Loretta. After she's gone, I'll go straight to the hospital.'

'Will you be back this afternoon?'

'Would it make much difference if I wasn't? I'd like to spend some time with Zimmy and maybe have a look around the village.'

'I'll put everything off until tomorrow.' She hesitated, then said, 'You might find changes in the village. It's not as – friendly as it was.'

'Too many tourists, perhaps?'

'That. And other things. Your father didn't tell you?'

'He said there'd been some local hostility since an accident at one of the building sites – actually, I read about it in England. He didn't seem to think it was too serious.'

'I expect it'll blow over eventually. But there's been an unpleasant feeling ever since it happened. Two brothers named Azano – local men – were killed. It was the fault of the contractor, a man named Rodrigo Leon.' She shrugged. 'The trouble is intermittent, though. You probably won't even notice it.'

She was turning to leave when a woman swept through the door without knocking. She was tall, painfully thin, with a haggard, lined face and dead black hair dragged back into a coil at the nape of her neck. She was wearing a loosely-fitting, filmy black dress that blew backwards as she came towards them. Paul had the impression of a witch flying without her broom-stick.

'Dear Paul, welcome home! I came as soon as I heard . . .'

He would not have recognised her, but the harsh voice, which Max had once said sounded as though it had been marinated in Spanish brandy, gave him the clue.

'Victoria!'

'My little love!' She kissed him and he caught a whiff of alcohol on her breath. She stepped back and put both hands on his shoulders, her head thrust forward like a bird's as she peered at him short-sightedly.

Beyond her, he saw that Marian's mouth had tightened. She stepped forward. 'Miss Ansaldo, I've been trying to contact you to arrange a meeting . . .'

Victoria did not bother to look at her. 'Always business, Paul! It's all Miss Lewis cares about. But not today. Today I am too worried about my Max to talk business. And you and I have so many years to catch up with!' Her manner had a frenetic vivacity that was new to Paul. He looked at the sticklike figure, the wide eyes and sun-crinkled skin. There was no grey in her hair, but in appearance she could have been any age from sixty to eighty. In fact, she was not yet fifty.

She was the only member of the Ansaldo family who had openly maintained contact with the Ravens, though Max alleged that it was more to annoy her brother, Rafael, than out of true friendship. Paul had always thought her a pathetic woman, spoiled, lonely, discontented with her life in the female-dominated Ansaldo household, but lacking the will to escape.

'So much to talk about,' she said. 'We will go to the swimming-pool bar, my love, and have a little drink as you tell me all about yourself. But first, how is Max? I was distraught . . .'

'He'll be okay, they say, but it will take time. Victoria, it's great to see you, but can we save that drink for later? I have a few things to catch up on.'

'I understand. We have plenty of time. I met Manolo on the way in. He said you were staying until Max is better. For me, that is wonderful news, but I think he is not so pleased. I remember that you were not friends.'

'He'll get used to the idea. As long as he goes on doing his job, I don't expect we'll clash.'

'He is Max's right-hand man. You can depend on his advice, Paul.'

'I'm sure I can.'

'And when you are free, we'll have that drink. After all these years, we will not stop at one! And there is a certain matter we must discuss. But for now . . .' She waved dramatically, and departed, leaving an almost visible wake of alcohol and expensive perfume.

'Jesus!' Paul said. 'She's aged a hundred years since I last saw her. Is she always so hyped-up . . . what's she on?'

'Alcohol. When she's not drunk, she's hung-over,' Marian said contemptuously. 'Now, I'd say she's halfway between.'

'At ten in the morning? And Max puts up with it?'

'They've been friends for a long time, I gather. You remember her brother, of course?'

'I do.' In his mind's eye he saw the short, immaculately-dressed figure of Rafael Ansaldo as he had stood beside Elena's bed, the square face which seemed to wear a permanent sneer, the dark eyes which rarely looked directly at anyone.

'He hates her coming to the Club.' Marian paused. 'I'm afraid she's involved in one of the problems we'll have to talk about.'

'Something to do with the sale of the Campo Negro?'

'You've heard about that?'

'From Loretta, last night. Look, I must go, or she'll think I'm not coming.'

'I'll see you tomorrow. In the meantime, if you don't object, I propose to close up this suite.' As she spoke, she was tidying away the papers that lay on the desk. She locked the filing-cabinet and desk drawers and put the keys in her pocket.

Loretta hardly spoke as they drove to the airport in Max's Porsche. Her eyes were heavy and red-rimmed.

Outside the terminal Paul looked for a parking-bay, but they were all occupied, mostly by the Club's fleet of Cadillacs, awaiting new arrivals.

'I'll let you out and try to find a place,' he said.

'Darling, you're Max Raven's son, driving Max Raven's car. Stop in front of the doors. If you wanted to drive into the hall, no one would dare to stop you.'

As he ran the two onside wheels up onto the pavement, a butter-yellow BMW 723 cruised up. Seeing the Porsche, the driver pulled in behind it. Immediately, two airport officials hurried out. There was a brief argument and he pointed at the Porsche. The officials were unmoved and one gestured towards a *guardia* who was standing nearby. Eventually the BMW moved out with an angry whirr of tyres on the gravelled roadway. The driver glared at them as he passed.

'If you're feeling sorry for that slob, don't,' Loretta said. 'That's Wayne Bridger.'

The name was familiar, but he could not place it. 'Bridger?'

'The Reading bank robbery in England a few years ago,

remember? The police arrested two of them. Bridger's the one that got away.'

'Is he living here now? Not at the Club, surely?'

'Max won't have him in the place. He has a villa a few miles up the coast. He spends his nights in the casinos and his days lolling around his pool in the company of a collection of imported blondes with the biggest boobs you ever saw.'

As a porter took her luggage away on a trolley he followed her into a small lounge that was reserved, she told him, for Max and his personal friends. It had its own bar.

'Drink?' he said.

'No thanks. Too early.'

'Not for Victoria Ansaldo.'

'She's a lush. Watch out for her, Paulie. Max has been trying to get her to confirm the sale of the Campo Negro, but she keeps putting the price up. He really wants that land. He doesn't seem to understand that a development there would be all wrong. It could cause big trouble in the village.'

'I don't see myself taking any major decisions until he's well. Anything that hasn't been finalised can go on hold in the meantime.'

'Well, watch out for Bridger, too. If he can think of anything which might damage Raven Enterprises now Max isn't around, he will.'

'Why? What's he got against us?'

'He isn't allowed to join the Club. That's one thing. Also, he wanted to buy it, and Max wouldn't even consider it. He loathes Max.'

'Christ, the Club's worth millions! Could he raise that kind of money, even from robbing banks?'

'It isn't only him. A few others like him have settled on this part of the coast and they've formed a kind of consortium.'

'All bank robbers?' He was finding it hard to take the conversation seriously.

'No. One's an American broker who made a packet from insider dealings, and there's a German who's said to have been a high-class fence. Stolen artworks, mostly. Two others are English con-men who left London just ahead of the police.

When Bridger told Max they wanted to buy the Club, he laughed at them.'

'Why on earth should they want it, if they've already made their pile?'

'So they can have somewhere to go, I imagine. They're not exactly popular. The Spaniards feel they're polluting the coast and won't have anything to do with them. The resident Brits avoid them.'

'If Max has dealt with them, I don't expect I'll have any trouble.'

'Probably not. Anyhow, you've got Maid Marian to keep you straight.'

'I'm sorry I won't have you, too. Won't you change your mind, Retta?'

She shook her head and stood up as a stewardess beckoned her towards the doorway which led through the Immigration and Passport controls.

'At least tell me where you're going,' he said.

'Still haven't decided. I'll probably spend a few weeks in Paris. After that, who knows? Maybe Palm Beach. Like I said, I haven't thought of anywhere more promising.'

'Will you keep in touch?'

She ignored the question. 'I've left a letter for Max at the house. Will you give it to him when you think he's well enough.'

A few lines to a sick man was a hell of a way to end a marriage, he thought. Maybe Max didn't deserve any more, but he and Loretta had been together for fifteen years. There must have been some good times.

She touched his arm. 'Paulie, there's something I want to say before I go. You know Max, when he makes a play for a woman, he's hard to resist. But his fancies come and go. If you can, give Elena another chance.'

His face hardened. 'I haven't yet reached the point where I'm prepared to pick up my father's discards.'

'No . . . well . . . it's just that I've always felt that in a way I was to blame for your first separation, when you were eighteen. If I hadn't forced you to come with me that night, you'd have met Elena and maybe . . .'

'And maybe not,' he said flatly. 'Let's not talk about it.'

They had reached the stewardess, who was waiting in front of a mirrored wall beside the door. Loretta caught sight of her own reflection and checked her perfectly-groomed hair, smoothed her cream linen skirt over her hips, settled her Hermes scarf, lifted her chin to tighten sagging flesh, and straightened her shoulders. When she was satisfied, she flashed Paul a quick smile, raised a hand in farewell and walked gracefully out of the terminal.

As he drove up to the hospital, he thought that Max had done well by the San Felipans with this development, at least. It was a low white building which stretched along a bluff above the beach, so that most of its rooms would have a view out to sea. There were blue shutters at the windows, and the lawns, like those of the Club, were green and well-kept. Separated from the frenetic pace of the holiday-makers, it was a tranquil place.

Just outside the oleander hedge that surrounded it, he passed a small villa, behind an iron-barred fence. Two old men were sitting on a raised terrace in the sun, their heads protected by wide-brimmed straw hats. One was reading, the other was asleep, his chin resting on his chest. They looked at peace with the world.

In the foyer, a nurse told him she had been instructed that he might see his father, but he was please not to show any reaction to his appearance. Although the effect of the stroke was probably temporary, it would not be good for him to see that it caused shock.

The room was filled with flowers, many of them out-of-season, so they must have been flown in. There were roses, orchids, day lilies, carnations. Vases stood on every available surface.

Max was lying in bed, propped up on pillows. He appeared to be asleep. In spite of the warning, Paul was unable to control an intake of breath as he looked at the ruined face, with its half-open, sagging mouth, the left eye drawn down by collapsed muscles.

As on the previous day, Max seemed to sense his presence,

and opened his eyes. But this time the blue was blurred, the lids heavy. He tried to speak, and a dribble of saliva ran down onto his chest. His words were slurred and incoherent. His mouth, on its undamaged right side, twitched with the effort. After a painful moment, when he realised that he was not making himself understood, expression came into his eyes, not the despair that might have been expected, but a look of intense anger.

Instinctively knowing that sympathy was the last thing he wanted, Paul spoke matter-of-factly. After a brief greeting he said, 'I'm staying until you're back in harness. Sanchez says that should be in a month or so. In the meantime, I'll try to keep the place from falling apart.'

Max began to splutter at him again. He leant forward, trying to make sense of the sounds, and was concentrating so hard that he did not hear the click of high-heeled shoes along the corridor. Nor was he aware of the arrival of a girl in the room, until he heard a gasp and a stifled cry behind him. He swung around. She was standing against the wall, staring at Max, one hand pressed against her mouth. A nun, her robes fluttering with agitation, hurried in, took her arm and pulled her towards the door.

'Come out at once, Senorita!' she said. 'Only the family . . . his son . . .'

The girl moved obediently, but when she reached the door, she looked back and shuddered. Her words echoed through the room: 'He's horrible!' She had made no attempt to lower her voice.

As she and the nun disappeared, Paul looked back at his father, momentarily hoping that he had fallen asleep and had not heard, but then the closed eyelids snapped open again and he gestured with his right hand towards the bedside table.

A Pentel and a pad lay there. Paul picked up the pen and put it in his hand, then held the pad in front of him. With immense effort, he began to write. The message was a scrawl, but legible: 'Only you . . . won't see anyone else. Not even L . . .'

Conscious of a blockage in his throat that he had not experienced since he was a child, Paul nodded. 'I'll see to it. And I'll come every day to report. You mustn't worry. I've met Marian Lewis and we'll get on. Everything's quiet, no problems. If there are, I'll let you know, and you'll tell me what to do. Okay?'

Max blinked his understanding, then gestured towards the pad again. This time, Paul laughed aloud when he read the words: 'Get rid of those fucking flowers . . . not dead yet.'

'I'll tell them.'

Max dropped the pen, and relaxed. Paul looked down at him for a moment, then left the room and hurried to the reception hall.

The nurse who had greeted him was still behind the desk. He passed on his father's messages, then asked who the visitor had been.

'She said she was a – a good friend of your father. She had just heard what had happened. She was hysterical, Senor.' Her voice became shriller with indignation. 'She insisted that he would close down the hospital if he were to find out that we had kept her from him. I did not think she should be allowed to go in, in her state, so I called Sister Magdalena, and she agreed with me. But the young lady took no notice, and ran away. She opened every patient's door until she found the right room. Poor Sister Magdalena had to chase her.' She glanced out of the window, which overlooked the drive. 'She is still outside.'

The girl was leaning against a Cadillac from the Club's fleet. She was very young, and swathed in layers of creased cotton which he recognised as one of the jokes played on Englishwomen by cult Japanese designers. She would have looked at home planting rice in a paddy-field, and had probably paid more for the garment than the average peasant would make in a decade. She was attractive, but he was in no mood for admiration.

'What the hell d'you think you were doing in that room?' he snapped. 'You had no right to be there, for a start, and then to tell a sick man that he looks horrible! Jesus!'

She gulped, and he wondered if she was going to throw up, but she only whispered, 'I slept with that *old* man!'

'You and a number of other women, but they don't do what

you did. What sort of insensitive bitch are you? Are you staying at the Club?'

'Yes.'

'Then I'm telling you to leave. Today.'

The shock brought her to life and she looked at him for the first time. 'Who are *you*?'

'I'm Max Raven's son, and I'm taking over while he's in hospital. I'll have your bags packed as soon as I get back.'

'I haven't unpacked them yet. I came especially to be with him. He was to meet me at the airport, only he didn't turn up and I heard he was in hospital and I knew he'd want to see me. Nobody told me . . . it was the shock . . . I thought it had only been a car accident, or something . . .'

'How old are you?' Some of his anger had evaporated.

'Twenty.'

'My father is sixty.'

'That didn't matter. He doesn't – didn't – look it. He was no age. He made every other man seem so boring . . .'

She was delicately pretty, with a skin that needed no cosmetics, and long straight hair whose shine was brighter in contrast with her sludge-green dress. Now that she had recovered from her shock, she was standing straight, her chin arrogantly high. Her voice was pure Sloane Square. Daddy has a house on Cheyne Walk, he thought, and there's Our Place in the Country for weekends, when she's into the Barbour jacket and green wellies. He was puzzled: she wasn't immediately recognisable as Max's type. In the past he had preferred sophisticated women: young, but not *that* young. But he was ten years older and it appeared that his taste for younger woman had increased in direct ratio to his age.

Looking at Paul with interest now, she held out her hand. 'I'm Caro Jarvis. What's your name?'

'Paul Raven.'

Her fingers tightened on his. 'I'm sorry for what I did in there. Please don't ask me to leave.'

'How long were you planning to stay?'

'A week. Then I have to go to Cannes to meet my parents. They don't know I'm here, actually. They think I'm in Portugal with friends.'

'You lead a complicated life. I suppose you can stay for a week, but if you go near Max again, you're out. Understand?'

'I promise. Actually, I couldn't bear it. I hope you and I will be meeting at the Club . . .?'

There was an unmistakeable invitation in the grey-blue eyes, in the tongue that moistened her smooth pink lips, and he realised that for the second time today he was being offered his father's empty shoes. He disengaged his hand. 'I'm going to be pretty busy, but I expect we'll run into each other,' he said. 'Have fun.'

Not waiting to see her into the car, he walked across to the Porsche. She was still standing, looking after him, as he drove away. Anger added weight to his foot on the accelerator.

Almost without realising where he was going, he found himself making for the Plaza San Juan. Although Spaniards rarely ate their mid-day meal before three o'clock, the tourists stuck to their own hours and were already crowding the bars for pre-lunch drinks. As he steered the car slowly around the encircling roadway, he saw that while San Felipe had changed in many ways, in others it remained much as it must have been when his grandparents had lived there. The long, shallow cement troughs where local women used to scrub their clothes on wash-boards had been carefully preserved as quaint relics of the past to amuse tourists. The same tree spread its branches over the groups of tables and chairs, the same red and gold notice indicated the Bar Jiminez.

Hoping that in the village, as well as at the air-terminal, Max's car would be regarded by the police as a sacred cow, he stopped outside the entrance to the bar, and went in. Two young, good-looking Spaniards were serving and he saw that the place had been enlarged, to spread into the houses on either side, with many more tables both inside and out. None of Zimmy's girls were in evidence and he wondered whether they still used the upstairs rooms. The last time he had been here, Zimmy had been in her usual place, perched on a kind of dais at a till, where she could keep a sharp eye on staff and customers. Her girls – one or two of them, he remembered, getting a bit long in the tooth – had their own tables, at which they received their clients.

He edged up to the bar and asked for Senora Zimmy – the married- woman's title had been awarded long since in recognition of her position in the San Felipe social hierarchy – in the unaccented Spanish which he was already finding he could again use as naturally as English.

'Not here,' the barman said, passing a tray of brandies over the counter to a waiter.

'Where can I find her?'

'At her home, perhaps. The Senora doesn't often come in now.'

'Where . . .?' But the barman had moved away to another group of customers.

The place was hot and noisy. Exasperated, Paul began to push his way back through the crowd. He had almost reached the entrance when he felt a touch on his arm. An old woman with a red, veined face and grey hair was beside him. She was wearing a brightly-flowered dress which clung around her overwieght body.

'You are looking for the Senora Zimmy?' Her mouth was painted with silvery lipstick and her teeth were yellow and broken.

'Can you tell me where she might be?'

He could not catch her answer above the rising decibels in the bar, so he steered her outside towards the car, which had gathered a circle of what he assumed at first were admirers.

As he pushed his way through them, he saw that not all were looking at it with good-natured envy. Two young local men were standing by the driver's seat and one was reaching for the wing-mirror. His intention was obvious, and Paul reached him just in time to knock his hand away. Before he could say anything, the man had fled. He turned to the old woman and said indignantly, 'Did you see that? He was trying to break the mirror!'

But she was looking up at him, her raddled face split into a beaming smile. Her voice was high and excited. 'You drive *El Hidalgo*'s car . . . you're Paul! Pablito! I am Pepita!' She patted his arm and reached up to kiss his cheek. 'Little Paul! The Senora Zimmy will be so pleased! She has been waiting for you ever since the dreadful news. You have seen your father?'

He remembered Pepita as a smooth-faced, dark woman who wore a rose in her hair. Now she was like an ancient, painted pug-dog. Even more than the sight of his father, her appearance made him aware of the cruelties inflicted by passing time. But the genuine pleasure in her greeting reminded him of Titi, and he bent to return her kiss, feeling the sweat on her fat cheek, smelling her cheap powder.

'I'll take you to the Senora. It isn't far, we could walk in two-three minutes, but you must move the beautiful car. You cannot trust these foreigners.'

And not only the foreigners, he thought.

They were sitting under the vine-shaded arbour behind Zimmy's house, which overlooked the village beach. On the table in front of him stood a *copita* containing sherry of a quality he had not tasted for years, and Pepita had brought dishes of tapas: olives, garlicky mushrooms, shrimps in olive oil, squid, croutons of fried bread.

Zimmy's walking-stick had been a surprise, but she had dismissed his inquiry. 'I have a touch of arthritis. Nothing to worry about.'

'You haven't changed, Zimmy.' He meant it. She seemed no older than she had been, except that she was handsomer. Her hair was silver now, where he remembered it as pepper-and-salt, and was wound into a plait on top of her head. Her eyes were dark and lively. She was still plump and the smile-lines that crinkled her olive skin added character rather than age. It was the lived-in face of a woman who had suffered her full share of troubles and come through with her compassion and humour intact.

'But you have,' she said. 'When you left, you were still a boy – in English, wet behind the ears, isn't it? Now you are dry, I think. It's good to have you back.'

'It's good to be here. I mean with you, not necessarily in San Felipe.'

'Loretta told me she'd asked you to come. I wasn't sure whether it was a good idea, but now Max has had the stroke – so unfair, when I am fifteen years older and in excellent health – I have changed my mind. He needs you.'

'I'm only staying until he's better.'

'You're on the defensive. Why?'

'I've been wondering whether he arranged things just to get me back,' he said wryly. 'He's never stopped writing to tell me this was where I should be, and every time he came to London, he talked about it.'

She smiled. 'Most things I would not put past your father when he wants his own way, but even he wouldn't arrange such an attack on himself. And on Elena Ansaldo.'

'Did you know about them?'

'No. And I'm sorry for it. She belonged to you. I always hoped it would be that way again. It's the one thing for which I am finding it hard to forgive Max.'

'Me, too.'

'Have you seen her?'

'For a moment, in the hospital. She wasn't awake, and Rafael was there. He looked as though he wanted to kill me. As a substitute for Max, I expect.'

'I hear that Loretta has left. I can understand why, but it's a pity. In her own way, she was good for Max. He has never been faithful to her, but I believe he was more fond of her than any woman since your mother.'

'She was bitter about Elena. I was wondering how to break it to Max, but fortunately he doesn't want to see anyone except me for the moment, so he needn't be told yet. How did you hear she'd gone? I only saw her off this morning.'

'I have my pipelines. People come to see me. They tell me things.' She paused, then said abruptly, 'Have you heard about this plan of your father's to build a supermarket and holiday camp on the Campo Negro?'

'Yes. Loretta told me about it.'

'It must be stopped!'

'She said there was opposition. I'm not sure why the people feel so strongly. It's not as though the Campo Negro is used. It's a few hectares of waste land. The only thing on it is the little shrine and it could stay.'

Her brown, veined hand clenched on the blanket which covered her knees. 'The Campo Negro has a special meaning for us, Paul. It must not be desecrated. I had planned to go to

Max this week and persuade him to find another site. Now I must ask you.'

'If he's made up his mind, the best I can do is try to convince Manolo to hold off for the moment, then you'll have a chance to talk to Max. But I can't believe Victoria will sell it. Rafael and her mother would never allow it.'

'Victoria wants to get away from here. She needs money and that's the only asset she has.'

'Oh, come on! The Ansaldos can't be broke.'

'When Don Luis died, he left several thriving properties, as you know. They've all gone. Rafael's a bad manager, Paul. His only interest is breeding horses, and he hasn't even been able to do that successfully. He's always left the administration of his land to incompetents and he's been cheated by most of them. First the olive groves near Granada had to go, then the oranges at Coin. I understand that even the vineyards were virtually owned by Alex Bellini, which probably means they're Elena's now.'

'She could stop Max from building by taking over Victoria's land herself.'

'I doubt that's been suggested yet. Nobody seemed to know that she was coming back, and from what I hear, she's too ill at the moment to think of such things.'

'Yes.' A vision of Elena's beautiful, battered face sprang into his mind. 'Well, I'll see what I can do. I hate the thought of a bloody supermarket there as much as you do. It's the last stretch of unspoiled land in the village.'

'Everyone is against it. If Max were to go ahead, I'm afraid of what might happen.'

'I still don't understand why the feeling is so strong. I mean, they've watched him destroying the coastline for years without making a fuss. Loretta said it had something to do with the Civil War, but that was a hell of a long time ago.'

'You can't understand. You didn't live through it. Paul, this village was torn apart. People were killed by members of their own families. We saw our friends turning into animals, tearing at each other. It went on until something so bad happened, that we – all of us who knew about it – decided that nothing like it must be allowed to occur again and that it would never be spoken of. We wanted to forget it and get on with our lives as best we could. The shock drew us together again, and gradually what had happened on the Campo Negro was covered by layers of years. But I don't think any of us *have* forgotten. Don't ask me what it was. It's not my secret. Other people were more involved than I was, and they still won't talk about it. They all have their own reasons for wanting to keep the Campo as it is.'

'What has Max said?'

'He hasn't taken them seriously. He was a child at the time of the incident, facing the loss of his parents and just about to leave for school in England. By the time he came back, it had been – smothered. He thinks the objections are superstitious nonsense. As, I suspect, you do. You and he are . . .'

'Don't say it! I'm getting a little tired of being told I'm like him. In the present circumstances, I don't find it a compliment.'

She smiled. 'From me, it was meant to be, but I can see that it was tactless.'

He pursued a thought that had strayed into his mind. 'I went through the garden after I left Loretta at the house last night, and saw the ruins of the old place. Your incident didn't have anything to do with the death of my grandparents, did it?'

She shook her head. 'No, that was something else.'

'What *did* happen to them? I know there was a fire . . .'

'We could only guess. They were packing to go to England, and the floor of your grandfather's studio was covered in wood-shavings. It was assumed that an oil-lamp fell over – the house had no electricity – and set them alight. The room was full of his canvases and paints. The fire must have gutted the house in a very short time.'

'Rough on Max.'

'Yes. It was the first of his tragedies. He was only eleven. Have you heard nothing of this before?'

'Not really. Max never talked about it. I just picked up bits and pieces in the village.'

Pepita came from the house. 'Lunch, Senora. Senor Paul.'

He stood up. 'I didn't realise it was so late. I hadn't meant to force myself on you for a meal.'

'You could never be an imposition, and I will be upset if you leave. We've been looking forward to this, haven't we, Pepita? She's been preparing your meal ever since Marian Lewis told us you were coming.'

'*Rinones al Jerez*,' Pepita said proudly. 'And *natillas* to follow.'

'Are you a cook now, Pepita?'

'She is the only one of my original girls who is still with me,' Zimmy said. 'We live together here, in this house your father insisted on buying us, and we get on beautifully, because she loves to cook, and I love to eat.'

He raised an eyebrow. 'So you've both retired from business?'

Leaning on her stick, she walked slowly towards the wide French doors. 'I had achieved everything I wanted, Paul. Many years ago I told Andrew Raven that one day I would have the best house in Andalusia.' She winked. 'I'm not sure what he would have thought if he'd known that his little son would help me to achieve it.'

'Max did?' Some shade of his Scottish Presbyterian ancestors jerked into brief, disapproving life at the thought of his father being a partner in a brothel.

'He gave me the house. Bought it and presented it to me as a gift, with a red bow on its front door, one Christmas.' The bright, perceptive eyes were amused as she looked up at him. 'He was never involved in its administration, my dear. I am out of it, too, now, but Pepita likes to go to the Bar every now and then for old times' sake. And five years ago I gave it to my girls, who now run it as a co-operative.'

His roar of laughter frightened half-a-dozen sparrows into flight. 'A tarts' co-op! Jesus! Only you, Zimmy . . .'

He followed her into the house. When he arrived, Pepita had steered him around the building into the arbour, so he was unprepared for the luxury inside. Zimmy had chosen light, locally-crafted furniture, which she had set on a hand-knotted red and yellow rug, against plastered white walls. At one end of her airy living-room a huge fireplace was now, in warm weather, filled with pots of scarlet geraniums. Their colour was picked up by a painting on the opposite wall, and

Paul laughed again as he looked up at it.

'You know what Max used to call that picture?'

'Portrait of an Old Goat,' she said calmly. 'Also it is a portrait of my Mamma. You know, of course, that the old goat is your great-uncle – no, two greats – Henry?'

'That's true, is it? I remember being told, but it seemed so improbable that I couldn't believe it.'

'He was Henry Raven, the uncle of Andrew and Moira, and it was through him that they came here. He was also, for many years, the lover of my Mamma.'

A round table had been set for two under the painting. Pepita served their calves' kidneys, which she had cooked in a sherry sauce, and hovered anxiously until Paul had tasted and approved.

Zimmy ate heartily, but he was aware that she was looking at him speculatively, and after a few minutes she said, 'You know very little about your family background, don't you? What do you know about your father's childhood, for instance?'

He thought for a moment. 'Not a lot, I suppose. He never volunteered much information.'

'Have you not wondered about him? What made him – the man he is?'

'When I look back, we had so little time together . . .'

'So what *do* you know?' she persisted.

'I know he went to school in England after his parents died. He was in the Army for a while, wasn't he? And he married, and was divorced after a few years. I suppose he treated that wife the same way he has treated Loretta. He seems to have been a different man when he was married to my mother. He never talked about her after she died, but I remember they always seemed happy together and she was warm, loving, funny, beautiful . . .'

Zimmy's grey head was nodding like a clockwork doll. 'She was all that. Go on.'

'After her death, all he cared about was the Club. When I came back for holidays, he was mostly too busy to come swimming or go for walks, or even talk. By the time I finished school, I thought of England as my home. That's where I wanted to be. I was shocked when I realised that he expected me to make my life here. I hated the Club.'

'And made no secret of it. You hurt him very much.'

He looked at her in surprise. 'I can only remember making him angry.'

'You were too bound up in yourself to try to see below the surface. Not entirely your fault, I suppose. You were just a child . . .'

'Do kids ever analyse their parents?' he said. 'All they want is loving-kindness . . .'

'Your father was never unkind to you!'

'He never hit me, or even abused me. His unkindness was by default. He didn't show any affection, I never felt I could go to him with a problem. Oh, shit, Zimmy, I'm not meaning to sound sorry for myself. It's only in the last few years I've even thought about this. I had a happy childhood, in most ways. I had you to turn to. You, never Max. I always assumed he had no real interest in me.'

There was a silence as they both looked down at their plates. Then, as she helped herself to some salad, Zimmy said, 'I think, *chico*, that it is time you learnt to know your father a little better . . .'

Part 4

1936–1944

1

Max would always remember Zimmy's breaking voice as she told him about his parents' death.

The impact of her words seemed to fling him over the edge of a cliff. He felt himself falling, his stomach churned and he was sick over the bed. After that, the hours were blurred.

He was passed from one person to another, embraced and wept over. Then there was only Zimmy, her skin blotchy and red, the tears flowing. She talked to him, trying to explain the inexplicable, and he pleaded with her to tell him it wasn't true.

Yesterday he had been preparing to leave for England with his father and mother. He hadn't been particularly moved by the fact that they were going, because they would be together, and eventually they would return together. He would not believe that today Andrew and Moira were dead, killed in the fire that had left their *finca* a blackened stone shell, and he was alone.

For a week, others took over his life, and neither his opinions nor his inclinations were explored, nor was he capable of clear thought. He stayed in his little white room, scarcely aware of what was going on around him. Nothing was real, people were shadows. At some point, Don Luis, pallid and grim-faced, came to tell him it had been decided that his parents' wishes should be carried out. They had wanted him to go to school, so he would be leaving on schedule. The following day, he and Zimmy were driven in the Hispano-Suiza into Malaga, where clothes were bought for him to replace those which had been burned. He accepted apathetically her choice of a wardrobe which she considered suitable for an English public schoolboy. Later he was to discard most of it.

Then he was on the ship, moving out into the ocean, and Zimmy's small, waving figure, clad in one of her 'ladylike' dresses, was no longer visible. Even the Rock had shrunk to the size of a pebble on the horizon.

He sat on his bunk, too shy to venture out of the cabin, trying to come to terms with the knowledge that for the first time in his life, he had no one but himself on whom to depend. After half an hour, a knock rattled the door. His first reaction was apprehension and he remained silent, thinking that if he did not answer, whoever it was would go away. Instead, the door opened, and he saw a large, red-headed man wearing a uniform with gold on the sleeves and shoulders.

'Mr Raven?' the man asked formally.

Max blinked, and nodded.

A freckled hand with ginger hairs on the back was held out, and shook his own. 'Welcome aboard, laddie. Name's McPhee. Had a message that you were travelling on your own. Everything all right?'

'Yes, thank you.'

'Thought you might like to have a look over the ship. Get your sea-legs. Things are quiet, so I've a few spare minutes. I'm the Captain, by the way,' he added, as an afterthought.

That was the beginning of Max's re-entry into a world not peopled only by ghosts. It emerged that Don Luis was acquainted with the shipping-company's agent in Gibraltar and McPhee had received a message that one of his passengers would be a newly-orphaned boy of Scottish ancestry. A warm-hearted Glaswegian, with several sons of his own, he needed no further urging to take Max under his wing.

The *Goddess Athena* was a cargo-boat, with cabins for a dozen passengers, the rest of whom were middle-aged to elderly. Several of them were former residents who, like the Ravens, had decided to leave Spain, and the escalating Civil War, while they could. It wasn't long before they all knew Max's story, and he was treated with general kindness. The crew followed McPhee's lead and set about filling his days, so there was little time left for him to brood. He spent hours on the bridge and in the engine-room. He was allowed to polish the brass bell and the compass and, an even greater privilege, to rise at dawn and help the seamen as they holystoned the decks to powdery whiteness.

By the time the ship reached Liverpool, the sharp edge of his misery had been blunted, although he still woke sometimes at night and cried silently for his mother and father.

He suffered a last-minute panic at the top of the gangway, and said to McPhee: 'Captain, do I have to go? Can't I stay on board, as a cabin-boy, or something? I don't want to go to school in England.'

McPhee laid a hand on his shoulder. 'You're worth something better than a cabin-boy's job, laddie. Get yourself an education, then you can choose what you want to be.'

Max hesitated, then burst out, 'What's it going to be like? I mean, I don't know anything about English boys. I suppose they'll think I'm a foreigner, won't they?'

'What if they do? Don't let them know you care what they think. Make *them* care what *you* think. That's the way to get on.'

'I'm not sure I can.'

'Old Glasgow saying, laddie, never let the bastards grind you down! Remember it.'

Max repeated the words, liked the sound of them, and marched down the gangway into his new life with a stiffened spine. He never forgot the Captain, never forgot the words.

He did not return to San Felipe for three years.

As he sat in the dusty bus that was bringing him around the coast from Gibraltar, long-buried memories surfaced. He looked out of the window and saw, not the harsh yellow landscape, but smoke from the flames that had incinerated his parents: he heard, not the bus's engine, but Zimmy's voice, breaking the news. The bus wound into the village, past the wall that bordered the Ansaldos' property. On the far side of it, not visible from the road, was the *finca* – or what was left of it. He had never seen the ruins, because Zimmy had insisted that he should be kept away from the place during the week before he had left for England. His last memory of it was when he had turned to wave good-bye to Andrew and Moira as he rode off on Burro, and he had shouted: 'See you the day after tomorrow!' The remains of the house were his now, but that meant little to him. He had been dreading his first sight of it, sure that the memories it would evoke, of happy days that could never return, would be hard to bear.

He wished he had not come back. What would the village be like after so long? Would anything be the same? He knew that he was a different person. What about Zimmy and Esteban and Manolo and Titi? They might have become strangers. He should have spent the summer, as he had spent the previous ones, with the Matsons in Scotland, or with Don Luis's widowed sister in Chelsea.

At first sight, San Felipe appeared to be unchanged. There were a few people in the Plaza San Juan, and though he did not recognise any of them, they might have been frozen there throughout the three years he had been away: the same small men in their dark blue cotton work clothes and berets; the black-clad women gossiping in groups. It was all so familiar that he began to lose his apprehension.

The bus stopped outside the Bar Jiminez, and Zimmy was waiting. She flung her arms around him. Almost immediately, her three girls hurried from the bar, to kiss and pat any part of him they could reach. It was a shock to discover that he was taller than they were.

When the greetings were over, he picked up his suitcases, knowing that he had come home. 'Let's go up. Am I in my old room?'

Zimmy's exuberance seemed to dim as she gestured towards a nearby table. Don Luis Ansaldo was sitting there, watching them, with a glass of brandy in front of him. He rose. 'Welcome back, Maxwell!'

'Thank you, sir. I'm glad to be here.'

Don Luis looked older, thinner. There were dark shadows under his eyes, but there was genuine warmth in his smile. 'You have become a proper Englishman! Let's go, then. Rafael and his mother are waiting for us.'

Max looked questioningly at Zimmy.

'You're staying with Don Luis, *querido*,' she said. 'You'll come and see me . . .'

He was too shocked to be polite. 'I want to stay with you!'

But his suitcases had already been loaded in the car and she was guiding him towards it. Before he could gather his thoughts to protest again, he was in the front passenger seat, being driven out of the Plaza, and Don Luis was chatting amiably, covering his silence with family news to which Max scarcely listened: '. . . Christina, alas, is not with us. She stays in Switzerland. Would you believe it, she's engaged! Too young, of course, but she refuses to wait. Her fiance is eight years older, and already a successful publisher in Zurich. Doña Maria thinks it will be an excellent match . . .' He paused. 'Now tell me, how are things in England? Will there be a war?'

It took Max a moment to realise that a reply was required, because he was planning the words he would use to announce that he had no intention of spending his holiday with the Ansaldos.

'Some of the papers say so,' he said. 'No one seems to be worrying too much. Not the people I know, anyway. Mr Chamberlain said there wouldn't be.'

'My sister writes that she is not optimistic. You saw her before you left, I believe. How is she?'

'Very well. She's been nice to me . . .'

He had stayed with Emilia Bartolomé for the first time on his way from Liverpool to his school in Sussex. The childless widow of a Spanish diplomat who had died during his London posting, she was several years younger than her brother but seemed prematurely aged. Her house in Chelsea was dark and gloomy, festooned with religious paintings, and rarely heard a young voice. On that occasion, he had found it depressing, but later she had invited him for a weekend and they had begun to establish a *modus vivendi*.

It became clear that she had no intention of trying to entertain him. She was prepared to give him a bed, and her staff would provide his meals, but apart from that, he was on his own. When he realised this, he had begun to enjoy himself. On that and subsequent visits he had explored London from

Knightsbridge to the East End, from Hampstead to Brixton. He spent hours in the Natural History and Science Museums, or wandering through the great art-galleries.

Delighted that nothing more was expected of her and that she could still carry out her brother's request to keep an eye on the boy, Emilia had given him an open invitation to visit her whenever he had a free weekend or needed accommodation during the holidays. As they came to know each other, she would occasionally summon him to her sitting-room after dinner and regale him with long, rambling reminiscences of the Ansaldo family. He endured them as a price he had to pay for the opportunity to be in London.

He had expected to go back to Spain at the end of his first term at school, but both Zimmy and Don Luis had written to tell him it would be unwise. The Civil War's violence had increased and the whole country was in chaos. What he had experienced before leaving had been no more than a taste of what was happening, and no end was in sight. So he had spent his holidays with Emilia or, as his circle of schoolfriends widened, with them and their parents. During the past year, he had mostly stayed with his best friend, Henry Matson, whose father owned a shooting-lodge in Inverness.

As Don Luis pulled up outside his house, Max kept his eyes averted from the wall beyond which his own land lay. He wanted to be by himself when he first saw the *finca*, because he was by no means sure that he would not cry, and no one must be allowed to witness that weakness.

Doña Maria appeared at the front door, with Rafael behind her. She watched, unsmiling, as Max took his cases from the car, and made no attempt to greet him.

'You've been a long time,' she said to Don Luis.

'The bus was late. I had a brandy while I waited.'

'At the Bar Jiminez?'

'Where else? That's where the bus stops.'

'It's a disgrace to the village! I've said it before, I say it again: that woman should be driven out!'

Luis's face stiffened. 'Maria, our guest is waiting. Rafael, will you show Maxwell to his room?'

The boys looked at each other. Max had always been the

taller, now he topped Rafael by six inches, though the other boy was thicker and heavier. His face was showing hints of the jowls that would develop later, and Max was to notice that he had a habit of looking sideways when he was talking to anyone, avoiding their eyes.

He was wearing elegant riding clothes: a grey waistcoat with silver buttons over an open-necked silk shirt, tightly-fitting trousers and highly polished boots. Max felt clumsy and juvenile in his grey flannels and blazer, his cotton shirt and green and black striped school tie.

Having nodded to each other, they did not bother to make conversation as they went up the wide staircase and into a small bedroom on the first floor. It was minimally furnished with a single iron bedstead, a wash-stand on which stood a china ewer and basin, a heavy oak chest of drawers and a wardrobe. A large, garishly-painted crucifix hung above the bed.

Rafael leant against the door-frame as Max put his suitcases on the floor and looked around. The room was no more welcoming than his school dormitory and he did not relish the prospect of sleeping directly under the pain-wracked, accusing eyes of the crucified Christ.

As he knelt and opened a case, Rafael said abruptly, 'What's your school like?'

'All right. How about yours?'

'It's near Lucerne. There's a swimming-pool and riding. It's the most expensive school in Europe.'

'I don't know what mine costs,' Max said indifferently.

'I do. It's much less than *Les Chênes*.'

'How do you know?'

'Because my father's paying the fees, of course.'

Max stared at him. 'Don't be silly! it was all paid for before my father died.'

Rafael smiled, and Max was reminded how much they had disliked each other. 'Your mother and father didn't leave any money. Or not much, anyway. My father said they'd been counting on selling his paintings to raise enough for the school. But all the paintings were burnt in the fire. My father felt sorry for you and he's been paying. And giving you an allowance. Didn't you know?'

'I don't believe it . . .' But as he said it, he realised that Rafael could be telling the truth. No one had actually said that his father had paid the fees in advance; he had simply assumed it. And when his house-master had handed him instalments of his generous allowance, he had accepted without question that they had come from the same source. He said, as much to himself as to Rafael: 'But why? I mean, why does he?'

Rafael shrugged. 'I don't know. My mother was very angry. She said there were more deserving charities in Spain.' He looked at his watch. 'It's time for lunch. She doesn't like us to be late.'

Max followed him downstairs and into a vast, dim dining-room, where Don Luis, Doña Maria and a thin child with long, dark hair, who he assumed was Victoria – no-one bothered to tell him – were already sitting at the table. As he ate, he tried to absorb Rafael's revelation, and found himself increasingly disturbed by the obligation it imposed on him. If Don Luis was paying for his education, did that mean he was now part of the Ansaldo family? Was he being adopted? Don Luis was all right, but he did not look forward to spending much time with Doña Maria and Rafael, who clearly liked him no more than he liked them.

It was a silent meal, because the Ansaldos talked little. Doña Maria, whose appetite was enormous, gobbled her food and rebuked Rafael and Victoria for their table manners once or twice, but Don Luis opened his mouth only to eat. They were waited on by two silent maids wearing black dresses, white caps and aprons.

The meal ended with sweet, almond-studded pastries, then Don Luis wiped his mouth with the napkin that had been tucked into his collar, and stood up. 'Maxwell, I think we must talk a little,' he said.

He led the way into a room which was made marginally more cheerful than the rest of the house by book shelves and by a couple of paintings of snow-scenes which hung on one wall. They looked familiar, and Don Luis followed Max's glance. 'Those were done by your father's uncle, Henry Raven. I bought them many years ago, during a particularly hot summer. They are of the Scottish winter, and looking at them made me feel cooler.'

'We had some that were almost the same,' Max said. 'I suppose they were burnt in the fire.'

'I'm afraid so. Everything was lost, my boy. That was one of the things I wanted to talk to you about . . .' He sat behind his desk and motioned towards a chair facing him.

Before he could say anything more, Max interrupted. 'Don Luis, Rafael says you've been paying for my school and sending me my allowance. Is that true?'

'Rafael had no right to tell you, but yes, it's true.'

Again Max said, 'But why?'

Don Luis looked down at his hands, which were folded tightly together as they lay on the desk. 'Your parents were my good friends. You will remember how often I visited them. Whenever I had – problems, I would go to your father's studio and sit with a glass of wine, and watch him paint. I envied him. Your mother was one of the most beautiful women I have ever seen. Andrew was a happy man, and he made me feel happy. They died because they had come to my country. I am not poor, and I felt that I owed them something.'

'Didn't they have any money? None at all?'

'Your father had an account in a bank in Gibraltar. It doesn't contain much, but it might help you to get started in life when you're older. The property belongs to you, of course. You will probably want to have the building demolished. The land isn't worth a great deal now, but it could increase in value.'

To his distress, Max felt a lump in his throat and tears threatening to swamp his eyes. With difficulty, he said, 'It's awfully kind of you, sir. I wish you didn't have to . . . I mean, all the money in the bank . . . I'll use it to pay you back.'

'We won't talk about that now. I must tell you that two years ago I applied to the Spanish court to be officially appointed as your guardian until you are eighteen. It was granted, because although we tried, no one was able to trace any of your relations in Scotland. Your father kept all his papers, which might have given us a clue, in the *finca*.'

'I'm not sure I have any relations. Neither my mother nor father had brothers and sisters, and the only person they talked about was Uncle Henry Raven.'

'I became your guardian only for your protection. It won't change your life in any way – except that I hope you will regard us as your family now. I instructed your school that you were not to know about this. I wanted to tell you myself and you'd have heard much sooner if it hadn't been for the war. I also asked your headmaster to send me copies of your reports. I've been very pleased with them.'

'Thank you.' He swallowed. 'Don Luis, thank you for everything.'

'Now that's been said, I want you to enjoy your holiday, and we've been making plans. Do you ride?'

'A bit.'

'You must ride with Rafael. He has two horses now and he goes to the beach for a gallop at least once a day.' For the first time, he sounded hesitant. 'I was wondering whether you might like to accompany me to the vineyards occasionally? Rafael isn't interested, but you might find it amusing to learn a little about wine-making.'

'I'd like to.' Wandering around rows of vines with Don Luis did not, in fact, sound particularly appealing, but he knew he was in no position to show reluctance. He gathered his courage and said, 'Could I go and see Zimmy this afternoon? If you don't want me for anything else.'

For a moment, he thought Luis was going to refuse, but after a pause, he nodded. 'I know she's an old family friend. But one thing: you understand about her . . . profession?'

'Yes.'

'It isn't one that commends itself to ladies. It would be better if you did not see her too often, and if you didn't tell my wife where you're going today. If she asks, simply say you're going for a walk. I would not want to upset her.'

In the event, Doña Maria showed no interest in his movements. When he emerged from the office, she had disappeared, and so had Rafael. He saw only maids when he came down from his room after unpacking and changing into less formal clothes.

'. . . So he said he was my guardian. Did you know about this?'

They were sitting side by side on a sofa in Zimmy's little sitting-room behind the bar, and she was holding his hand, a smile in her dark eyes as she watched him.

'It's as though you were never away,' she said irrelevantly. 'Yes, my dear, I knew, but Don Luis wanted to break it to you himself.'

'I was thinking about it on the way down. I don't really want to live with them all the time when I'm not at school.'

'I used not to like Don Luis, but he was so distraught when your parents died that we found something in common,' she said. 'It was almost as though he blamed himself. He didn't come out of his house for two days, and when he did, he was determined to do what he could for you. We had some meetings, because I knew more about Andrew's affairs than he did. He made the final arrangements for your trip to England, and insisted that he would pay your school fees. When he said he wanted you to stay with him during the holidays, it wasn't possible for me to argue.' She paused, and sighed. 'He is still a Fascist, but Spain has become a Fascist country, and we all have to live together now.'

'I must owe him an awful lot. I'll pay it back some day.'

'I have a feeling that all the payment he will want is, perhaps, some affection. He gets little enough from his own children. That is not a happy house.'

'Isn't it? Why?'

'Doña Maria is – difficult. A jealous woman. He talks to Angelina about her and she, of course, tells me.'

'You mean he's Angelina's – her customer?'

'Yes, but don't you dare even hint that you know!'

Flattered that she was treating him as an adult, he said, 'Of course I won't. How's business, anyway?'

'Improving. The war was dreadful. We had only the Republican soldiers – no Nationalists were admitted – but the girls didn't like them. Many of them never bathed and treated them like animals. In. Out. *Gracias* . . .' She stopped, and looked at him severely. 'You're too young for such talk!'

'No, I'm not!'

'Nevertheless, we will change the subject.'

'Okay. Tell me about Esteban. Where is he? I can't wait to

see him and the others: Titi, Manolo, Jaime . . . how are they?'

Her shoulders sagged: 'I have been waiting for you to ask. Esteban is dead, my love.'

He stared at her, then whispered, 'Killed in the war?'

'He left here the night of the fire. I never saw him again. That was a terrible night: you lost your parents, I lost my best friends, and my brother.'

'How did it happen?'

'One of Esteban's friends came much later to tell me about it. His name was Juan. He had lost a leg and the war was over for him. He and Esteban were with a group of Republicans who were on their way to the front up north. One day they camped outside a town and went in to drink a little brandy and pretend for a while that there was no war.

'The church bells rang to warn of an air-raid, and ten minutes later, bombers flown by Germans who were fighting for the Nationalists came over the town. They were part of what was called the Condor Legion of the Luftwaffe. First they dropped their bombs, then they machine-gunned the people from the air. Juan said it was a massacre. Men, women and children were killed as they ran for shelter.' She was clasping his hand so tightly that his fingers were crushed.

'When Juan saw Esteban for the last time, he was carrying a little girl who was covered in blood. Then an aeroplane swept low, with its machine-guns firing. Esteban fell. Juan was himself trying to help two old women, so he couldn't go to him. When it was over, the town had been destroyed and most of the bodies were unidentifiable.'

Max remembered the tall, brown-haired young man who had given him rides on his motor-cycle, with whom he had walked and swum and talked. Even when Esteban had been urging the villagers in the plaza to rise against their masters he had seemed too polite and gentle to be a revolutionary.

After a moment, he said, 'It won't be the same without him.'

'I never stop missing him,' she said. 'And now I am going to tell you a secret: you and Esteban were related.'

His mouth fell open. 'Me and Esteban?'

'He was the son of your great-uncle Henry.'

'But he was your brother! Are you and I . . .'

'He was my half-brother only.' Seeing his 14-year-old mind struggling to understand, she spoke more slowly. 'My Papa was an invalid for some time before he died. My Mamma loved him, but she needed also someone for whom she was more than a nurse. She loved Henry Raven, too, and he gave her Esteban, who was born just before Papa died.'

He was too interested to be embarrassed by this revelation of adult sexual peccadilloes. 'But what did your Papa say? Wasn't he angry?'

'For the last few months, he wasn't capable of anger. He was a vegetable. He knew nothing of Esteban, but everyone else accepted that the baby had been conceived before he became incapable. I did, too. My Mamma only told me the truth just before she died.'

'Did you mind?'

'No. I loved Esteban and I loved Enrique. I hope you don't mind that I have told you.'

'Of course not! So you and me are sort of step-cousins, or something. Did my mother and father know?'

'I was never sure. I think they might have suspected. One day, if they'd lived, we would have talked about it. I could never bring myself to tell them then, because I was afraid it might spoil things between us.'

'Why should it?'

'My work. We were friends, but that's very different from finding yourself with a family connection to a woman who runs a – a house.'

'Well, I think it's terrific! I'd much rather be connected to you than to Don Luis. Only I wish Esteban was still here, too.'

'He's not the only one you will find missing, I'm afraid. There's been so much bad news during the past three years. Have you had enough, or will we get it all over now?'

He thought for a moment. 'Now. I'd rather hear it from you than anyone else.'

'Jaime's gone,' she said. 'And Gil, and one of Aquilina's boys. Aquilina herself was shot during an attack by the Falange and has gone to live with a daughter in Sevilla. She cannot leave her bed. Marcos's son was killed. He was on the other side, but we were still sad. Almost every family has lost someone and I sometimes think that I'm the only woman who doesn't wear mourning. I can remember Esteban just as well without looking like a black crow.'

For months he had been looking forward to seeing his friends. Although he had read news of the Civil War at school, it had not occurred to him that it would affect him personally. His parents' death had been a dreadful accident, nothing to do with the conflict. Even the violence he had seen before leaving had been more exciting than frightening. Now, for the first time, he began to understand what had been happening to Spain.

Afraid of the answer, he said, 'Titi . . .?'

'He isn't dead, but his mind has been hurt.'

'What happened?'

'After his father was killed, he ran away. So many dreadful things were going on that for a while I didn't notice he'd gone. Then someone said he had been seen in the hills, so I took Burro and went to look for him.'

'Did you find him?'

She nodded. 'There's an old shepherd's hut in a valley about ten kilometres back in the hills. It was one of the hiding-places Esteban and his men had used, and the only one I knew about. I found Titi crouching inside, and he wouldn't speak. I asked him to come with me, but he didn't seem to understand. Then I tried to pull him up from the floor, and he ran. I'd taken some food with me, so I left it, and came home.'

'Where is he now?'

'Still in the hills. I told others about him, and we went to him, sometimes one by one and sometimes in groups, trying to bring him back, but every time we came too near, he ran away. We had to give up. His brain was always weak, you remember, and the death of his father had been too much of a shock for him to bear. Every few weeks one of the girls or I load supplies on Burro and leave them in the hut. We've taken a mattress and blankets so he doesn't freeze in winter.'

'Do you see him?'

'Oh, yes. I think he realises now that I won't try to force

him to leave. He even says a few words sometimes, though they don't make much sense.'

'Can I come with you next time?'

'I'd like you to. Who knows, you might be able to persuade him to come back.'

'What about Manolo? Is he . . .?'

'Manolo's a survivor! Through the war, he followed whichever side was on top at the moment. He begged and stole from everyone. But maybe he isn't totally bad. Once or twice, he and Luisa sheltered our men who would otherwise have been shot.'

'Are they still living in the cave?'

'Yes. Luisa is ill. She has the social disease. Do you know what that is?' He shook his head. 'It is from lying with too many men who are unclean. She's had it for years, but she'd never go to the doctor. Now she's in great pain and her mind is being affected. Manolo won't let anyone else look after her. He stays with her and only comes into the village when she needs something to ease the pain.'

'I hope I'll be able to see him.'

'I'll get a message to you next time he's here . . . but you'd better not tell Don Luis. A few weeks ago someone painted 'Falange pig!' on his car. He was convinced it was Manolo, and sent the police after him, but he and his mother swore they'd been together all evening.'

Max began to see that his life in San Felipe could become complicated. Don Luis had said that Doña Maria must not be told he was seeing Zimmy: Now Zimmy told him Don Luis should not know about Manolo. It seemed that all his surviving friends had to occupy separate pigeon-holes, and he was reminded of how he had always had to keep Manolo and Rafael apart.

Zimmy stood up. 'Now you've heard the worst, my dear, and we will think of more cheerful things! Would you like to go for a walk?'

'Could we go to the beach? In England beaches are mostly made of pebbles and I haven't seen real sand for years.'

'That's one thing that hasn't changed here. We'll take Burro with us for his afternoon stroll.'

To his embarrassment, she took his hand as she used to when they walked at the water's edge, but he didn't want to withdraw it as long as there was no one around to see. The little grey donkey trotted beside them. It was Burro Dos, Zimmy explained; Burro Uno had died a year ago.

As they walked, he told her about England, and his school, his friends, his holidays in London and Inverness. Whenever he slowed down, she shot questions at him, avid for detail. At one point she said, 'Do you know, the furthest I have been from San Felipe is Gibraltar. Here I am, over thirty years old, and you're only fourteen and travel all over the world by yourself without thinking twice.'

Although he murmured, 'It's not exactly the world,' he felt himself immensely sophisticated.

He was so absorbed in his monologue that he didn't notice the horse and rider coming towards them, until they had drawn level. He looked up, raised his hand and said, '*Hola*, Rafael!' The other boy ignored the greeting, dug his heels into the horse's side, and cantered on.

'What's the matter with him?' Max said indignantly.

Zimmy shrugged. 'Maybe it was because you are with me. His Mamma does not approve of the Bar Jiminez.'

'I wish I didn't have to stay with them.'

'There's no help for it. You'll just have to keep out of Rafael's way.' She shook her head. 'His Mamma is devoted to him, but he's a sad disappointment to his father. He doesn't do well at school. He only cares about horse-riding.'

'I suppose Don Luis told Angelina this,' he said.

'I have said too much today! It's the excitement of having you back, and finding a man I can talk to instead of a little boy. You will kindly forget my gossip!'

He squeezed her hand. 'I won't tell anyone. It's between you and me. And I don't care about Doña Maria, I'm going to come and see you whenever I want to.'

When he returned to the Ansaldos, he heard raised voices in Don Luis's office: Don Luis himself; Doña Maria, sounding tearful. He paused at the bottom of the stairs, trying to make out what was going on, but the door opened and Rafael emerged, closing it behind him. As he saw Max, he said, 'They're talking about you.'

'Why?'

'You'll find out.'

'I bet you told your mother about seeing me with Zimmy this afternoon.'

'What if I did? She keeps a brothel.'

With concentrated venom, Max said: 'At my school, we *pack* sneaks!'

'What does that mean?'

'It means that kids who go around telling tales get *packed* on by everyone else in the dorm at night. Once we broke someone's wrist.'

Rafael sniffed. 'I wouldn't let anyone do that to me!'

'Want me to try?' Max took a step towards him and Rafael's arrogance turned to apprehension. At that moment, the door opened again and his mother appeared. Her face was flushed and her eyes watery, but there was a distinct look of satisfaction in the glance she shot at Max. She beckoned Rafael to follow her.

Max went up to his room, wondering how to fill the hours until supper. During the journey from England he had read all the books he had brought, and he did not feel sufficiently confident to ask if he could look through the shelves. Then, from the window, he saw Don Luis drive out of the gates and turn his car towards the village. He felt suddenly desolate, with the knowledge that his only supporter in the household had deserted him.

The holiday stretched drearily ahead. More than ever, he wished he had stayed in Britain. The visit to Zimmy had been a brief pleasure in a generally disappointing day, but even that had been saddened by her news that three of his friends, Esteban, Gil and Jaime, were dead; that Titi seemed to have lost contact with reality; that Manolo was occupied with his mother. Only Zimmy herself hadn't changed, but he'd bet that Doña Maria had been trying to talk her husband into forbidding him to see her. Just let him try, he thought.

He walked restlessly around the small room, aware of the dead eyes following him from the crucifix. At least he could put a stop to that. He reached up and unhooked the carving, then slid it under his bed. Doña Maria would probably be furious, but he didn't care. One of the things he had most disliked about the day had been the discovery that he was the recipient of Ansaldo charity, and he was sure that Rafael would take every opportunity to remind him of the fact. For the first time, the importance of money was brought home to him. He'd never had to think about it before.

He wandered back to the window. It was a warm evening and the sun was shooting up red rays as it sank behind the hills. To the east, beyond the village rooftops, he could see the horizon, which curved around until it was lost behind the high stone walls over which, on that memorable afternoon, Christina had stared, open-mouthed and shocked, at himself and Manolo. Beyond the wall . . .

Five minutes later, he was walking along the road which led from the Ansaldos' gates to the *finca*. There was no fence around the property. Rough ground, dotted with trees, reached to the road, bisected by a path which led up to the little farmhouse. Jaime had never had a chance to create more than a patch of lawn in front of the terrace, but Moira had managed to grow pelargonium bushes and even a few roses in the sandy soil.

Dreading the moment of recognition, he did not raise his eyes from the weeds which covered the gravel path until he had almost reached the terrace. Then he stopped, and looked. The place was derelict. It had no roof; the walls were streaked with soot; there were no doors, no window-frames, only empty rectangles. It could have been one of the ruined crofts in Inverness which he and Henry Matson explored. The lawn, like the path, had disappeared under weeds, but Moira's pelargoniums were in full bloom, great patches of purple against the sun-dried grass.

He went inside, through what had been the front door. There must have been rain within the past few days, because the stone floors were wet. They were covered by rubbish: blackened beam-ends, riddled with termites; twisted, unidentifiable pieces of metal, shards of crockery. There were piles of ashes in what had been Andrew's studio, where cooking fires had been made by tramps and gypsies seeking shelter from the winter, and these gave him his first sense of possession: this was *his* house, and he resented the strangers' intrusion.

He kicked a pile and as unburnt slivers of wood scattered, he saw, lying on the flat-stones, one of his father's palette knives, eaten into by rust, but recognisable.

He remembered how Andrew would step back from his easel, the paint-caked knife in hand, stare at his picture, then swoop forward like a great bird to attack it with fast strokes which would turn a flat expanse of green into an olive-grove, or a greyish blob into a peasant woman, her back bent under a load of fire-wood.

In the remains of other rooms, there were other memories: of his mother in the kitchen, slapping her fan against the stove to bring up the heat; of the table in the *sala* where they played dominoes or snap in winter, their feet warmed by the charcoal-pan; of Moira in his bedroom, turning out drawers as she looked for clothing to give to Manolo or Titi; of himself perching on the edge of the terrace on fine evenings, while his parents drank wine and talked. He saw the pictures as though they were on a screen, and there was no sadness in them. Three years had passed, he was into a whole new life. His anticipation of the emotional impact had borne so little relationship to the reality that he felt a weight had been lifted from his mind. The ghosts that haunted the ruins were of two people he still loved, but could now see only dimly.

He spent half an hour in the *finca*, then made his way back to the road. As he reached it, he turned for a last look, and saw that there was beauty in the shape of the stone ruins against the sky. Don Luis had said he would probably want to have them demolished. In that moment, he decided that he would leave them as they were, in memory of Moira and Andrew.

Supper that night was no more lively than lunch had been, and again Doña Maria ate more than anyone else. Neither she nor Rafael addressed a word to him. Don Luis made an effort, asking him questions about his school, and he answered politely, but briefly. At ten o'clock, he excused himself and went to bed.

He overslept the next morning and when he arrived in the dining-room, his was the only place that remained at the table. One of the silent maids brought him a cup of chocolate and *churros*. Accustomed to boarding-school breakfasts of baked beans, sausages or fried eggs and as much soggy toast as he wanted, he was unsatisfied by the fried dough. Peasants, who had to rise early, would eat again at about eleven o'clock. The Ansaldos' *comida* would not be served until two-thirty at the earliest.

But there would be something to eat at the Bar. No one had yet said that he might not go and see Zimmy. No one, in fact, had said anything to him. He might not have existed, he thought resentfully.

He left the house quietly. The sprawling area called the Campo Negro, which belonged to Don Luis, offered a short cut, so he crossed it, leaping deep furrows, jumping down rocky outcrops, breaking into a run across a wide, flat, grassy shelf. As he regained the road at the edge of the village, he saw the Hispano-Suiza coming towards him. With a sinking feeling in his stomach, he stopped, wondering whether he was going to be forbidden to go any further.

The car drew up beside him and Don Luis opened the door. 'I was coming to look for you, Maxwell.'

Sullenly, Max climbed in beside him, and waited for the blow to fall.

Instead of driving on, Don Luis switched off the engine. 'I imagine you were on your way to see Senorita Zimmy,' he said.

'Yes.'

'How would you like to stay with her for the rest of your holidays?'

It was so unexpected that for a moment Max did not realise what he was being offered.

'I'd hoped to keep you with us, but there seem to be – difficulties,' Don Luis said carefully. 'My wife is a busy woman . . . religious duties . . . her charitable activities. Rafael has his own interests, of course . . .' The unconvincing excuses droned on, but Max hardly heard them. He felt as though he had been given parole from a life-sentence.

Half-an-hour later, he had re-packed his belongings, been driven back into the village and was settled in his little white room above the bar.

What had promised to be a disastrous vacation became one which he would always remember with pleasure.

He scarcely set eyes on Doña Maria or Rafael, but spent much of his time swimming, wandering in the hills as he used to, chatting with Zimmy and helping out in the Bar in the evenings. It was a few days before he realised that he hadn't seen Pepita, Angelina or Sonia ushering any clients up to their rooms, though he had heard occasional bangs on the door downstairs late at night.

'Aren't they working, then?' he ask Zimmy.

'They are having a little vacation, too,' she said. 'It was my arrangement with Don Luis.'

'Is it because of me?'

'He said that if I could not close down while you were here, he would have to find other accommodation for you. It seems that la Senora is too busy . . .' She raised her eyes and turned down the corners of her mouth '. . . to have a guest. Such nonsense. All she does is pray and eat. But of course I was not going to miss the chance! Anyhow, he is paying the girls a little compensation.'

'I wouldn't mind about the customers. I know what it's all about. Don Luis knows I know.'

'Nevertheless, we have our arrangement.' She chuckled. 'Only do not be surprised if Don Luis himself drops in some evening. The ban does not extend to him.'

But Don Luis prudently confined his visits to the daylight hours and, whatever his wife's objections might have been, regularly drank a brandy as he sat in the sun on the plaza. If Max was about, he would be invited to join him, and a tentative friendship began to grow between them.

As Max settled back into village life, he learnt more about the changes which had resulted from three years of bitter civil conflict: San Felipe was a community licking its wounds, some of which would leave permanent scars.

Where the plaza had once been a meeting-place for all

generations, there was now a gap. Black-clad housewives still gathered at the washing-troughs, with small children. Old men sat over their brandies or rough red wine. But the evening *paseo*, when he rememebered groups of young men dominating the plaza as they ogled the well-chaperoned village girls – at eleven, he had looked forward to the day when he would be old enough to join them – was now made up largely of women. It seemed that almost a whole generation of men, aged between twenty and forty, had vanished, and of the survivors, many were disabled.

Apart from the Machados, there had been no beggars in San Felipe. Now Max saw gaunt, sunken-eyed men, often with a limb missing, standing on corners with their hands outstretched. Others, sightless, squatted in the dust trying to sell a few boxes of matches. Curious stories circulated of Republicans still lurking in the hills, too frightened to return now their enemies were in power. At least one family was believed to have a refugee still concealed in their house.

But he was too occupied with his own life to let the tragedies disturb him, and Zimmy hid her sorrow so successfully that he was scarcely aware of it. Esteban, like his own parents, belonged to the past.

A week or so after his arrival, Don Luis took him on an expedition to the family vineyards near Jerez. The Ansaldos had owned the property for two generations, growing small, but profitable, quantities of the sweet Pedro Ximinez grape, whose juice was blended into sherries produced in the Jerez *bodegas*.

There was a house among the vines, which was maintained by a staff for his monthly visits.

Somewhat to Max's surprise, he enjoyed himself. Don Luis's enthusiasm for viniculture was infectious, and when he discovered that the boy responded, he was happy to talk for hours about wine, from the great red *riojas* of Castile, to Andalusia's sherry, which was his personal passion. He was rarely without a *copita* in his hand.

Max learned how the juice was trodden out of the grapes by men wearing heavy boots with nails in the soles to catch the pips; how the *mosto* was fermented in the *bodegas*, sometimes frothing with such force that it flew up to the ceiling; how different sherries were blended to create the sweet or dry quality required by a shipper; how they should be served cold, but not icy.

By the end of the holidays, he had acquired a good working knowledge of the wine-making process, and Don Luis was obviously touched by his attention, and grateful for it. He remarked sadly that he had hoped Rafael would eventually take over the business, but that he had so far shown little interest in it.

Apart from the vineyard expeditions, Max's holiday in that last, pre-World War summer was punctuated by three highlights: his meetings with Titi and Manolo, and the night when Pepita came to his bed.

Exploring a shed which leant against the back wall of the Bar one day, he had discovered Esteban's old motor-cycle, covered in blown sand and spiders' webs.

Two days later, having obtained Zimmy's permission, he had cleaned and polished it, and filled the tank with *gasolina*. At first he took it, cautiously, into the narrow village lanes, but as he became more familiar with it, he made longer and longer forays into the surrounding countryside, delighting in the freedom it gave him.

One stifling afternoon, when the sun blazed down from a blue-white sky and a wind was swirling sand into dust-devils, he made for the hills, where trees might give at least an illusion of coolness.

Nearing the base of a slope which led into a remote, rock-fringed valley, he saw, away to his left, an old wooden hut. Remembering what Zimmy had told him about Titi, he turned the bike towards it. The track had long since petered out and he bounced over the rough ground.

An umbrella pine, blown by the wind so it leant at a forty-five degree angle, shaded the hut, which rested against it so they looked as though they were holding each other up. He put the motor-cycle on the ground and went cautiously towards it. A wooden door sagged, half-open, from one hinge. As he reached it, he called: 'Titi? You there?'

There was no response, so he looked inside. A pile of

blankets lay in one corner. On a wooden box which seemed to serve as a table, there were a few plates holding scraps of half-eaten food, where ants grazed busily. There was no sign of Titi.

He went back to the motor-bike and started the engine. As it burst into life, he saw movement near a rocky out-crop to the left of the hut. He waited, the bike's engine panting.

Minutes passed, then a small, ragged figure moved slowly out of the shadows of the rock and stood, staring at him.

'*Hola*, Titi! It's me, Max!' He switched off the engine and went forward, his hand outstretched. When they were a few feet apart, Titi began backing away, so he stopped. 'I'm not going to hurt you,' he said. 'I've come to say hello, that's all. I'm here for the holidays. I'm staying with Zimmy at the Bar . . .'

He went on talking as they faced each other, and Titi gradually relaxed; he smiled and even muttered a kind of greeting. But then Max took another step forward, and it was all over: he turned and fled, losing himself among the trees.

Max went back the next day and this time Titi was waiting for him, sheltering beside the rocks as though they were his fortress. Knowing better than to try and go too close, Max squatted on the ground and studied the little boy who, at thirteen, was no taller than he had been three years before. His eyes were wide and blank, as though they were shuttered from the outside world. His naturally round face had fallen into hollows and his dark hair was matted. His hands and feet seemed little bigger than a baby's. He wore no shoes and his clothes, gathered by Zimmy from mothers whose sons had grown out of them, hung on his scarecrow-thin body. After a while, he edged closer, and Max saw that he was looking, not at himself, but at the motor-bike. He stood up and began to push it forward. But again he had moved too quickly, and Titi fled.

When he told Zimmy that night, she said, 'You must have patience. Already you've probably been closer to him than I have. He's never been visible when I arrive. He hides until he sees who it is. He comes out eventually for me and the girls, but there are some who never set eyes on him.'

Patience was not one of Max's virtues and, in fact, it was not to be tested this time. The next afternoon, Titi was again waiting at the rocks. Step by step, he advanced towards the motor-bike, then he looked up at Max and raised his hands, with fists closed as though they were clenched on the handle-bars.

Max said softly, 'I'll give you a ride, if you like.'

Instead of running away, Titi moved his head in the slightest nod.

Max depressed the starter pedal. Titi moved in slow motion, but eventually he was astride the pillion, sitting upright, his arms down by his sides.

'If you don't hold me, you'll fall off,' Max said. There was no reply, but after a moment he felt hands resting on his shoulders.

He circled the hut, then he went up the slope which led towards the track into the village. Behind him, Titi laughed excitedly.

They swooped and swerved between rocks, up and down hills, and when they pulled up outside the hut, Titi's thin face had come alive and there was colour on his cheekbones.

He jumped down from the pillion and Max said, 'I'll come back tomorrow. Maybe we'll go down and ride on the beach.'

The eye-shutters came down as Titi gestured round the valley. '*Aqui*! *Aqui*!' he muttered.

'We can't ride here all the time. You like Zimmy, don't you?' Titi nodded. 'Well, we'll go and see her first. She'll make us a *torta*. She's got a melon, too. There won't be anyone else. Only us.'

Whether it was the promise of cake and fruit, another ride, or the guarantee that his company would be restricted to Zimmy and Max, Titi mounted the bike without hesitation the next day. His only indication of apprehension as they neared the inhabited area was the tightening of his grip around Max's waist.

It was siesta and the streets were almost deserted. Zimmy was waiting at the Bar, and whisked him straight into her sitting-room.

He stood, wide-eyed, looking around at the comfortable

chairs, the bobble-fringed green velour cover on the table, the sewing-machine, draped with a bright, flounced skirt she was making for Sonia, the walnut-framed photographs of her mother and father on the wall.

He hardly spoke, but ate everything he was offered: pastries stuffed with wine-soaked fruit, cinnamon-flavoured cakes and slices of melon. Max could actually see the food swelling his concave stomach.

Then they went to the beach. He had a moment of panic when he saw a few fishermen sitting cross-legged on the sand near their boats, mending nets, but recovered when they hardly glanced at him. For an hour, Max raced the bike back and forth on the hard sand at the water's edge, faster and faster, until they were both shouting with exhilaration.

When they returned to the Bar, Zimmy said, 'Titi, I have a little room ready for you. Wouldn't you like to sleep in a bed for a change?' His body stiffened and he shook his head with small, frantic movements, like a clockwork toy. 'It's all right, my love,' she said quickly. 'No one will make you stay. Max will take you back.'

'What's made him so frightened?' Max asked later.

'It was what happened to his father . . .' He thought she was going on, but she stopped.

'Does Titi know how he was killed then?'

'I don't know what he knows.' She changed the subject abruptly. 'Do you realise that this was the first time he had been inside a real house for three years? Maybe you have brought him back to us.'

'It wasn't me. It was the bike.'

'It was you and the bike together. He always loved you. The first step has been taken, the next ones should be easier for him.'

She was right. By the time Max returned to school, Titi had been into the village several times. Though he still shrank away when other people came near, he gained confidence every day. Often, when Max arrived at the hut, he would be racing around it, pretending to be riding the motor-cycle, imitating the sound of its engine. His speech was becoming less garbled and his old, sweet smile was lighting his face more frequently. One hot night, he even agreed not to return to the hills. He refused to sleep in Zimmy's room, but wandered off to the beach and curled up in a fissure between two rocks.

One thing that would always send him back into his trauma was any mention of his father. When Max had tried to express sympathy, the shutters had fallen. He had stared blankly ahead for a moment, then fled. Max had caught up with him on the motor-cycle as he was trudging back to his hut. He had refused a ride. By the next day, he seemed to have forgotten the incident, but Zimmy warned Max never to mention Jaime again.

He did not renew his friendship with Manolo until his holiday was half over. Zimmy had heard that Luisa was dying, and decided to go to the cave and see if there was anything she could do to help. 'We are, after all, members of the same profession,' she said wryly.

'Can I come too?'

'If you wish. It might not be very pleasant.'

'I don't care. I'd like to see Manolo.'

To reach the cave, Max walking and Zimmy mounted on Burro, they had to cross the clearing where, years ago, he had found Clara's body. He could not avoid looking at the spot, remembering the splayed, naked form, the suffused face, the ants crawling, unhindered, into the mouth.

'This is where that poor child was killed,' Zimmy said casually. 'Clara. Do you remember?'

'Yes.'

'She was not a good little girl, but it was sad. They never found out who did it.'

For a moment, he was tempted to tell her that Manolo believed he knew, but keeping his own involvement secret had been a habit for so long that he could not find the words. He was pleased that she dropped the subject.

The cave was not far from the tree where Manolo had caught up with him that day. It reached into a cliff-face and an old, torn piece of oil-cloth had been hung over the narrow entrance.

Zimmy tied Burro to a tree, and Max peered curiously over

her shoulder as she drew the oil-cloth aside. The stench that came from the darkness made them recoil. They heard a sound and, as their eyes became used to the gloom, they saw Manolo standing beside a rough iron bedstead on which Luisa lay, motionless.

Zimmy went to the bed and looked down. Then she said softly, 'How long ago . . .?'

'Yesterday, I think.'

'You should have come to me. We must make arrangements . . .'

'I didn't want her to go away.'

Manolo's face had lost its boyishness. His eyebrows had thickened and his full mouth had coarsened. The dark, sly, gypsy eyes were red and there were tear-tracks down his cheeks.

Zimmy put an arm around his shoulders and turned him away from the bed. 'It's necessary, Manolo. The hot weather . . . Come with us and we'll send the *funerario* to fetch her.' Her peasant lack of sentimentality in the face of death seemed to hearten him and after a moment, he said, 'All right. You go. I'll stay with her until they come.'

'Are you sure? Perhaps Max . . .?'

He desperately did not want to stay in this filthy hovel, with a dead body, and was grateful when Manolo said, 'I don't want him. I just want to be here by myself.'

The next day, they were the only three mourners at her hastily-arranged funeral, and as soon as it was over, Manolo disappeared.

'Will he be all right?' Max said.

'Luisa was all he had, so he is unhappy now, but he'll get over it. We all do.'

Again, she was right. A few days later, Max found him waiting outside the Bar, composed and self-confident as ever. They picked up their friendship as if it had never been interrupted, though during their first afternoon together Max was dismayed to discover that he was expected to support Manolo when he begged from visitors. They were few and far between these days, since the war had discouraged foreign tourists and they had not yet returned, but the buses from Malaga occasionally yielded a few pesetas from Spaniards seeking sun and sand.

After that first occasion, when he retreated, trying not to be noticed as Manolo whined for money, he refused to take part in the exercise.

'What's the matter?' Manolo said. 'I've always done it. You never minded before.'

'I was never with you. I hate taking money from other people.'

'That's stupid. Everyone's got more than me. I'll get it any way I can.'

It was true, Max thought. And in a way, there wasn't much difference between Manolo and himself. They both had to depend on charity.

'One day I'm going to have my own money,' he said. 'I'm going to earn it myself and never have to take it from anyone else.'

Manolo smiled mockingly. 'You can give some of it to me, then. I won't mind taking it.'

He didn't see much of Zimmy's girls. Pepita had stayed, but Sonia and Angelina had taken advantage of their unexpected vacation to go to Barcelona.

'Have they gone to see their mothers and fathers?' he asked Pepita.

She laughed. 'Angelina's parents died when she was a baby. Sonia wouldn't dare to go home to hers.'

'Why not?'

'You are an innocent, aren't you, Little Max? They have gone to Barcelona because there is money to be made there. Sailors love Barcelona, and sailors are generous. Don't you know that mothers and fathers, especially in Spain, do not like their daughters to become whores?'

Uninhibited with Zimmy, the word 'whore' from Pepita embarrassed him. It was a word whispered in the dormitory after lights-out, with speculation about what 'it' was like with 'them', salacious fantasies, ribald suggestions, uncomfortable laughter.

Then their eyes met and he felt an unusual excitement. She

was wearing a dressing-gown which had fallen open at the front, and he was reminded of the night she had come to his room. If she hadn't left so suddenly, he might have learned more than, he guessed, any of the boys in the dormitory who pretended to be so knowledgeable. Maybe this was his opportunity. He realised that she shared his thought when she took a step towards him.

Then Zimmy bustled in and ordered her sharply to go and make herself decent.

Their chance finally came two nights before he was due to return to England. Zimmy's elderly barman, Jorge, had indulged in a drunken debauch and she had sent him staggering back to his wife and taken over the bar herself.

Max had started his packing when Pepita appeared at his bedroom door.

'I came to see if I could help you,' she said.

'I can manage, thanks . . .' He hesitated, then added. 'You can stay if you like.'

She moved to his bed and lay back among the pillows, smiling at him. He gulped. 'Where's Zimmy?'

'The bar is busy. She will be there for the rest of the evening.' Her body quivered as she laughed. 'She sent me up to ask if you needed anything.'

This was it, then. He went to the door and slipped the brass bolt into its catch. When he turned, Pepita had already removed her blouse and was slipping out of her skirt.

Her love-making was a revelation, and for some time afterwards he erroneously assumed that hers was a natural talent shared by all women.

When it was over he felt more relaxed than he had ever been, and only wanted to sleep. But there was something to discover first.

'Did I do anything wrong?' he asked anxiously.

'Oh, Little Max! I would never had believed it was your first time. Never! I have known very few men like you! You are so beautiful . . . and you were *esplendido*!'

He felt ten feet tall, a man above other men. 'So you can stop calling me Little Max now,' he said.

'No. That is my name for you. You are my *pequeno* Max,

and I will never forget this time we have had.'

'I won't, either and there'll be other times when I come back.'

But there never were. By the time he returned to San Felipe he had acquired new standards of womanhood and had already been able to choose among many who showed themselves eager to go to bed with him. Pepita, in the way of Spanish women, had aged quickly. Overweight and overpainted, her physical appeal for him no longer existed. Later he realised that it was a mark of her generous spirit that she accepted his indifference without protest and their relationship settled back into its former casual affection.

During the last week of August he left San Felipe in a Spanish cargo boat to return to school, expecting to be back for Christmas.

In fact, it was to be six years before he saw the village again. For the second time, a war changed the course of his life.

2

He returned to London at the end of August, and found the country preparing for war, bubbling with excitement, confusion, apprehension and determination, spiced with pinches of panic.

The day after his arrival, on the first of September, Germany invaded Poland, and on the third, at 11.15 in the morning, he and Emilia Bartolomé, with whom he was staying until his school term started, crouched over her old bakelite wireless set and heard the 70-year-old Prime Minister, Neville Chamberlain, breaking the news the British people had been dreading.

Rigidly under control, the tired, elderly voice said: 'This morning, the British Ambassador in Berlin handed the German Government a final note, stating that unless the British Government heard from them by 11 o'clock that they were prepared at once to withdraw their troops from Poland, a state of war would exist between us. I have to tell you now that no such undertaking has been received, and that consequently this country is at war with Germany . . .'

Less than fifteen minutes later, air-raid warnings were heard over Greater London, but the skies remained empty. There was a general sense of anti-climax when the All Clear sounded.

Briskly, Emilia informed Max that he would see even less of her than usual, because she was already taking driving and first aid lessons in preparation for war work.

Schools, industries and families were rushing plans for evacuation from the capital – many had already left. Summer vacations ended abruptly as holiday-makers hurried back from the coastal resorts. In August, thousands of Service reservists and the Territorial Army had been called up, and it was announced that the Fleet had been mobilised.

Max found his explorations in London more than usually interesting. Every second person seemed to be wearing a uniform; there were piles of sand-bags in the street and arrows pointing to air-raid shelters. Black-out curtains were drawn across windows at dusk and the city became an eerie maze of almost unrecognisable streets enclosed by darkness, while the sky was criss-crossed by searchlights.

The day before term was due to start, he took the school train from Waterloo.

Henry Matson was sitting on the steps of the quad when he climbed out of the bus which had brought him from the station, and ran forward, talking with scarcely a pause for breath: 'Hey, you're late! I've been waiting since this morning. Come on, I'll help with your trunk. Gosh, Raven, I wish you'd come to Scotland this summer. There wasn't anyone except my parents and Nancy, and Daddy made me go out shooting rabbits . . . there's a plague of them.' He paused briefly as they manhandled Max's trunk up the stairs that led to the dormitories.'Then, one of the keepers hung them up by their ears and stuff dripped out of them. I'm never going to eat rabbit again. What was your holiday like?'

'Not bad, thanks.'

They reached their four-man dormitory. Max began to transfer clothes into his wardrobe.

'What did you do?' Henry said.

He had been rehearsing how he would describe the episode with Pepita, but now that the opportunity had been handed to him, he no longer wanted to. Men who knew what it was all about, he decided, didn't need to boast. 'Oh, nothing much. Swam. Learned a bit about wine-making. Saw my friends.'

'Sounds about as dull as my holiday. Daddy says you can still come to us whenever you want to.' He winked slyly. 'Nancy hopes you'll come, too. I think she's a bit . . . you know . . . about you.'

'Don't be silly. She's sixteen. Anyway, she's not my type.'

Nancy Matson, two years older than the boys, was as different from Spanish women as could be imagined. She was thin and pale, with light blue eyes fringed by fair lashes, and lank brown hair. Her features were regular, but her skin was almost colourless and the pastel colours she wore did not enhance her looks. Her character was as pallid as her appearance, and Max tended not to notice when she was present, except once or twice when he had caught her looking at him in a way that reminded him uncomfortably of Christina Ansaldo.

He was pleased to hear that his long-standing invitation to spend holidays with the Matsons had been renewed. Henry had been one of the first school friends he had made, and their relationship had survived the years. He was an ebullient youth, tall and bony, with a cheerful, open face and hair which, to the distress of his house-master's wife, he wore long enough to brush his collar. A high-bridged nose and the same pale skin as his sister gave him an aristocratic look that belied his parentage, for there was nothing aristocratic about Sir Cedric and Lady Matson.

Henry told Max that when he had first asked if he might invite his friend to stay, Sir Cedric had said, 'Spanish, is 'e? One o' they bloody foreigners.'

In keeping with this unpromising welcome, Max did not much like Sir Cedric when they met. He was later to discover that few people did.

At 50, Matson was a large, beetle-browed despot, who had begun his working life in the north of England as an apprentice plumber.

At twenty, he had married a red-headed girl named Sarah Blessing, whom he had known since they had lived in back-to-back terrace houses in Barnsley.

Five years later, he had started his own plumbing business. Within another ten years, he had expanded into other business activities and property dealing, moved to London, and was close to becoming a millionaire. He had eventually bought his title by the judicious distribution of cash to high-profile charities in which various members of the Royal Family were known to be interested.

When Max met Henry, the Matsons had a house in Belgravia, a cottage in Devon, and the shooting lodge, with a couple of miles of salmon-river and 800 acres of grouse-moor, in Inverness.

Success, combined with money and his title, had added pomposity and self-importance to Sir Cedric's other qualities. They had not softened his Yorkshire accent, his habit of blunt speaking – rudeness, in some people's language – nor his ambition.

On the other hand, he had remained faithful to Sarah and was proud of his two children. He was delighted with what he described as their 'posh' accents, acquired at the best educational establishments. It was a constant embarrassment to Henry that his father would frequently comment approvingly, in company, on his pronunciation of English.

Despite his original reservations, Max's speech and manner had impressed him. 'He said you're an arrogant young bugger,' Henry reported. 'That means he likes you.'

A natural bully, he was accustomed to dominate any company. Henry became a shadow of his outgoing self in his father's presence, and Nancy had been turned into a mouse.

But Max discovered that if he assumed an even 'posher' accent than his normal one, Sir Cedric could often be worsted. Faced by the boy's ice-blue, unwavering gaze and patronising drawl, his bluster would subside into stammering irritation.

He enjoyed his holidays in Devon and Scotland. Sir Cedric frequently had to be in London looking after the various companies of which he was chairman, and the children did much as they liked. Lady Matson, lazy and good natured, rarely took any interest in their activities.

His unpacking finished, he and Henry carried the trunk to a store-room and went outside to watch the buses disgorge their cargoes of boys.

'Is the war going to make any difference to your father?' Max said.

'He's going all out for defence contracts. Some generals were at the Lodge a couple of weeks ago and when they'd gone I heard him telling my mother that he was set to make another fortune.'

'I wonder how long the war will last. Did you ask the generals?'

'I hardly even spoke to them. They were talking business all the time. I don't suppose it will be long enough for us to get in it, though. They won't take you until you're eighteen.

'That's four years away. We'll never make it,' Max said disgustedly.

A few weeks after term started, he received a letter from Don Luis suggesting that he might be safer if he returned to Spain to finish his education. He wrote a polite, but firm, refusal, pointing out that he was in no danger and would prefer to stay where he was. Even if he was too young for the Services, he was determined not to miss the excitement of war at close quarters.

His school, situated in countryside off the main aircraft routes to London, suffered little from the Luftwaffe. A few stray bombs fell in nearby fields, but there were no direct hits on the buildings. The cellars had been turned into air-raid shelters, but were rarely used. A London school was evacuated there and the dormitories became more crowded as room was made for the newcomers. After a few initial skirmishes the two sets of boys got on reasonably well. Minor inconveniences included a shortage of paper, and classes were instructed to abolish margins and start their work at the top of each sheet. Max was severely reprimanded for making paper darts from pages of his exercise book. Food became stodgier, but there was usually enough.

He and Henry joined the cadet corps and drilled every Saturday. They became experts at aircraft recognition and could identify any enemy aircraft, from a Heinkel 111 to a Messerschmitt 109. The school years passed quickly and enjoyably. He did well enough in his examinations, played cricket in the First Eleven, and Rugby in the First Fifteen. He had a wide circle of friends, though Henry remained the one to whom he was closest.

They followed the war's progress on maps on which coloured pins indicated the various fronts, and he often chafed at the thought of the excitement he was missing.

He continued to spend summers in Scotland and went to

Devon for Easter. Christmas he spent with Emilia, on whom the war had had an enlivening effect. She joined the WVS as a driver, transported supplies of food and tea to their various centres and won universal praise for her willingness to give shelter in her home to neighbours whose houses had been bombed. Hers was one of only three in her street which remained undamaged after the Battle of Britain in 1941.

When the American forces began to arrive early in 1942 she held open-house for their officers and Max sometimes wondered just how far her hospitality extended, for she seemed to be on remarkably intimate terms with many of them.

The summer before the boys turned eighteen, Sir Cedric called them into his den at the Lodge.

'I've fixed it for you two,' he said abruptly. 'Had a word last week with General Thomas. You go straight to an officers' training school, then into 7th Armoured Division as Second Lieutenants.'

'But I want to join the Air Force . . .' Henry began.

'No, you don't , lad. I'm not having my son and heir flying aeroplanes. Too bloody dangerous. You'll go into the Army, and that's an end to it. Off you go, now.'

Henry was almost in tears when they left the room. 'I won't do it!' he said. 'I don't care what he says. I'm joining the RAF. What about you?'

Max shrugged. 'I just want to get over there. If that's the quickest way, I'll do what he says. If we don't get moving, it'll all be over.'

Two days before his eighteenth birthday, Henry disappeared. By the time he was traced, he was in training at an Air Force base in Wiltshire. To Max's surprise, Sir Cedric was not displeased. It was the first time Henry had defied him, and he said, 'Shows the lad has more guts than I thought.'

Max stayed with the Matsons in London while he awaited his summons from the Army. Lacking Henry's company, he turned to Nancy, who was on leave from the ATS. He had not seen her for nearly a year and thought she had improved. The uniform suited her slim figure. Her hair, cut short under her cap, had a curl which softened her rather sharp features.

She still had little to say for herself and he did not find her company stimulating, but he was at an age when any female was better than none.

Since Pepita, his experience of women had been limited. There had been one episode during a shooting-party at the Lodge, when the twenty-nine-year old wife of an industrialist had found her way to his bedroom. She had claimed to be impressed by his sophisticated love-making, but he had found her uninteresting. Pepita had created a high standard. There had been a couple of maids at school who had been eager to accommodate him, but they, too, had been disappointing, and after an experimental coupling in each case, he had discarded them.

One evening he took Nancy to the cinema to see a new film called 'This Happy Breed.' As they sat in the dark he was astonished to feel her hand creep into his. It was a small, bony hand, but he enjoyed holding it. Another night he took her to the Hammersmith Palais, to dance to Lou Preager's band, and her body moulded itself to his in a way that made him wonder whether she was as innocent as she appeared. He was entertaining serious thoughts about carrying their budding romance further when his Army summons arrived.

The next time they met, he was wearing the uniform of a second lieutenant, and she had been allowed leave to attend her brother's funeral. Henry had been killed by a bomb which had fallen directly on the hangar in which he was being instructed in aircraft maintenance.

After the service, Sir Cedric said to Max: 'When's your next leave, son?'

'In two weeks.'

'Come to us, will you? Nancy'll be home and if you were there . . . it'd help.'

Henry's death seemed to have diminished him, and his black suit was slack on his big frame. He was clinging to Sarah's arm, and Max felt a stab of pity. It was the first time he had seen Sir Cedric as a vulnerable human being. It was also to be the last.

* * *

The house in Belgravia seemed cold and empty without Henry.

Sir Cedric had sent word that he would not be home until late on Saturday. As he had predicted, he was making a second fortune from his defence contracts, and often worked far into the night. He had moved his headquarters into a luxurious office building in Ealing, where it was in less danger of being bombed than it had been in the City of London. Nancy arrived during the afternoon and in the evening she and Max found themselves alone. Lady Matson was at a WVS meeting and the one old servant who remained with the family had left to spend the week-end with her sister in Bushy Park.

Supper had been left for them, and when Nancy opened the larder door to bring out the dishes, Max saw that its shelves were packed with food: tinned salmon, tinned meats, tinned fruit of all kinds, chocolate, sugar, tea, in amounts which no family's ration points would cover – even if the goods had been available.

She saw his raised eyebrows. 'It's legal,' she said hurriedly. 'Daddy gets his American business contacts to send it over.'

He thought of the tired mothers, the undernourished children he had seen playing in the streets near Victoria Station as he had walked to Belgravia. 'Does he ever give any of it away?'

'Daddy's never given anything away in his life.'

There was no condemnation in her voice. She was simply stating a fact. He found himself wondering what she would do when the war ended. Would her time in the Army have given her the courage to live permanently away from home, or would she remain under her father's thumb for the rest of her life?

'How have they taken it . . . Henry, I mean?' he said.

'Mummy cries a lot. Daddy won't talk about him.' She paused. 'Do you miss him, Max?'

'Of course I do.'

'At the funeral, you didn't seem to care. I mean, your face was just ordinary, as though you were standing in a bus-queue.'

It was the first time she had ever made such a directly personal comment, and he was surprised into candour. 'I wanted to cry,' he said. 'Only I've always found it makes things easier if people don't know you care too much . . .' He floundered, seeking the right words. 'It sort of gives them an advantage if they can see what you're thinking.'

'Don't you ever like to share your thoughts?'

'Not often. Not my private ones. Henry and I shared a lot, and there's someone in Spain . . . no one else.'

'You're lucky to have one person.' There was an undertone of bitterness.

'Don't you have anyone?'

'No. Mummy lives in a world of her own and she isn't interested in anything much apart from money and clothes. I don't make friends easily.'

'How about your father?'

'He's not the sort of person you can talk to. Actually, he sometimes frightens me.'

'I met a chap once,' he said. 'He told me that if you're frightened of someone, you should keep saying to yourself, "Never let the bastards grind you down!" '

Her eyes blinked nervously. 'Do you do that?'

'Often. When I was bullied at school, or called up in front of the headmaster.' He laughed. 'He'd have had a fit if he'd known what I was thinking while I was standing in front of him. I do it with your father, too. You should try it.'

The exchange seemed to have cracked her reserve and after that they talked more easily. He set out to amuse her with stories of service life and enjoyed hearing her laugh.

When they had finished eating, she made coffee from real beans, the taste of which he had almost forgotten. Although it was not rationed, coffee was in short supply, and the brew produced by Army cooks often tasted like boiled boot-polish.

They moved from the kitchen into the blacked-out drawing room, with its rich furnishings and the Bechstein grand piano which no one could play, and were listening to the radio when the air-raid warning sounded. London was being battered nightly by flying bombs – the V.1s – which had already killed thousands of people and caused destruction comparable with that suffered at the height of the Battle of Britain.

'Into the shelter?' Max said.

'What for? If one falls on us, no shelter's going to save us. Let's stay where we are.'

She had turned off the room's central chandelier and in the dim light of one standard lamp she looked more attractive than he had ever seen her, in a long cotton house-gown, her hair fluffed out around her face.

'You're not afraid?'

'Oh, yes. But I'm afraid of lots of things – as well as my father.' She smiled, and he felt a wave of affection for her. He moved to the sofa where she was half-sitting, half-lying.

They heard the swelling roar which warned that a flying bomb was on its way towards them, and he put his arm around her.

They looked up at the ceiling, as though they might see the missile through it.

Then there was a 'crump,' and they relaxed. They were safe. Someone else had lost life, home, family.

Almost before he knew what was happening, he found himself kissing her, and she was responding. He began to fumble with the fastening of her dress, but he was too slow for her. She stood up and ripped it off, then flung her underclothes on the carpet beside it. Her eagerness was almost too much for him, but in the end, they reached their climaxes together, unaware that three more flying bombs had landed within a mile of them.

Afterwards, they dressed quickly, and when Sir Cedric arrived home half an hour later, they were sitting sedately on separate chairs, drinking mugs of cocoa.

He stayed in Belgravia two more nights, and on each of them, she came to his room. His experience of women had widened since he had joined the Army. He and Nancy didn't talk much, but he found their love-making more enjoyable than many of his other encounters.

She returned to her unit on Monday morning. He was not due to go back to camp until the evening, so after a necessarily restrained farewell, he went to see Emilia Bartolomé.

He found her preparing for the arrival of some American officers and, since she was already putting up a local family whose house had been demolished by a V.1 the previous week, she needed the room he always used. When he left school, he had sent his trunk to her and it was stored in her loft. Now he offered to take the rest of his clothes from the drawers and pack them away.

'There's masses of stuff I won't need any more,' he said. 'I'll sort it out, and you can give it to the Red Cross.'

When he opened the trunk and squatted down beside it, it was like entering an already-forgotten world. He lifted out his old green blazer, his green and black ties, his cricket flannels and the straw cheese-cutter with its green and black band which he had avoided wearing whenever possible because he felt ridiculous in it.

Under the clothes, he found a cardboard box stuffed with letters he had received from Don Luis and Zimmy while he was at school. Both had written to him regularly.

Idly, he leafed through them, and as phrases caught his eye, he suddenly wished he was back in Spain. He wanted to feel the dry heat; to walk bare-foot through the sand which, in summer, burned the soles of one's feet; to wander in the hills with Manolo, or ride the motor-cycle with Titi behind him; to sit with Zimmy, drinking a glass of wine and eating his favourited garlic-flavoured croutons. Then he thought, maybe it wouldn't be all that long before he was. Despite the V.1s, everyone said the war was already won, that the Allied landings in Normandy had been the beginning of the end. He bitterly resented having missed D- day and even now, side by side with his nostalgia for San Felipe, he was still hoping that there might be some war left in which he could take part.

He came upon a letter Zimmy had written a couple of years previously to tell him that Titi had moved back to the village. She had found him one day, curled up on the ground in a deep alcove in the ruins of the old Moorish fortification. He had resisted all efforts to remove him and simply said that this was his *casa* now. 'He is comfortable, for he had brought down his blankets and his mattress from the hills,' she wrote. 'But I worry about what will happen to him in winter – the hut at least had a door he could close.'

In a later letter, Max remembered, she had said that Don Luis had sent a carpenter to set a little door into the alcove and to repoint the old stones so that the tiny room was draught-proof. 'The war changed that man,' she added. 'Sometimes, now, he does think of the poor people. They say that he is paying his workers a few pesetas more than he needs to. And he is not the only one to be kind: so many people leave food for Titi that he cannot eat it all.'

Nearer to the top of the pile was a letter he had received from Don Luis.

After the usual salutations and information that his wife and Victoria were in good health, that it was warm in San Felipe, that the vines were doing well and he hoped for a good harvest, his writing seemed to became less well-formed, as though he was setting down what he had to say more quickly, perhaps to get it over.

'I hope you will be returning to us when you finish your education,' he had written, 'Before you do, I feel you should know that Rafael is now fighting on the side of Britain's enemies. With my encouragement, he volunteered for the so-called Blue Division, which was formed by the Generalissimo under the command of General Munoz Grandes. The Division consists of some 45,000 Spanish volunteers, members of our Falangist party, and they have joined the German Army in Eastern Europe. My reason for supporting his decision has nothing to do with my feelings for Britain – as you know, I love England. But Rafael has been going through a difficult time lately, and has been in some trouble. It pains me to tell you this, but even though I will not be your guardian for much longer, I will always regard you as a member of my family. We have had some letters from Rafael, and conditions are very hard. I am praying for his survival, and that he will return a man. Whatever he has done, I love my son very much.'

During the school holidays Don Luis always wrote to Max care of Emilia, and they had discussed the letter as they drank tea together.

'Do you know what sort of trouble Rafael was in?' he said.

'There was a girl in Malaga whom he made pregnant. Luis had to buy her off. He's been constantly in debt, and most recently there was the matter of a cheque he had forged in his father's name. If he hadn't volunteered, he would probably be in prison now. He is a bad boy.'

'I'm going into the Army soon. Wouldn't it be funny if we found ourselves facing each other on opposite sides?'

'Not funny, no. And unlikely. The Blue Division is fighting on the Russian front. The dreadful winter and the Russians' defence of Stalingrad have caused the Axis to suffer huge losses.' She paused, and added slowly, 'I hope Luis will not regret persuading the boy to volunteer. Rafael is not a strong character. Who knows what such an experience could do to him.'

The afternoon light was fading when Max locked his trunk and went downstairs. He had wondered whether he should throw the letters out, but decided not to. One day maybe, he would have a son who would like to read them. He wished that he had some such reminder of his own parents.

Emilia called him from the kitchen, where she was preparing the evening meal. 'Spam, Spam, Spam,' she grumbled. 'I have a dinner party, yes? What do I give my guests? Spam, boiled potatoes and mashed parsnips. Disgusting.'

'Doesn't Don Luis send you food parcels?'

'Not one! It is that wife of his. She spends thousands of pesetas on her children – ah, that Rafael was so spoiled! To anyone else she is . . . I like the English expression . . . mean as dirt. Which makes me remember: there is a letter for you from Luis in the drawing-room.'

He opened the envelope and perched on the kitchen table as he read it.

'Tell me what my brother says,' she commanded. 'I have not heard from him for months. The last time, there had still been no word from Rafael. Perhaps by now there has been a letter.'

'No, ' he said. 'No word. He says it's been a year now, Doña Maria is convinced he is alive, but Don Luis hasn't much hope.'

'Ah, my poor brother. I have never approved of his politics, but he doesn't deserve such a tragedy.' She regarded her plate of Spam slices with distaste, and placed a sprig of parsley in the centre. 'Nothing can make this stuff look appetising. He's very fond of you, Max. He was disappointed that you did not go straight back to Spain when you finished your education.'

'Well, I'm fond of him, too. I wasn't at first, but I got to know him when we went to the vineyards. He's been awfully good to me. I'd like to repay him some day.'

'Will you go back when the war is over?'

'Of course! It's *home*.'

She smiled at him. 'I think that will be enough repayment for Luis.'

Half an hour later, he was on his way back to camp. Two days afterwards, he was in France.

3

He would always see the war as a series of photographs preserved in his memory. Suddenly, a picture would surface of the mountains of stone which were all that had remained of the devastated city of Caen; or a peasant, blank-faced and dazed, staring at the bombed-out remains of his farmhouse; or a nun, holding a child who had been blinded by shell-splinters; a British soldier whose head had exploded as a German sniper's bullet hit it; the peaceful cider orchards of Normandy, littered with dead cattle and dead men.

Sometimes he would see liberated Paris: trees along the Seine in full leaf; the hastily-donned FFI arm-bands flaunted by Parisians anxious to be recognised as *resistants;* the buses, running on gas-cylinders; German officers sitting in a defeated group on the floor of the Hotel Majestic, their former headquarters, as they awaited transport to a prison camp; Parisian women, sleeker, better-dressed than their London counterparts.

War was not the romantic adventure his schoolboy imagination had painted. As part of a small unit which moved across Europe, mopping up in the wake of the advancing Allied Forces, he became hardened to tragedy, killing and destruction. He learned that death could strike from a hedge, a house or from the air, that a beautiful stone barn in the middle of a field of corn could contain an eighty-eight millimetre anti-tank gun.

He found himself reacting cynically to smiling, waving French townspeople as he wondered how many of them had welcomed the German invaders with the same appearance of joy. Everyone said that the war was in its last stages, but men were still being killed, and killing.He spent wet nights crouching in the mud under trees or hedges, hearing enemy bombers flying overhead. The unit was always within sound of artillery as the Germans were driven back towards the Rhine.

War, he discovered, was dangerous, exhausting, uncomfortable, and often boring.

But, true to Captain McPhee, he preserved an appearance of impassivity that won him a reputation for fearlessness which he knew he did not deserve.

For week after weary week the unit drove through France, moving steadily towards the east. In mid-August they heard that the Allies had landed on the Mediterranean coast, and taken Marseilles and Toulon.

Sometimes, when they reached a small town, they would find that the occupiers had fled and the Resistance was already taking its revenge on local people who had been branded as collaborators.

In one hillside village they came upon the bodies of a man and a woman who had been shot less than an hour before. The swarthy town Mayor informed them that the dead man was a local businessman who'd had black-market dealings with the Germans. The woman had assisted him by providing drink and sex for his contacts.

'They are only the first,' he said. 'We will seek out and execute every traitor!'

'Where were they tried?' asked one of the British officers, who had been a lawyer in civilian life.

'There was no need for a trial, m'sieu. We have dossiers.'

'You didn't allow them a defence?'

'For what these people have been doing, there is no defence.'

A legalistic argument developed which ended when the Mayor stormed off, shouting that all British were Fascist sympathisers; in France, it was well-known.

That evening, an order was issued to the unit that there must be no interference in French local affairs, no opinions publicly expressed on the summary justice being administered. 'None of our business,' they were told. 'The French have been living under the Occupation for five years. We have no right to tell them how to deal with their own people.'

One morning in late September,they marched into a mountain town which was still occupied by the remnants of a German unit which had been by-passed by the main sweep of battle. Snipers opened up from several buildings and fighting raged through the streets and squares until, late in the afternoon, a small, sullen group of soldiers emerged from the Town Hall with their hands up.The rest had been killed or wounded.

Exhausted, the British platoon left the town, watched silently by a few local people, who seemed to have been dazed by the eruption of violence, and showed no emotion at their liberation.

They made camp a few kilometres further on, knowing that the hills and woods around them could be sheltering scattered enemy forces, possibly regrouping for a counter-attack.

Dusk was falling when Max was summoned by the C.O. He found him talking with two Frenchmen. The younger had thin features, with small, furtive eyes; the other was older, with a square, sullen face. Dressed in baggy blue cotton trousers, shabby jackets and berets, with cigarettes drooping from their mouths, Max thought they were not a prepossessing pair.

Major Hammond, a tall, brisk Yorkshireman, spoke rapidly: 'These men claim to be members of the local Resistance. They say there's a party of Jerries hidden in a manor house – the Manoir de Montclair – just beyond the next village, about three kilometres away. They don't know how many there are, but estimate four or five. Raven, I want you and Bredon to take half-a-dozen men and clean 'em out. I wouldn't trust these two to give me the right time, but we can't risk ignoring them.'

Dan Bredon was the closest friend Max had made in the Army, despite backgrounds so different that it was unlikely they would have met in civilian life. Short, with a mobile, comedian's face, he was an exuberant son of the music-halls, whose parents had been a song-and-dance act called Lenny and Lena.

But under his ebullience, there was a streak of toughness

that equalled Max's own. In skirmishes they backed each other up so efficiently that after the first few weeks senior officers habitually thought of them as a team.

Less than an hour later they entered a village which seemed to consist of a few houses, a bar-restaurant and a *boulangerie* gathered around a central square. For all the life they saw, it could have been deserted. Only chinks of light through shutters in some of the houses indicated that they were inhabited. They moved quietly out through the one street and were surrounded again by the unique night silence of the French countryside. Even the sound of distant gunfire had ceased. No vehicles moved; no birds sang; no breath of wind ruffled the trees.

A few hundred yards beyond the village they found themselves walking parallel with a high stone wall which had been described by the Resistance men. A little further on, they reached a pair of sagging, iron-barred gates which reminded Max of the entrance to the Ansaldos' house, except that this property was clearly in an advanced state of decay. The gates were hanging off their hinges and held together by a piece of knotted rope, so rotten that it needed only the touch of a knife to sever it. The gates squeaked as they swung open, and the men froze.

But there was no challenge, and they went through, each with a weapon to hand.

The ground was a wilderness of weeds and bushes, and the outlines of a house loomed ahead of them.

It was a clear night, and a waxing moon helped them to make out details. The house was substantial, with three storeys and a pepper-pot turret at each end. The upper windows were shuttered. From the ground floor, French windows on either side of a heavy oak front door led onto a terrace, from which steps descended to what had once been a drive.

They reached the terrace, and felt their way along the wall. The front door was locked and all the French windows were shuttered except one. It was heavily curtained, but light glowed behind the heavy fabric.

Max and Bredon moved in opposite directions around the house, which was U-shaped, the shorter arms edging a stone court-yard which was stacked with rubbish: boxes, wine-bottles, uncleared garbage. Two rats scuttled from one of the piles. Every window was shuttered, every door locked.

'What do we do now?' Bredon said.

'How about knocking politely and saying, "Excuse me, but may we come in and arrest you?" '

'That should do it . . . more or less.'

A few minutes later, the men were in position, guns trained on all the exits.

Bredon cupped his hands around his mouth, and shouted: 'This house is surrounded! You are ordered to surrender! Come out with your hands on your heads and there'll be no shooting. You have two minutes before we fire!'

As the reverberations died away, the silence seemed deeper than ever.

'Maybe they don't understand English, ' Max said. 'You know any German?'

'A few words.' Again the voice rang out: '*Achtung! Achtung! Auskommen! Hände hoch*!'

They waited. The doors remained shut.

After two minutes, Max aimed his sub-machine gun over the roof and gave it a five-second burst. The noise was tremendous. When it stopped, the front door began to open.

A woman came slowly across the terrace towards them.

She paused at the top of the steps, her figure outlined against the faint yellow light in the house behind her.

Her voice was low and clear and her English was almost without accent. 'Why have you come here? What do you want?'

She took another step, and swayed, as though about to fall, then sagged against the balustrade.

Max went forward cautiously. 'We have had a report that there are German troops in this house.'

'They've gone,' she said. 'I'm alone.'

She turned, and they followed her into a hall, with a double staircase rising to a first-floor gallery, and a huge stone fire-place at one end. It was empty of furniture, the stone floor uncarpeted. Only the mounted head of a wild boar broke the expanse of wall.

She led the way into a room which was lit by two oil-lamps. It contained a couple of sagging arm-chairs, an oak table and an eight-foot high, carved *garde-robe*. Again, the floor was uncarpeted, the walls bare.

She sank into one of the chairs, which was next to a lamp, and looked up at them. Max saw her clearly for the first time. His eyes widened, for she was an exceptionally beautiful woman. Her face, though gaunt and fleshless, was heart-shaped, with wide, high cheek-bones and a pointed chin. Her skin was creamy and her eyes, huge and shadowed, were grey-blue, surrounded by thick dark lashes and arched eye-brows. Light brown hair was drawn back into a knot at the nape of her neck. Her body was hidden by a shapeless grey smock. She was wearing a wedding ring.

She, too, seemed momentarily mesmerised as their eyes locked, then she took a deep breath, and said, 'You will find the bodies of two German soldiers upstairs.'

Bredon left the room at a run, followed by three of the men.

'Four of them came last week,' she said tiredly. 'Two were badly wounded. The others left them here and went away. They took all our food. One of the wounded men died almost at once. I did what I could for the second, but he died a few days later.' A shudder shook her thin body. 'I couldn't move them.'

'Where did the others go?'

She lifted her shoulders almost imperceptibly, as though she had no energy for greater movement. 'They thought their friends were hiding in the mountains. They were going to look for them.'

'Did you say you had no food? Surely . . . your husband? Neighbours? You must be able to get food from somewhere.'

'My husband was killed nearly three years ago.'

'Friends?'

'I have no friends here.'

Bredon reappeared at the door. 'One's been dead a while. We'll have to bury them.'

'No sign of anyone else?'

He shook his head. 'I went through the whole place.'

When he had disappeared, the woman said hesitantly, 'I

wonder if I might ask . . . do you have anything to eat?'

'How long is it since you've had a meal?'

'Three days.'

'Christ! Wait a minute.' He came back holding two small bars of chocolate. 'That's all I could rake up, but I've sent a couple of chaps to scavenge. We passed a farm a little way back. They had hens.'

'They won't give you anything.'

'They won't be asked. My corporal tells me he's a farm boy. He can wring a chicken's neck before it knows what's happening. In the meantime, have some chocolate.'

As he undid the wrapping, she said, 'It's not for me . . .'

He looked at her with sudden suspicion. 'I thought you were alone.'

She raised her voice. 'Véronique! It's safe. You can come out.'

One of the *garde-robe's* doors opened. A girl stepped into the room. Skinny and white-faced, she looked about twelve, but was, he discovered later, nearly fifteen. Her fair hair was tied back with a piece of string. The woman held out the chocolate. She reached for it, then withdrew her hand. 'No! You must have it. You gave me the last potato.'

'There's another one. And did you hear? They're going to steal a chicken for us! We can have soup!' She turned to Max. 'This is my daughter, Véronique.'

Over the girl's head, his eyes met hers again and he felt suddenly breathless. He had to force himself to break the contact.

'Are they going to bury those men? There's an awful smell upstairs.' Véronique spoke English almost as well as her mother. Her voice was matter-of-fact.

The promise of food seemed to have given the woman back some of her strength. 'I have to thank you for what you're doing, monsieur,' she said. 'I am more grateful than I can express.'

'There are questions . . . Your identity . . . I'll have to make a report to my C.O.' The words were stiff, but she smiled up at him, and his heart lurched. This woman, he thought, was having a most peculiar effect on him.

'Well . . . my name is Anne-Louise Meredith . . .'
'Meredith? That's not French, surely?'
'My husband's father was English. John was born in France, though he went to school in England.' Her mouth tightened.'He was a writer. A poet. When the Germans came, he said there was no need for us to leave Paris, because there was no reason for them to harm us. He was not a practical man, but he was very brave. We had many Jewish friends, and we hid two of them in our apartment. One day when Véronique and I were out, the S.S. came and found them. John was arrested. A neighbour met us near the apartment and warned me not to go home. He said we must leave Paris, because they were looking for us, too. A week later, they shot John.'
'Why did you come here?'
'I had inherited this house from an uncle. I suppose I was as naive as my husband. It didn't occur to me that the Germans would bother to occupy such a remote area. Véronique and I arrived with nothing. I had just enough francs in my purse to pay our fares. All our clothes, everything had been left in the apartment. At first we felt safe enough. I sold nearly all the furniture in the house so we would have something to live on, then I tried to find work. That was when I discovered that the people in the village would have nothing to do with me.' She stopped, as though she needed to gather her strength to continue.
'Because you were a stranger?'
'Mainly, it was because my uncle, many years ago, had made pregnant one of the village girls, then discarded her. She had killed herself. This is an inbred society, Lieutenant. They are mostly related to each other, so if an injury is done to one, they all take it personally. In France there are many villages like this one, where the peasants are almost illiterate and they know nothing of the world outside. The only thing that matters is what happens to *them*, and they nurse grudges for ever.'
Her voice trailed away. Her shoulders slumped and the heavy lashes swept down over her eyes. Véronique leant forward anxiously.
'Are you all right?' he said sharply.
'I'm a little tired, that's all.' She tried to smile.
'You can tell me the rest later. Why don't you relax for a

while? We'll see what we can do about getting you both a meal.'

Two hours later, the smell of poaching chicken had spread through the house, and he was alone with her. The bodies had been buried. Bredon and the men had returned to headquarters. 'I'll follow when I've finished interrogating her,' Max said.

Despite near-starvation, she ate hardly anything, though she drank a cup of broth. Véronique, too, held back, and he realised that she had been estimating how long they could make the meat last.

As the chicken revived them, they asked him about himself, and he told them about San Felipe, about Zimmy and Manolo and Titi, about his school and the Matsons, and life in London. With amusement, he realised that they were interrogating *him*, and they watched him with fascinated eyes as he reintroduced them to a world they had almost forgotten. At half-past ten Véronique, her eyelids drooping, went to bed – or rather, to her pile of blankets on the floor of a room near the kitchen.

'I'd better go, too,' he said reluctantly.

'Can't you stay a little longer?' Anne-Louise said. 'It's been a long time since I had anyone like you to talk to.'

So he stayed, and even found, hidden in the cellar, one remaining bottle of wine. Having been laid down by her uncle, it was long past its best, but he sipped the red, vinegary liquid without tasting it, trying to imprint her face on his memory as they talked about everything except the war.

She told him about her life in Paris, her travels as the daughter of a French diplomat, her husband's poetry, their happiness with Véronique.

At one point, she asked him how old he was.

Without even thinking about it, he lied, not wanting her to know how many years separated them. 'I'm twenty-six.'

'You look younger. I am thirty-five.'

At last, he reluctantly brought her back to the present, knowing that Hammond would ask about her contact with the enemy.

She paused for so long that he thought she was going to refuse to tell him, then, looking down at her hands, she began to describe the day the Germans had arrived in the village.

'Someone told them about this big, empty house, and their senior officer came to see me. He was – polite. I explained that we had almost no furniture, nor food, but he said that he needed only a bed and he would supply us with rations. While he was here, Véronique and I had enough to eat.' She lifted her eyes and looked directly at him. 'I had to pay for it.'

It was a moment before he understood. He was shocked into brutality: 'You mean you slept with him?'

'Yes. Two months ago he was posted back to Germany. I have not heard from him since.'

With an effort, he said, 'Were you in love with him?'

'No! Karl was a big, blonde Prussian with no back to his head and hair growing across his shoulders. He clicked his heels every time he came into the room and he talked only of the war. But he was not a bad man.'

Loathing the German, he saw in his mind the bare, hairy back as he had made love to this woman whom he, Max, had already decided he would give almost anything to possess. It didn't matter that she was older than himself, that he had only known her for a few hours, nor even, he realised, that she had been the mistress of a Nazi.

'What happened after he left?'

'It has not been easy. Even people who had at least said good-morning pretend they don't see me. We have had to scavenge for potatoes, anything we could find. Then I became . . . unwell. A few nights ago, when Véronique was trying to steal some eggs, a farmer shot at her.'

Again, a wave of exhaustion overtook her, and she seemed to shrink into the chair.

He stood up. 'Anne-Louise, we're moving out tomorrow, but I'll be back before we leave. I'll bring you some supplies, and in the meantime . . .' He took a handful of francs from his pocket. 'I'm leaving this. I'll send you some more as soon as I can.' She hesitated. 'For Véronique,' he said.

They were facing each other. She raised a hand and touched his cheek. He kissed her gently, and left.

Major Hammond listened to his story in silence, then said, 'So the daughter's half-English?'

'Yes, sir.'

'All right. You can collect what supplies we can spare and take them to her in the morning. Only Raven, don't assume this is a precedent. We're not going to maintain every pretty girl you pick up on the way to Germany.'

'There won't be any others, sir.' And he added silently to himself: not ever. At the time, he believed it.

It was ten-fifteen when he and Bredon, who was driving the Major's Jeep, entered the village beyond which the Manoir lay. The square was ahead of them, and it was crowded with shouting, gesticulating people.

As they edged around the perimeter, Max had an impression that, despite the noise and some laughter, there was no gaiety in the atmosphere.

They pulled up. The people were packed in a tight mass, and were all looking in the same direction.

He stood up on the passenger seat, which gave him a view over their heads, and saw that they were gathered around an open space, in the centre of which a figure was tied to a chair with ropes. He could not tell whether it was a man or a woman, because the head had been shaved. Little globules of blood had formed where the skin had been nicked. Beside the chair, a man was dipping a brush into a can of black, viscous liquid. Max recognised the younger of the two who had reported the presence of Germans at the Manoir.

His eyes flicked around the audience and he saw Véronique, held by two women so she was facing the chair. Her head was thrown back and tears were pouring down her face. Then he knew that the shaven prisoner was Anne-Louise.

He vaulted out of the Jeep and pushed through the crowd, shouting, elbowing them to left and right.

He had almost reached the open space when his arms were gripped and he was surrounded by men. He fought, but they held fast. From behind, one of them slid an arm around his neck and squeezed, so that he started to choke. He heard a voice, speaking broken English. 'It is not your business, Tommy! We punish Nazi whore!'

He began to struggle again and one of the men raised a heavy walking-stick.

Before the blow could fall, he heard a burst of fire, and instantly, there was silence. His captors released him as they turned towards the Jeep, where Bredon was standing, holding a sub-machine gun.

He said, 'The next person who touches that woman or that officer, gets it.' Whether or not they understood English, his meaning was clear.

When Max reached Anne-Louise, Véronique was kneeling beside her in the dust, trying to undo the ropes. He cut through them. Sickened, he saw that during the short time he had been fighting his way towards her, a swastika had been daubed on her head and paint was dribbling down onto her forehead.

He tried to lift her, but she resisted. 'I will walk!' she hissed.

She moved steadily, looking straight ahead, and the crowd made a path for her. Véronique, still sobbing, followed.

She stumbled as they reached the Jeep, and he helped her in. There were a few catcalls, a woman laughed as they drove off, but when he looked back, the square was emptying.

Anne-Louise said nothing, even when, unable to bear the sight of her defaced scalp, he handed her his scarf. She made no attempt to put it on, so he did it for her, draping it over her forehead and winding it around her throat.

By the time they reached the Manoir, the strength had drained out of her and she made no protest when he lifted her and carried her inside.

'Heat up some soup,' he told Véronique. 'I suppose there's no brandy?'

She shook her head and disappeared towards the back of the house. Outside, Bredon was unloading the supplies.

Anne-Louise sat down in her chair and rested her head against the back. With the scarf hiding her scalp she looked, he thought, like a Botticelli Madonna.

He took both of her hands and, for the first time in years, felt tears in his eyes. 'I wanted to kill them all!' he whispered.

'I have been waiting for it to happen since I learnt what was going on in other parts of France. Now it's over, and there won't be any more trouble.'

'How can you know that?'

'I think they will turn their attention to others now. I am not the only woman in this village who slept with Germans.'

'How are you feeling?'

'Ugly! Unhappy because you have seen me like this. Otherwise, I am all right.'

'That bastard with the paint-brush . . . he was one of the two Resistance men who reported you to the C.O. last night.'

She looked thoughtful. 'He was never a member of the Resistance. I know him. He is a brother of the girl whom they say my uncle drove to suicide. Most of the people there were of the family. Her other brother, too . . .'

'A thickset chap? Looks like a thug?' She nodded. 'They both came to the camp.'

'Then I will tell you something. I don't think that what has just happened had anything to do with the Resistance and my contact with Karl. I think that was just an excuse. And first they reported me to your officer so that he would send men to make sure the Germans had all gone and the coast was clear.'

Véronique came in with a steaming mug, followed by Bredon.

'Mamma, we have food to last for ages! And they have brought money!'

Bredon said warningly, 'Max, time's getting on.'

'We can't leave them like this.'

'You must go . . .' Anne-Louise began.

At that moment, they heard movement outside. A man and a woman were standing at the French windows, making urgent signs.

'Who are they? D'you know them?' Max said sharply.

Véronique answered. 'They are Monsieur and Madame Varenne. They keep the Bar.'

'Shall I open the door?'

Anne-Louise shrugged. 'Why not? They cannot hurt us.'

Varenne was a middle-aged man with broad shoulders and a face that might have been carved out of rock. His wife was half his size, plump and red-faced. She was wearing a full-skirted, ankle- length dress, an apron and a head-scarf, and she was carrying a basket.

As soon as they were inside, Varenne started to speak, slowly and carefully, as though it was a speech he had prepared. He kept his eyes down and twisted his beret in his hands. When he stopped, his wife darted forward and put the basket on the floor, beside Anne-Louise, then she, too, spoke rapidly. Max's school-boy French was too poor for him to pick up more than a few words, but he recognised that there was no hostility in them.

When she stopped, they stood, awkwardly silent.

'What was that about?' he asked.

'They were apologising,' Anne-Louise said. 'I hardly know them, they have not been here long, but I think they have been working with the Resistance. M. Varenne says they had nothing to do with what happened.'

'Then why the hell didn't they stop it?'

'They left early this morning to see their daughter, who lives on a farm nearby. They have only just come back. Madame has brought us some eggs and vegetables.'

Varenne burst into speech again, this time too impassioned to have been rehearsed.

She translated: 'He is furious with the Picard brothers. He says what they did shames the village and that whatever happens in the rest of France, he will see that no other woman here is physically humiliated.'

Bredon touched Max's arm urgently.

Anne-Louise stood up. 'It is all over, Max. These people will look after us. Véronique and I will never forget what you have done.'

He wanted desperately to have a last moment alone with her, but the Varennes and Véronique were standing in a protective group around her and Bredon was tapping his foot impatiently. All he could do was raise her hand to his lips.

As he reached the French windows, he turned. 'I'm coming back, you know.'

4

The Allied advance moved inexorably towards Germany and, for Max, Christmas, 1944, passed almost unnoticed. In the first weeks of the New Year, news came that the Red Army had opened a major offensive in East Prussia, and in April the forces which had been driving eastwards linked up with the Russians in the Elbe. Soviet troops reached Berlin and, at the end of the first week in May, the Germans surrendered unconditionally.

But Max's war was not yet over. In June, he arrived in Berlin as a member of the Occupation forces.

The memory of Anne-Louise had remained with him. On three occasions he had sent her money, accompanied by letters, but had received no acknowledgement. The possibility of reunion in the near future still seemed remote.

He was quartered in a former German barracks in Spandau, on the outskirts of the city, part of a force whose days were filled with patrols, guard duty, parades and keeping control of the disparate elements which had taken over the shattered city. Appalled by what he saw, he had only pity for the defeated citizens who wandered among the ruins of their homes, dazed and hopeless.

'This is a dreadful place,' he wrote to Zimmy. 'It is totally grey. There isn't a flower or blade of grass to be seen, only piles of rubble. Three out of four houses have been gutted by our air-raids. Many of the people seem apathetic, as though they don't know how to put their lives back together. They have little money, and there isn't much food, but already a black-market has sprung up, and some of the troops are cashing in on it. You can buy anything from a woman to an oil-painting for not much more than a few cigarettes or a packet of soap. I'm told that before the war there were ten women to every nine men in Germany. Now the ratio is seven women to two men, so it's the women, on the whole, whom one sees trying to keep themselves and their children alive. They scratch among the ruins, looking for anything useful, from an undamaged can of food to an old scrap of blanket. Babies are dying like flies.

'There are refugees, too, from all over Europe. One job facing the Allies is to round them up and get them into camps where they can be sorted out and, hopefully, reunited with their families. They include civilians fleeing from the Russians, and soldiers from the Eastern Front. Some of these have lost fingers and toes from frostbite, others don't seem to know who they are. Their eyes remind me of Titi's.

'The Russian troops are a problem. The Germans are terrified of them. They bully, loot, rape, get fighting drunk and have no regard for hygiene. When we moved into our barracks, following a Russian division, we found them in a disgusting state, stinking with rotten garbage and excrement.

'But however awful Berlin is, life goes on. Already people are moving back into the ruins, clearing away the rubble and creating shelters in the cellars. The Tiergarten, which was a bombed wasteland of tree-stumps, is being cleared and I even saw an elderly couple digging a little vegetable patch.

'There are night-clubs, too. Some of them are operated by racketeers and are pretty vicious – out of bounds for our troops – but others are like London clubs, with dancing and cabarets.

'You can spend an evening at, say, the Femina, where every table has a telephone on which you can call up a pretty girl at another table . . . and, believe me, there isn't a girl in Berlin who doesn't want to latch onto one of us and share our "riches": cigarettes, soap, sardines, and so on. The Americans are doing particularly well with them.

'The Femina is cheerful, noisy, has the best cabaret, plenty to eat and drink (at a price) and is patronised by both Russians and Yanks. It's supposed to be out of bounds for us, but occasionally one breaks the rules and risks being picked up by the Military Police. I've been lucky so far.

'In the early hours, you walk out of a Club, warm, well-fed and well-wined, into the derelict streets, and throw down a cigarette butt. Figures come from nowhere – often they're children – and dive on it, then melt back into the darkness.

'Occasionally you look down at a tiny light below street-level and it's a candle in one of the inhabited cellars. Berlin is eerie after dark, and that's the time when I most miss San Felipe.

'I often think of you all. Haven't had any letters for a while, but I've written to Emilia Bartolomé and asked her to send mail on to me here, care of the Spanish Consulate.

'I've just heard that I'm due for some leave next month and am going to London, via France, where I have someone to see.'

When he had finished the letter, he sat for a few minutes, warmed by the reminder of Spain's sun, sea and colour. He was so far away that he was not aware Bredon had come in, until fingers clicked sharply in front of him.

'Dreaming of France again? Come back to earth, mate!' Bredon was the only person who suspected how he felt about Anne-Louise, though he refused to take it seriously. 'Want to risk the Femina tonight?'

Max nodded. 'Okay. I've heard they're going to lift the ban soon, anyway. But I wasn't dreaming of France. I was in Spain.' He tipped his chair onto its back legs and gazed into space. 'It's mid-summer, so hot that you can't walk on the sand in bare feet, and the water's like silk. You can swim out as far as you like, then turn on your back and see the little white buildings, and it's all clean and peaceful. There's no Femina there – Christ, there isn't even a restaurant, only the Bar Jiminez, where I practically grew up. In the evenings, you can sit in the plaza and Zimmy or one of the girls will bring out *tapas,* and people say hello to you and the wine's cheap and good, and the girls are small and dark – I'm sick of big blondes!'

'You going back when you're demobbed?'

'Of course.'

'What'll you do there? What work, I mean.'

'I don't know. I'll have to find something. I've got this bit of land, with a burned-out ruin on it, and a few pesetas in the bank, but even with my gratuity, I won't be able to spend the rest of my life lying on the beach, which is what I'd like to do.'

'I'll come and visit you sometime.'

'What are you going to do?'

'I'm going to be a Star of Stage and Screen!' He paused, and the irony left his voice. 'I've always enjoyed performing, preferably making people laugh. My Mam and Dad have been with ENSA since the beginning of the war. Maybe they'll know someone who'll give me a chance.'

Max thumped the chair back on its four feet. 'You'll make it. And there'll always be room for you in San Felipe when you want to get away from the responsibilities of fame.' An idea stirred in his mind, and he said thoughtfully, 'Maybe that's what I could do. I've got the land. I won't have enough money, but I could probably raise it . . .'

'What for?'

'A hotel, with a restaurant. Nobody's been able to travel freely for years. Spain's been almost cut off. First there was the Civil War, then this one. People must start to move around Europe again soon. They'll want holidays in the sun . . .' He stood up, and stretched. 'Ah, it's probably a crazy idea. How the hell could I run a hotel?'

But the seed had been sown and every now and then his mind returned to it: a hotel on his land, overlooking the sea, surrounded by landscaped gardens. Zimmy would help. Her establishment wasn't exactly a hotel, but she knew how to conduct a business. And maybe . . . just maybe, Anne-Louise would come out . . .

A couple of days later he went to the Spanish Consulate to see if there were any letters for him.

He was so accustomed to the sight of refugees that he hardly noticed the groups of thin, ragged men hanging about outside the building: Spanish nationals who, for one reason or another, had been caught up in the war and were desperate to be repatriated. Many of them, he knew, had no means of proving their identities and it could be months before they were returned to their own country. The problem was not confined to Spaniards. For some of the occupying troops it was an afternoon's entertainment to stroll along to one of the stations where trains bearing refugees from the East arrived, and watch them spilling into the city. There were Ukrainians, Poles, Czechs, Austrians, even Swedes, who had fought for the Germans and now had to be dealt with by the various agencies operating in Berlin. Many wore bandages, some were blind, others crippled.

There were several letters. He took them outside and flicked over the envelopes. One from Nancy, one from Emilia, two from Zimmy, one from Don Luis, several from former schoolfriends, and girls whose names he barely remembered. For the past nine months he had looked for one with a French stamp, but it had never come, and each time he had to remind himself that there was no way Anne-Louise would know where to address a letter. But he still looked.

It was a warm, sunny day, which made even the city's devastation seem less depressing. He perched on the remains of a stone wall and lit a cigarette, deciding to read Nancy's letter as an hors d' oeuvre, and save the rest until he returned to barracks.

As usual, it was short, written in her childish, back-sloping hand. Her mother and father were well, and so was she. It was nice that the war was over, and she hoped to be discharged from the ATS soon, but wasn't sure what she would do then. Daddy wanted her to take a course in shorthand and typing so she could be his secretary. He had made a lot of money during the past five years and was going to buy a house in one of the Nash terraces in Regent's Park. It had ten bedrooms. She hoped that Max would be back in London soon. She would stop now because she had no more news. She was his loving Nancy.

Her laboured letters always left him with a feeling of irritation. He stood up and dropped the last inch of his cigarette onto the road. A man scurried from behind him and fell on his knees, scrabbling for it. As he was stuffing it into a pocket of his ragged jacket, he looked up. It was Rafael Ansaldo.

For a moment, Max thought he must be wrong. This

unshaven beggar, with filthy, shaking hands, in torn clothes which had been made for a bigger man, could not possibly be Rafael. The bullet head, with its black stubble, seemed too heavy for his skinny body. But there was recognition in the hollowed eyes.

Disbelievingly, he said, 'Rafael?'

'Max? Max Raven?' It was as though he couldn't believe it, either. Then, with no further greeting, he said in Spanish: 'You've got to help me! I'm so hungry!'

'Jesus, of course I'll help you! Come on, we'll get you a meal. What the hell has happened to you?' They walked away from the Consulate. Rafael's head was lowered and he kept his eyes fixed on the ground.'When did you get to Berlin?'

He licked dry lips. 'Two days ago. I've been outside the Consulate ever since. I've lost my papers and I haven't any money. I told them who I am, who my father is, and they wouldn't believe me. I thought that if I stayed there, I might find someone who'd help.' His face twisted bitterly. 'It had to be you, didn't it?'

His hostility was unmistakable. Shocked, Max said, 'You're bloody lucky it's me! You might have had to hang around for weeks.' Then, looking at the pathetic figure shuffling beside him, in cracked, unlaced boots, he regretted his sharpness.

They reached a small cafe with a few wooden tables, marked with the rings of countless beer tankards. There was a pervasive smell of hops, stale cigarette smoke and drunken men. A few words were chalked on a blackboard outside: KARTOFFELSUPPE! BRATWURST! SAUERKRAUT!

A couple of workmen sat over their beer at the back, drinking in silence. Max's British uniform caught their eyes for a moment, then they looked away indifferently.

The potato soup was as thick as glue. Rafael plunged his spoon in and hardly took breath between swallows. A plate of sausage and sauerkraut, too, disappeared at lightning speed.

When he had finished, Max handed him a packet of cigarettes and said,'Want to tell me about it?'

'There isn't much to tell . . .' But when he started to talk, it was as though he could not stop. He spoke in Spanish, and the hoarse, monotonous voice went on and on . . .

When he joined the Blue Division on the Eastern Front, he had found himself in the company of terrified men already being driven back by the Soviet Army. He had fought through the Russian winter, inadequately clothed, in cold such as he had never imagined. The only thing that had saved him from frost-bite had been stealing newspaper that lined the boots of a wounded German, and putting it in his own. He had watched Spaniards who had scarcely known a temperature below 15 degrees celsius fall into sleep, a coma, then death from the cold. He had heard others screaming with pain and fear as they lay, wounded, in the snow, and there was no one to help them. In Spring, he had been terrified of falling and suffocating in mud that was several feet deep.

After a Soviet attack, he had been separated from his Division and found himself lost in Russia. For months, he had trudged over roads which, after rain, became almost impassable; through endless fields of maize and dense forests and kilometre after kilometre of yellow sunflowers taller than himself. He had to skirt a marsh the size of Andalusia, in which one careless step would have caused him to drown. He begged or stole food where he could. It was luxury to spend a night in a peasant's barn, despite the filth with which it was littered. His greatest fear was that a Russian would take him for a German, and kill him, so he had discarded his uniform and stolen civilian clothes from a farmer. He had lost count of the months he had wandered on his own.

Eventually, he had joined up with a group of retreating Finns. They had reached a railhead and proceeded in long, weary hops between stations, sometimes spending days waiting in the open for a train. Other starving refugees added to their number and at last, crammed into cattle-trucks, they had come to Berlin.

Max realised that whatever he had faced during the war was insignificant compared with the sufferings of this pampered son of a rich Spanish family. And it hadn't even been his war.

When Rafael lapsed into silence, he said, 'Have you been able to let your father know you're alive?'

'How could I?'

'I'll send a cable. In the meantime, we'll find you somewhere to stay.'

Half an hour later, he left Rafael in a first-floor hotel off the Alexanderplatz. It had been partially bombed, but there were still a few rooms intact. The manageress only agreed to allow him to stay when Max paid for a week in advance. A further liberal dispensation of money persuaded her to heat up enough water for him to take a bath.

Max sent off a brief cable to Don Luis: 'rafael alive berlin stop requires documents of identification before repatriation can be arranged.'

Two days later, a reply came: 'Arriving berlin soon as possible with documentation.'

'What's he coming for? I only want the papers.' Rafael said.

'For Christ's sake! He wants to help. He's your father!'

'He sent me there! if it hadn't been for him, I'd never have gone to Russia.' He paused. 'I won't forgive him. Ever.'

A week later, when his father arrived, some new clothes and regular meals had improved his appearance. His stubble of hair was longer, his face and body had gained a little flesh. In contrast with the creature who had scrabbled in the dust for a cigarette butt, he was a different being. But when Max saw Don Luis's stricken face, he realised how little resemblance he must bear to the boy who had left Spain.

By making use of powerful friends, Don Luis had obtained all the documentation needed to enable him to travel. Cables, including one from Franco's Cabinet Office, had wrought a remarkable change in the Consulate's attitude and every diplomatic assistance was given to secure seats on an aircraft to London, thence to Madrid.

The night before they were due to leave, Max called at the hotel. Don Luis was waiting for him in the dusty little reception room.

'I will never be able to thank you enough for what you have done for my son, Maxwell,' he said. 'I will not forget it.' There were tears in his eyes as he put out his hand.

'All I did was turn up in the right place at the right time.' Don Luis's hand was thin and dry, his grasp without strength.

He looked worn and old, but that was natural enough, Max thought, after months of worry.

'There is something else I wanted to say. You know that I have never wished to interfere in your life, but I would like to know if you have made any plans for your future.'

'Not really.' There was his dream of a hotel, but that could hardly be dignified into a plan. 'I haven't had much chance to think about it.'

'Will you come back to Spain?'

'Yes. It's my home.'

'Would you consider moving to Jerez, to live on my property and learn how to run a vineyard?'

He was too surprised to react for a moment, then he said, 'I'd never thought about anything like that. I know so little about wine . . .'

'You showed interest and intelligence during our visits. I thought perhaps you might try it out. If you were sufficiently enthusiastic, we could eventually consider a partnership.'

'That's very generous of you, sir. I'm pretty sure I'd like it very much, but I don't know how long it'll be before I'm discharged.'

'There's no hurry. Think about it, then let me know.' He smiled. 'I'll probably last for a year or so yet, and I imagine by then you'll be out of the Army.'

Assuming that he had made a joke, Max returned the smile.

That evening he said to Bredon, 'I think I'll take him up on it. It'll mean I'd be able to go straight into a job, and I did enjoy what I learnt about the wine-business when I was a kid.'

'You'd be crazy not to. And you send me a case or two every Christmas.'

The next morning, while Rafael was collecting his final papers from the Consulate, he told Don Luis that he would like to accept his offer. He would return to Spain immediately he was discharged, prepared to start work at once.

'Nothing could please me more!' Don Luis looked suddenly younger as he grasped his hand. 'And now you've decided, I can tell you something else, which I want you to keep to yourself for the moment. I propose to add a codicil to my will.'

'A codicil?'

'Which will specify that after my death, you will inherit the house and vineyards.' He raised a finger as Max began to stammer his thanks. 'You were deprived of so much. Your mother and father, family life. I wish you to have the land, Maxwell. In return, I will ask only one thing: that when I am gone, you will keep an eye on my wife, and on Victoria. Christina, of course, has her husband. If they need help, I would like to think that they can turn to you.'

'Of course! I'll do whatever I can for them. But there's Rafael . . . and, anyway, it's going to be a long time before you're not around.'

'Perhaps. My wife and children will, of course, inherit everything else in equal shares, except that my little Victoria is to have the Campo Negro. It's worth nothing, but it will be something of her own,' He looked speculatively at Max. 'She is growing into a very pretty girl. Who knows . . . perhaps in a few years . . . when you have settled back in Spain . . .'

Nervously, Max said, ' I haven't thought that far ahead, sir.'

'You're very young. Twenty, is it? And Victoria is still a child. There's plenty of time.' To Max's relief, he waved a hand dismissively. 'We will talk no more about it.'

Rafael appeared, and he lowered his voice: 'I ask you to say nothing about the will. I must, of course, tell my wife first, and then my attorney will draw up the codicil.' He looked across at his son.'There is no need for anyone else to know about it.'

An hour later, he and Rafael were on their way to England, and Max was warming himself with the thought that he was now the heir to a substantial property, even though it was likely to be many years before he came into the inheritance.

5

A month later, Max, on leave, drove into the quiet square of Montjoli. It was lunch-time, and there was no one about. An autumn silence hung over the village, but his imagination peopled it with the crowd which had filled it before. He saw the coarse, Breughel faces surrounding the chair, Véronique's tears, Anne-Louise's shaven head with the swastika daubed on it.

He reached the stone wall, then the iron gates of the Manoir de Montclair. They were no longer tied with rope, but swung open, creaking as a light breeze moved them. The ancient car, which he had hired at the station, bumped over rough ground to the house. The weeds were, if anything, taller and thicker than they had been, the bushes wilder. The house looked the same, except that even the shutters that had been open, were now closed. There was a general air of dereliction about the place that made him uneasy.

He tugged an iron bell-pull that hung to the right of the door. He heard no clang inside, so he beat on the panels with his fist. With a curious sense of *déjà vu,* he knew that no one would come. As he had the last time, he circled the house, and saw the same locked windows and doors. It looked as though it had been deserted for years.

He had an absurd urge to shout, as Bredon had: *Achtung . . . Achtung . . . Auskommen*!' Maybe,like 'Open Sesame!' they were the magic words.

Instead, he drove back to the village and parked outside the Varennes' bar. Inside, a woman was reading a newspaper which was spread out on the zinc. She glanced up as he said, '*Bonjour, Madame. Je cherche Monsieur Varenne.*'

'*Il est parti, Monsieur.*' She looked at him with interest. 'You speak English?'

'Yes. Could you tell me where I can find him?'

'I am his daughter. Can I help you?' Her English was heavily accented, but fluent.

'I'm looking for Madame Meredith, who lived at the Manoir de Montclair. I thought M. Varenne would know where she is.'

She raised her eyebrows. 'But she went away many months ago, with her daughter.'

He stared at her. For some reason, during all his fantasies about meeting Anne-Louise again, it had not occurred to him that she would not be there.

'Where did she go?'

'I do not know. Maybe to Paris. She live there before. Perhaps she want her baby to be born there.'

'Her . . . baby?'

Obviously pleased to pass on gossip, she settled her elbows comfortably on the bar and said, 'You did not know, Monsieur? Madame Meredit' was the mistress of a German officer, who made her pregnant. My father told me that the people here did not like her. Because of what she had done, they cut off all her hair. A few weeks after that, she left.'

Too numbed to question her further, he turned towards the door. As he reached it, he heard her call, 'Wait, please!' She took a packet from under the bar and peered at it. 'Is it that you are M. Raven?'

'Yes, I am.'

'My father has looked after these for a long time. The envelopes have your name on the back. He said someone would perhaps come for them.'

For a second, he thought that she must have left him a message. The disappointment was almost too much to bear when he looked down at his own letters.

He became aware that the woman was speaking. 'Are you ill, Monsieur? Would you take a cognac?'

He shook his head, then tore open each of the envelopes, extracted the francs he had enclosed, and pushed them over the bar. 'Give these to M. Varenne, please. They're with my thanks for – for what he did for Madame Meredith.'

It had taken him more than twenty-four hours, by train, bus and car, to reach Montjoli. It was another twenty-four before he arrived in London, with only a few days of his leave remaining. He didn't care. All he wanted was to get back to work in Berlin, and forget Anne-Louise.

He realised how naive he had been not to recognise the indications of her pregnancy: her loose grey smock, her weakness and lack of appetite; Véronique's concern. Then came anger: he had admired her honesty in admitting that she had slept with the German, and the courage with which she had faced the villagers. But she had only been half-honest, and her insistence that she would not be attacked again must have been because she had already decided that she was going to leave Montjoli, using the money he had given her.

His emotions swayed from one extreme to another. Sometimes he would cringe with embarrassment at the fool he had made of himself, and be thankful that he had not advertised his feelings to anyone except Dan Bredon. Then he would see in his mind the ethereal face, the grey eyes with their curtain of dark lashes, the rare smile that transformed her into a young girl, and wonder whether there was any way he could trace her. This thought, in turn, was replaced by bitterness at the knowledge that she would now have borne the German's child.

Unexpectedly, it was Nancy Matson who helped him to regain his equilibrium.

He found her at the pretentious house in Regent's Park to which her parents had moved, preparing to join them in Scotland – war or no war, Sir Cedric had never missed the grouse-season.

She at once despatched a telegram, saying that she had been delayed and would not be in Inverness until the following week.

They had the house to themselves, and although he found her no more stimulating a conversationalist than before, he was always to remember the cathartic passion with which they made love, time after time, to the point of exhaustion.

By the end of the week, he had almost convinced himself that he was lucky Anne-Louise had left Montjoli and that he'd escaped a promiscuous and dishonest woman.

One of his few excursions was a visit to Emilia Bartolomé, which produced a shock.

Having cross-questioned him about what she insisted on calling his 'rescue' of Rafael, she said sadly, 'I only pray that he does not let Luis down again during the little time he has left.'

He frowned. 'What do you mean?'

'He didn't tell you? Luis was never one to demand sympathy. He has the cancer. He was given less than six months to live. His time is almost up.' She added, acidly, 'I hear that Maria has already gone into mourning and has hysterics daily.'

It was in his mind to mention the generosity of his promised legacy, but he had been asked to keep it to himself, so he remained silent. He was distressed at the news, but at the same time he could not resist a secret moment of pleasure at the thought that he would be a property-owner sooner than he had expected.

6

'I'm having no bastards in this family. You follow me?'

Max was sitting, frozen, in Sir Cedric's study while the old man paced the room, his voice steadily rising as he lashed out at his morals, his ingratitude, his lack of principle or conscience, the infamous advantage he had taken of an innocent girl.

The attack had started the moment he entered the room, a cheery greeting on his lips. Sir Cedric had simply pointed to a chair opposite his desk and snarled: 'Sit!'

Carried away by the flow of his own invective, it was some time before he revealed its reason: Nancy was pregnant; preparations for the wedding were already under way; Max was to be the bridegroom. There would be no arguments.

He tried several times to interrupt, but for once, even Captain McPhee's advice did not help, because Sir Cedric gave him no chance to speak. Gradually, as the enormity of what was happening sank in, he shrank back in the chair and a kind of dull hopelessness overtook him.

Two days ago, he had bought Dan Bredon a drink to celebrate his summons to London, which had come out of the blue.

'You lucky sod! I bet it's your demob,' Bredon had said. 'You must know the right people.'

'I wasn't expecting it so soon.'

'Don't query it. Take the money and run.'

'I will. All the way to Spain, as fast as I can.'

He remembered his own words as Sir Cedric's thick Yorkshire vowels battered him: 'I pulled strings to get you out of the Army, lad, and I'm taking you over now. I'm not having my daughter tied to a jobless, penniless layabout. You'll come into my property business, and you'll bloody work your fingers to the bone, and you'll keep Nancy – and my grandchild – in the way they ought to live. Understand?'

He paused for breath, and Max had his chance, 'If the baby's mine, of course I'll marry Nancy. But I've got a job waiting for me back in Spain.'

'*If* the baby's yours? What are you implying? My girl's no whore! It's yours, all right, she's admitted it. And if you think my grandchild's going to be brought up by foreigners, you've got another think coming. You'll do as I say!'

Max was nearly twenty-one years old. He had fought a war and taken on responsibilities many an older man would never meet. N.C.O.s twice his age called him 'Sir'. But facing his future father-in-law, he could only nod as his life was rearranged.

'You can go now,' Sir Cedric snapped. 'Nancy's waiting for you.'

He found her in the drawing-room. She was sitting on the sofa, and her pallor reminded him painfully of Anne-Louise, who had presumably been pale for the same reason.

They looked at each other in silence.

'Oh, Christ . . .' he said. 'I'm sorry, Nancy! But can't we do something about it? I mean, there are ways, aren't there?'

'An abortion? No! I *want* the baby, Max. Anyway, Daddy would kill me.'

She went to him and put her head against his shirt. 'Daddy's angry now. He'll come round. He only wants me to be happy.'

'What Daddy wants, Daddy gets,' he said bleakly.

During the next two weeks he sometimes woke in the early hours of the morning with a sense of claustrophobia, feeling that he was being smothered by Matsons: by Sir Cedric, loud-voiced and domineering; by Lady Matson, who was preoccupied by what she would wear to the wedding and refused to acknowledge anything abnormal in the situation; by Nancy, silent and morning-sick; by his unborn, unwanted child.

The days passed all too quickly. Each morning, he reported

for work at Matsons' headquarters. Sir Cedric had bought up properties in Central London throughout the war years, many at giveaway prices asked by owners fleeing from the bombs. Now he was planning to convert them into flats.

'With all them that ran away wanting to come back, and discharged Servicemen, a good flat'll fetch the earth,' he said. 'When we've done renovating, I reckon one floor will bring in more than a whole house cost.'

Max's job involved chivvying Government departments and councils for planning permission; getting estimates for building work; applying for war reparations on houses that were being derequisitioned.

He hated every minute of it.

Living with the Matsons on a permanent basis was very different from carefree school holidays. Each evening Sir Cedric put him through a rigorous cross-examination on his day's work, usually finding some fault. Lady Matson talked only about clothes and her latest diet. She had improved her figure, but her temper had grown shorter with every pound she shed.

Nancy's period of independence as a member of the Auxiliary Territorial Service had had little effect on her. Since Henry's death, Sir Cedric had focussed all his love (and his need to dominate those whom he loved) on her, and she seemed content that the status quo should be maintained.

In Max's attitude to her, guilt, resentment and pity warred. The one certain thing was that he did not love her, and the prospect of spending the rest of his life under the Matson umbrella was a nightmare. At first, he told himself that after they were married he would be able to persuade her to defy her father and they could escape.

The hope was dashed one day when he said tentatively, 'How would you feel about living in Spain?'

She looked frightened. 'Oh, I couldn't! I don't know the language. We'd have no friends. What would happen to our baby in a place like that?'

'I have friends. And Don Luis Ansaldo, who was my guardian, wants me to take over his vineyards. We could live pretty well.'

She shook her head with unusual determination. 'Daddy would never allow it. I'm all he's got, now Henry's gone. And he'll be able to do so much for the baby, Max.'

The night before their registry office wedding, he wrote to Don Luis and Zimmy. He had started several letters already, but each time he had torn them up, wanting to delay as long as possible what he was convinced would be a final break with the life he had loved. Don Luis would certainly cancel the promised codicil to his will . . . why should he leave property to someone whose future home, perforce, was in another country?

Years later, Zimmy was to say to him: 'Didn't it ever occur to you to leave them? You had a little money. You could have got away before the wedding.'

'Oh, it occurred to me,' he said bitterly. 'But how could I? I'd made Nancy pregnant. I couldn't desert her at that stage. Christ, I couldn't have lived with myself!'

The wedding ceremony was brief and brisk, attended only by the Matsons and two members of Sir Cedric's staff, who acted as witnesses.

Their honeymoon was three days in a hotel in Brighton. Nancy was not feeling well, so they didn't make love. He found conversation with her increasingly unsatisfactory, because, watching him adoringly, she simply agreed with everything he said. He was irritated by her insistence on clinging heavily to his arm whenever they went out.

The one pleasurable moment was his discovery of three of his father's paintings in a small art-gallery in the Lanes.

They were hanging on a side wall and he recognised them immediately. One was of an umbrella-mender in the Plaza San Juan, another of a basket-weaver sitting on a chair outside her house as she worked – he knew the precise house. The third showed a fisherman mending his nets on the beach, with the village in the background. A flood of nostalgia swept over him as he pushed open the door of the gallery.

The pictures were for sale, the gallery's owner told him. He had acquired them from a deceased estate and would accept twenty pounds each. The artist was a Scot who had died tragically young.

When they were on their way back to the hotel, Nancy said,

'I don't, understand why you bought them, Max. I think they're a bit . . . chocolate-boxy, don't you?'

'No, I don't,' he said shortly. 'My father painted them.'

'Oh, I'm sorry! I mean, I didn't know your father was an artist.'

She had never asked him about his background. In fact, he realised, she always changed the subject when he mentioned Spain, as though she was afraid that even talking about it might endanger her security.

Sir Cedric was equally dismissive when he saw the pictures. He had become a collector of paintings as well as properties, and fancied himself something of an expert on early Victorian landscapes.

Ignoring Andrew's fine draughtsmanship and delicate use of colour, he said. 'What'd you pay for them?'

'Twenty pounds each.'

'You were done.'

When he reached the room he and Nancy shared, a letter from Zimmy was awaiting him, which must have crossed his own announcement of his marriage.

'I have sad news for you, my dear. Don Luis died last week. I believe it was for him a happy release, not only because he is now free of pain, but it was already clear that Rafael's war experiences have not changed him. At first – so weak and thin! – he seemed subdued, but after a few weeks he became as feckless and arrogant as ever, showing no interest whatever in helping to run the family properties. Also, he would scarcely speak to his father. It is said that he blamed him for all he suffered in Russia.

'I understand that Don Luis's fortune is divided equally between the three children and Doña Maria, with a special legacy of the Campo Negro to Victoria.

'Sometimes, when Don Luis felt well enough, he would come and sit with me on the plaza and we would talk about you. He was very fond of you, Max. He mentioned that he had made plans for you, and that your future was secure. Perhaps he talked about this to you . . .'

The letter ended with the words, 'Surely, now, it cannot be too long before you are back with us again!'

When he had finished reading he sat, frowning down at it. He felt a genuine sadness at Don Luis's death, but it was curious that Zimmy should seem to know the main contents of the will, but nothing about the codicil. Surely, official news of his inheritance must soon be forthcoming.

Excitement rose in him. Somehow, he would have to find a way to persuade Nancy to come to Spain, even if they had to wait until the baby was born. At least, she couldn't refuse to spend a holiday there. Remembering the large white villa near Jerez, with its shaded terraces, set among vines, he told himself that when she saw it, she would soon change her mind about the rigours of living in a foreign country.

He felt that a door was opening into a future that was no longer bleak.

Part 5

The Present

Marian was awaiting Paul in Max's office. He greeted her, yawned and passed a hand over his hair. She raised her eyebrows, but made no comment. It was nearly ten o'clock on the morning of his first full working day.

She looked fresh and efficient in an olive-green cotton dress, with a wide belt and strappy tan sandals. A pair of glasses hung around her neck on a gold chain.

He sat down behind the desk and picked up a clip-board that lay in front of him.

'Staff list. Guest list. Messages that came for you yesterday and this morning. Your appointments for today,' she said briskly.

His eyes skimmed over the top sheet: '10.15-10.30: Chef and restaurant manager. 10.30-10.45: House-keeper. 10.45-11.45: Attorney (Sr Alvarez) and Accountant (Mr Petrie) . . .' As far as he could see, no minute of the day was unaccounted for.

With restraint, he said, 'Is this a normal time-table for Max?'

'Rather lighter than usual. I've allowed extra time for you to get to know the staff. And Max always fits in one or two quick patrols through the Club, to show interest in the guests. There are sure to be droppers-in, too, with complaints or queries, or people with nothing better to do who just want to chat. I try and filter most of them out, but there are a few who won't be filtered.'

He glanced at his watch. 'Fifteen minutes before the first appointment. Are you allowing me time for a cup of coffee? I skipped breakfast.' As though by magic, a waiter appeared at the door with a silver tray containing a pot and two cups. Paul blinked. 'I must have rubbed the lantern without realising it. Okay, what's next?'

She handed him his coffee.

'The Hon. Caroline Jarvis hopes you will meet her in the bar this evening. She seemed to know you.'

'Never heard . . . oh, yes, I have. She burst into Max's room at the hospital yesterday.'

Marian nodded. 'She's one of his chasers.'

'His what?'

'That's what he calls them. Single girls, widows, divorcees, wives who are here without their husbands . . . there are always a few pursuing him like hounds after a fox. The Hon. Caroline's a recent addition to the pack.'

'I rather think she's given up the chase since she saw what the stroke has done to him.'

'She's very young. You don't need to reply to her. It wasn't a formal invitation.'

'Any more?'

'I believe you might be pleased with this one. Dan Bredon would like to see you, at your convenience, any time of the day or night.'

'Dan's here? That's the best news I've heard since I arrived.'

'We all love him. He comes for a few months whenever he's finished a film. He was looking for you yesterday.'

'But when am I going to have a chance to see him?'

'If you'll read your programme more carefully,' she said severely, 'You'll see that I've arranged for you to join him for dinner at nine o'clock this evening.'

'That's fine.' He yawned again.

'Late night?' she said. 'I didn't see you come back.'

'I spent the afternoon with Zimmy, then went straight to the house. I'm going to stay there rather than at the Club. And if you think my late night was spent carousing, think again. I was reading Max's letters, written from school and while he was in the Army.'

'Interesting?' All trace of formality had disappeared from her manner.

'Very. Zimmy gave me a box full of them. She said that they might help me to understand him.'

'Did they?'

He nodded. 'I haven't read them all yet. But I'm beginning to think she was right. I never have really known him.'

There was a tap at the French windows. Titi was standing outside. He waved, then grasped the handle-bars of his imaginary motor-cycle and made a circuit of Max's private terrace, accompanying himself with the appropriate noises.

Paul laughed and, forgetting Marian, joined him on a second circuit, leaning into the corners, pulling up with a squeal of brakes. Delighted, Titi patted his arm, then trotted off to the service quarters.

He realised that Marian had been watching them and said, defensively: 'Well, he enjoys it.'

'Don't apologise! Your father does the same. It's a kind of tradition with him and Titi.'

'Does he often come to the Club?'

'Every few days. He delivers parcels from the village. Max insists that he's given a good meal each time. It isn't that the people in the village neglect him – far from it. But he hands out most of the food he's given to children. Max has made him a place in a store-room off the kitchens. He has his own table and chair there.' She looked thoughtful. 'I've often wondered about his relationship with the people in the village. It's almost as though he's on their consciences. They can't seem to give him enough, from cast-off clothing to hot meals.'

Having grown up in San Felipe, it had never occurred to Paul that there was anything unusual in such charity. 'His father was killed in the Civil War. I expect it's just become a habit to look after him.'

'Everyone loves him. It's so sad . . .' She smiled. 'I'm being sentimental. Shall we get back to work?'

As the day progressed, he realised that the smooth flow of Marian's schedule, with each appointment tucked neatly into its allotted space, bore little relation to the reality.

By mid-day, his head was swimming with confused details. He'd discussed menus, the state of the cellars, the dismissal of a trainee chef who had been caught licking cream off his finger, the inefficiency of a local laundry, the need to replenish linen supplies. At first, he entered into discussions, but he soon realised that each member of the executive staff was,as Max had said, perfectly capable of dealing with normal problems, and he was only required to accept their suggestions. He had also read and signed agreements which gave him the right to draw cheques on both the Club account and Max's personal bank account.

Between appointments, he answered queries about Max's health, dictated a letter to his partner in London, detailing work outstanding on their current projects, and okayed the purchase of a list of plants produced by the head gardener.

As Max's attorney, Ramon Alvarez, left, Manolo marched in.

Without a greeting, he said: 'I'm going ahead with arrangements to buy and clear the Campo Negro, according to your father's instructions. I understand you'll be signing cheques for the next couple of weeks. I need a deposit for Victoria Ansaldo to confirm our offer.'

'I told you yesterday, Manolo, I'm confirming nothing until I've talked with Max.'

'She's getting impatient. She needs the money.'

'She's owned that land as long as I can remember. Max might think it's a good site for a supermarket. Nobody else has ever wanted it, as far as I know. She can wait.'

'I warned you not to interfere! This will cause trouble.'

Paul stood up. Several inches taller than Manolo, he looked down at him and said, 'And I'm warning *you*. After what I heard from Zimmy about the feeling in the village, I'm going to do my damnedest to talk Max out of developing the Campo Negro.'

'What makes you think you can come here and wreck everything we've worked for? I'm going to the hospital to see Max!'

'He doesn't want to . . .'

But Manolo had gone. Paul knew he had abrogated his rights to Raven Enterprises years ago, so there was some justification for Manolo's anger. But equally, what gave him – and Max – the right to impose on the village a development which apparently nobody wanted?

He went into Marian's office, which was between his own and the reception-hall.

'I'm sorry about that,' she said. 'He came through like a hurricane. I couldn't stop him. More trouble?'

'He wants me to write a cheque for Victoria for the Campo Negro. Just how far have the negotiations gone?'

'She offered to sell it some weeks ago, but she keeps adjusting the price – upwards. Max brought in architects and they worked out this supermarket and camping-site scheme. He's very enthusiastic about it.' She paused. 'Not least, I think, because it will infuriate Rafael Ansaldo. He knows nothing about it, incidentally. Victoria made that a condition of the sale, though I've a feeling she won't be able to keep it from him for much longer. Everyone in the village seems to know about it. It's only because Rafael keeps himself apart that he hasn't heard already.'

'Loretta and Zimmy said there's a lot of opposition.'

'Yes. Especially among the older people. It's not my place to say so, but I don't like the idea of that land being developed, with such feeling against it.'

'I wish I knew what it is about the Campo Negro that means so much to them. I could use it as an argument.'

'You're going to try to persuade Max to give it up?'

'I don't suppose there's any chance, but I'll have a go. Who else have I got to see this morning?'

She glanced at her appointment-book. 'Only me. I was reserving the next hour or so to introduce you to our filing system.'

'If that can wait, I'd like to go to the hospital.'

'Of course. We can meet when you get back.'

'Why don't we lunch together? It would be a good opportunity for you to fill me in on anything else I should know.'

'Max has his own table in each of the restaurants. Do you want to eat Spanish, French or American?'

He threw up his hands. 'Decisions! Decisions! You choose. At home, my only problem would be whether I have a ham sandwich with or without mustard.'

Manolo was leaving the hospital as he arrived, and his expression was angry. Without a word, he climbed into his car and drove off.

The nurse at the reception desk was looking distraught. Messengers were coming and going, and the entrance hall was filled with baskets of flowers and fruit, boxes of chocolates, and champagne bottles bedecked with coloured ribbons.

'All for Senor Raven!' she said despairingly. 'And he refuses to have them in his room. We have filled the wards with flowers. We have given the children enough chocolates to make them sick. And so many visitors come, and are angry when we turn them away. That man . . . did you see him as you came in? . . . he was quite violent, senor!'

'But he didn't see my father?'

'Sister Magdalena told him she would call the police if he didn't leave. Doctor Sanchez said Senor Max was not well enough for visitors, and she is standing guard outside his room.'

'How is he?'

'He is making progress, but he is listless. Stroke victims often become apathetic. It is something we must help him to fight.'

When Paul saw Max, he understood her concern. Where yesterday he had been able to summon up the energy to write messages and order the removal of flowers from his room, today he was too languid even to acknowledge Paul's arrival. He sat in a chair beside the bed and started to report on his morning's work, hoping to jog him into a response, but Max simply closed his eyes. After ten minutes, Paul realised that it was not possible to bring up the problem of the Campo Negro. With a cheerfulness he did not feel, he passed on get-well messages, made a joke of the little nurse's despair at the rising tide of gifts, talked about his visit to Zimmy the previous day.

It was not until he rose to leave that Max spoke. More clearly than he had been able to manage the previous day, he said: 'Loretta?'

'She's fine,' Paul said heartily. 'You said you didn't want to see her, and she understood. She asks after you all the time and she sent her love.' Max nodded, and his eyes closed again.

As he walked back along the passage, Paul paused at Elena's door, which was shut. For a moment, he was tempted to go in, but what was the point? It would be like reopening a wound.

Even if her father was not there, why would she want to see him? Max was the one to whom she had turned as soon as her husband had died.

Marian rejected his suggestion that they should have a quiet lunch in the suite.

'You should be seen. The guests have been asking for you – this Club depends so much on the owner's personality. One of them said that when Max isn't here, it's as though the lights have been turned out.' The businesslike voice softened. 'He has that extraordinary ability to make everyone feel like the most important person in his world.'

'I know. I remember when I was a kid, I used to watch him paying attention to people I thought thoroughly boring, and wonder how he could keep it up. I've never known anyone else with the same ability to hide his real feelings. He'd have made a bloody good actor.'

'Well, right now, you're his understudy. We'll have a drink first. Ready?'

He followed her onto the swimming-pool terrace, with its tables under fringed umbrellas, each one a different colour. He was aware of heads turning towards him, and heard whispers: 'Max Raven's son . . .' '. . . Paul, I think . . .' 'Doesn't look like his father . . .' '. . . Wonder if he's married?' And one clear female voice, 'He's gorgeous!'

Max's table was at one end of the pool and they were no sooner seated, with Margaritas in front of them, when a small procession began to move towards them.

During the next half-hour he was introduced to Princess this, and Countess that, and Lord and Lady something else, and the Marquis of . . . and Baron von . . . and even a few plain misters and their wives, some of whom he recognised from films or television. They came in all shapes and sizes, but his general impression was of sleek, good-looking people whom money had burnished to a high gloss. He began to long for just one plain, homely face. But he plastered a smile on his lips and adopted Max's trick of looking directly into their eyes as he shook their hands.

He was relieved when Marian decided it was time for

lunch, and shepherded him into the French restaurant, where the table-cloths and napkins were pink, the silver and glasses gleamed and bottles of red and white wine stood on every table. But once again guests came up one after another to be introduced, until their faces blurred into a kaleidoscopic mass.

It was almost a relief, as he was finishing his rapidly-cooling *Cailles aux Raisins en Timbale*, to see someone he recognised.

He stood up. 'Miss Jarvis.'

'I hoped I might meet you,' she said. 'Did you get my message?'

She was wearing a pink silk button-through skirt, which was mostly unbuttoned, revealing long slim legs encased in brief shorts. Her matching shirt was knotted at the front, above an expanse of bare midriff. Her clear skin was flushed from the sun.

'Yes. It was kind of you, but . . .'

'Why don't we have a drink, to show you've forgiven me for yesterday?'

She was younger and more appealing than most of the other women he had been meeting, and the reminder of Elena at the hospital had brought back some of his previous unhappiness. So why not? If he were to spend the rest of his time in San Felipe mooning after a lost love, life would be intolerable.

'Fine,' he said. 'I have a dinner date at nine, so we'll make it seven-thirty. Okay?'

When he arrived at the bar that evening, Victoria Ansaldo was perched on a stool next to a tall man whose arm was around her shoulders. Caro Jarvis was sitting a few yards away from them. She beckoned, but Victoria saw him at the same time, and slid to the floor, wavering slightly as she sought her balance.

'Paul, my dear! You must come and have a drink with Paco and me.' She swayed towards him and kissed him.

'I'm meeting someone, Victoria . . .' He gestured towards the girl.

'That child? But she must join us, too. We'll find a table.

Paco, darling, you will order drinks for four.'

Caro looked sullen as she was swept towards the table, and Paul made an apologetic face.

When Victoria's companion arrived back with the drinks, she said, 'Paco, this is Max's son, whom I have known since he was a baby. Paul, this is Paco Orlando – but you must have recognised him! And this is . . .' She waved a vague hand towards Caro and didn't bother to finish the sentence.

The man shook hands. Orlando was rangy, olive-skinned, with thick brown hair and deep lines incised from his nose to the corners of a wide, thin mouth.

'I saw you play at Queen's . . . what? Eight years ago?' Paul said. 'In the quarter-finals, wasn't it?'

'Maybe,' Orlando said indifferently. He lounged in his deeply-cushioned cane chair, his fingers playing with Victoria's hair.

Paul vividly remembered the match. Orlando had been the worst-tempered player of his decade, loathed by umpires, feared by his opponents. Fans flocked to watch him, as much for the anticipation of his explosions on court as for his tennis. After the match Paul had seen, he had thrown his racquet at one of the linesmen, knocking him to the ground. There had been a media scandal, he had been fined and temporarily banned from competitive tennis. Soon after that, he had retired, and little had been heard of him since.

There was a brief silence. Caroline was clearly annoyed at having an anticipated *téte á téte* subverted. Orlando looked bored, and Victoria was watching him, Paul thought, with the longing of a child outside a toy-shop.

'You staying here long?' he asked.

Victoria came to life. 'But darling, don't you know? Paco's been the Club professional for the last five years.'

'I didn't know. Sorry. I haven't had time to catch up with everyone yet.'

'Are *you* staying long?' Orlando said.

'Depends on my father's health. I'll be here until he can take over again.'

He saw Victoria and Orlando glance at each other. 'How is dear Max today?' she said.

'Making slow progress, according to the hospital.'

'Who'll be looking after the – the business side of the Club in the meantime?'

'Business side?'

'Salaries, *hombre,*' Orlando drawled. 'Some of us work for our living. We need to be paid.'

'Everything will continue as if Max were here.' Paul felt a stab of irritation. Orlando's eyes shifted to a group of women on the other side of the room.

'Paul, my love, I would like to have a little private talk with you,' Victoria said abruptly.

'Of course. Some time tomorrow?'

'Now.'

'Can't it wait? This isn't the most convenient time.'

'It will take only ten minutes. Paco will wait here for us, won't you, darling?'

He turned to Caroline, whom Victoria had ignored. 'Do you mind? I'll be back as soon as I can.'

Tight-lipped, she said, 'Don't hurry. Some friends of mine have just come in. If you'll excuse me . . .'

Victoria linked her arm in his and drew him away. 'We'll go to Max's suite. Never mind that little girl, she'll be back.'

When they reached the sitting-room, she made purposefully for the bar, poured them each a drink, then sank into a chair.

'I want to talk to you about our project, Max's and mine,' she said. 'You have heard of the Campo Negro development?'

'Yes, but I'm afraid it'll have to wait until Max is better. I can't take the responsibility of going ahead without him. Anyhow, I have to tell you I think it's a pretty bad idea, given the local feeling.' After her rudeness to Caroline Jarvis, he made no attempt to hide his irritation.

'What you think is of no importance. Max has offered to buy my land. I have decided the price and I need the money within a week. Manolo told me you would make trouble. I can see he was right.'

She drained her glass and he watched her as she went to the bar again. He remembered her as a reasonably attractive woman, though she had always been too thin, her constant pursuit of amusement too frenetic. Now there was desperation in the expression on her gaunt face.

'I'm sorry, Victoria,' he said. 'But it really isn't up to me.'

'Manolo says you're going to try to talk Max out of it.'

'The Campo Nergo is the last piece of unspoiled land in the village. Why do you want to sell it?'

'I told you. I need the money.' She downed her drink in one long swallow, then said, more quietly, 'That money's going to buy my future, Paul. Max understands.'

'What do you mean?'

A nervous tic was causing her left eye to blink constantly and the fingers of one hand were clenching and unclenching. 'All my life, I've had to live in that house with my mother and Rafael. His wife died after a couple of years – anyhow, she was only a shadow. For a while, Christina moved back with her two dull daughters. Elena escaped when she was eighteen. Our servants are women. We always seem to have been a household of widows and old maids, apart from Rafael, who likes to pretend he's the sultan in a harem. I can't stand it any longer!'

'Surely you could have left years ago?'

'How? The only money I have is what Rafael gives me. My father was supposed to have left me part of his property – he told me he would – but somehow my mother and Rafael got control of everything except the Campo Negro. It wasn't worth anything, so they didn't want it. It's all I've got, and I'm going to sell it to Max so I can get away before it's too late.'

'You won't mind seeing a supermarket and a camp site just beyond the wall of your own house?'

'Why should I? I won't be here.'She leant forward. 'Paco and I have a chance to buy a tennis ranch further along the coast.'

'What will Rafael say?'

'You can guess. He mustn't know until it's too late for him to stop me. That's why I need the money *now.*'

'And you'll hand it straight over to Orlando?'

'We're going to be married. Call this my dowry if you like. But nothing's going to stop me. It might be the only chance I'll have to get away.'

He watched her unhappily. He was sorry for her, but his determination remained unshaken.

'I promise I'll discuss this with Max as soon as possible,' he said. 'In the meantime, I'm sure Orlando can postpone confirmation of the ranch deal.'

She rose and moved unsteadily across the room. When she reached the door, she turned. 'I always thought we were friends, Paul. If you won't help me, I'll have to find someone who will . . .'

'I felt such a heel!' he said. 'Christ, she's a pathetic creature. She thinks Orlando's going to help her to escape from Rafael, but Lord knows what she'd be getting herself into. I wonder if he'll really marry her? She implied herself that if she doesn't get the money, it could all fall apart.'

He and Dan Bredon were sitting in Bredon's villa, drinking coffee and brandies. Dan had ordered dinner to be served there, and Paul had been able to relax away from the public eye for the first time that day.

He had always loved Dan, and although they had not met for some time, their easy, affectionate relationship remained unchanged. Neither time nor fame had altered Bredon: his hair was thinner and greyer, but the round face was as mobile as ever. Paul had seen him occasionally on the screen, starring in the comedies which had made his name, and during the past couple of hours he had been entertained by his Hollywood stories. After the meal they had moved onto the little terrace overlooking the villa's private pool and, in the warm darkness, Bredon became listener rather than performer. Almost before he was aware of it, Paul was telling him about Victoria. He did not remember until he was well into the account that her plan to marry Orlando was supposed to be a secret.

'I wouldn't pass on anything you tell me,' Bredon said. 'But you needn't worry about breaking a confidence. The entire Club knows about their affair. Everytime she gets drunk – and that's most evenings – she tells anyone who'll listen. You have good reason to wonder what could happen to her . . . he's a right bastard. He's a heavy drinker, and there are remours that he accepts payment from rich ladies for his off-court services. Did she tell you that Max has threatened to fire him a couple of times?'

'No!'

'He's only kept him on because he's sorry for Victoria. But even Max's charity is likely to be withdrawn if there's any more trouble.'

'I've never thought of Max as particularly charitable,' Paul remarked.

'Then you don't know him very well.'

'Oh, Christ, you too! Anyhow, Victoria said he's the only person who understands why she has to sell the Campo Negro. You've been coming here for years, do you know why the village is so set against its development?'

Dan shook his head. 'They're a funny lot, the San Felipans. As a tourist, you think at first that they're jolly and friendly and out-going. But as you get to know them, you start to see the dark side: they're superstitious, secretive and clannish. The Campo Negro's bound up with all that. Even Max doesn't know why.'

He reached for a half-smoked cigar that was lying on the ash-tray and re-lit it, puffing until it glowed red against the shadows. 'I'll tell you something else: there's an underlying violence here, that seems to be increasing. Last year two tourists were beaten up by local lads. More recently, a couple of Spanish maids from the Club were walking home after dark. They were raped by a group of men – all Spaniards. The girls couldn't – or were too afraid to – identify them. An old woman who did some ironing for the Club, and lived alone, was tied up and robbed. She died of a heart attack. There have been other cases. You'll hear people say that it's the tourists who have brought violence. That's not entirely true. Of course there are louts among the visitors . . . look what happened to Max and Elena Ansaldo . . . but there's no doubt that the locals are involved, too.'

'I don't remember anything like this happening when I was a kid.'

'There must have been some violence in the past . . . I remember Max told me once about a girl who was murdered.

He and Manolo found her body.' He hesitated. 'D' you realise that the victims in all the recent cases were connected with the Club?'

'I'm told that the rot set in a couple of years ago, when two workmen were killed. But, hell, that was an accident. Raven's has created jobs for virtually everyone, and brought money into the village.' He was surprised to find himself defending his father's enterprise, and added hastily: 'Not that I hold any brief for what Max has done to this part of the coast.'

'It's also brought jealousy. The people watch us here, at the Club, throwing our money around like confetti. We're the masters, they're always the servants. There's resentment, especially among the young ones.'

'But surely the Club's guests are a minority? Most of the package-deal tourists are ordinary people who have saved for a year to have a fortnight's break.'

'Sure, but for that fortnight, they're at leisure, too and they set out to spend all they've got. They can *pretend* they're rich. The San Felipans never see them scraping and saving, and they must wonder how it is that they've never managed to cut themselves a slice of the same cake.'

For a moment, Paul was silent then he said, 'So it's Max, in fact, who's entirely responsible for what's gone wrong. Apart from destroying the landscape, he's destroying the people.'

Bredon said sharply, 'Don't be so quick to condemn your father! If you want to blame any single person for what's happened to San Felipe, blame Rafael Ansaldo.'

'Oh, come on! Rafael's an arrogant, selfish old snob, but he's fought Max every inch of the way on each new development.'

'And never managed to stop one. Ever wondered why?'

'Max's back-handers to the right people, I suppose.'

'Right. Including Rafael.'

'He's bribed *Rafael*?'

'Certainly. And every time, through his lawyer – they've had no personal contact – Rafael's accepted the bribe. That's one reason why he hates Max so much.'

'You'll have to explain that.'

'Rafael's always been too damn lazy and inefficient to manage the properties his father left him. He's sold them off one by one, and spent the money. Doña Maria still has a certain amount that she inherited, I understand, but according to Max, even she finally jacked up on financing Rafael's life-style: constant trips to Madrid and Paris, his stable, expensive clothes, women . . .'

'Rafael's never struck me as a lady's man.'

'He's a normal male. After his wife died, the story is that he's set up a series if mistresses in an apartment in Malaga. They've been expensive, so he's taken Max's money, in return for withdrawing his opposition to the developments.'

'I don't see why that should make him hate Max any more than he did already.'

'Each time he gave in, it was another humiliation. Spanish aristocrats like the Ansaldos have always had this pride in being proud, if you see what I mean. Max says that every peseta Rafael has accepted from him has been another little erosion of his self-respect.'

'Okay, I can understand that. But you still can't blame him, rather than Max, for San Felipe's problems.'

'It was his greed that started the whole thing – with his mother's connivance. If it hadn't been for them, Max would probably be a contented wine-farmer on his own property near Jerez.' He shrugged. 'I don't suppose that in the long run it would have made much difference to the village, though. This is too beautiful a place to have been left in peace by the tourist industry. Development was inevitable.'

'What about that wine-farm? I was reading Max's wartime letters to Zimmy last night – he mentions you quite a bit – and the last one I looked at asked her to try to find out what was happening about Don Luis's estate, because he hadn't had any word about the land he'd been promised.'

'You never heard that story?' Bredon smiled happily. 'Have another brandy, and sit back, son. You're about to hear the next chapter in the life of Maxwell Raven. It's the one I know most about.'

Part 6

1945–1956

1

Hands in the pockets of his old Army shorts, Max stood at the edge of his property, reckoning up his worldly wealth. It was an uncomplicated calculation: he owned four hectares of virtually uncleared land, on which stood the burned-out shell of a house, and a few hundred pounds in banks in London and Gibraltar. That was it.

There was no vineyard near Jerez, no white villa with marble floors, for Don Luis's entire estate had gone to his own family.

The Spanish sun was warm on his back, the view from where he stood was beautiful, with San Felipe's little white houses clustering on the hillside to his left, and the sunburned land sweeping down to the sand. The sea's green shallows deepened into indigo under a pale blue sky in which floated a few puff-balls of white cloud. He did not see any of it, for his mind was flooded with a cold anger as he thought back over the past few days.

It was several weeks after Don Luis's death that he had finally written to Zimmy and told her about the old man's promise, asking whether she had heard any more about the will. He had already written his commiserations to Doña Maria, but received no reply.

Zimmy had answered at once: 'I do urge you to come out so that you can discuss the matter. I have made some inquiries, but all I can discover is that the estate is generally believed to be divided among the family. You could write to the Ansaldos' attorney, Senor Pinilla, but it would be better if you were here in person. Apart from this, dear Max, you have been away from us for too long. Do come!'

At breakfast the next morning, he had faced the Matsons with his announcement. 'I'm going to have to go to Spain for a few days. It's a matter of an inheritance.'

As Nancy stared at him, Sir Cedric said: 'What's this, then? Spain? An inheritance? You never said anything about this before. What about your job? You can't expect to take days off whenever you feel inclined, lad, even if you are the chairman's son-in-law.'

'I know that, sir. But this is a special case. Of course, I'll be taking leave without pay.'

'You *will* be taking leave? Suppose I say you *won't* be taking it?'

Max smiled as the ghost of Captain McPhee whispered encouragement. 'I'm afraid there's no room for argument, sir.'

Two days later, when he boarded the aircraft that would take him to Madrid, he had felt that he was flying into freedom. Nancy had been as angry with him as her father was, but where Sir Cedric blustered, she sulked, and had hardly spoken to him.

As their child had grown inside her, he had become increasingly aware that their marriage was a farce. The one attraction she'd had for him was her appetite for sex. Now, it seemed, she had lost even that. 'It could hurt the baby,' was her excuse. Her Army service might never have taken her away from home, for she was still subservient to her father, and it was his allowance which bought clothes for the unborn infant and furnished its nursery. It seemed to Max that now he had given it a name, he had no further function within the family. Outside it, Nancy, proud of her triumph in having captured such a spectacularly attractive man, was suffocatingly possessive.

His heart had begun to lighten the moment he closed the door of the Regent's Park mansion behind him.

From Madrid he had, without realising it, followed the route that had originally brought him to San Felipe with his parents: by train to Malaga, then a taxi to the village.

His welcome from Zimmy and the girls was as warm and affectionate as it had been the previous time, but now there was no Don Luis waiting at his table on the plaza. The following morning, he had gone to the Ansaldos' house and asked for Doña Maria.

Followed by Rafael, she came into the gloomy drawing-room, with its dark family portraits around the walls. She was swathed in black and looked like a nomad's tent. She greeted him curtly as he bowed over her hand. Rafael said nothing. They had stood side by side and stared at him, waiting.

'I've come . . . I mean . . . I want to tell you how sorry I was to hear about Don Luis's death,' he said.

She inclined her head. 'It was a great loss to his family.'

'Yes. Ah, Doña Maria . . .' How, without sounding crass, did you ask a widow what her husband had left you in his will? He started again. 'I saw Don Luis in Germany . . .'

'He told me.'

'Just before he and Rafael left, he said . . . he said . . . that when I came back to Spain, he wanted me to manage the wine-farm.'

'I know nothing of that.'

Rafael spoke for the first time. 'I'm taking over the vineyards.'

The old Rafael had come back to life. There was no trace of the hollow-eyed skeleton who had arrived in Berlin by cattle-truck. Now he was smooth-skinned and well-fed, his hair glossy, the side-burns longer than they were normally worn in England. He was wearing his favourite costume of tight trousers, tucked into boots, and an open-necked shirt. He carried a leather riding-crop.

Max ignored him, and spoke directly to Doña Maria. 'I have to tell you, Senora, that Don Luis informed me that he intended me to inherit the property near Jerez.'

Her face remained expressionless. 'That is not possible.'

'He was going to let you know when he got back from Germany.'

'My husband would never have deprived his children of family property.'

'I assure you . . .'

Rafael said, 'You can assure us of anything you like. You weren't mentioned in my father's will. If you have any doubts, you can go and see our attorney, Juan Pinilla.'

Max did that, the same afternoon.

Pinilla was an old man with a face as scaley and wrinkled as a tortoise. Throughout the interview, his brown, veined hands fiddled with a paper-knife on his desk.

As nearly word for word as he could remember, Max had repeated his last conversation with Don Luis. Pinilla had heard him out, then said, 'Had Don Luis intended any such thing, he would have told me. I recognise your name, but only because I helped him in the transfer of funds for your schooling. I suspect that on reflection he realised that he had already been sufficiently generous to you.'

'May I see a copy of his will?'

'It isn't any of your business, but if it will satisfy you . . .'

He went to a wooden filing-cabinet and brought out a rolled document, tied up with red tape. Dated December, 1936, its terms were unequivocal: Don Luis's entire estate was left to his wife, his son and his two daughters. There was no codicil.

Max had found an attorney of his own in Malaga, and put the problem to him, but following a brief investigation, an interview this morning had killed his last hope.

The attorney had been sympathetic, but definite. 'I'm sorry, Senor Raven. I'm assured there was no codicil. There's no way I can help you.'

'I can't understand it,' Max said. 'It wasn't like Don Luis to make a promise and then go back on his word.'

'In view of the fact that Pinilla has known the family for a long time, would there be any possibility that, as a favour to the widow and children he might have persuaded Don Luis against the codicil?'

'Persuaded him?' He looked at the lawyer with narrowed eyes. 'There's another possibility, isn't there? Doña Maria and Rafael could have *persuaded* Pinilla to pretend the codicil never existed.'

'There are, regrettably, a few attorneys who are open to – persuasion.'

'And if that's what happened, there's not a damn thing we can do about it?'

'Not a damn thing, Senor, short of going to the Courts, which would be a long, expensive, and probably fruitless exercise.'

Back in San Felipe and needing to be alone with his thoughts, he had changed out of his city clothes and gone up to the deserted *finca*. His resentment at having been cheated – he was now certain of this – grew with every step he took, for not only had the Ansaldos annexed property that was rightfully his, but they had deprived him of the chance to make a new future.

He walked around the land; crossed and recrossed it; leant against the blackened stones of the old farm-house and stared, unseeing, out over the sea; walked some more. By the time the sun began to set, he had come to a decision: he was not going back to England. Somehow, he was going to find a way to make a living in Spain.

Instantly, he began to feel better, more aware of his surroundings. He ran down to the empty beach, flung off his shirt and shorts and dived into the water. When he came out, he stood, looking up towards the *finca*, waiting for the warm wind to dry his underpants.

A path divided his property from a tract of rough land below it, which extended down to the beach. It was a gentle slope, several hundred metres wide. Perhaps six hectares in all, he thought, and it seemed less rocky than other sites around the village.

An idea, shelved when he had anticipated becoming a *vinador*, crept back into his mind: a hotel, with its own private access to the beach, which would attract tourists from all over the world. As he had in Germany, he saw it in his mind's eye, set into the slope: a long, low, white building, with terraces shaded by bougainvillea; a restaurant; every bedroom with its own bathroom; suites planned so that each had a balcony overlooking the sea.

He dressed and hurried back to the village.

Zimmy, wearing one of her shiny red 'madam' dresses, a rose tucked behind her ear, was in the bar. There were no customers. 'I've got to talk to you. It's important,' he said.

She poured glasses of wine for them both, then joined him

at a table. Putting his plan into words seemed to clarify it. The more he talked, the more feasible it seemed.

She was infected by his enthusiasm, though with reservations. 'Would foreigners come to this little place? I remember your father said once that bad roads and the fact that there's nothing to do except swim in the sea and walk in the hills might save San Felipe from what he called the invaders.' She paused, and added thoughtfully, 'I must say, I've sometimes thought that we could do with something to liven things up. We have almost too much peace and quiet.'

'People would come,' he said with certainty. 'I've often been asked about Spain. The English think it's romantic – bullfights, guitars, flamenco . . .' He smiled at her. 'Pretty women with roses in their hair. Northern Europe's grey and drab, and food and clothing are still rationed. Now the war's over, people will make for the sun, you'll see. We'll advertise, tell them how cheap Spain is compared with anywhere else. That's important, with foreign currency allowances being so small, especially in England. I could make a go of it, Zimmy!'

She looked at him affectionately, thinking how attractive he was – but no longer her little Max. He was six feet tall now, with broad shoulders tapering to narrow hips. His dark hair was roughened after his swim and his face was alive with enthusiasm. That young wife of his must be mad to let him loose without her, she thought, and continued the thought aloud: 'What about Nancy? Will she join you?'

'I'm here to stay. When she's had the baby, she can come out if she wants to.'

'You must buy that land. You will have to build your hotel. Do you have enough money?'

'No. But I'll go to Senor Valino at the bank for a loan. He should realise what a good thing it would be for the village.'

She looked dubious. 'Valino has never liked lending money. If only I had enough . . .'

'I wouldn't take it. Don't worry, I'll be able to persuade him.'

Impulsively, she kissed him. 'I'm sure you will. And, oh, it will be so good to have you back with us!'

He patted her cheek absently. 'I'll sound out a few people.

Builders, an architect. I'll get estimates so Valino will know exactly what the money is for. And the land. I think I have just enough cash to pay for that. There's a perfect site a few hundred metres below the *finca* . . .'

He ran on and on, his words coming faster as new ideas tumbled into his mind.

Two days later, most people in San Felipe knew that Max Raven was thinking of building a hotel on old Tia Carlota's useless strip of coastline, which she had said she would be pleased to sell to him. There was cautious optimism: foreigners were rich, and would probably spend their money in the shops and bars; fishermen might find an increased market for their daily catches of *langustinos* and *boquerones*, there could be work for many more people.

Max himself worked from morning until late evening, preparing his submission for the bank. Almost the only time he relaxed was a few hours one day, when he took Titi for a ride into the hills on his old motor-cycle.

As news of his activities spread, and the San Felipans began to realise that their moribund village was about to be reborn, everyone appeared to be delighted.

Everyone, that is, except the Ansaldo family.

Max was pacing out Tia Carlota's land when Rafael came towards him, flicking at grasses and flying insects with his riding crop.

When they were a few yards apart, he stopped. 'What's this nonsense I hear about a hotel?'

'It isn't nonsense.' Max said mildly. 'Building will start as soon as my bank loan is confirmed.'

'You must be mad! It will be visible from the windows of my house. We would never allow it!'

Max looked at the white villa, which was further up the hill, behind its high stone wall. Rafael was right.

He went on with his measuring.

Trying to keep pace with him, Rafael's voice rose: he would take legal action, give orders that no one in the village was to work on the site, stop the land-sale . . .

Max sighed and tucked his pencil into his pocket. 'The land's mine already. I paid Tia Carlota for it this morning. And what makes you think *you* can order people not to work for me? You've never done a damn thing for this village. A hotel will provide jobs and bring in money. You can take any legal action you like. Talk it over with my attorney in Malaga. I'll give you his address. But you'll be wasting your time. He's already told me there's no way I can be prevented from building a hotel here.' He paused, then added softly, 'Just as there was no way I could prove that you and your mother had monkeyed with Don Luis's will.'

Rafael's face was suddenly red with fury, and he raised his riding-crop. Instead of retreating, Max took a step towards him.

Their eyes locked, and Rafael was the first to look away. He turned, and hurried back up the hill.

The next morning, Max made his way to San Felipe's only bank, which occupied the ground floor of a narrow house in an alley leading off the plaza. He was shown into the office of the manager.

Valino was a small man with thinning grey hair. He was wearing a grey suit, white shirt and grey tie, even his skin had a tinge of grey.

He listened without expression as Max explained his project, but did not even glance at the figures he had prepared.

Then he said, 'I'm afraid I do not see my way clear to making you a loan, Senor Raven.'

'But you haven't even looked at my estimates!'

'I've heard what you had to say. It was enough. In a village like this, it would not be profitable to build such a hotel. There is nothing to attract tourists.'

'For God's sake! How would you know? Have you ever been to England or France? I've *talked* to people there. We have everything that they want after five years of war. They'll come, all right.'

'That's your opinion. I disagree with you.' He stood up.'If that was all . . .?'

'But a hotel would create jobs! Everyone I've talked to is in favour of it.'

'Not everyone, I think.' He waved a dismissive hand.

Then Max understood. 'Rafael Ansaldo!'

'This decision has been mine alone, Senor.'

Max was so angry that the people and places he passed after leaving the bank blurred in front of his eyes. He thought, they can't win a second time! There must be some way . . .

Hearing a beggar's whine, 'Senor! Senor!' he swung around as a grimy hand clutched his arm. He found himself glaring at Manolo, who flinched.

'Hey, Max! It was a joke. I heard you were back. I only wanted to say hello!'

'*Lo sieno tanto*! How are you, Manolo?'

He spread his hands. 'Look at me. How would you think?'

His clothes were worn and patched and he was bare-footed. He was the same Manolo, as dirty and unkempt as ever.

'You still living in your cave?'

'Where else?' he said bitterly. 'It's not easy to make a living these days. No tourists with big pockets. I might even have to go to work some time. It's a hard life.'

Max laughed in spite of himself. 'Come and have a beer. We can talk.'

They turned into a tiny bar near the beach that was largely patronised by fishermen. Now, at eleven-thirty in the morning, it was deserted.

When they were seated at a table, and Max had ordered two Victorias, Manolo said, 'You look good, my friend. You're rich now, hey?'

'I've just spent my last peseta on a piece of land I can't do anything with. I'm broke.'

'Word is that you're going to build a hotel. That takes money.'

'Which I haven't got . . .'

Manolo listened in silence as he described his encounters with Rafael and the bank manager. 'I could try other banks in Malaga, I suppose. But what have I got to offer, apart from an idea? I've no securities, no experience, nobody knows me.'

'You have a rich father-in-law, so I heard. Why don't you borrow from him?'

'First, because he wouldn't lend me a peseta. Second, even if he would, I wouldn't take it. I don't like him.'

'What about the Senorita Zimmy?'

'She'd give me all she has, but I wouldn't take it from her, either. She's had a struggle for the past few years.'

Manolo's heavy brows drew together as he looked down at his glass. 'If you were to find out . . . if I told you something that would help you to get the money you need, what'd you do for me?'

Max recognised from childhood the calculating expression on his face and was disinclined to take him seriously. 'I presume my gratitude wouldn't be enough?' Unsmiling, Manolo shook his head. 'You'd have a job with me for life. How's that?'

'It might do. That's a promise?'

'Sure! If you can help me to get the hotel built.'

Manolo put his elbows on the table and leant forward. 'Do you remember that day we found Clara?'

'I'll never forget it.'

'I found something else . . .' The low tones took Max back to the clearing in the hills, where the dead, naked girl lay under the trees, her clothing in a heap beside her. He was reminded that Manolo had picked up a small object from the ground, and thrust it into his pocket.

'You asked me what it was, and I told you it was only a pebble,' Manolo said.'But it wasn't. It was half a cuff-link, with a piece of fine chain attached to it. It was gold. I thought I might be able to make some money on it.'

The day after Clara's body had been found, he had gone back, searched among the flattened grass where she had been lying, and found the other piece of the link. 'It *had* to belong to the man who'd killed her. The chain must have broken while they were struggling.'

'Did you know whose it was?'

'Not then. I took it home and cleaned it. The piece I'd found first was oval, about a centimetre long, and it had initials on it. They were swirls and loops in a kind of pattern, and I couldn't make them out. I went to see the Russian, Kulik.'

Max remembered Kulik. He was a gentle, elderly man who had fled from the Russian Revolution in 1917 and, after months of wandering in Europe, had fetched up in San Felipe. He had managed to keep himself alive mending watches and making small pieces of jewellery which he sold in Malaga. His Spanish remained poor and he lived quietly by himself in a single room where he worked, cooked, ate and slept.

'I thought he might know what it was worth. When I got there, he was working. I asked him what he was doing, and he told me he was making a cuff-link for a man in the village. His wife had given him the set and he didn't want her to know he'd lost one, so it had to match exactly. I saw the one Kulik was copying.'

'It was the same?'

'No mistaking it. Same size, shape, initials.'

'Come on! Whose was it?'

'It belonged to Valino.'

Max sat back and exhaled in a long sigh. 'What did you do?'

'I went home and thought about it for days. I did – nothing.'

'You didn't go to the police?'

'Maybe you don't remember: the police and me . . . we've never been exactly friends. I knew what would happen. That pig Julio had been waiting for years for an excuse to arrest me. He'd have found some way to make it look as though I'd stolen the cuff-link. Valino would have backed him up, wouldn't he? Who'd believe my word against his? I might even have ended up being charged with the murder.'

'Did you keep the link?'

'Sure. I've always thought it would come in useful some day. All you have to do is tell Valino you've got evidence that he murdered Clara. You'll get the loan.'

'Blackmail? Christ, I couldn't!'

Manolo's lids dropped over the dark, sly eyes. He shrugged. 'Forget it, then. Let the Ansaldos have their own way.'

After a moment, Max stood up. 'So maybe I could. Let's go, before I change my mind again.'

When he returned to the bank, the gold cuff-link was in the breast pocket of his shirt.

A secretary was sitting at a typewriter in the outer office.

'Is Senor Valino alone?' he said.

'Si, Senor. But he is busy . . .' He pushed past her.

Valino looked up. 'I told you we had nothing further to discuss.'

Max put the cuff-link on the desk.

'Where did you get that?' His voice was hardly audible.

'It doesn't matter where I got it. The important thing is that I have it. I can prove who the owner is and where it was found.'

'It isn't possible . . .' He pulled a handkerchief from his pocket and wiped his forehead. As he raised his arm, the jacket sleeve slipped back, revealing an identical link. They stared at each other for a few seconds, then he said, 'What do you want from me?'

'From you, nothing. From the bank, a loan.'

'You will give me it back to me?'

'When the papers have been signed.'

'I will have them ready for you tomorrow.'

At the door, Max turned. 'You don't look the kind of man . . . What made you do it?'

Valino's hands were shaking as he lit a cigarette. 'I never meant . . . I still have nightmares about it.' He cleared his throat and his eyes looked back into the past. 'My marriage has never been . . . satisfactory. Clara was young, but she liked older men. She was always hanging about the plaza. She would lean over me and touch me with her breasts.

'That day, I said I would take her for a drive. We left the car beside the road and walked up into the hills. I thought . . . I was sure . . . she would let me make love to her. She began to undress, to show herself to me. I pulled her down onto the grass, but she fought. I couldn't stop, I needed her so badly. I must have put my hands around her throat to keep her quiet. I don't remember. When it was over, and I discovered that she was dead, I could not believe it. I remember shouting, "No!" then I ran.' He shuddered. 'And the nightmares started.'

'I found Clara,' Max said. 'I was nine years old. I had nightmares, too.'

Manolo was waiting for him a few yards away from the bank. 'You don't look happy,' he said. 'Didn't it work?'

'Oh, it worked, all right,' Max said, flatly. 'Welcome to Raven Enterprises.'

A few years later, he was to watch Valino becoming thinner and more bloodless as cancer ate into his lungs, until he was taken to hospital in Marbella, where he died.

After the funeral, Zimmy told Max that Susanna Valino was being forced to move out of her house. Inexplicably, the bank-manager had left her almost destitute.

A pinch-mouthed woman with a permanent look of resentment etched into her face, she was packing when Max knocked at her door.

'He worked all his life, but he left nothing!' she said bitterly. 'I'm going to my daughter in Seville. She doesn't want me. I don't want to go there. But what else can I do?' Despair briefly replaced her anger. 'He never told me. Years ago, he said that there would be money, some business he had with Rafael Ansaldo. I bought new furniture for the house. I thought there would always be enough, so I never stinted. He never told me . . . Now there are debts.' The anger returned. 'The other day I went to Senor Ansaldo and he said my husband had let him down over a deal they'd made, so it had been cancelled.'

The following day, Max bought her house and asked her to stay on in it as care-taker, for which he paid her a small wage for the rest of her life. She showed no particular gratitude, and when she died, he sold the house at a profit.

2

Three months after he received his loan, the hotel was taking recognisable shape. He had moved into a caravan, which he parked a few yards away from the *finca*, overlooking the site.

His builders, recruited locally, found themselves working harder than they ever had before. He chivvied them from morning until night, and anyone who did not turn up for work was instantly fired. They put up with him good-naturedly and, in fact, respected him, because he was paying them more than the going rate, and because he worked beside them, carried hods, mixed cement, provided beer or wine for the mid-morning break, shared their *tortillas* and *churros*.

Manolo worked as hard as anyone and Max soon found that it was profitable to leave him to hire the labour. His free-floating years in and around San Felipe had provided him with a detailed knowledge of local people and conditions. If a plasterer went sick, he would produce a replacement like a rabbit out of a hat; if a mason dropped a chunk of stone on his foot, he knew exactly how much compensation would be fair.

Max himself set rates of pay, but left him to hand out the wages. A few weeks after building started, he discovered that Manolo was creaming a few pesetas off every pay-out for himself. When he protested angrily, he was informed that he'd been away from Spain too long, and did not understand how business was conducted. Anyway, the men were still receiving more than they could earn anywhere else.

It was Max's first lesson in what he could expect as Manolo's employer, and he accepted the condition. The gypsy had already made himself too valuable an ally to lose.

Also, Max never forgot that without him, there probably would not have been a hotel.

Titi, too, joined his work-force. He simply appeared each morning and unobtrusively made himself useful. At the end of a week, Max presented him with a handful of pesetas. He looked at them with astonishment, then shrugged and put them in his pocket. Later Zimmy reported that she had seen him sharing them among the village children, as he shared the food left outside his hole-in-the-wall.

There was a curious incident one day when Max, needing a screw-driver he had left in his caravan, asked Titi to fetch it. A look of horror crossed his face and he shook his head violently.

'Why not?' Max said. 'Only take you a moment.'

But Titi's head went on shaking, as it had years ago when Zimmy first suggested that he might move from his hut in the hills. The same shutters seemed to fall over his eyes, and he fled.

The next morning, he turned up for work as usual, but Max watched him more carefully and noticed that though he trotted happily around the building site, he would never set foot on the *finca* land.

When he told Zimmy about it, she said sadly, 'Who can tell what's in his mind? It's like a locked room. The key was lost when Jaime died.'

He thought about Nancy only occasionally. He had written to tell her of his decision to stay in Spain and added that she might feel like joining him after the baby was born. When he read the letter over, he recognised that the invitation was hardly enthusiastic, but he posted it anyway. She did not reply.

As the weeks passed, his life with the Matsons receded into a kind of limbo, and he found it hard to convince himself that he was a married man, with a child due to be born any moment.

The San Felipe Hotel was ready for occupation ten months after building had started. As it progressed, he had tapped the water-supply from the hills, so green lawns seemed to have sprouted by magic. Gardens were laid out, and wide, shallow steps led down to the beach. Each guest room was furnished differently, each had a balcony and a tiled bathroom, as he had planned.

When the last nail was in place, he threw a party for everyone in the village, whether or not they had been involved in the building. As far as he could tell, the only people who did not come were the Ansaldos and the Valinos. Even the other land-owners, who were friendly with Doña Maria and Rafael, accepted their invitations out of curiosity.

The party went on for twelve hours and when the last person had gone, he wandered through the deserted rooms, knowing that nothing in his life so far had given him more satisfaction than this creation.

Now he only needed guests to fill it.

He had already sent out dozens of personal letters to friends, acquaintances, anyone whose name he could remember, offering reduced rates to the first fifty people who made bookings.

An instant acceptance bounced back from Dan Bredon, long since demobilised and working in repertory in Edinburgh.

His arrival was followed by others, including several of Max's former schoolfellows, some of whom were married and had started families.

Without exception, they loved San Felipe. They didn't mind bumping into the village over the rough roads and, with the strain of the war still showing in their pale faces, were happy to relax in the sun and find what entertainment they could on the beach and in Zimmy's bar. Among the single men, her girls' business improved dramatically.

At her suggestion, Max imported a chef from Madrid, but otherwise employed only local people, who were so pleased with the fulfilment of their hopes that they were as determined as he was to make the venture a success, and served the guests with cheerful enthusiasm. To the British, existing at home on a few ounces of meat a week, with sugar, sweets, ham, bacon, butter, clothes and petrol still rationed, bananas unavailable and eggs in short supply, Spain's abundance seemed like paradise.

Max found that he enjoyed the role of host. His good looks and easy charm, although they attracted women, did not antagonise the male guests, with many of whom he formed enduring friendships.

Even the villagers whom he did not employ directly could find no fault with the development in those early days. Tourists had money to spend, and plans were soon under way for new shops around the plaza.

Only the Ansaldos remained bitterly opposed. Max followed their reactions at second-hand, because Rafael kept well out of his way. Zimmy, with her ear to the ground as usual, reported that he had been furious when he had been told that Valino had agreed to the loan. With raised eyebrows, she said, 'I still don't know how you managed it, my love!' and Max replied casually, 'A little gentle persuasion, that's all.'

Doña Maria now kept her front windows shuttered, although the house was at least five hundred metres away from the hotel.

There was another outburst from Rafael when his gardener informed him that he was leaving in order to work for Max. In the bar that night, Miguel reported that he had shouted: 'I will never employ anyone who has worked for that man! You think he's almost royalty now: *El Hidalgo!* Let me assure you, in a year, he'll be bankrupt, and you'll all be out of jobs.'

From that moment, Max was *El Hidalgo*, the Grandee, to the village. When Zimmy told him about the nickname, he said solemnly, 'I'll have to live up to it, won't I?' and bought himself a wardrobe based on Rafael's: long, hand-made boots, well-tailored grey trousers, beautifully-cut white silk shirts and several expensive leather belts, ornamented with chased silver, from Toledo. Because he laughed at himself, the village laughed with him and, as Zimmy said, beside him Rafael looked like a peasant.

Several weeks after the opening, he was working at his accounts in his office behind the reception desk when he heard a car pull up outside.

Two minutes later, the pretty girl receptionist came in and told him that a lady wanted to see him. 'She hasn't made a reservation, senor, but she says she will be staying. She would like to see you. She has a baby with her.'

The room's temperature seemed to drop to zero as he walked stiffly towards the hall.

Nancy was clutching a shawl-wrapped bundle. They looked at each other, and there was shock in her eyes as she took in what she was later to call his fancy-dress.

Her first words were: 'You look so . . . so *foreign*!'

She, on the other hand, looked no different: colourless skin, untouched by cosmetics, pale lips, large, apprehensive eyes. Her pink and blue Liberty cotton dress, with puffed sleeves, hung loosely on her thin body.

She shifted the baby from one arm to the other, holding it tightly against her as though for protection. In spite of his dismay, she looked so nervous that he felt sorry for her. He put his arm around her and kissed her cheek. 'Why didn't you let me know you were coming? Why didn't you write?'

'Because I didn't know whether I could bring myself to leave until the last minute.'

There was a smell he didn't care for emanating from the shawl and he stepped back. 'How long are you staying?'

'I haven't decided yet.'

A pile of luggage stood just inside the doors. 'I'll call someone to take your stuff upstairs,' he said.

'Max?'

'Yes?'

'Don't you want to see your daughter?'

Appalled, he saw that she was holding the bundle out as though she expected him to take it. He stepped back, hands clasped behind him. Aware that the receptionist was watching interestedly, he looked into the folds of the shawl. There was a yellow stain on the wool, and he smelt the same unpleasant smell. Holding his breath, he leant forward until he could see a small round face from which two light blue eyes stared up at him without expression. The lashes and brows were so pale as to be almost invisible. A couple of bubbles appeared at the corner of the child's mouth. It bore, he thought, more than a passing resemblance to Sir Cedric.

'She's beautiful, isn't she?' Nancy said.

'What's her name?'

'Jennifer.'

'That's nice.' With false heartiness, he repeated, 'Nice. Jennifer Matson. Right, well, we'd better get you both into a room. You must be tired.'

He signalled the receptionist to summon a bell-boy and heard Nancy's tight, furious voice: 'Her name is Jennifer Raven! She's *your daughter*, Max.'

They didn't speak to each other again until he had shown her into a vacant suite and she had set the baby down between pillows on the double bed. She looked around. 'This isn't your room?'

'No. Mine's at the back. It's small. You'll be more comfortable here.'

She stood, facing him, and her back seemed to stiffen. 'We have to talk. But first I want something to eat and I must feed Jennifer. I've brought a supply of tinned milk. I need hot water to warm her bottle.' Her voice became an accusation. 'I didn't have enough milk to breast-feed her. The doctor said it was because of all the worry.'

As Max's knowledge of the care and feeding of infants was non-existent, he understood only that he was to blame for her apparent failure to be a normal mother.

'I'll send one of the women to help you,' he said. 'A couple of the housemaids have children. They'll know . . .'

He retreated out of the door and almost ran along the corridor, back to his office.

An hour later, she joined him, and put a large parcel on his desk.

'What's this?'

'Open it.'

Under layers of brown paper, he found his father's three paintings of San Felipe.

'I thought you'd want them,' she said. 'Anyhow, Daddy wouldn't let me hang them at home.'

He was touched. 'Thank you. I've been missing them. Sit down. Drink?'

'No, thanks. I've just got Jennifer off to sleep. I asked that woman you sent to listen for her, but she didn't understand a word I said.'

'Someone will hear her. Spaniards love babies.'

She watched in silence as he poured himself a rather larger brandy than normal, then said, 'Why do you wear those funny clothes, Max?'

'I like them. They're practical for the life I lead.'

'I've never seen a hotel-keeper dressed like that.'

He said abruptly, 'Nancy, why did you come?'

'You're my husband. Jennifer's father.'

'That's not enough. I wrote to you. You never answered. I assumed you'd decided to divorce me.'

'I didn't write because Daddy wouldn't let me. I truly believe he wanted to kill you, Max.'

'Then how did you persuade him to let you come here?'

'He didn't know. He and Mummy were in Scotland. I left him a letter, saying I was going to try to persuade you to come back with me.'

'No! Nancy, try to understand: my life is here. This place is taking off. I'm making a profit already. If you want to stay on, you'll have a good life. But as far as I'm concerned, you're free to make up your own mind.'

'You mean you don't care whether I'm here or not.' Her mouth set stubbornly. 'I'm staying, Max. At least for a while. I'm sick of having a baby, but no husband. I'm sick of making up lies, and telling people you've been away on business.'

He forced enthusiasm into his voice. 'I promise you'll love it here when you get used to it.'

He soon realised that it was a promise he could not keep. She disliked San Felipe, hotel life, Spanish food, Spanish people, the language she made no attempt to learn, the servants, whom she thought over-friendly. Most of all, she disliked Zimmy.

He took her, with Jennifer, into the village a couple of days after her arrival.

He had bought himself a second-hand Seat, and when he pulled up outside the Bar Jiminez, there was an eruption of women. Zimmy, Pepita and the younger girls who had replaced Sonia and Angelina, clustered around, twittering over the baby. The girls were dressed in their working clothes, and their satin dresses glittered in the rays of the evening sun.

Seeing Nancy's nervous expression, he said in Spanish, 'For Heavens sake, girls, give her a chance to breathe!'

Zimmy waved them away, took Nancy's face between her hands and kissed her on both cheeks. 'Welcome to San Felipe! We have been longing to see you and the *niña*. Our Max a father! I couldn't believe it. When he arrived here he was small enough for me to pick him up and cuddle him!' She winked, 'Maybe I would like to do that now, too, but alas, it isn't possible. Instead, I will take his daughter.'

She held out her arms, but Nancy said, 'She doesn't like strangers. I'm sorry, it would upset her.'

'Oh, come on, Nancy . . .' he began.

'No, no!' Zimmy said quickly. 'I understand. We must wait for her to get used to us. We will drink some wine, but inside, I think, so we will not be disturbed.'

She led the way through the bar to her sitting-room. Nancy sat upright on a sofa, and he saw her eyes widen as they focused on a point behind his head. He glanced around, and laughed.

'Oh, God, Zimmy! I haven't seen that for years!'

'I decided to bring it down from the room upstairs. Why should only outsiders have the pleasure of looking at my Mamma?'

He turned to Nancy. 'Picture of an Old Goat,' he said. 'Would you believe it, that's my great-uncle Henry, a much-respected Scottish landscape painter. It's a self-portrait.'

She said nothing. Indeed, she hardly spoke from that moment. Max maintained a conversation, but her frigid presence loomed large out of all proportion to her physical size. He was relieved when Jennifer began to howl and he could announce that it was time to leave.'

As he hugged Zimmy, he whispered, 'I'm sorry. Give her time.'

'Don't worry. It's strange to her. Later, we make friends, perhaps.'

But the afternoon's difficult encounters had not yet ended.

He was walking around the car to help Nancy into the passenger seat when he heard her scream. Titi had appeared beside her and was tugging at the baby's shawl. 'Max! Make him go away!'

'Calm down,' he said. 'This is Titi. He's my friend. He loves children. Here, give her to me.'

Before she could protest, he lifted Jennifer out of her arms, unwrapped the shawl and went down on one knee. Titi put out a finger and touched her cheek, then he said softly, '*La munequita*!'

'She's a baby, *amigo*, not a doll. Would you like to hold her for a minute?'

Titi held out both arms, making a platform, and Max was about to lay her on them when Nancy swooped. 'Don't you dare! Give her to me!'

She grabbed the child and climbed into the car. Frightened by the sudden movement, Titi backed away.

'It's all right,' Max said gently. 'You haven't done anything wrong.' He lowered his voice. 'I'll let you hold the baby some other time, okay?'

Instantly happy, Titi grasped his imaginary handle-bars and the sound of his motor-cycle engine receded into the distance.

Max moved the car off with an angry grating of gears, but he kept his mouth shut, afraid if he spoke at all, it would be to say too much.

Nancy had no such inhibitions. 'Max, who are those people? Why did you make me go there?'

'I told you about Zimmy. She's my oldest friend.'

'You didn't tell me about that – that place. Nor about those other awful women.'

'You never asked me. In fact, you've never shown the slightest interest in my life here. I'd have told you . . .'

'They look – they look like tarts!'

'They are,' he said calmly.

'Are you telling me that place is a brothel?'

Through clenched teeth, he said,'Yes. It's a clean, well-run brothel that provides a necessary service for lonely men. Zimmy owns it, and I was practically brought up there.'

'I can't believe it! You took our daughter there! And *she* tried to kiss her! What sort of diseases . . .' She shuddered. 'Hurry up, please. I must get her into a bath at once.'

'Don't be so silly! My parents loved Zimmy, and so do I. You behaved very badly.'

She swept on: 'And that disgusting picture on the wall! If I'd only known . . .'

'You wouldn't have come?' His voice was soft. 'Nancy, why don't you go home to your father?'

'You'd like me to, wouldn't you? Well, I won't. You're my husband.' She squeezed the child too tightly and it whimpered. When she had quietened it, she started again, like a rewound gramophone. 'And that hideous dwarf! You were going to let him hold Jennifer! What kind of a parent are you, Max?'

He began to lose control of his temper. 'Do you realise that in less than an hour, you've succeeded in hurting two gentle, affectionate people who only want to be your friends?'

Her mouth set in the stubborn line that always reminded him of Sir Cedric. 'I will not have people like those near my child.'

The anger drained away and a cloud of depression enveloped him. 'Don't worry, I won't inflict them on you again.'

As the months passed, she made no move to return to England, although she had received a letter from Sir Cedric soon after her arrival, which had made her cry. 'He isn't angry with me,' she reported. 'He only wants me to come home. He says . . .' She sniffed. 'He says, "your old Dad will always be here, love, waiting for you." '

With an effort, Max said, 'Why don't you suggest that he and your mother come out and stay at the hotel for a while?'

'Oh, no! He wouldn't do that. He says he won't ever see you again. I'm sorry, Max.'

He tried to keep the relief from his face.

She corresponded with her father regularly after that, and made Max take photographs of herself and the baby to send to him.

His feelings for Jennifer were confused. He found it almost impossible to believe that his sperm had produced this child in whom, try as he might, he could not feel any real interest. At the same time, there were moments – usually when Nancy was not present – when he would look down at her and feel a stirring of something that might some day develop into affection.

He was relieved when Titi never again attempted to touch the 'doll,' though sometimes – again only when her mother was not there – he would stand by her pram out in the sunny courtyard, and watch her, smiling. Nancy would never leave her entirely alone, and insisted that one of the maids sat by her on the rare occasions when she herself was elsewhere.

She scarcely ever moved beyond the grounds of the hotel, and took no interest in its running. To preserve appearances, she had insisted on moving into a room next to Max's, but when his need for sexual relief became too much and he joined her in bed, two times out of three she was too tired. The third, she would receive him with dull resignation. The appetites which had sent her creeping into his room before their marriage seemed to have been smothered by motherhood.

He had his first affair, with a statuesque and uninhibited Swedish painter whose husband was a timber millionaire. He was, she assured him, 'very understanding', and would be pleased that Max had made her so happy. It was a light-hearted, uncomplicated liaison, which lasted until she regretfully departed to rejoin the understanding millionaire. After that, instead of forcing himself on his wife, he discovered that there was usually a compliant female guest who was happy to serve his needs.

In public, Nancy continued to show the possessiveness which he had found irritating from the beginning. Sometimes she would sit at a table in the bar, with a glass of wine in front of her. From politeness, and because he was sorry for her solitude, he would usually join her. There were no awkward silences, because they were constantly interrupted by members of the staff, with queries, or guests wanting to buy them drinks. Numbers around the table would swell into a cheerful, chattering crowd. Max enjoyed this, but was uncomfortably aware that she remained on her own little island of silence, rarely taking her eyes off him. If she was sitting next to him, she insisted on holding his hand. People who tried to make conversation with her were soon intimidated by her reserve and turned away.

Years later, he was to say to Zimmy that he wondered whether she had ever regarded him as anything more than a possession. 'It was the same with the baby. She couldn't bear anyone else to touch her. Maybe, if she hadn't been so possessive, I might have got closer to Jennifer.'

'Poor girl. She must have known that eventually she would lose you, and then she would only have her child,' Zimmy said. 'I think she loved you, Max, but apart from that, capturing you was a triumph for a girl like her, and she didn't want to give you up.' Her eyes narrowed. 'I think you don't altogether understand the effect you have on women, my love. I watch them when you are in the village. You look at them all as though you want to take them to bed!'

'I mostly do! I like women.'

'And you aren't afraid to show it . . . that is unusual for an Englishman, I think.'

By the end of the hotel's first year of operation, reservations were being made months in advance. During one rare quiet period, Max had invited a party of travel writers from England to come out for a week as his guests. Their enthusiastic reports in magazines and newspapers brought a new flood of bookings.

He began to buy more land for development, and drew up a scheme for a larger hotel to the west of the village, which would be followed by the first of a series of holiday apartment blocks.

Whenever news of his plans leaked out, Rafael Ansaldo did all he could to whip up opposition. Thanks to Manolo's knowledge of local officials' weaknesses, and Max's liberal dispersion of money, he finally gave in each time.

Remembering how he had been cheated of his inheritance, Max had no inhibitions about extending his property until it virtually surrounded the Ansaldos' house. Through an agent, he even made an offer for the Campo Negro, which belonged to Victoria. It was rejected, since Rafael knew perfectly well from whom it came. For once, no offer could persuade him to change his mind, and Victoria was too young to defy him, though the land meant nothing to her.

In the management of his own lands, Rafael's inefficiency was already causing financial problems, according to village gossip. Although he occasionally toured the orchards and olive groves, he was really only interested in spending the money they produced. From the start, he left the management to others, whom he paid badly and who therefore had little incentive to maintain them as Don Luis had done.

'I hear he's thinking of selling the olive trees,' Zimmy said. 'He claims it isn't economic to have properties scattered over such a wide area. The only thing that seems to interest him is the wine-farm, because he can use the house for his extravagant parties.'

Had Rafael shown the slightest wish for a reconciliation, Max might have met him half way. But he seemed determined to maintain their feud, to the extent that he would even turn his car off the road if they were driving towards each other.

Fortunately, with his plans for expansion going ahead, Max was too busy to brood either about Rafael or the failure of his marriage.

One morning, a small, colourful tribe of gypsies came down the steep road from the hills, leading two mules. Half an hour later, they had spread through the village.

As once they had when Manolo appeared, the shop-keepers fluttered like frightened hens. When one of the gypsies entered a shop, or walked through the market, suspicious eyes were constantly on him. They were easy to keep in sight: the men in ragged trousers and tightly-belted cotton shirts, with scarves knotted around their heads; the women in long, bright skirts, hoop ear-rings and fringed shawls. Nevertheless, their passing was nearly always followed by the discovery of thefts. 'You have only to blink, and a kilo of oranges disappears,' wailed Ignacio, the fruiterer.

Even the beggars, who had their pitches in the plaza and doorways, resented them. Their takings had improved with the influx of tourists, but many were immobilised after having lost limbs during the Civil War, and could only harass passers-by vocally. The gypsies had the business of begging down to a fine art. The men were aggressive, clinging to sleeves and jackets until money was forthcoming. The women clutched their babies and whined about poverty and starvation. They let no potential marks off the hook, following them down to the beach, squatting in front of their tables in the plaza, huge, pleading eyes fixed on the food and wine, until they were paid to go away.

With an unerring instinct for the richest pickings, they filtered towards the hotel. Some took up positions at the gates, with their hands outstretched, while others entered the grounds, the reception hall and the courtyard, where Nancy snatched Jennifer out of her cot and fled inside.

Max ordered Manolo to get rid of them, which he did, by a combination of abuse and bribery.

That evening, they camped outside the village with their mules, and the next morning, small boys who had been hanging around the camp, reported that they were preparing to move off.

In the afternoon, reassured that they had left the area, Nancy ordered one of the housemaids, Catalina, to take Jennifer outside and keep an eye on her. Suffering from an attack of diarrhoea, an ailment which debilitated her regularly and which added to her resentment of things Spanish, she retired to her room.

At five o'clock, she was awakened from a doze by Max's unceremonious entry. 'Get up! Jennifer's gone!' he said.

When she ran into the reception hall, hair flying, eyes still crinkled with sleep, Catalina was sobbing beside the empty pram. Nancy shook her, shrieking hysterically, while Max's shouts to them both to shut up heightened the decibels. An interested crowd of guests had gathered.

Eventually, the story emerged. Catalina had been knitting in the shade of a tree when her *novio,* who was one of the porters, had joined her. Taking the opportunity to steal a few minutes together, they had moved out of sight of the hotel's windows, at the same time out of sight of the pram, and enfolded each other. When they had disentangled, Jennifer was gone. They had heard nothing.

Nobody doubted that she had been kidnapped by the gypsies. Within minutes, the police had been informed, and a full-scale search was instigated. A pilot flying overhead during the following hours would have thought that the countryside was crawling with oversized ants as Max, several guests who had cars, and the tiny local police force scoured the hills. They found no trace of the gypsies. As darkness fell, a violent storm made it impossible to continue the search.

It was still raining, with intermittent thunder and flashes of forked lightning, when Manolo and Max, together with the senior police officer, Juan Aranda, returned wearily to the hotel. Nancy, exhausted with crying, had been persuaded to rest in her room.

Aranda was a large, pessimistic man with drooping moustaches. 'There will be a ransom demand, senor,' he said. 'You might receive it tomorrow, or not for a week. Sometimes these people will wait, so the parents' anxiety is greater and they do not try to bargain.'

'There'll be no bargaining,' Max said. 'I'll pay whatever they ask.'

'They must have known that you could afford to pay. Your reputation has spread: everyone on the coast has heard of *El Hidalgo*.' He yawned. 'There is nothing further we can do tonight, senor. Tomorrow, we search again.'

After he had gone, Max went to Nancy's room. She was lying on her bed, asleep. Her face was flushed and puffy, her cheek resting against her hand. With her pale lashes and brows, her indeterminate features, she seemed little older than Jennifer. His heart lurched as he thought of the baby, frightened, with strangers in unfamiliar surroundings. From a distance, the gypsies had looked exotic; at close quarters in the village, he had seen their bare, dirty feet and the black under their fingernails; the unwashed hair and stained clothing; the fierce eyes.

Nancy woke, and jerked upright when she saw him. 'You've found her! She's dead, isn't she?'

'She's still missing. There's no point in searching any longer tonight. She'll be okay, Nancy. We'll find her.'

'She's dead,' she repeated. 'They'll ask for money, and then all we'll find is her body. Like the Lindbergh baby.'

'For God's sake, that was fifteen years ago! And it was in America. This is Spain. Spaniards don't harm babies.'

She lay back, and her face was as white as the pillows. 'I should never have brought her here . . .'

He sat on the bed and put out a hand to stroke her head, but she turned away. 'Don't touch me, Max! It's your fault as much as mine. *We* killed her!'

'Nancy . . .'

'Leave me alone.'

Unnerved by her hostility, he made a hopeless gesture and left the room. Who, he wondered, had said that shared troubles brought people together? This crisis had only proved how far apart he and Nancy were.

He slept restlessly, and awoke at first light. He dressed and went to the kitchen, where he made himself a cup of black coffee. He was sure that if the gypsies had taken to the hills, they would have been found. Where the hell could they have gone? Then he thought, suppose they hadn't left the area, but were in hiding close by, awaiting an opportunity to make their ransom demand?

To the east, the coast was scalloped by inlets, some with tiny beaches backed by steep cliffs. As children, he and Manolo had climbed down to the sea and explored caves that had been cut into the rocks by centuries of battering by the waves.

He drove out of the village, parked his car on a patch of turf and began to walk, carrying his binoculars. He paused every now and then to scan the cliffs. The storm had washed all dust from the air and left the landscape fresh and clean, but the sea was still disturbed. He had a sudden, sickening vision of a small body being rocked on the white-caps, then sinking slowly below the surface.

He had walked for two or three kilometres, and the sun was high when, standing above an inlet, he heard a sound over the breaking of the waves. He held his breath, and listened. It came again, unmistakably the braying of a mule. He focused his glasses and spotted a rough, almost vertical track that wound down the cliff-face to a narrow strip of sand. Then he caught a flash of red against the dark mouth of a cave.

He raced back to the car.

Less than half an hour later, the cliff-top was ringed by armed police and volunteers, including Manolo.

Automatically, Max assumed command, and his authority, acquired in the Army, was sufficient to persuade the police to accept his leadership.

'I'm going down first,' he said. 'The rest of you follow me. There can't be more than half a dozen men, but we need to surprise them, so they don't have a chance to harm the baby. Ready . . .?'

As he stopped speaking, he became aware of a scrabbling noise below his feet, then the sound of voices. He dropped onto his stomach, worked his way towards the edge, and looked over. A procession was scrambling up the path. At its head, two men were leading reluctant mules, cursing as they hauled them up the steep incline. They were followed by the rest of the tribe. His heart was hammering as he watched. Some of the women, carrying bundles on their heads, were tall for Spaniards, with proud carriage. Two were carrying babies, slung in shawls on their backs. With an intake of the breath, he focused his binoculars on them, but the infants' heads were hidden. Which one . . .?

He crawled backwards until he could stand up without being seen from below, put a finger to his lips and motioned his little army to stand back. Within a few minutes, a mule's head appeared above the precipice. It was whipped onto level ground by an old, ragged gypsy, who stopped dead when he saw the circle of men, some uniformed, with their hands on pistols. A look of terror crossed his face, but before he could warn his followers, Max and Manolo had grasped him. Max clapped a hand over his mouth. The second mule appeared, then, one by one, the other gypsies.

Their reactions echoed the old man's: astonishment, followed by fear. The two groups stood, facing each other, then Max went to a woman who was carrying a baby. Anger replaced her fright as he pulled back the shawl. She whirled, with a raised hand, ready to strike him. But he had already seen that the infant was dark-skinned, with a fluff of black hair and great black eyes. He went to the second woman. Her baby, too, was a gypsy.

The let-down made him feel physically ill, and he stood with clenched hands, swallowing the bile that rose into his throat.

When he regained control, the silence had been broken as the gypsies recovered from their shock and began to shout questions. Their Spanish was so guttural, so larded with words in an unfamiliar language, that it was difficult to follow, but their anger was obvious.

It increased when Aranda ordered his men to search the big basket-work panniers on their mules. Fights broke out as the gypsies tried to stop them. Outnumbered, they were soon subdued and the panniers were upended on the ground. They revealed a variety of items, from loaves of bread to saucepans and bolts of cloth. There was no hidden child.

The old man who had led the first mule was the most vociferous protester, and when the search had ended and the tribe was sullenly repacking their belongings, Max began to question him. As he understood the accusation, he roared with indignation. Kidnap a *goy* baby? They were honest people, travelling up to the annual Romany festival at Stes-Maries-de-la-Mer in France. They had enough babies of their own!

Manolo interrupted: 'If you didn't take the child, why did you hide? How did you know about the path down the cliff?'

Another gypsy, with a red scarf tied around his head, stepped forward. He indicated the old man, and said, 'He was here many years ago. He knew there was a cave where we could shelter. The storm was coming.'

A bizarre suspicion struck Max as he looked at the three men. Even in his distress, he registered Manolo's physical resemblance to the other two: squat, broad-shouldered, low-browed, with full red lips and bold eyes. Snatches of words he'd heard from his mother came back to him: 'Five of them, three men and two women, with a donkey and a camel . . . Luisa said the baby was coming . . . the next morning, the other gypsies had gone.'

His thought was interrupted by an outbreak of violence. Manolo's temper had exploded. He had the old gypsy by the throat and was systematically throttling him as he hissed threats.

Max, the other gypsy and a policeman dragged him off. His eyes were reddened with anger as his struggles subsided.

'That's enough,' Max said. 'Let them go. I don't think they had anything to do with it.' Slowly, the tribe moved off. They said nothing, but shot venomous glances back as they went towards the road.

'You're a fool!' Manolo snapped. 'They should have gone to prison until they confessed. *Dios*, how I hate those people!'

Max glanced at him curiously. 'They seemed harmless enough.'

'I'd kill them all, if I could.' His face was a mask of bitterness, and Max knew that he was remembering his childhood: the cave in which he had shivered through the winters, the constant hunger, the mother who, deserted by his father, had become a diseased, drunken whore.

'I don't think they did it,' he repeated. 'Come on, I'll drive you back.'

As they got into the car, Aranda came to the window. 'We will continue looking for her, Senor, you can be sure of that, but . . .' He raised his hands dejectedly.

Driving towards the hotel, where he faced breaking the news to Nancy, Max had just passed Titi's cupboard in the wall when he had to brake sharply to let a procession cross the road. About twenty people, all wearing black, were moving slowly towards the Campo Negro. Most were women, their heads bent over rosaries, but there were a few elderly men, and Titi was among a small group of children.

'What the hell . . .?' Max said.

'It's the annual pilgrimage to the shrine on the Campo Negro,' Manolo said.

The last of the pilgrims crossed the road. Titi, recognising them, raised a hand and smiled shyly.

'I don't suppose he has the faintest idea what it's all about,' Max remarked. 'Come to think of it, I'm not sure myself. Something to do with the Civil War, isn't it?'

Manolo didn't reply. Max glanced at him and saw that he was looking after the procession, his eyes narrowed. He did not speak until they reached the hotel. Then he left the car and, with a brief goodbye, went back towards the gates.

Max was too occupied with his own immediate problem to be curious.

Nancy was waiting in his office, staring straight ahead, her hands clasped in her lap. As soon as she looked up, he knew she had recognised his failure.

He told her what had happened. When he fell silent, she said, 'They've killed her. They heard you coming, and they put her into the sea. She'll never be found.'

'The police searched the cave. There was no indication that she'd ever been there.'

'How would there be? They took her, then they threw her away like a piece of rubbish.' She stood up and walked out of the room.

The hours stretched emptily ahead of Max. He could go out in the car again, or he could try to take his mind off his lost baby by working as though nothing had happened. In the event, he did neither, but simply sat at his desk, thinking about Jennifer. He had never felt she belonged to him, had never made any attempt to show a father's love. She had been an object which belonged to Nancy. Now, his regret at the wasted opportunity was almost unbearable.

He was still sitting when his door opened.

Manolo stood there, and he held the baby in his arms. Pausing only to say, 'Is she alive?' he ran along the corridor, shouting for Nancy.

When the first rejoicings were over and Nancy had closed herself away to bath and feed the child, Manolo said: 'It was while we were coming back. We'd just passed Titi's cupboard. I noticed that the door was closed, but I didn't think anything of it. Then we saw him in the procession. It's a fine day. Even when he isn't at home, he only closes the door if it's raining. I wondered about it, so I went back. I remembered that you'd told me he thought she was a doll and sometimes came to look at her. She was lying on his bed, wrapped up in his blanket. I think he'd fed her on a bit of *tortilla*. She was happy enough.'

Max poured him a brandy. 'I'm in your debt again, my friend.'

'*De nada.* Titi came back while I was there. He kept saying, "*la munequeta,*" and trying to kiss her. What are you going to do about him?'

'He meant no harm. If we'd let him play with her here, he'd never have done it. We'll forget it. I'll tell Aranda.'

Nancy was not so charitable. She demanded that Titi be punished, and any joy they might have shared in the baby's recovery was cancelled out by an argument.

Max stood firm, and eventually she left him, sobbing that from now on, she would never have an easy moment.

Late in the afternoon, he went to her room, bearing a bottle of champagne as a peace offering. Her door was open, and as he was about to enter, he heard her talking on the telephone. She was half-sobbing. '. . . as soon as I can, Daddy. I can't stand it any longer. Oh, you were right! . . . Yes, of course Jennifer will be with me . . .'

She put the receiver down, and saw him in the doorway.

'I'm taking Jennifer home.' she said. 'You don't have to pretend you'll be sorry. I'm going to divorce you, Max.'

He put the champagne on her table. 'You can celebrate with this.' He left the room.

3

'A lady to see you, Senor Max.'

'What?'

Aquilina's grand-daughter, serving her first week in the hotel, wondered what she had done wrong. 'I'm sorry . . . but she said she knew you, from a long time ago.'

It couldn't be, he thought. They were divorced. There had been no contact. It was only the echo of that evening, years ago, that had made him think of her. Nevertheless . . .

Dreading the reply, he said, 'Is she English?'

'She speaks English,' Juana said doubtfully. 'But she doesn't look like the English ladies who are staying here.'

He followed her into the hall. A girl was standing by the fountain that splashed from a cherub's cornucopia in the centre of the marble floor. It was not Nancy.

She was tall, with long fair hair rolled into a pleat at the back of her head. Slim and graceful, she was wearing a jacket in pale grey silk over a turquoise shirt. A full skirt swirled around her calves and a pale grey suede coat was slung casually over her shoulders. There were gold chains around her neck, gold studs in her ears, but these were details he was not to notice until later, because his eyes were fixed on her face.

'Anne-Louise?' he whispered.

'No. Not Anne-Louise. I'm Véronique.'

'Véronique?'

'Her daughter. I would have recognised *you*.' She looked amused as he studied her, trying to find some resemblance to the skinny fourteen-year-old he had met so briefly. 'Don't you believe me?' She held out her hand to be shaken.

'I have to believe you! But you've changed so much . . . and you're the last person I expected.'

Her amusement faded. 'Should I not have come? I understand you would rather it was my mother.'

Good manners came to his rescue. 'Not at all. I'm delighted to see you. Are you staying here, with us?'

'This is a club, no? I had not realised that before I came. I will go to a hotel.'

He was rapidly recovering from his shock. Questions were tumbling into his mind – too many and too important to be snapped out in a few minutes. 'You'll do nothing of the kind. It's our off-season. There's plenty of room.'

'Thank you. But I must think about it.' She glanced around the luxurious hall, which had been redecorated when he had converted the hotel into the San Felipe Club a year ago.'I didn't dream it would be like this.'

He took her arm. 'Come into my office. We can have coffee while you make up your mind.'

After a brief hesitation, she nodded.

His new office was part of the suite he'd reserved for himself during extensions. It was modern, almost stark, but comfortable. The walls were off-white, as were the corduroy-covered armchairs. His huge desk was polished rosewood and the floor was a chequerboard of black and white ceramic tiles. The one touch of colour was a scarlet rug.

She threw her coat over the back of a chair, then said, almost to herself, 'What a difference . . .!' He understood that she was thinking of the house in which they had met.

A waiter arrived with their coffee and she sat down in one of the chairs he had set around a low, glass-topped table. She looked around and he saw a momentary frown crease her forehead.

'Something bothers you?' he said.

'This is so elegant! But you have no flowers! Or are you the kind of man who believes that it is effeminate to have flowers in your office?'

From another woman he had just met he might have resented the unsolicited criticism, but he was still under the spell of memory. He recalled that even in the dreadful *manoir*, a glass jar of wild flowers had stood on the table beside Anne-Louise's chair.

'I've never thought about them one way or another, though I do tend to connect flowers with funerals. But if you say so . . .' He pressed a button on his desk. When Juana appeared, he waved a lordly hand. 'Flowers, Juana! Lots of them, in vases.'

As she scuttled off, Véronique said, 'At the touch of a button, you can have anything you want. I'm impressed.'

He laughed. 'I was showing off. This suite, the buzzers, they're new toys.' He filled her coffee cup. 'Now it's question-and-answer time. My questions, your answers.'

She was looking at him steadily. Her eyes were a curious smoky grey that almost matched her jacket. The heart-shaped face and the dark, curved eyebrows, dramatic against her fair hair, were inherited from Anne-Louise. He rarely thought about her these days, but looking at Véronique, it was as though he had parted from her only yesterday.

'You want to know about my mother.' It was a statement, not a question.

'Yes.'

She spoke without emotion. 'She died six months ago. She had been ill for a long time. It was cancer of the bones. At the end, it was quick. I was glad for her.'

He remembered Anne-Louise's fragility as she stood alone on the terrace, facing his guns; the swastika daubed on her shaven head; her insistence on walking, unaided, through a mocking, hostile crowd.

In the same flat tone, Véronique said, 'She was brave. I miss her very much.'

He said, with difficulty, 'I went back, you know.'

'Did you? I didn't know that. We never went back. I expect I own the house now, but I won't go there again. Let it rot!' Her voice was suddenly hard.

'When did you leave Montjoli?'

'A few weeks after you did. We were not attacked again because the man who owned the bar protected us, though even he did not like to speak to us. His wife used to leave us food, otherwise we'd have starved. No one would sell us anything. You had given us enough money to pay our fares to Paris. We still had friends there, who didn't know anything about what had happened in Montjoli. An S.S officer had been living in our apartment, and he had been a thoughtful care-taker. All our furniture was intact, and there was even a little money which my father had hidden under the floor-boards before he was arrested. People were kind to us. Later, my mother took a job with a publisher who had been a friend of my father, so I was able to go to school. Then I was apprenticed in a fashion-house.' She shrugged. 'That's all, I think.'

'What about your . . . the child your mother had?'

'You knew she was pregnant?'

'Monsieur Varenne's daughter told me when I went back.'

'The baby was never born. She had a miscarriage just after we arrived in Paris.'

'I wish I'd known that,' he said slowly. 'Maybe, if I had, I'd have made more effort to find her.'

'You couldn't stand the idea that she was carrying a Nazi's child?'

'She was the first woman . . .' He stopped.

'You were very naive,' she said. 'And transparent. My mother and I both knew that you had fallen in love with her. It was the one happy memory of her life in Montjoli. We often talked about you.' She paused. 'How old are you, Max?'

'Twenty-seven.'

'So you have the secret of eternal youth. You have aged only one year in seven.'

He laughed. 'I didn't want her to know how young I was.'

'We guessed you had lied. I think she was flattered.' Her face lightened.

He said, 'Would you like me to show you around while we talk? I hope it might persuade you to stay for a while.'

They walked through his sitting-room, onto the terrace. It was an early Spring day with warm sun, but the air was refreshingly cool. The garden fountains were playing. A few guests were swimming, others were sitting at tables with long, fruit-filled drinks in front of them.

He showed her the new villas, with their little private

pools, the central courtyard, bright with tubs of flowers, palm-trees and climbing plants, the block of exclusive shops, the two new restaurants, and the bars. As they strolled, he noticed heads swivelling to look at her. Though he did not suffer from false modesty, he was unaware that much of the admiration was for the picture they made together, rather than for her alone. Her hair was as fair as his was dark, they were both tall, straight-backed, impeccably dressed. Both moved with the ease and grace of perfect health.

They paused at the top of the steps that led down to the beach, where more people sat under thatched umbrellas.

'How did you find me?' he said. 'This is a hell of a long way from Montjoli.'

'Don't you remember that you told us about San Felipe that night? Not long before my mother died, she said, "Some day, go to Spain and find Max Raven, and tell him that we never forgot what he did for us." So I came, because I had promised myself a holiday.' She looked sideways at him. 'I did not expect it would be so easy, though. When I got off the bus from Malaga, I asked the first person I saw if he knew you. I don't understand very much Spanish, but I think he said, "Everyone knows *El Hidalgo*!" ' There was mockery in the grey eyes.

'It's a silly nickname – but I rather enjoy it, particularly as it annoys the real lord of the manor!' He paused to greet a passing guest with genuine and flattering warmth, then said, 'Well? Have you made up your mind?'

'I would like to stay for perhaps a week, if you will let me.'

'Of course. And then what?'

'Back to Paris. I've been a *vendeuse* with Dior for the past twelve months, but I was bored with it, so I left. I must find another job.'

'Find one here,' he said impulsively, and instantly regretted the words. He didn't even know this girl, and certainly he did not want her to assume that he was prepared to take responsibility for her.

'That would be difficult. I don't speak Spanish well enough.'

'No. Well, you can think about it later.' He changed the

subject, with the uncomfortable feeling that she was reading his thoughts. 'D' you feel like a swim?'

'I'd love one. And I mustn't keep you from your work any longer. Thank you for the tour. I'll go to my room and unpack now, then to the beach.' With some surprise, he realised that she was dismissing him. Véronique Meredith was a girl of independent mind.

'Have dinner with me tonight?' he said.

'I'd like that.' Willing, but not as appreciative as she might have been. He was accustomed to more enthusiasm when he honoured a guest with an invitation. Intrigued, he decided that she might reward closer acquaintance.

They dined at his table in the Spanish restaurant, where he had already ordered the meal. They talked like old friends. She spoke of her mother, of their life together in Paris, of her work. In return, he found himself telling her about his marriage, his return to San Felipe, the formation of Raven Enterprises, and his divorce.

'Were you very unhappy when Nancy and the baby left?' she said.

'In some ways, but it was more regret that I'd made so little effort with Jennifer. Mostly, I felt as though a weight had been lifted. Poor Nancy hated it here, and the kidnapping was the last straw'

'You haven't seen them since?'

'No. I used to send the baby presents. They were never acknowledged. Then I heard that Nancy had married again. He's an accountant who works for her father; it was in *The Times.* I thought it was best not to try and maintain the contact. I hope the accountant is a better father than I was.' He realised that she was the first person, apart from Dan Bredon and Zimmy, to whom he had ever talked freely about his marriage.

'That is sad. But you are no longer unhappy or lonely?'

'I don't have time to be. This is a full-time job. A couple of years after we opened, we were turning people away. We built another hotel at the far end of the village where it is cheaper to stay, but we were still over-booked, and I was having to refuse regulars. Then an old friend of mine, Dan Bredon . . .'

'But I know him,' she interrupted. 'He was with you at Montjoli.'

'Of course. And you even remember his name!'

She sipped her *rioja.* 'I remember everything about that time. He was a little man, with a cheerful face.'

'He's still little and still cheerful. But he's an actor now. He's made some films and lives in Hollywood. He comes here every year. You'll meet him.'

'I'd like that.'

It was only later that he realised they had both talked as though it was a foregone conclusion that her stay would not end after a week.

'He suggested that I should turn this place into a private club, with a limited membership. It costs the earth to join, and I can pick and choose who we accept. We have a waiting-list already.'

She mopped up the last drops of her *gazpacho* and sighed happily. 'I could make a whole meal of that. What comes next?'

'*Ternera a la Sevillana.*'

'Which is?'

'Veal in a sherry sauce with green olives. Then I've ordered a cheese called *Queso di Cabrales* for you to try.'

'I haven't heard of it.'

'It's made from a mixture of goat's and sheep's milk by country people in Asturias and matured for months in mountain caves. I don't think you can get it outside Spain. After that, you are allowed to choose your own pudding.'

Awed, she said, 'Do you eat like this every day?'

'I usually have a plate of *tapas* in my own room.' He looked around the restaurant, and acknowledged waves from several guests who caught his eye. 'I sometimes get a little tired of being on-stage.'

'Have you no place of your own where you can get away?'

'I will have soon.'

'You're buying somewhere else?'

'I'll show it to you after dinner.'

* * *

It was nearly midnight, and a soft glow from lights set under trees and on tall lamp-standards made walking easy as he led her around the back of the hotel. They reached a high brick wall which now divided the hotel grounds from those of the *finca.* He took a key from his pocket and unlocked a door that was set into the brickwork.

He took her hand to help her up a steep, winding path then, when she stumbled, put his arm around her waist.

A building loomed ahead of them, its white-washed walls almost fluorescent under the sickle moon. They stepped up onto a terrace and he pressed a switch. She gasped as floodlights illuminated graceful arches above which a long balcony with lacy, wrought-iron railings extended the length of an upper storey whose walls were almost uninterrupted sheets of glass.

'Turn around,' he said.

With their backs to the house, they looked out to sea. Below them, the Club's gardens were patterns of light, with silhouettes of the trees and shrubs creating mysterious shadows. The fountains winked in spotlights like continuous fire-works. To the left, the lamps of the village were yellow pinpoints spattered on an indigo background.

'It's beautiful,' she said. 'And this is your house?'

'My getaway. It's just finished. I only have to furnish it and then I can move in.'

He unlocked the front door and they walked through the big, airy rooms, with their floors of marble and ceramic tile. She laughed with pleasure at the indoor-outdoor pool that was his special pride.

The only decoration was his father's three paintings of San Felipe, which he had hung in the *salon.* She went from one to the other, spending a few seconds in front of each.

He put his hands on her shoulders and she turned to him. He kissed her for the first time.

Later he was to tell her, not entirely joking, that their relationship had been in the balance until the moment she had reacted to the pictures.

'If you'd mentioned chocolate-boxes, or amateurs, it would have been all up.'

'I've forgotten what I did say.'

'I remember every word. You touched the one of the fishermen on the beach and said that you hoped San Felipe would always be as peaceful as that. But even if it wasn't, I was lucky to have the pictures to remind me how it had been. It was exactly the right thing to say.'

'That was the only reason you decided to marry me?'

'Just about.'

Their wedding took place six weeks after her arrival in San Felipe. A month after that, they moved into the house, which she had decorated with a taste and style that surpassed all his hopes. From the first day, the rooms were never without fresh flowers.

She passed a second test with honours when he took her to meet Zimmy and Titi.

After her experience with Nancy, Zimmy at first treated her with reserve, but when Véronique revealed a voracious appetite for reminiscences about Max's childhood, she dropped all barriers and they became close friends and confidantes. She was vastly amused by the painting of Great Uncle Henry and Mamma Jiminez.

Titi fell instantly in love with her. He visited the hotel often and, when she became pregnant, would sit quietly beside her as she sewed or knitted in the suite at the Club. But he would never visit her in the new house. Any suggestion that he should do so brought the shutters down.

Only Manolo was impervious to her charm and his undisguised hostility was the one small cloud on her horizon. Not wanting to worry Max, she discussed it with Zimmy, who told her to ignore it.

'He's jealous, is all,' she said sagely. 'He regards himself as second only to Max in Raven Enterprises. He thinks you've usurped his place, and he doesn't like it.'

'That's absurd! Max turns to him all the time.'

'I know, and it worries me. Max feels that he owes a lot to Manolo. I sometimes wonder if Manolo's loyalty is as strong as his.'

'Surely it must be. Max has done so much for him. He told me once that Manolo's home before he came to the hotel was a cave in the hills.'

'His mother was a prostitute – not, you understand, that I condemn that, but she was of a type to give the profession a bad name – and he lived by begging and stealing. He attached himself to Max, I think, because he knew that he was going to be a success. Manolo is interested only in his own advancement.'

'I'm sure he would never do anything to hurt Max. I just wish he'd realise that I have no intention of taking his place.'

It was Paul's birth, in 1955, which eased the tension because, for the first few years at least, Véronique spent much of her time with him at the house and Manolo felt he was maintaining his position.

Max was steadily improving the Club and, unique of its kind at that time, it was increasingly attracting the rich, famous and titled from all over the world. He never gave up his right to control the membership and money or social position was no guarantee of acceptance.

He added a gymnasium and a casino, bought a couple of power-boats for water-skiing, built three hard tennis-courts, and started planning a golf-course. In summer, he organised aquatic festivals, when villagers, tourists and Club members competed in water-sports. For local colour, he regularly imported troupes of flamenco dancers from Granada, hired world-famous guitarists for recitals and bought blocks of seats for the bull-fights in Malaga, Seville and Granada.

Manolo pressed him to cash in on the exploding tourist market by building blocks of holiday apartments. This had indeed been part of his original plan, and the reason why he had bought up virtually all the available land around the village, but Véronique was unenthusiastic.

'It would be a pity to spoil this place with great concrete fingers growing out of the cliffs,' she said. 'With the Club and the hotel, we have enough visitors, without overcrowding the village.'

Because his life was so full and contented, he agreed with her. Manolo made no attempt to hide his displeasure. He had succumbed to the lure of the casino and regularly lost his salary there. Without its topping up from fiddles he could organise when new projects were under way, he felt himself hard done by.

Those years after his marriage were the happiest of Max's life. Sophisticated, witty, gregarious, uninhibited in her attitude to sex, Veronique was everything Nancy had not been. They were friends as well as lovers, and she was the only person with whom he felt totally relaxed, and from whom he had no secrets. He had admitted the affairs he'd had after Nancy left, and found her unmoved. 'All I would ask is that if you sleep with other women after we are married, I am not told about it,' she said. He was never to put her tolerance to the test.

She persuaded him to take holidays, something he had not done since his return to Spain, and they went to London, Madrid, Paris, Vienna. She loved music, and introduced him to the great symphonies and operas, infecting him with her enthusiasm.

In return, he taught her to play tennis and water-ski, and she was soon as proficient as he.

Sometimes, on a summer evening, they would sit on their balcony, drinking champagne and watching the lights come up as they listened to *Bachianas Brazilieras* or Victoria de los Angeles singing old Spanish songs. With Paul asleep in his room behind the plate glass, Max knew that this was happiness, and could see no reason why it should ever end.

Part 7

The Present

Paul was trying to make sense of Raven Enterprises' balance sheets for his daily report to Max when Marian told him a delegation from the village wanted to see him.

He looked up impatiently. 'What kind of a delegation? Christ, Marian, these things might as well be in Arabic!'

'I'll go through them with you later.' Trim and elegant as always, in a brown shirt and white linen skirt, she said, 'I think you should see them. I suspect it's about the Campo Negro.'

'Okay, but I don't know what I can tell them. I haven't been able to talk to Max about it yet.'

They followed her into the office and stood awkwardly in front of the desk: two small men in dark blue work clothes, berets squarely on their heads. He noticed that they had both shaved in honour of the occasion. Neither looked friendly, neither offered to shake hands.

He looked at the older man. ' I know you, don't I? Hey, it's Eduardo, surely!'

The man nodded. He had been a gardener at the Club, and Paul, as a small boy, had trailed around behind him, 'helping' by trundling his wheel-barrow and gathering up pelargonium prunings. The high spot of his day had been when he had sometimes been allowed to snip off dead-heads. He had always got on well with Eduardo, but there was no recognition of the former relationship in the man's cold eyes.

Paul tried again. 'It's good to see you. How's the family?'

He ignored the question and indicated the younger man. 'This is my nephew, Jesús.'

Jesús nodded sullenly. He was examining the luxurious office with undisguised antagonism.

Into a brief silence, Paul said, 'What can I do for you, Eduardo? I understand you're a – delegation.'

'It's about the Campo Negro, Senor.'

'I thought it might be. Before you go on, I have to tell you that I'm not involved in my father's plans. I've heard that he wants to develop the site, but he's been too ill to talk about it. Any discussion will have to wait until he's better.'

'The Campo is a shrine! It would be like dishonouring a church . . .'

Jesús broke in impatiently. 'It's not only that. We have told Machado that no one in the village will work on the project. Yesterday we heard that he is arranging to bring in outsiders. We won't allow it! If necessary, we'll fight to keep them away.'

Surprised, Paul said, 'As far as I know, Machado has no right to do anything of the kind. You know very well that my father has always insisted on work going to local men.' But does he still, he wondered? Things had changed during the past ten years. He went on slowly: 'I told you this was none of my business, and it isn't. All I can say is that I'm not in favour of developing the Campo, either. I promise that I'll put your case to my father as soon as he's well enough.'

'You'll support us?' Eduardo insisted.

He felt as though a net was closing around him. Whatever his personal feelings, this wasn't his fight. 'I'll speak to Senor Max. That's the best I can do.'

'And Machado?'

'I'll talk to him, too.'

The younger man said, 'Talking won't be enough! *El Hidalgo* . . .' There was a sneer in his voice. '*El Hidalgo* and Machado have thought they could run San Felipe for too long. Maybe in the old days, but there's a new generation now. This is *our* country, and we're tired of foreigners arranging our lives.'

Marian appeared as they left.

As he finished describing the interview, Paul frowned and added: 'There's something about Jesús I should remember, but I'm damned if I know what it is. I don't think I've seen him before, but . . . Eduardo's nephew? Hell, yes! The builders who were killed a couple of years ago . . .'

It had been a wet morning in London, and the weather was holding up the projects on which he and Alan were working.

He was flicking moodily through *The Times* when a filler at the bottom of a page had caught his eye:

> Two builders were killed when a balcony on a British-owned block of flats collapsed in the Spanish holiday resort of San Felipe del Mar. The building, still under construction, is owned by Raven Enterprises, one of the major development companies on the Costa del Sol. It is believed that faulty cement, allegedly used in an effort to cut costs, caused the tragedy. The company's chairman, Maxwell Raven, said the accident was being investigated.

He read it aloud, and Alan had commented: 'That's not going to do your father's image much good.'

'You're right. Curious, though. It's not like him to skimp on materials. He's always been pretty fierce about keeping up building standards.'

A week later, he had received a letter from Loretta: 'You will probably have read about our local scandal. The newest block of apartments was to have been the jewel in Max's crown, but it seems that some cowboy contractor named Rodrigo Leon, hired by Machado, used cement that had too much sand mixed in it. I don't know the technical details, but that apparently makes it dangerously crumbly. Two brothers, Pepe and Pedro Azano, were killed when the fourth-floor balcony on which they were working, broke away from the wall.

'There's a lot of resentment because of it, but it was really nothing to do with Max. The contractor seems to have disappeared and Machado's making all kinds of threats about what he'll do to him when he gets his hands on him. In the meantime, Max has paid substantial compensation to the boys' family.'

Paul said, 'The men who were killed were Jesús's brothers, weren't they?'

Marian nodded. 'You were lucky not to be here. People said Max should have taken more safety precautions.'

'Surely, if anyone was to blame, apart from the contractor, it was Manolo.'

'Oh, they blamed him as well, but it was Max's project. Zimmy told me once that they'd never really forgiven him.'

'What happened to the contractor? Was he sued?'

'No. That was another extraordinary thing. He disappeared, and a few weeks later his body was found on the rocks at the bottom of a cliff to the east of the village. He was half in, half out of his car, which had been smashed to pieces. Apparently he'd committed suicide.'

'Couldn't take the guilt?'

'I suppose so. It was the beginning of the deterioration of our relations with the people here. If it hadn't been for that, they might not be so hostile to the new project.'

'I must see Manolo as soon as possible. D'you think Max told him to hire outside labour?'

'I can't imagine it. He didn't say anything to me, and he never has in the past.'

'Is Manolo on the premises?'

'I'll send someone to look for him.'

But Manolo couldn't be found, and no one knew where he was.

An hour later, Paul was driving Zimmy to the hospital to see Max.

He had told her about the visit from the Azanos, and she had agreed that his father must hear about it as soon as he was well enough.

They were on a narrow stretch of coast road which had been cut into the face of a cliff, with the sea on their left. Paul was enjoying the wind in his face when, from the corner of his eye, he saw an object hurtling down towards them. There was no room to swerve. His reaction, pumping the brake to prevent a skid, was instantaneous. Had he been a fraction slower, the brick would have hit either himself or Zimmy. As it was, it exploded on the car in front of him, pieces breaking off and flying against the wind-screen. When he came to a halt, there was a deep dent in the bonnet, the paint was cracked and striated.

Impelled by rage, he leapt out of the car and clambered up the steep, rocky rise. When he reached the top, two figures, running at full pelt, were disappearing into a grove of trees a couple of hundred metres ahead of him.

He was shaking when he returned to the car. 'Are you all right? My God, they could have killed us!'

Zimmy was calmer than he.'Did you see who they were?'

'They were too far away, but I think they were kids. I'd like to beat the bloody daylights out of them!'

Relieved that the car did not seem to have suffered any internal damage, he started the engine. When they reached the wider road that covered the last few kilometres to the hospital, Zimmy said thoughtfully, 'This is a distinctive car, Paul. Everyone in the village knows it belongs to Max.'

'So?'

'So I wonder if this was something more than silly little boys throwing stones at anyone who happened to be passing.'

'You mean it was *meant* for us? Why? And who'd have known that we'd be there at that moment?'

'It couldn't have been planned. But parents talk in front of their children. It could be that some village boys were playing on the cliff, and when they saw the car, they decided to show their disapproval of Max's plans for the Campo Negro by frightening his son.'

'They achieved that.'

'Is Max well enough to be worried by all this?'

'He's getting better every day. His diction's clearer, and the paralysis isn't as bad as it was. The trouble is, he doesn't seem to care about anything. I tell him what's going on at the Club, and he falls asleep – or pretends to fall asleep. I'm never sure.'

'Has he been seeing many people?'

'The nurses have told me Manolo's been there every day, asking to see him. They finally gave him a few minutes yesterday, after asking Max's permission. I don't know what they talked about. I just hope that Max didn't order him to go ahead with the development.'

'Didn't you ask Manolo whether they'd discussed it?'

'I wouldn't even have known he'd been allowed in to see Max if the nurses hadn't told me. He's avoiding me. I asked Max, but he just closed his eyes and said he was too tired to talk. He does tire quickly. You're the first person he's agreed to see. Marian wanted to come, but he said no. She was pretty hurt.'

'She would be. She adores him. Now Loretta's gone, she must be wondering if her chance has come.'

'With Elena around, she hasn't a hope,' he said grimly.

'Have you seen Elena yet?'

'No.'

'Why not? At least you could show that you care enough to find out how she is.'

Giving himself away, he said, 'I know how she is. I ask Sister Magdalena every day. Physically, she's better, but she sleeps badly and she has nightmares. She keeps asking the Sisters about Max. They said she was distraught when she heard about the stroke.'

'I still think you should try to see her. I wouldn't be surprised if Rafael had given orders that she was not even to be told you're here.'

'He does hate us, doesn't he? It's only since I've talked to you and Dan Bredon that I've begun to understand why.'

'The feud goes back to when he and Max were children. And then there was his humiliation in Berlin.'

'D'you think it's true that he and his mother cheated Max out of the vineyard?'

'I'm sure of it. Don Luis would never have broken such a promise.'

'It back-fired on them, though,' he said. 'Rafael could never have anticipated that Max would stay and take over his own village.'

He slowed the car as they passed the white cottage which stood outside the hospital entrance. He had become accustomed to the sight of the two peaceful old men he had noticed on his first visit, sitting in the sun on their terrace. There were worse places, he thought, to spend one's declining years. Today their chairs were empty and the door that led into the house was closed. He spared them a passing thought, hoping all was well with them.

Max was propped up on pillows. Each day now, there was visible improvement in his facial muscles, and his eyes had regained some of their brightness.

Zimmy hugged him, and settled in a chair by the bed, holding his hand. His voice was still slurred, but there was no longer any need for him to use the pen and pad.

The three of them chatted generally for a few minutes, and Paul made his report on the Club. It wasn't until he said, 'We have to talk about the Campo Negro,' that Max seemed to sag.

'Not now.'

'We must! The whole village is turning against us. Nobody wants a development there. Old Eduardo Azano and his nephew, Jesús, came to see me about it this morning. Some kids even slung a brick at Zimmy and me as we were on our way here.'

His interest sharpened. 'Anything happen to my car?'

'Nothing that can't be fixed. But that's beside the point: we want you to cancel the project.'

He looked to Zimmy for support. 'I really don't feel up to discussing business. You deal with it.'

She said, 'Paul, it's too soon. He's not well enough. It can wait for a few days.'

Max's eyes closed, but Paul was no longer prepared to be sympathetic. 'He was bright enough a few minutes ago. He does this every day! As soon as anything important is mentioned, he goes into a slump.' He glared at his father. 'Right. Well, if he won't make a decision, I will. I'm telling Victoria the deal's off.'

The eyes snapped open. 'You'll do nothing of the kind! I want that land. You'll go ahead right *now* and give her a cheque.'

'Do I detect a recovery? So maybe we can talk about it like reasonable people. Zimmy, tell him what you think.'

'I'm sure it would be a mistake, my dear,' she said. 'You have no idea of the opposition. People don't want the Campo Negro vandalised.'

'Who said it would be? It's the land I want.'

'Then what's all the fuss about?' Paul said. 'Loretta told me you brought people out from England to do a feasibility study. You've had plans drawn up – I saw them in your file. And Manolo's said to be hiring out-of-town labour. Everyone's talking about it.'

'Maybe I've changed my mind. I haven't decided yet. But I still want that land.'

'For God's sake, why?'

A smile lit the mobile side of his face, so that it looked like a comedy-tragedy mask. There was little trace of weakness as he tapped one finger after another on the quilt. 'One, because it will get Victoria off my back. She's become a liability at the Club. Two, it will buy her that drunken tennis-player – though why she should want him, I can't imagine. Three, I don't want anyone else to have it, and four, it will annoy the hell out of Rafael and Doña Maria.'

'But you might not develop it? Have you told Manolo?'

'All I've told him is that you're in full charge. That you're making the decisions now.'

'No! You're not conning me that way! I'm leaving the minute you're on your feet. Or even in a wheel-chair. My limit here's a month. After that, whatever your health, I'm going back to England and you can take your own chestnuts out of the fire.'

As though he could no longer summon the energy to argue, Max said wearily, 'Just handle this one thing for me. Give Victoria whatever she's asking for the Campo Negro.'

There was a knock at the door, and Sister Magdalena appeared, in a flutter of controlled agitation. 'Senora, could you come for a moment? The doctor would like to see you.'

A look Paul did not understand passed between Zimmy and the nun, but her movements were unhurried as she kissed Max. 'May I come again?'

'As soon as you can. Bring Loretta next time. Maybe she'll be able to stand looking at me now.'

Paul wondered whether this was the moment for them to break the news that Loretta had left, but Zimmy had already followed Sister Magdalena, so he decided to say nothing.

He turned back to the bed. 'I'll see you tomorrow, and I'll

try to fix things with Victoria this evening. What should I tell Manolo?'

'Whatever you think best. Have you seen Elena Ansaldo yet?'

The question was so unexpected that Paul took a moment to answer. 'No. I don't intend to.'

'Why not?'

'I'd have thought the reason was obvious. I'm not going into competition with you.'

For a moment, he thought his father looked surprised, then a satiric gleam came into his blue eyes. 'You give up quickly. There she is, lying helplessly in her room, and here I am, no good to any woman. If you want her, why the hell don't you fight for her? You've had it too easy all your life!'

'I've had it easy? Shit, you've always made everything as difficult as you could for me!' He paused, then he said: 'You don't love Elena, do you? I think you only moved in on her to hurt Rafael. So maybe I *will* fight you. You've asked for it.'

This time, instead of passing her door as he was on his way out, he knocked. There was no reply. He waited, then opened it. A few fading flowers drooped in vases, but the bed was empty.

He stopped a nurse who was hurrying along the corridor.

'The Senora was discharged this morning, senor,' she said. 'Don Rafael took her home.'

All thought of the village's problems were relegated to the back of his mind as his determination to take up his father's challenge hardened. But Rafael would never allow him into the house. He'd have to find some other way to see her.

He was still exploring possibilities when he walked out of the hospital. Unusually, the reception desk had been deserted and as he looked around, he saw Zimmy limping along the drive towards the gates, flanked on either side by a nun. Dr Sanchez was jogging ahead. Three white-jacketed male nurses were converging on them from different directions.

He broke into a run, and caught up with them as they reached a gate which led into the back garden of the cottage where the two old men lived.

Shouts for help were coming from inside. Sanchez took a

key from his pocket, unlocked the gate and everyone followed him around to the front door. He flung it open. Taller than the other men, Paul looked over their heads at a scene of devastation: upturned furniture, shards of glass and china on the tiled floor, broken pot-plants, scattered soil, pictures torn from the wall.

In a corner, half-hidden by an upturned table, flailing an umbrella to protect himself, was one of the old men, his glasses askew on the end of his nose.

The other was crouched threateningly in front of him, supported by a crutch under one arm. His hands were outstretched, the fingers curved. His face was distorted and there was no mistaking his intention to attack.

Two of the male nurses plunged forward, but Zimmy told them sharply to stop. At the sound of her voice, the aggressor turned, lips drawn back from his teeth in an animal snarl. Paul started towards her, but Sanchez grabbed his sleeve. 'Leave her,' he whispered. 'She can manage him.'

She reached the old man. 'It's all right, *querido*,' she said. 'It's all over. I'm here.' Gently, she stroked his head.

He looked up at her, then, slowly, his face smoothed out. When he straightened, he peered around as though uncertain where he was: a gaunt figure with sunken eyes and long, thin strands of white hair almost covering his ears. Despite the day's warmth, he was shivering. Zimmy put her arm around him as his quarry emerged from shelter.

She turned to the watching group. 'You can leave us now. Will you send someone to clear up this mess, Sister Magdalena? Paul, bring the car to the gate.'

The rest of the party were already on their way out as he backed towards the door.

'Are you sure . . .?'

'I'm all right. I won't be long.'

When she emerged, he was waiting outside the cottage. Helping her into the passenger seat, he said, 'Are you going to tell me what that was all about?'

'First, we go back to your house, where you will give me a drink. It always takes me a little time to recover.'

'Always?'

'This happens about twice a year, usually around the same time, the anniversaries . . .' She put her head back against the seat. For the first time, she looked her age, but she was still able to smile. 'When I have a brandy in my hand, I will be better.'

He settled her in an arm-chair overlooking the indoor pool, and poured her a stiff drink, a lighter one for himself. The sun was coming in through the open French windows and he could hear bird-song in the trees outside. The violence he had just witnessed could have been a dream.

After a few minutes, as the brandy brought life back to her face, he could contain his curiosity no longer. 'Who *are* those two?'

'They are my brother, Esteban, and his friend, Gregorio.'

Bewildered, he stared at her. 'But your brother died years ago!'

'We thought he had. For forty years, as far as I knew, he was dead. Then he came back . . . you want me to tell you about it? You have time?'

'Of course I have. I can't believe it! All I know about your brother is that he was the illegitimate son of Max's great-uncle Henry. I wouldn't even have remembered his name.'

'Why should you? He was gone before you were born. My poor Esteban . . . his war lasted too long.'

She began the story slowly, but her voice gained strength as she progressed, her eyes looking past him, back over the years.

'The night your grandparents died, Max was staying with me, in that small room over the Bar, where you slept sometimes when you were a little boy.

'I was going to bed when I heard someone tapping at the door downstairs. It was Andrew, and he was very agitated. He told me that Esteban was at the *finca*, badly injured, and he wanted me to bring Burro. He had to get to a boat that was going to take him up the coast to join the Republican forces. Andrew said he couldn't walk, but he thought he could ride the donkey. In those days, of course, almost nobody here owned a car.

'Esteban and his men were leaving. They had been conducting a guerrilla war from the hills against the Fascist Nationalists, but they'd decided that they could be more effective as part of a larger group. In those days, Paul, the political tension was almost unbelievable. The Falangists, known as Nationalists, were on one side; the Republicans, many – but not all – of whom were Communists, were on the other. Here, most of them had known each other all their lives, but every single one would have killed his own brother for supporting the opposition. Many of them did. Someone, we never found out who, had told the Nationalists that Esteban and his little army were going to move. When they came down from the hills, on their way to the coast, there was an ambush, and he had been shot. He didn't know what had happened to his friends.

'Although he was wounded in the thigh, he had managed to reach the *finca*, where your grandparents took him in. He was bleeding, and Andrew said Moira had nearly fainted when she saw this figure standing outside in the darkness, its bloody hand reaching out to them. Fortunately, your father was staying with me, and he was sound asleep.

'Andrew and I went back with Burro. Moira had been looking after Esteban, and we helped him up onto the donkey. He was in pain, but we knew that if he didn't get to the boat, he would be killed.

'Andrew insisted on coming with us. There was no moon, and the path was rough. It took us a long time to reach a little cove where the fishing-boat was waiting, because we had to keep stopping to make sure no one was following. We were just in time.

'He was taken on board, then we came back. Andrew said goodnight to me at the Bar, and walked home.

'I was very tired. I went to bed, and slept heavily. It wasn't until the next morning that I heard about the fire. Max said later that he had woken up and had seen the smoke, without suspecting where it came from. All I can guess is that when Andrew went into the *finca*, he must have knocked over an oil lamp and it set fire to some paint or wood shavings. His body was found in the studio, and Moira's was near him.' She shivered. 'I still think about it sometimes, when I can't sleep. If I hadn't let him come with us, he wouldn't have died. I had to break the news to Max.'

She held out her glass and he poured her another drink. 'Go on about Esteban.'

'It was a long time before I heard from him. I thought the boat might have been attacked, or perhaps he had died from his wound. But then a letter came, to say he was with a Republican force in Catalonia.

'I heard nothing after that, until one of his friends came here and told me that he had been killed during an air-attack on a little town near where they were camped. Juan had seen Esteban fall. He had himself been shot and had to lie for hours before he was found.

'In fact, a bomb splinter had penetrated Esteban's stomach, but he had been dragged into a cellar by a local man. Eventually, he was taken to a field hospital, and for weeks the doctors thought he would die. When he recovered, he went back to the front.' Her face was bleak. 'It should never have been allowed, but his people needed every man. He's vague about that period of the war. I think much of the time he must not even have been aware of what was going on, except for the killing. He told me that he can still see in his mind faces of the men he killed. His stomach wound reopened and had to be stitched up again, but he kept going.

'And in the long run, it was all for nothing. At the beginning of 1939, he was with the remnants of his force near the French border. The Falangists had won the war. Republicans were pouring towards the border, desperate to escape reprisals. At first the French didn't want them, then they said only civilians and wounded men could cross, but in the end they had to allow everyone in, knowing that otherwise they would all have been killed.

'Esteban found himself in a refugee camp. There was no shelter, no water, no food. They were like prisoners, surrounded by barbed wire and guarded by black French troops from North Africa.

'But he made friends with a young Basque named Gregorio Aguirre. They decided to leave the camp together and make their way back to Aguirre's family, peasants who raised sheep for milk in the mountains not far from the French border. Gregorio said they would be safe there.

'They walked, travelling at night, hiding from the Falange during the day. It took them weeks to reach the farm. It was little more than a stone hut, tucked away in the hills, a long way from civilisation, but Esteban was happy there. He told me he found peace for the first time in years. And Gregorio . . .' She hesitated briefly: 'With the freedom today, I need not be shy about these matters: Gregorio and Esteban became lovers. When I learnt about it, I was not too surprised. Esteban had never shown any interest in girls. And I was happy that he had found someone to look after him.

'He meant to come home, meant to write, but the time passed, and he recovered slowly from his wounds, both of the body and the mind.

'In that same year, the other war broke out, which was none of his business, and he never thought to be mixed up in it. All he wanted was to tend the sheep and be with Gregorio.

'But one day, some Frenchmen came. They were setting up an escape route for Allied airmen who had been shot down, Jews, members of the French Underground who were on the run from the Germans. Guides were needed to lead them over the mountains into Spain.

'Gregorio and Esteban agreed to help. It wasn't for money: what Esteban remembered was those German airmen who had machine-gunned women and children. The Germans had fought on the side of the Falange, so in a way, he reasoned, this new war was his.

'He and Gregorio went backwards and forwards over those mountains, in deep snow and in the hot summers, leading men into safety. Sometimes they had to carry them on stretchers because they were unable to walk. I don't know how many they rescued. I often wonder if there are still some alive in England or America who remember them.

'One night, they were in charge of two Americans who had been shot down near Lyons, and had been passed from one Underground cell to the next, until they reached the border.

'The Germans were angry about the number of escapes,

and had sent extra troops there to try and stop them. Esteban and Gregorio knew this and were pushing their refugees as fast as possible. They were climbing an almost perpendicular, rocky track where snow was falling, when one of the Americans slipped and tumbled back, rolling over and over, sending a river of stones down into the valley. At first, they thought he must have been killed, then they heard him call. Gregorio wanted to leave him, but Esteban said he would go back, while the other two kept moving on.

'He found that the American had twisted his ankle, but he could still walk, with help. They started up the track again, with Esteban half carrying him. It was very slow, and they displaced more stones.

'They were nearly at the top when there were shots from behind them. One killed the American. He was holding on to Esteban, and he dragged him down, so they both slid back. The Germans, who had been attracted by the falling stones, were waiting for them.

'They took Esteban for questioning. They wanted details of the escape routes, so they tortured him. He had to give Gregorio time to reach the border, and he stayed silent for as long as he could. Finally, they twisted wire around his toes, and hung him, head down, from a tree branch. Then he talked.

'The next day, Gregorio came back for him. He knew ways across the mountains that would never be found. Esteban was lying under the trees, almost naked, freezing. The wire was still around his toes. Gregorio carried him to a hiding place and found two other Spanish guides to help him. Eventually, they got him to a doctor. Gangrene had set in on his left foot and his toes had to be amputated.

'When he was well enough, Gregorio took him back to the farm. But what he suffered had affected his mind. He started to take what Gregorio calls his "fits." Sometimes he would be found wandering miles from the hut they lived in, with no idea how he got there. Other times, he would think that he was still fighting a war, and that everyone was his enemy, to be attacked and killed. That's what you saw today.

'But Gregorio loved him. They went on living together in

the same hut, tending their sheep. Esteban lost the will to come home. He only wanted to be left alone.

'That lasted until, as they grew old, he began to talk about San Felipe. Life was hard in the mountains, and all the other Aguirres had died off, so Gregorio decided to bring him back. Out of the blue, I had a letter, saying they were coming. A letter from the dead! Can you imagine how I felt?' She paused. 'I think he has been happy here. And we know now how to deal with his fits.

'They happen around the anniversaries of his escape from San Felipe, and of his torture. And the sight of violence – youngsters fighting, even in fun – can bring one on.'

'Surely it's dangerous for Gregorio to live with him?'

'I think, without Esteban to look after, and worry over, Gregorio would die. They have been like husband and wife for a long time. After they'd been here for a few months, Max built them that little house. They're watched over by the hospital staff. There are bells in every room, so in a crisis Gregorio can call for help.'

She reached for her stick and levered herself to her feet. 'I am hoarse with talking! But I think it has done me good to face again what happened, and know it is all in the past. Thank you for listening, my dear. Will you take me home now?'

He linked his arm in hers and they walked to the car. He said, 'Does Max ever see Esteban?'

'Of course! They see each other two or three times a week. Your father is the kindest and most generous of men, Paul, not only with money, but with his friendship.'

'I've never thought of him as kind. Sometimes I have a feeling you and I are talking about different men.'

'You only see him as your domineering father, whom you think neglected you when you were a child. Has it ever occurred to you that, however misguidedly, he was trying to protect you? So many people he loved had died tragically. He told me once that after Véronique's death, he thought he went a little mad, because he found himself wondering whether he was a – what is it in English? – bringer of bad luck.'

'A jinx?'

'. . . on the people around him. He was afraid to be too close to you. There was another thing: you were so like your mother that for a long while he found it painful even to look at you. When he finally readjusted to life without Véronique, you were no longer friends, and he didn't know how to undo the damage.'

As they drew up outside her house he said abruptly: 'He told me I should fight him for Elena – as though she's a ribbon to be won in a horse-race.'

'With men, I am told, a fight can clear the air, and this is one Max deserves to lose. Women spoil him, Paul. He thinks he has only to crook his little finger and they come to him. Unfortunately, he is usually right. But I've noticed that even when he tires of them, he manages to keep their friendship. He's never cruel.'

'Loretta might not agree with you.'

'Her misfortune was that he married her. The only wife he ever really wanted was Véronique. Loretta should have remained his mistress.'

Before leaving her, he said, 'I'll like to go and see Esteban one day. Is it allowed?'

'Of course. I was going to suggest it. He isn't a prisoner. He often goes up to the Club to see Max. It's unlikely there will be another fit for months. He'd love you to visit him.'

As he drove off, Paul was uncomfortably aware of a need to answer a few questions about himself. Had he been too quick to condemn Max for an apparent lack of affection? Had he been too self-absorbed in his own grief after his mother's death, to try to understand what Max must be suffering? In each case, he had to admit, the answer was yes. For the first time, he found himself regretting wasted years. Maybe if he'd been less selfish, he and his father would have become friends, instead of challenging each other at every turn. But there was still the most important challenge to be met: Elena. Somehow, he had to see her. His problem was how to break through the Ansaldo cordon.

He had reached the plaza without solving it when his eye was caught by the ugly depression in the car's bonnet. A Guardia patrolling the street directed him to a mechanic who, he said, was the best on the coast, and would rent him a car until the Porsche had been resprayed.

The repair shop was about fifteen kilometres inland. The road was empty and he was able to put his foot down. The car leapt forward like a released cheetah and the tension in his mind relaxed in the exhilaration of speed.

Half-an-hour later, in a small rented Seat, he was driving back along the same route at a more sedate pace, able to enjoy the scenery. White villas studded the landscape, many of them as spectacular as Max's house, others smaller, with red-tiled roofs, set among olive trees.

On a slight rise, a few kilometres out of San Felipe, he noticed a large villa with a terrace into which a swimming-pool was set, with loungers and sun-umbrellas around it. His eye was caught by two blondes who were sauntering out of the house. They were a spectacular sight, with pneumatic breasts bursting out of bikini tops that were little more than strips of ribbon, narrow waists and swelling hips below which two tiny v-shaped pieces of fabric were tied together with strings. And to think that not too many years ago public notices in the village used to direct female visitors to remain decently covered at all times. Even sleeveless dresses and shorts had been frowned upon, he remembered.

He slowed the car to a crawl and watched the girls move sinuously towards two men who were sitting under an umbrella, with drinks on a table in front of them. One was wearing swimming-trunks over which his fleshy stomach drooped, and sun-glasses. The other, in a crumpled grey suit over an open-neck shirt was – Paul blinked to make sure he was not mistaken – Manolo Machado.

Because their eyes were fixed on the girls, they did not see the Seat pass.

'Who lives in that big villa to the west of the village, with the raised sundeck and pool in front?' Paul asked Marian.

'Blue and white umbrellas? Blondes?'

'That's the one.'

'It belongs to our token villain – every village on the coast seems to have one. They're mostly English and they managed to bring out ill-gotten fortunes one jump ahead of the police. Ours is said to have been the Mr Big behind a bank-robbery. Wayne Bridger.' She saw recognition in his eyes. 'You know him?'

'Not personally. Loretta pointed him out at the airport. How come Manolo knows him?'

'I didn't realise he did. But he came here once or twice before Max found out who he was and banned him. I suppose Manolo met him then.'

'They must be pretty friendly. They were drinking together this morning on Bridger's terrace.'

'That's curious. Max wouldn't be pleased to hear that.'

'Loretta told me Bridger had tried to buy the Club.'

'Max wouldn't take him seriously. He was very annoyed. Incidentally, did you talk to Max about the development this morning?'

'He insists on buying the land, but he said that he might – only *might* – have changed his mind about building on it. He kept saying I should deal with it, but I'm damned if I know how. I mean, suppose I announce that there won't be any development, and he changes his mind back again? That could cause even more trouble. I suspect he's trying to get me so deeply involved here that I'll decide to stay and run the bloody business for him. Well, I'm not going to!'

She spoke like a nanny soothing a petulent child. 'It's because he's ill, and maybe he's wondering whether he'll ever be well enough to cope by himself.'

'He's well enough already . . . when it suits him.' He fiddled absently with some papers that were lying on the desk.

'That's your programme for the rest of the day.' She smoothed a sheet that he had pushed out of place.'I've put aside an hour to talk finance; you have several meetings; then cocktails with Lord and Lady Rogers at eight. And the Hon. Caroline has been looking for you.'

'She can wait. So can everything else. I want some lunch. Join me?'

When she had ordered their lunch, she said, 'In spite of the damage he's been accused of doing to this part of the coast, Max really does love San Felipe and the people. He could have finally realised that there's something about the Campo that means more to them even than the gratification of *El Hidalgo*. He might think it's only superstition, but he would never want to hurt them.'

'I hope you're right,' he said.

At eight o'clock, he left the Rogers' villa party, wondering how his father managed to endure such gatherings night after night. Most of the older guests in the Club had been invited. High-pitched, strangled English vowels fought for attention with nasal American, Australian drawls, German, French, Italian and Greek. He had waved to Dan Bredon, who was amusing one group with tales of Hollywood scandals, acting out all the characters.

He was on his way to the Spanish Bar, where he hoped to find Victoria, when Dan joined him.

'You catch my performance in there?'

'A good audience?'

'Not bad. Except that three of them couldn't understand English and laughed in all the wrong places.'

'Do you go to many of these bashes?'

'As few as possible. I get asked somewhere almost every night, because people know I'll sing for my *sangria*. I only accept when I like the hosts.'

'How can Max stand this sort of thing all the time?'

'Parties? He rarely goes to them.'

Paul frowned. 'Then why the hell am I going? I thought it was obligatory for mine host to put in an appearance. Marian didn't tell me I could refuse.'

'You can, but only if you do it as gracefully as your father. He says no, thanks, with the kind of charm that convinces them having to refuse causes him unbearable disappointment. He has it down to a fine art.'

'He's a hard act to follow.' There was reluctant admiration in Paul's voice.

'He is, indeed. Join me for a drink?'

'Could we make it later? I have to find Victoria Ansaldo.'

'That shouldn't be difficult. She'll be in the bar, or the bar. I'll be in my villa.'

The first person he saw when he entered the bar was Caroline Jarvis. He had written an apology for the unfortunate end to their previous meeting, but since then her only recognition had been a frigid nod in passing. He'd noticed that she was often accompanied by a weary-looking, middle-aged Italian count. Tonight she was alone, and obviously bored. He remembered Marian had mentioned that the Countess was due to arrive that day.

She waved, and this time, there was nothing cold about her greeting. 'Have a drink with me, Paul! It will be a change to talk to someone under forty!'

He felt suddenly sorry for her. Whatever she had expected from this holiday had certainly not been fulfilled. And maybe he could do with some company that would take his mind off Elena, at least for a while. 'I have to see someone first, but what about meeting me for dinner in the French room at about ten?'

Her face lit up. 'I'd love that.'

Victoria was sitting with Paco Orlando and several other people on the far side of the room, so he pushed through the crowd towards them, nodding in response to a dozen greetings.

It was a noisy group, already well-primed with Margaritas and Tequila Sunrises, and he saw that Victoria, if not yet drunk, was on the way.

He tapped her shoulder. 'Could I have a word with you?'

'Darling! How lovely to see you. Come and have a drink.'

'Not now, thanks. Can you spare me a minute? I have a message from Max.'

'How is dear Max?'

'Much better. Let's go to his sitting-room. It's quieter.'

'Not now, darling. I'm with friends.'

'This won't take long.'

'Paulie, dear, you're being very rude. I can't possibly leave.'

He leant towards her and said quietly, 'For Christ's sake, Victoria! It's about the Campo Negro. You don't want the world to hear.'

She looked as though she had no idea what he was talking about, then said, 'But we agreed that there was no hurry about that, didn't we? I'm sure Max's message can wait.'

'We didn't agree anything of the kind. You wanted a decision. I have one for you.'

Deliberately, she turned away and called across the table. 'Paco, glasses are empty! Drinks for everyone.' Then, to the group: 'Isn't it a shame Paul won't have one with us, but we all know how busy he is. We won't keep you any longer, darling.' She presented her shoulder to him and began an animated conversation with her neighbour.

The tennis-player met his eyes and a curious expression crossed his face. Contempt? Triumph? Insolence? Paul could not identify it. He realised that there was no point in making any further attempt to talk to Victoria. She was probably less sober than she appeared. Tomorrow he'd try to catch her before the first drink.

He found Dan Bredon sitting under a palm-tree beside the tiny private pool attached to his villa.

'Help yourself to something. I'm too lazy to get up,' he said.

'Thanks. I stuck to tomato juice at the party. Maybe that's why I found it such a bore, but it's not easy to control your drinking habit in a place like this.'

'Drinking and screwing . . . that's what most of 'em come for.'

'You, too?'

'Hell, no! I get all of that I want in L.A. It's what I come here to get away from.'

'How many times have you been married now, Dan?'

'Three.'

'Any more wives on the horizon?'

'No way. Alimony keeps me broke already. Anyhow, I'm looking for a woman like Zimmy, and I'm afraid the mould was broken after her.'

'Why look for anyone else? Marry her.' He was joking – Zimmy must be rising eighty – but Dan didn't smile.

'I asked her years ago. She wouldn't have me. She was so badly burnt once that she said she didn't intend to go near the fire again.'

'What does that mean?'

'Didn't you ever hear about the time she fell in love? The earth shook.'

'I remember there was some man. I didn't realise it was serious. Come to think of it, it never occurred to me that Zimmy was a woman with an emotional life of her own. She's always been just my surrogate mother.' He paused. 'I'm beginning to realise that I've hardly ever thought of Max, nor Zimmy I suppose, in any context that didn't involve me. Who was the man?'

'He was a chap I'd brought here as my guest. An English writer named Nicholas Maitland. We were working on a screenplay together and he met Zimmy at a dinner-party Max gave.' He smiled reminiscently. 'Remember how he used to invite her to be his hostess? She'd turn up, dressed like a grand lady, and behave like one, too. But if there were any stuffed shirts – or blouses – among the guests, she and Max would make sure that her profession was made known. It amused them both, and Max says he could judge peoples' characters by watching how they reacted.

'Nicholas reacted impeccably. When he discovered she ran the local house of ill-fame, he was neither shocked nor patronising, just genuinely interested, and clearly attracted to her. She was in her fifties then, but looked years younger. Her figure was trim and her skin was like a girl's and her eyes sparkled. Max told me that in her young days she used to wear what she called her "madam-dresses," which were pretty hectic, but she'd given them up, and she was an elegant woman. Sexy with it.

'She fell for Nicholas. He was only supposed to be here for a few weeks, but he managed to spin out the screenplay for nearly three months. They were together most of the time, and I was jealous as hell. They used to go for long walks, and she said later that she'd never talked so openly to anyone except Max. She told him all about herself and her problems and her girls and their clients, and some of *their* problems.

'She thought, from hints he dropped, that he would eventually ask her to marry him, but he left without saying anything, and he didn't even write. She mooned around like a ghost, waiting, though she never whined.'

'I wasn't here when the final blow came, but Max told me about it. One day, a book arrived in the post for her. It was called *Twilight Sunshine*, and had a sub-title: "A frank, witty account of life with a Spanish madam." It was, of course, written by Maitland, and it detailed everything she'd told him, everything they'd talked about, everything they'd done together. She was shattered, didn't come out of her room for days. The final insult was that he dedicated it "to Zimmy, with gratitude." '

'What a shit he must be!'

'He is, as she then realised, and she was very angry. She told me she found anger is the best possible way to overcome unhappiness.'

'Was that when you proposed?'

'I waited until I thought she'd recovered. I didn't want her on the rebound. But she wouldn't have me. She said that years ago she'd told Max's mother, Moira, that she was looking for a "respectable" man, and one whom *she* could respect. After Nicholas, she decided that such a man didn't exist. She was laughing at herself, but unfortunately, she meant it.' He stretched and swallowed his drink. 'Maybe it's better that we've stayed just friends. I haven't made the greatest husband in the world.'

Paul looked at his watch. 'I've got a date in the dining-room. Thanks for the drink. Having you to relax with makes this place more tolerable.'

'Max is hoping you'll stay on.'

'I know he is, but there isn't a chance.'

As he went to the restaurant to meet Caroline, he was rather regretting his invitation, thinking that he would prefer to be returning to the house to spend the evening drawing up plans for a Sussex barn he and Alan were going to restore. He seemed to have worked hard since the day he arrived in San Felipe, and yet there was nothing to show for it, none of the satisfaction he felt after a day's labour on an old, run-down cottage in an English lane, slowly returning it to its original beauty.

Caroline was awaiting him at his table. She was wearing a white blouse that sagged off one shoulder, showing her newly-acquired tan, a chunky necklace that seemed to be made of nuts and bolts strung on wire – which he guessed had probably cost Daddy the earth – a bunchy black skirt reaching almost to her ankles, and flat ballet shoes. She looked very young. The contrast between her and the varnished, bejewelled wives and mistresses at other tables was dramatic. Rich and spoiled she might be, but so far she retained a freshness and an innocence – or the appearance of innocence – that most of the other women had lost.

She had laid aside the arrogance that had irritated him at their first meeting. Even her voice lost its social affectations and they chatted easily. Her sly dissection of her fellow-guests' characters was often amusing.

As they sat over coffee, he said, 'I'm afraid it must have been a pretty boring holiday for you, without Max.'

She brushed a stray crumb off the table, then said, 'I really was in love in him, Paul. I'd never met anyone like him. He was the best-looking, the most charming . . . every woman who comes here falls for him, you know. Sixty, thirty, his age didn't matter. I had to have him.' She laughed. 'He didn't have a chance! I was here by myself for a few days, and when Daddy arrived, he was furious. He kept saying that Max was old enough to be my grandfather. That's why I couldn't tell him I was coming back this time.' She sighed. 'I have to leave tomorrow, by the way.'

'Sorry it had to turn out as it did. Want a brandy with your coffee?'

'I'd rather have a Tia Maria. But can't we have it somewhere quieter?'

'We could go to Max's suite, if you like.'

'That would be super. I'm having a lovely evening.'

They looked at each other. Her tongue flicked out and she licked her lips, as she had done outside the hospital.

Leaving the restaurant, he put his hand under her elbow and she pressed it to her body, so he could feel the ribs under her soft flesh. There was little doubt, he thought, that if he wanted her tonight, she would be available. But did he? His last attempt to exorcize the memory of Elena, with Loretta, had been disastrous.

She curled up in a corner of the sofa and, as he handed her a glass of Tia Maria, patted the cushions invitingly.

When he sat down, she shifted until she was leaning against him, and lifted her face. Feeling that it was only polite to respond, he kissed her. The tastes of his brandy and her coffee-flavoured liqueur – a drink he particularly disliked – blended unappetisingly. Her lips were soft and yielding and it was, he thought, like kissing a marshmallow. Elena's kisses, on the other hand . . .

To his relief, the question of whether he was prepared to carry the kisses to their logical conclusion was resolved by an imperative knock on the door.

An elderly porter was outside. 'Sorry to interrupt, Senor Paul, but we have a little problem with the Senorita Ansaldo. Could you come?'

'Where is she?'

'We've taken her into the accountant's office.'

He turned to Caroline, and spread his hands in a gesture of resignation.

'I'll wait for you,' she said.

He recognised that this was the kind of determination that must have won her a place in Max's bed. Caro's scrubbed innocence disguised the appetites of a man-hungry piranha.

'I might be away for some time.'

'Never mind. I'll be here.'

He followed the porter to the accountant's office. Victoria was sprawled in a chair, asleep, her mouth open, her legs and arms spread ungracefully. Her unnaturally black hair had come loose and snaked around her head in Medusa strands. Two hefty young waiters were standing beside her.

Paul regarded her with distaste. 'What happened?'

The porter said: 'She was with the tennis-player, and he was talking to another lady. The Senorita Ansaldo thought he was not paying her enough attention, and she slapped him. Senor Orlando then left with the other lady. Senorita Ansaldo started to scream, and Cristobal and Tomas escorted her here.' He added expressionlessly, 'It was much as usual, Senor.'

'This happens often?'

'Perhaps every six weeks or so.'

'So what now? What would my father do?'

'He would call a car, and have her driven home. She has to be carried into her bedroom. I have taken her myself once or twice, but usually the chauffeur is Guilliermo. Shall I call him?'

'They don't wake up the rest of the family?'

'If they hear, they take no notice. They ignore her.'

An idea burst, fully-fledged, into his mind. 'It's late. You needn't disturb Guilliermo. I'll take her home.'

Cristobal and Tomas carried her to his car, and she lay along the back seat. Before driving off, he instructed them to make his apologies to the young lady in Senor Max's sitting-room and tell her that he would not be back tonight.

The windows of the Ansaldo house were dark, most of the shutters were closed, as he pulled up at the door. The porter had described the location of Victoria's rooms on the first floor. She had not stirred and her limbs flopped like a rag doll's as he hauled her out of the car. She was so thin that it felt as though he was carrying a child. It took him a moment to find the right key on the ring she carried in her bag, then for the first time in his life, he entered Elena's home.

A dim lamp burnt on a landing, giving enough light to show him the stairs. 'Turn left at the top, and go along the corridor to the door facing you at the end,' the porter had said.'That is her sitting-room, and her bedroom is beyond it. The rest of the family sleep in another part of the house, I think.'

As a child, meeting him at the wall that separated the two properties, Elena had pointed out her bedroom window. It seemed to him that it must have been near Victoria's. Would she, a visitor now, still be using the same room?

As he mounted the stairs, Victoria began to mumble, repeating Paco's name. He was almost at the top when her body jerked. To prevent himself from losing his balance, he released her feet, which landed on the floor as he reached for the banister. The movement disturbed her drunken sleep and she let out a wail.

'Shut up!' he hissed.

'Where's Paco?'

'He's not here. I've brought you home. For Christ's sake, be quiet!'

'I want Paco!' She began to sob.

He heard movement nearby. A door ahead of him opened. A figure appeared, silhouetted against the light that flooded into the passage.

'Who's there?' A woman's voice.

He stepped into the light.

Elena's eyes were huge as she looked up at him, then at his burden. 'Paul? Is it you? What are you doing here?'

First things first, he thought. 'I've brought Victoria home. She's drunk.'

'We must get her to her room. Hurry, before my father wakes up.'

She opened the door at the end of the passage and he dumped Victoria on the bed. Elena swiftly removed her shoes and pulled a blanket over her, then she whispered. 'Come with me.'

He followed her into the room from which she had emerged, and was able to see her properly. Her thick hair fell around her shoulders. The swelling around her mouth had gone, but her face was still disfigured by a dark bruise on the cheek-bone, and there were contusions along her jawline. She was wearing a pale blue night-gown, cut low at the front, revealing bruising above her breasts. Her left wrist was bandaged.

Suddenly self-conscious, she picked up a robe and put it on, hugging it around her.

They stared at each other, then as he held out his hands, there was a strangled cry behind him. Rafael Ansaldo was standing in the doorway. He was wearing a maroon and silver brocade dressing-gown, his thinning hair was uncombed. He advanced on Paul, a fist doubled up.

'Father!' Elena slipped between them. 'Paul brought Victoria home!'

'Liar! He came to see you . . . creeping into my house . . . treating you like a whore!' The rage had built, and he shoved her aside so roughly that she almost fell.

Towering over him, Paul grasped his arms. 'Stop that!

She's right. I brought your sister home. And if I did want to see Elena, it's none of your damn business! We're not children any more.' Suddenly, he was back at the *feria* in Seville, when he had confronted Don Rafael for the first time.

'Get out of my house!'

'Paul, please . . . I can't bear this!' Tears were running down Elena's bruised face. He stepped back. 'Go away, please,' she whispered.

'I did come to see you,' he said. 'I thought we should talk.'

'Not now. You must go!'

He drove back the few hundred yards to Max's house, his mood matching the darkness that closed around him. There had been a moment of hope then, with Rafael's arrival, it had faded. She had been quick to back up her father. And there had been no welcome on her face when he had appeared, only shock.

So that's it, he thought bitterly, Max has won.

It was dawn before he fell asleep. For years, having given her up as lost to him for ever, he had found it too painful to remember the past. Seeing her, even for a brief moment, had brought it to life and his childhood came rushing back. Then, it had been fun to defy Rafael and Doña Maria in order to meet. Elena had always been there, to talk to, to confide in when things were going wrong, to laugh with . . .

Part 8

1963–1976

1

Paul's first brush with the law came when, at the age of eight, he was arrested.

In many ways, his early childhood had been an echo of Max's: the same freedom, a happy home-life, loving parents. The Club was his playground, and he was made much of by the guests.

His favourite companions were Dan Bredon, whose clowning made him weep with laughter, Titi and Manolo, whom he trailed after like a puppy.

Véronique disliked Manolo, but Max saw no harm in Paul's friendship with him. Reluctantly, she accepted his opinion.

What neither of them knew was that Manolo had become a smuggler.

The sale of tobacco had long been a Government monopoly. Locally-made cigarettes such as Bisonte and Celtas were freely available, but American Chesterfields and Lucky Strikes, when they were obtainable at all, were heavily taxed, therefore beyond the reach of many Spaniards. This gave them a snob value, and a thriving post-war industry had grown up, with fast motor-launches bringing the cartons across from duty-free Tangier. A few miles off-shore, they would be loaded late at night into fishing-boats, and landed in remote coves. Within hours, they were on sale on street-corners all along the coast.

Looking for some way to augment his basic wage, Manolo realised that he had a captive market for smuggled cigarettes in San Felipe, too small a trading-centre for the big dealers to bother about.

The pause in Raven Enterprises' building operations had

left him with time on his hands and it wasn't long before he organised a contact in Tangier and a boat which plied regularly across the Straits. He recruited shop-keepers, who sold the cigarettes from under their counters, and touts, some of them little boys, who would sidle up to visitors, show the corner of a carton, hidden under their jackets, and whisper beguilingly low prices. Such furtive exchanges added spice to holidays, stories to tell afterwards. Local policemen, on whose doorsteps gift-cartons regularly appeared, generally turned a blind eye.

Manolo's Tangier contact was a fat Egyptian named Joseph, who had for years dominated Mediterranean smuggling, moving tons of contraceptives, penicillin and drugs as well as cigarettes. Reasoning that few purchasers of illegal tobacco would dare to complain of irregularities to the Guardia Civil, he added to his profits by replacing some of the packs in the cartons with others containing only sawdust. The substitution was so expert it was virtually undetectable until the purchaser opened the pack. In case anyone should be so untrusting as to check the carton before buying, a couple of genuine packs were left at each end.

Manolo was well aware of the racket, and had made it a condition of his custom that he would handle only cartons that had not been tampered with. This was not because he had any objection to the practice in principle, but it was too risky in a small village. In a crowded city, the distributors could more easily escape should an angry buyer attempt to pursue them.

The business flourished until Joseph made a mistake, and some cartons containing sawdust packs were included in a consignment for San Felipe.

Although Manolo did no direct business with customers, he kept a supply for emergencies hidden in his room at the Club.

One afternoon, he received a telephone call from a distributor who urgently needed several cartons. Unwilling to handle them himself, he cast around for an errand boy. His eyes fell on Paul, who was helping Eduardo in the garden.

'Hey, Pablito!' he called. 'One of the toasters needs repairing. Will you take it to the electrician for me?'

'Okay,' Paul said. It was a nice day, and he could call in and see Zimmy.

He set off, swinging the large, square parcel, which was done up in brown paper. It seemed heavy for a toaster, but he didn't query it.

He handed it over to the electrician and went off to the Bar Jiminez.

He was strolling home an hour later when a *guardia* whom he did not know, dropped a hand on his shoulder. 'I've been looking for you,' he said grimly. 'You're wanted at the *comisaria*.'

Paul was more intrigued than frightened. He knew most of the policemen in San Felipe, but had never been inside the *comisaria*.

When they reached it, he was taken into an office. The first thing he saw, on a wooden table, was a pile of cigarette-cartons, most of which had been torn open. Sawdust was spilling out of them. An angry American in a Hawaiian shirt was standing beside the table.

'Is this the boy?' the *guardia* said.

'That's him. I saw him from the shop. Shit, they go into the rackets early in this country!'

'Where did you get those cigarettes?' the *guardia* said to Paul.

'I didn't get any cigarettes anywhere.'

'You heard: you were seen. Six cartons of Chesters. Where did they come from?'

'I don't know! Manolo just asked me to take a toaster to be mended.'

The *guardia* looked at him in disbelief, but before he could continue the inquisition, another policeman, whom Paul knew as Jorge, arrived.

'*Hola*, Pablito! What are you doing here?'

'You know him?' the first policeman said.

'Sure. It's *El Hidalgo*'s son.'

Jorge translated the exchange for the American.

'And who the hell's *El Hidalgo*?' he demanded.

'Owns most of San Felipe. Runs the Club up on the hill.'

'Well, his son's a swindler! I was told to contact the guy in the electrical shop for cigarettes. He'd run out, but he knew where to get some, so I waited until this kid arrived. Only when I got back to the hotel and opened one of the cartons, I thought there was something funny about the packs. Sawdust! Six out of ten filled with sawdust!'

'But I didn't . . . Manolo gave me the *toaster.*'

'Manolo?' Jorge turned to his colleague and said quietly. 'We'd better talk about this. You're new . . . a few things you should know . . .'

'What's going on?' the tourist said. 'I want my money back!'

'Senor, you took part in an illegal transaction. You are as much at fault as the vendors of the cigarettes.' Jorge added briskly, 'Perhaps we will confiscate your passport . . .'

After a moment's thought, during which he remembered what he had heard about the problems of foreigners who became enmeshed in the Spanish legal system, the American's tone was suddenly conciliatory. 'Well, I won't press charges. After all, he's only a kid. What you do with him is your business . . .' He put his hand in his pocket: 'Perhaps a little contribution to police funds?'

'And what happened then?' Elena was enthralled.

'They put me in a cell and called my father. He gave them money, too, to let me out. He was very angry with Manolo and I heard him saying to my mother that he'd never buy him off again and if he didn't give up smuggling, he'd see that he went to prison.'

'How exciting! Nothing like that ever happens to me,' she said.

He sighed. 'Only Manolo doesn't like me now. He says I've ruined his business and he doesn't want anything more to do with me.'

The two children had been friends since they were six years old, and had called to each other over the wall between the two properties. At first, they had not understood that such contacts were not allowed, but one day Don Rafael found Paul sitting astride the wall. He ordered his daughter away and forbade her ever to talk to any member of the Raven family again. Shortly afterwards, one of his gardeners was observed setting broken bottle-glass into cement on top of the wall.

The only effect of the ban was to make them more cautious. Paul discovered a small cave on the Campo Negro, its entrance hidden by bushes. It was an ideal meeting-place, because the Campo, being Ansaldo property, was one of the few places where Elena was allowed to roam unescorted. Apart from the annual pilgrimage to the shrine, few other people ever went there. If asked about her absence from home, she would say innocently that she had taken some flowers to the Virgin. They would arrange assignations by leaving notes in a hole they had burrowed in crumbling cement between two of the stones in the wall.

Although she didn't complain, Paul realised that she was lonely. She had never known her mother, a frail, aristocratic woman from Madrid whom Rafael had married not long after Max's wedding. Two years later, she had borne Elena, and died.

'I wish I'd known her,' Elena said wistfully. 'Tia Victoria told me she didn't talk much. My papa used to go away often, but she stayed at home. I don't think anyone missed her when she died.'

'They had you instead,' he said practically.

She made a face. 'And Tia Christina, and my cousins.'

He had seen Christina in the village, a fat woman with small eyes and features that were lost in mounds of flesh. Her daughters were equally plain. After her Swiss husband died she had returned to live with her brother until, saying she did not want her daughters to grow up in a backwater, she had removed them permanently to Zurich.

'How do you like Victoria?' he said.

'She's nice. Only sometimes she and my Papa have rows because she goes to your Club. He says it's just a drinking den.'

'It isn't!'

'I know. And Victoria doesn't take any notice of him. She says she has to get away from the *mausoleo* or she'd go mad. What's a *mausoleo*?'

'I think it's got something to do with dead people. Are you

going to come to the Club, too, when you're older?'

'My father would never let me.'

'Do you do everything he tells you?'

'Well . . . mostly.' Then she said apologetically, 'I know he's funny about your family, but I do love him. And he keeps telling me that I'm all he's got.' A sadness, adult beyond her years, disturbed her face. 'Sometimes I'm so sorry for him. My grandmother treats him like a little boy, and Victoria keeps asking him for money. I think he goes to Malaga and Jerez to get away from them. It's awful without him. The house is so quiet and my grandmother's so strict.'

'I can't imagine what that would be like. There are always people around at my place. Only you'll be at school soon, won't you?'

'Papa says I'm going to boarding-school in Switzerland. What are you doing?'

'I'm going to my father's old school in England.'

'We won't be able to see each other for ages!'

'We'll have the holidays.' But he found himself already depressed by the thought of being so far away from her.

For years, Max had promised to take Véronique and Paul to Seville for Holy Week and the *feria* that follows it.

Paul was eleven when the promise was fulfilled.

They stayed in a hotel, which was an excitement in itself, and each morning of Holy Week, there were processions to watch. He was fascinated and frightened by the sinister Brotherhoods, who paraded in their long robes, their faces covered by hoods which rose into points nearly three feet above their heads. Only their eyes showed through two slits. Max explained that they were recreating the last walk of medieval heretics who had been condemned to death by the Inquisition.

There were floats bearing gorgeously-robed and jewelled statues of the Virgin, and the 'Jesus floats', on which men enacted the parts of Roman soldiers, in polished helmets and breast-plates, preparing to carry out the Crucifixion. Since Max, on the whole, supported the Marxist theory that religion is the opiate of the people, and said that his own life was too full to need drugs, Paul's religious education had been minimal, and he remained unmoved by the floats' significance. He thought that the barefoot penitents, carrying heavy crosses and dragging chains from their ankles, some of them beating their bare backs with whips, were rather silly.

The *feria* began after Holy Week and then, like everyone else, the Ravens turned night into day.

They rose late in the morning, to watch parades of magnificent horses, bearing on their backs women in flounced dresses, with combs in their hair, riding side-saddle behind men in flat Cordoban hats, ruffled, lace-trimmed shirts, with leather chaps covering their trousers; and ornate carriages, carrying beautiful girls who waved to them as they passed.

They would not lunch until four in the afternoon, and then, perhaps, go to the bull-fight – without Véronique. She hated it, and after the first time refused to go again, but Paul was dazzled by the colour and spectacle. As an alternative there was the horse-fair, where gypsies spent hours bargaining over horses, mules and donkeys, or one of the little circuses which had been set up in a park on the southern edge of the city, and came from Switzerland, Italy, Germany, even the Orient. There was always something new to see.

In the evenings, they had a permanent invitation to a *caseta* in which the host was Don Francisco Bario, a bodega-owner from Jerez. Every year, rows of private *casetas* were set up along the streets, little houses with walls and roofs of brightly-striped canvas, wooden floors for dancing, and tables laden with food and sherry. Guests came and went, and each evening was one long party.

Paul dropped into the habit of leaving Max and Véronique with their friends while he explored the streets, watching dancers, listening to guitarists and to singers performing the deep flamenco lament, *cante jondo*, enjoying the lights, the noise and the excitement. If Max had given him a few pesetas, he would buy some sugared almonds, a cake flavoured with sesame seeds and aniseed, a pastry, or one of the almost weightless fritters called *bunuelos de viento*. Sometimes he would be invited into a stranger's *caseta* and offered snacks or a glass of fino. There might be other children to talk to, dressed in folk costumes, and he would watch them dancing flamenco patterns as expertly as the professional troupes. He learnt to clap to the changing rhythms, was sometimes persuaded to join the dancers himself. He found, with some embarrassment, that the Sevillanos were fascinated by him: a fair-haired, blue-eyed boy, effortlessly bi-lingual in English and Spanish.

On the third evening of the *feria* he was perambulating as usual when he saw Elena, sitting on a chair in one of the *casetas*. Her thick, dark hair had been drawn up and folded on the crown of her head, where it was held by a tortoiseshell comb into which a red rose was tucked. Her dress was white, polka-dotted in black. The bodice fitted tightly and flared out into flounces at hip level. Each flounce was edged with scarlet. It had never occurred to him that she was beautiful. Now, coming upon her unexpectedly, he decided that, for looks, no girl he had seen could hold a candle to her.

She was sitting with her hands clasped in her lap, eyes down, looking infinitely bored. There were several adults in the *caseta*, all holding *copitas* of sherry. Victoria was among them, but Don Rafael was not.

He sidled close to the *caseta* and whistled softly. She saw him, and a smile spread across her face. She slipped from her chair, made sure that no one was watching, and joined him. Hand in hand, they ran. When they were out of sight of the *caseta*, he said, 'I didn't know you were coming to Seville.'

'I didn't either, but Tia Victoria had this invitation, so my father said I could come, too.'

'You didn't look as though you were enjoying yourself much.'

'We don't do anything except stay in the *caseta*. I asked Tia Victoria if we could go to a circus, but she said there was enough entertainment here. I'm sick of being with grown-ups. Let's go for a walk.'

'Won't your aunt be annoyed when she sees you've gone?'

'I don't care. I'll go back in a little while. She probably won't even have noticed.'

'Where's your father?'

'With his own friends. He doesn't often come with us.'

They wandered through the crowded streets, stopping every now and then to watch the dancing. They ate *churros*, and paused at a tiny street-circus consisting of a couple of tumblers, a juggler and a girl performing on a unicycle.

They reached the walk that ran along the Guadalquivir River, and there were new sights: strings of lights, yachts that had sailed up into the heart of the city and moored by the path. Deck parties were under way on most of them.

'Let's go and look,' she said.

'We should go back.'

'Not yet! We haven't been away long.'

He glanced at his watch. 'More than half an hour. Victoria will be looking for you. Come on!' He pulled her arm, but she tugged herself away.

'No! I'm not going back to those stupid people. You go, if you want to.'

She picked up her flounces and ran along the path, dodging parties of strollers.

He was a few metres behind her when his feet became entangled in the leash of a small white poodle. By the time he had picked himself up and apologised to its owner, she had been stopped by a large man with dark, tightly-curled hair, who was standing at the foot of a gang-way.

As he hurried up, he heard the man say in heavily-accented English, 'You the prettiest little girl in Seville! You gotta come aboard and have a drink with me.'

'Don't!' Paul said in Spanish. 'We must go back.'

'This your boy-friend? What he saying?'

With a defiant glance backwards, she ran up the gang-way. The man followed her. Angrily, Paul went after them.

There were about twenty people on the deck, all holding glasses. They wore garish holiday clothes and several, including Elena's host, reminded him of the rich Greeks he had occasionally seen at the Club. English, in a variety of accents, was the *lingua franca*. Champagne bottles were everywhere. A table was littered with the debris of a buffet supper.

The din of conversation quietened when the curly-haired man raised his voice.

'Look what I got! A Spanish doll!' He swept her up in his

arms and deposited her on the table, where she stood among the dirty plates and glasses and spilled food.

Everyone was looking at her, and suddenly, Paul knew, she was no longer having fun.

A man said, 'Think she's a dancer? Spikka English, baby?'

Although she had English lessons from a governess, and her understanding was adequate, she did not reply. She appeared to be on the verge of tears.

'Probably a gypsy,' said another man. 'Wouldn't be walking around without a chaperone otherwise. Let's see if she can dance. Hey, kid, you do this?' He stamped his feet and clapped his hands in a travesty of flamenco rhythm.

She stepped to the edge of the table and looked imploringly at Paul. He started forward, but the man blocked his way.

'I know what she wants,' he said loudly. 'Money. A Spaniard'll do anything for a few pesetas.' He pulled some coins from his pocket and threw them on the table. There was a burst of laughter as others followed suit. Some of the money hit her, and she cowered away.

An empty champagne bottle stood within Paul's reach. He picked it up by the neck and slammed it as hard as he could onto the knee-cap of the nearest of Elena's tormenters, who gave a howl of agony, and subsided onto the deck. As everyone turned towards him, she slithered to the ground. Paul grabbed her hand and they hurtled down the gangway.

When they stopped running, she was crying. He put his arm around her and drew her into a quiet doorway, where she clung to him, shivering.

'It's all right,' he said. 'I'll take you back to Victoria.'

'I shouldn't have run away! And I shouldn't have gone onto the boat. They were horrible!' He patted her shoulder, rather enjoying the dampness of her tears through his shirt. 'You were so brave,' she whispered. 'What would have happened to us if you hadn't hit that man?'

'Nothing much, I expect.' He remembered the insulting shower of coins and his anger returned. 'I hope I broke his knee.'

'I hope you did, too.' She looked at him with eyes full of admiration. Then she leant forward and he felt her lips touch his cheek. It was the first time she had kissed him.

Suddenly shy, he said, 'We'd better go.'

'Do I look all right?' She smoothed her hair and shook out the ruffles of her dress. The excitement had coloured her olive cheeks and tears clung like dew-drops to her eyelashes.

He swallowed. 'You look beautiful.'

She squeezed his hand. 'Apart from those awful people, this has been the nicest time I've ever had.'

As they approached the *caseta*, she said, 'Don't come any further,' and went ahead.

He saw what she had not: Don Rafael was there, peering along the crowded street, talking angrily to Victoria. As Elena scurried up, there was a moment when he seemed to freeze, then, even from a distance, Paul heard him shouting. He ran forward. 'She wasn't doing anything wrong,' he cried. 'I was with her. We only went for a walk.'

Rafael turned on him a face suffused with anger. 'You!' He made an obvious effort to control himself, and hissed, 'Your father will hear about this! And if you come near my daughter again, I will take a whip to you!'

'But, Papa, he was looking after me!'

'Be quiet! I'll deal with you later.' Still glaring at Paul, he said, 'Do you understand?'

'Yes, sir. Only, Elena shouldn't get into trouble. It was my fault.'

'Oh, I know that! You're your father's son . . .'

Elena was gesturing wildly for him to leave. Gathering what shreds of dignity he could, he walked away.

He did not take Rafael's melodramatic threats too seriously, confident that Max would be on his side, but reviewing the situation later, he knew that something had changed between himself and Elena. She had kissed him, and clung to him. He had been able to rescue her from – he thought dramatically – an unknown fate. The notion crept into his mind that it would be nice if he could always be around to look after her.

But their separation came earlier than either of them had expected.

The following day, he returned to the *caseta*. Neither she nor Victoria was there. When he got back to San Felipe the next week, he left a note in the wall, but it was still in place three days later.

As he was extracting it, a voice behind him said: 'They've sent her away. You won't be seeing her again.' Manolo was standing behind him, smiling unpleasantly.

'What do you mean?'

'She's gone to Switzerland.'

'She wasn't going until next month!'

'She left three days ago. She's staying with her Tia Christina. Funny she didn't let you know.'

He wanted to write to her, but no one he could ask knew her address. He tried to tell himself that she would be home for the holidays, but it didn't help. He missed her very much.

Weeks later, he received a letter from her: 'Papa brought us back from Seville and made me go straight to Switzerland. Did you find the note I left in the wall? I'm sorry it ended so badly, and I don't know when I'll see you again, because Tia Christina says I'm to stay with her during the holidays. I hope you didn't get into trouble. Thank you for looking after me. School is not bad, at least I have some friends, but I haven't been able to write before because our letters are read by the teachers. I'm paying one of the servants to post this. I hope you enjoy your school. I think of you all the time. With love . . .'

He found Manolo working on one of the power-boats that were used to tow the water-skiiers.

'While I was in Seville, did you take a letter from that place in the wall?' he said.

Manolo wiped his hands on a piece of rag. His hair was greasy with sweat and, stripped to the waist, thick muscles bulged under the dark skin. 'What are you talking about?'

'A letter was left. It wasn't there when I came back.'

'You accusing me of something?'

'You knew about our place, didn't you?'

Manolo grinned. 'I've known about it for years. But I never took your letter.'

Paul didn't believe him, but there was no way he could prove he was lying. That moment saw the flowering of his distrust of Manolo.

2

The small public school that Max had attended had challenged convention in the fifties by liberalising its curriculum to include a dozen unusual activities, from choral-singing to furniture-design.

Paul adapted quickly to his new life. He acted with the drama group, saw a naked woman for the first time in the life-drawing class, learnt to develop and print his own photographs, and how to use a lathe.

The activity he most enjoyed was called simply Restoration. An ancient, tumble-down flint barn, built in the 18th Century, stood in a corner of the school grounds, and some of the boys were repairing and renovating it for use as an exhibition hall. In his first year, he helped to lay a flag-stone floor, repoint the wall-flints, replace rotted beams and rafters. When the old, rat-infested roof had been removed, he learnt from a professional thatcher how to lay bundles of Norfolk reeds in courses and pin them down with U-shaped spars of hazel.

His love of old buildings dated from his work on the barn, though other factors were to contribute to his final decision to make their restoration his career.

In the meantime, school dominated his life for eight months of the year. He was a reasonable student, an excellent athlete, and he got on well with most people. A casual disregard for rules he regarded as unnecessary occasionally annoyed his seniors, but on the whole, his days were untroubled, and he was too busy to brood about his separation from Elena.

He was to return to San Felipe for the holidays, and particularly looked forward each year to the summer, of which the highlight was the annual water-festival which Max and Véronique organised.

Max had built a yacht marina between the Club and the village. It was an attractive addition to the landscape, with its curved breakwaters and moorings for about fifty boats, whose swooping sails added movement and colour to the bay.

The festival, which had been started when Paul was a baby, lasted for four days and included yacht-races, a swimming gala in the Club's pool and water-skiing contests. It ended with a beach-party, when barbecue fires were lit on the sand. There was music and flamenco dancers performed on specially-built platforms.

Flying back from England the year he turned fourteen, his only sadness was that Elena was staying in Switzerland. Her father had never allowed her to attend the festival, but as he had competed in the junior water-skiing competitions, he had liked knowing that she was watching from her window. The previous year, he had collected a plate of food from the beach and she had stolen out to meet him in their cave.

Having left behind a cold, grey English spring, the Spanish summer was particularly beguiling. The marina was filled with yachts and power-boats, the Club and the hotel were booked out, many of the villagers had opened their houses to accommodate the overflow of guests.

Véronique found herself increasingly confined to the Club, overseeing decorations, menus, guest-lists, organising extra staff, until, the day before the festival opened, she announced that she could stand it no longer. 'I am going stir-crazy in that kitchen, and I smell of garlic! I need salt water and the wind in my hair.'

Max always loved watching her water-ski, and he and Paul stood on the upper balcony of the house as she ran down to the power-boat, where her driver was waiting.

The boat accelerated, and she rose on the skis, a slim, graceful figure in a scarlet swimsuit, her fair hair floating behind her.

The little bay was out of bounds to power-boats other than those towing skiiers. There was no one else out, and she had the water to herself. She swooped and darted, leaving curves of white foam like a jet-stream, and her exhilaration communicated itself to the watchers. Some guests applauded her from the jetty. Paul heard his father laughing with pleasure.

Then a power-boat, bow lifted high out of the water, appeared around the point, directly in her path. Her driver had to swerve sharply to avoid a head-on collision. The movement was so fast and so unexpected that she was caught unaware.

Frozen with horror, hearing Max's agonised shouts, Paul saw her skis plough into the water.

Her body somersaulted, crashed down onto the stern of the invading boat, was hauled helplessly after it.

She was dead when they brought her ashore. A doctor later reported that her breastbone had cut the main artery to her heart, her neck and back had been broken, ribs had punctured her lung.

The ripples of the accident were to spread for a long time. The driver whose fault it had been was the son of an Italian motor-manufacturing magnate, who had been given the power-boat for his nineteenth birthday. A year later Max heard that he'd had a mental breakdown. Véronique's driver, a young Englishman hired for the season, left San Felipe immediately, although no blame was attached to him. He would never, he said, go near a power-boat again.

The festival went ahead, but it was a disaster. Max did not appear, and the staff, who had loved Véronique, carried out their tasks like zombies. It was the last water festival held in San Felipe.

For Paul, the days were unrelieved misery. He kept to the house, needing his father, but Max locked himself in his room and drank himself into oblivion. When he did emerge, unshaven, unwashed, red-eyed, he would shamble past Paul as though he did not see him. He refused to attend the funeral, which was orchestrated by Dan Bredon, who had flown in from Los Angeles.

Zimmy arrived at the house after the ceremony to find Paul huddled on a window-seat, hugging a yellow teddy-bear which he had long ago put away as too childish a play-thing. She took him to the Bar Jiminez and installed him in the little room in which, many years ago, his father had slept.

He stayed with her for nearly three weeks, by which time Max, alone in the house, had lost so much weight he was little more than a skeleton.

The Club, thanks to Manolo's assumption of power, and a well-trained staff, had resumed a semblance of normality, but its atmosphere remained gloomy. Véronique's ghost was everywhere.

Once again, it was Zimmy who came to the rescue. Handing Paul over to Titi for company one day, she mounted Burro Tres and plodded up to the house.

He was never to learn what she said to Max, but the next day he returned to the Club. Orders were issued to the staff that there was to be no further mention of his wife's death.

On the surface, he was on the road to recovery. But his character had changed: where he had been able to relax and enjoy leisure, now he seemed driven to activity every moment of the day. At night, he sought out guests whom he could cajole into sitting with him into the early hours.

When Zimmy accompanied Paul back to the house, he watched them coming up the path. Only she noticed him flinch and turn away, seeing Véronique in the fair-haired boy, unable to bear the thought that the resemblance was all he had left of her. When they reached him, he could manage only a cool greeting. For the rest of the holidays, he seemed to be determined that their paths would cross as infrequently as possible.

The beginning of Paul's school term was a relief. Although at first he often cried himself to sleep, the pain gradually eased, as the present came between him and his memories.

His father's letters changed, too. Where they had been light-hearted diaries of activities he and Véronique had shared, they were at first hasty, impersonal missives, mainly about the weather. But after a few weeks, news of a different kind began to creep in. He was building a block of holiday apartments at the other end of the village. It would probably be the first of several. He had plans for hotels, a second marina and a golf-course. 'We're working from morning until night,' he wrote. 'I'm going to turn San Felipe into the biggest and best resort on the coast.'

Paul spent that Christmas in Switzerland on a school skiing expedition. When he had written asking if he should join it, Max had agreed instantly, saying that he had so many new projects he would have little time to spare for Christmas activities. Paul stoically concealed his hurt and, in fact, enjoyed his first Christmas in the snow. At home, there would have been too many reminders of Véronique.

He was working on a new reconstruction at school. A former pupil had on his Hampshire estate a charming pair of 17th Century cottages which had fallen into decay. Impressed by the renovated barn, he offered them to the school. They were to be taken apart, each weathered brick numbered, then re-erected on a site in the grounds. They would be modernised by the installation of plumbing and electricity so they could become guest-houses. The owner would pay all expenses.

Paul and his best friend, Alan Hayes, were put in charge of the undertaking. They made a good team. Alan was fascinated by architecture; Paul loved historic detail and the re-creation of interiors. Their helpers changed from week to week as boyish enthusiasms waxed and waned, but the two of them worked steadily during every spare moment after school and at week-ends.

A London newspaper heard about the project and sent a writer and photographer to record it. Result was a feature about the two 14- year-olds who were, almost single-handedly, carrying out a major project in architectural conservation.

Reluctant to leave the work during the summer, Paul contemplated asking Max if he could stay in England, but a letter from Zimmy changed his mind.

'He needs you,' she wrote. 'He's working too hard, and he should relax. Perhaps you can persuade him to take time off.' She added ominously: 'I hope the changes here won't shock you too much.'

Max met him at Malaga Airport, driving a new silver-grey Jensen Interceptor. Physically, he was his old self: handsome, fit, tanned, attracting female eyes as he lounged against a wall. He wore a white, open-neck shirt, well-cut grey trousers tucked into his boots, and held his wide-brimmed hat.

But when he greeted Paul, they might have been the merest acquaintances. He shook hands, offered no embrace. There was a new hardness about him which Paul found intimidating. Once or twice he thought he caught a sidelong glance which was full of pain, but their conversation was polite, almost formal.

'You're doing pretty well at school, it seems.'

'Yes. Except at physics.'

'You're not likely to need physics in the future. Enjoying yourself, on the whole?'

'Yes, thanks.'

'How're the cottages going?'

'All right. They won't be finished for about a year.'

'We'll probably be able to use that kind of knowledge here when you leave school.'

They breasted the hill and looked down on San Felipe. The Club seemed to have spread since he left, and he saw that there were new tennis-courts. A golf-course was under construction. The village, nestled into its bay, seemed to be much as it had always been, but to the west an apartment block rose several storeys high. Beyond it, the land was scarred and bull-dozers were crawling over it like giant beetles. A new road was being slashed through the hills.

'What d'you think?' Max said.

'It's getting to be awfully big, isn't it?'

'This is only the beginning. We're planning two more blocks of flats and a couple of hotels. Apartments in the completed block are already booked for months ahead. This coast's taken off.'

'Lots of my friends seem to come to Spain for their holidays now.'

'We're still the cheapest country in Europe and we've got everything a visitor wants. Developers are throwing up hotels like sand-castles. And some of them no more stable.' His voice hardened. 'That won't apply here. San Felipe belongs to me.'

'Isn't the village going to be a bit crowded?'

'There's plenty of space. There'll be new shops and we're going to make a promenade along the main beach, with bars and restaurants. There's a hundred per cent employment here now. Even the beggars will soon be peseta millionaires.'

Paul was silent as they drove through the plaza, where the street had been newly tarmaced. A cafe proudly advertising ENGLISH FISH AND CHIPS had taken the place of the electrician's to which he had once delivered smuggled cigarettes. Shop-fronts had been modernised, plate-glass windows replacing the narrow doors which had made it hard to differentiate between houses and commercial premises. The old laundry-troughs were unused, the village pump more a decoration than a necessity now that most houses had water laid on. Telephone wires criss-crossed the roads. There were stalls selling post-cards, straw hats, bags made of leather patchwork, Spanish dolls and plastic buckets and spades. Another bar had opened, above which the village's first neon proclaimed COCKTAILS in red and green.

One of the few survivals, Paul was pleased to see, was the Bar Jiminez, which, apart from a new coat of paint, was as it had always been.

He wondered what alterations he would find at the house, but it was exactly as Véronique had decorated it, and her photograph hung in the alcove. Here time had stood still.

Zimmy and Titi also remained untouched by the changes, though Titi had become something of a tourist attraction, and visitors would exclaim at the dwarf who lived in a cupboard. He rather enjoyed the attention, smiled at them all, offered to share the food he had been given, and did not understand if the remarks they made were contemptuous or hurtful.

Paul went to the Bar as soon as he had unpacked. If his father's greeting had been disappointing, Zimmy made up for it. They sat in her room, drinking coffee, fussed over by Pepita.

When he stood up to go, Zimmy said happily, 'It's been like having Max here all over again. I've missed you.'

'Don't you see him any more?'

'Oh, yes, but he has so much to do that he can't spare the time he used to.'

He burst out: What do you think of all this building?'

'It's bringing prosperity. If it wasn't for your father, we'd still be a village of poor peasants.'

'I liked it then,' he muttered.

'So did I. But you and I were the fortunate ones. We were never in need. There are other people who regard Max as their saviour.'

'I think those apartments are ugly.'

'They mean progress,' she said flatly. 'We have a great deal to thank Max for.'

He knew that she would hear no word against his father, so he did not pursue the subject, but in his mind he compared the hard lines of the new building, stark white, studded with even rows of windows, and balconies like protruding teeth, with the old barn and the cottages in England: weathered and dignified, built with loving care to last for centuries. Restoring them was like bringing a sick person back to life.

Before they parted, Zimmy told him that Elena was at home for a month. Delighted, he left a note for her in the wall, and the next day there was a reply: 'I've been waiting! One of the maids told me you were here. Meet me in the cave tomorrow morning, eleven o'clock.'

He was already there when she pushed the branches aside. The cave was about four feet high, by the same wide, and extended six feet into the hillside. The sun was coming through the bushes, dappling the sandy ground, on which he had spread a layer of dried grass.

For a moment, they looked at each other, then he said: 'You've changed!'

She was no longer a child. Her hair fell, thick and shining, to her shoulders, and her figure was rounded. She was wearing a short denim skirt and a scarlet T-shirt, with red *alpagatas*, their tapes criss-crossed around her slim ankles.

She laughed. 'We're nearly two years older! And you're so tall! You're getting to look like your father.'

Almost without conscious thought, he put his arms around her, and kissed her.

It began chastely on her cheek, but she turned her face and their lips met, and clung. He felt her soft breasts against him and her back was warm under his hand.

After a moment, she pulled away. 'That's the first time anyone's kissed me properly.'

'Me too. Did you like it?'

'Yes.'

'Again?'

But she drew back and said slowly. 'No. Paul, have you ever . . . you know . . . with a girl?'

He shook his head. 'I know what it's all about, though. I've heard the sixth-formers at school talk about it.'

'So do I. Girls talk, too. And they say . . . things can happen to you.'

'Babies?'

'Yes. You can stop them, only I don't know how, so we mustn't take any risks.'

'I could find out . . .'

'No. Not yet. I – I'm a bit afraid. I'll tell you something, though, my first time will be with you, and yours must be with me.'

'Of course it will.' He could not visualise making love to anyone but her.

'Promise?'

'I promise.'

She lay back. 'Then that's that. We can kiss whenever we like. Now . . . do you realise we haven't even said hullo? Let's talk. I want to hear everything.'

Holding hands, they talked for an hour, and had not nearly covered their lives during what seemed to have been an endless separation.

At mid-day, she said reluctantly, 'I have to go. I told my grandmother I was going to the shrine.'

He remembered with affection the simple, arched shrine made of mountain stone which had always been a place of pilgrimage for old women of the village. Hands clasped in front of her, a brightly-painted statuette of the Virgin looked out benignly from behind a little glass door. Candles burned on either side of her, and there were usually fresh flowers in jam-jars in front of the shrine. It wasn't so much her religious significance that appealed to him, as her association with Elena's ability to escape from custody.

'Must you still make excuses? Isn't it any different now you're older?'

'No. They're like gaolers. It's because of the feud. As soon as my father hears you're home, he watches me like a hawk. Fortunately, he's away a good deal of the time, and my grandmother mostly stays in her room.' She giggled. 'They've told one of the servants to keep an eye on me, but I've given her a few pesetas so she won't say anything.'

'Is the feud as bad as ever?'

'Worse. My father hates all the new building.'

He said thoughtfully, 'It's a wonder he hasn't moved away from San Felipe. I mean, Max seems to own so much of it now.'

'He says he's not going to be driven from his family home by a foreigner.'

'Max isn't really a foreigner. And I'm certainly not. I was born here.'

'I know. Papa's unreasonable. I think that hating your family has become a habit.'

'Maybe when you're older he won't mind so much if we see each other.'

'Maybe. I met your father last holidays, when you stayed in England.'

'Did you talk to him?'

'Yes. I was out for a walk and he was taking a short cut through the Campo to see Senora Zimmy. He stopped and spoke to me. It's the first time I've seen him up close. Imagine, in a small village like this!'

'How did you like him?'

'Very much. We talked in English and he said my accent was excellent. He told me what you were doing, and when I had to go he said he understood that I wasn't supposed to talk to a Raven and that he wouldn't tell anyone we'd met. He's *so* good-looking.'

Paul felt his first pang of sexual jealousy of Max. 'Have you talked to him again?'

'No. But I've seen him in the distance and we've waved.' She sighed. 'I do wish I was allowed to go to the Club, just for a swim or a game of tennis. When you're not here, I hate my holidays. They all treat me as though I'm a child. I'm nearly fifteen!'

From his advanced age, six months older than her, he said, 'You're still a baby!'

She threw a handful of grass at him then, laughing, she crawled out of the cave, stood up and brushed herself down.

'See you tomorrow?' he said.

'I can't manage it too often. I'll leave you a note. Check the wall every morning.'

A few days later, his father informed him that he was to spend part of each day in the Club. 'Since it's not beyond the bounds of possibility that the place will belong to you one day, you'd better learn how it works,' he said.

'Belong to me?' Such a thing had never occurred to him.

'I might feel immortal, but I'm probably not. You'll inherit Raven Enterprises when I die. Before that, you'll join me as a partner.'

'But I don't . . .' He stopped.

'Don't what?'

'I don't want to own Raven Enterprises.'

'You will when you're a bit older, and think yourself bloody lucky to have the chance. There are very few kids your age who can look forward to a partnership in a successful business as soon as they leave school.'

'Would I have to live here all the time?'

'You could hardly run the Club from a Swiss mountain-top. Anyhow, this is your home. Where else would you live?'

'I thought I might stay on in England.'

'Nonsense! What would you do there? University? I suppose that's a possibility, but you won't need a degree for the future I've planned for you.'

'It isn't that. Alan Hayes and I want to, sort of, renovate houses.'

'Down here, you can *build* houses. I'm not going to discuss it now. You've got another three years at school. In the meantime, you can work in the kitchens for a week. Then, if you're lucky, I'll promote you to waiter in one of the restaurants.'

To his own surprise, Paul found that working at the Club was, on the whole, more satisfying than spending all his time lying around on the beach, and since Max only expected him to be on duty in the afternoons or evenings, he was able to see Elena whenever she was available. He washed up, chopped vegetables, waited at tables, learnt how to make a Daiquiri and a Harvey Wallbanger in the bar, helped the house-keeper in the linen-room, and found out something about the financial structure of Raven Enterprises.

One day, Max took him onto the site of the new building and showed him how an architect's plans would be translated into a block of apartments. Manolo was there, greeted him briefly, then ignored him as they discussed the work. When they'd finished talking, Max turned back to him and said jokingly, 'You've just about seen the lot now. Reckon you're ready to take over?'

Manolo's head swivelled and he stared at them. There was a frown on his dark face. Instinctively, Paul knew he had suddenly realised that one day he might be working for Max's son, and did not take kindly to the idea. He needn't worry, he thought grimly, I've got other plans.

It was a silent rebellion which was eventually to escalate into a major war.

Two nights before he was due to return to school, another wedge was hammered into his relationship with his father, when he discovered Max in bed with a woman at the Club.

He was helping in the terrace bar. By ten o'clock, most of the guests had drifted into the restaurants, but a few lingered. He normally finished work at that point, and went back to the house. Max was rarely there. He would return during the early hours of the morning, apparently able to maintain full energy on three or four hours' sleep.

This evening, the barman asked Paul if he would stay on for an hour while he replaced an absent waiter in one of the restaurants. He did not want to leave his assistant, a shy young trainee from the village, alone.

José and Paul cleaned the bar and chatted, enjoying the temporary peace before diners came out for their liqueurs.

It was after eleven when the first group returned, two Swedish businessmen and their blonde wives. The men were awash with good wine, boisterous and unsteady on their feet. One of them, making for the bar, did not see a low tub of geraniums at the corner of the pool, tripped over it and fell into deep water. Paul began to laugh, but sobered almost at once, as farce threatened to turn into tragedy. The man could not swim. Thrashing wildly, weighted down by shoes and clothes, he sank, came up, gasping, sank again.

Paul dived in, followed by José. The drowning man made the rescue as difficult as possible, struggling, pushing them under the water in turn. Eventually, they manoeuvred him to the side. His friend took his hands and, with Paul and José pushing from below, hauled him out and laid him on his stomach. He was coughing and retching, sounding as though his last hour was imminent.

Paul was trying to squeeze out his own clothes when a waiter hissed at him: 'Get your father, quickly!'

'Where is he?'

'Look in his rooms.'

He hurried to the terrace outside Max's sitting-room, and banged on the French windows. Behind them, the curtains were not fully drawn. He knocked again, then put his eye to the gap. It was as though he was watching a screen where the camera had focused on the action, cutting off any extraneous background. His father was sprawled over a naked woman on the sofa. Hearing Paul's knock, he raised his head and called, 'Who is it? What do you want?'

Paul was unable to answer.

Max stood up, pulled on his trousers and ran his fingers through ruffled hair. The woman moved to a heap of clothes which were lying on the floor. Max gestured towards the stairs and Paul heard him say, 'Go to the bedroom. I'll see what this is, and I'll be right with you.'

Dark hair fell around her shoulders. Her body was thin to the point of emaciation. It was Victoria Ansaldo.

Paul's eyes were wide with shock as his father opened the windows. For a moment, they stared at each other, then Max said, 'What the hell do you want?'

'I . . .' Why *was* he there? What he had seen had taken over his mind to the exclusion of all else. Max had loved Véronique . . . how could he behave like that with another woman?

'Well?'

He gathered himself. 'Someone nearly drowned. You'd better come.'

'Christ!' Buttoning his shirt, Max ran to the pool, where the Swede was now sitting up, spluttering threats of law-suits.

Paul walked slowly back to the house. He felt something close to hatred for his father, who had betrayed Véronique. It would, he knew, be a long time before he forgot what he had seen through the curtain.

3

As the years passed, their relationship remained cool. The closeness of the early years never returned. Although he worked willingly enough in the Club, Paul was stubbornly silent whenever any attempt was made to discuss his future. Neither did he make any secret of his dislike of the new buildings which were springing up like fence-posts along the coast, and one day, he said the unforgivable: 'My mother would have hated it!'

Max turned away, and avoided him for the rest of the day.

When he told Zimmy, she said sadly, 'Oh, my dear, don't you realise that if your mother were here, Max wouldn't *need* to build these places. Work is his way of stopping himself from thinking about her.'

'There must be other ways,' he muttered sulkily.

He continued to see Elena whenever possible, and Rafael never found out about their meetings. They kissed, and explored each other's bodies, but she always insisted on stopping short of the final act. It seemed to him that he took an inordinate number of cold showers during the holidays.

Apart from her, Zimmy, ready at any time to give him her full attention, was the only person with whom he could talk without inhibition. She told him once that having him with her was like filling in the years she had missed with Max, who had been away from fourteen until his discharge from the Army.

Having understood about her profession for as long as he could remember, he accepted it matter-of-factly. He was never as close to Pepita and the other girls as Max had been, but he regarded them as friends. His sexual fantasies centred on Elena, so he was not tempted to experiment with them.

During the year he turned sixteen, Max married Loretta Barrie, an American actress whom he had met while she was working on location in San Felipe.

His affair with Victoria had apparently been short-lived. During Paul's subsequent holidays, he had been constantly in the company of a beautiful Austrian divorcee, then a recently-widowed French countess, a Brazilian heiress, an English fashion designer and an Australian Olympic swimmer. It seemed to Paul that he changed his mistresses as often as he changed his motor-car, but as Zimmy was later to point out, they nearly always remained his friends. 'I sometimes wonder if there wasn't something between him and Victoria Ansaldo,' she said once. 'However badly she behaves, however he complains about her, he won't ban her from the Club – and I'm sure it isn't only to annoy Rafael.'

Paul said nothing. He had decided that he would never speak to anyone about what he had seen through the curtains.

For some years, Loretta had starred in a soap-opera which had been originally successful, but had slipped down the ratings, due to an increasingly banal script and, it was said, her wooden acting.

In a vain attempt to attract audiences back, the writers had sent their characters abroad to a variety of exotic locations, and the episode being shot in Spain turned out to be the last in the series. She received word while she was in San Felipe that it had been cancelled.

Although she was playing a 21-year-old, she was then in her thirties. Her short-lived marriage to the producer of the series ended when the cameras stopped rolling.

Heart-stoppingly beautiful, she had inevitably attracted Max's attention. When the rest of the unit departed, she stayed. After a quick divorce, she and Max were married.

When he arrived back for his next vacation, Paul said to Zimmy, with what he imagined was cool sophistication: 'What I can't understand is why he married her. He didn't need to bother, did he?'

For once, she spoke sharply: 'You do not say such things! I will tell you why he married her: he has been a widower for a long time. He is over forty, and he is lonely. You and he – well, never mind that. Loretta loves him. She is beautiful and elegant, a decoration for his Club. Also, he was sorry for the way her husband dumped her. He, if anyone, knows what it is to be unhappy. You understand?'

Only partly, Paul thought, but he nodded, reminded once again that it was unwise to criticise his father to Zimmy.

Although he was wary of her at first, he grew fond of Loretta, who treated him like a younger brother. He enjoyed having her in the house, in which he'd previously spent a good deal of time by himself.

That summer turned out to be one of the happiest he could remember since his mother's death. Elena was home, and his father seemed more relaxed, more amused than irritated – as he would later become – by Loretta's obsession with her appearance. He enjoyed the attention her beauty attracted and she accepted his teasing about her intellectual deficiencies with unfailing good-humour.

When Paul went back to school, she wrote him long, cheerful letters filled with gossip about the Club and the village, with frequent affectionate references to Max, from which he assumed that their marriage was working out better than might have been anticipated.

His eighteenth birthday was due to be celebrated a few days after he returned from school for the last time. He knew it would be a momentous occasion, because he would finally have to face his father with the fact that he did not intend to make his future in San Felipe.

When the cottages had been completed, he and Alan had received more publicity, this time in a glossy magazine, which had hardened their determination to go into partnership. Alan's parents had agreed to invest £5,000 in their project, if Paul would contribute the same amount.

During his plane journey home, he rehearsed his request to Max for a loan. The more he thought about it, the more nervous he became, and the more certain of opposition.

Loretta met him at the airport in one of the Club's chauffeur-driven Cadillacs. There was a suppressed excitement in her greeting, but when he asked what was going on, she said merely, 'You'll find out.'

As soon as they arrived at the Club, he realised that it was being prepared for a spectacular party. Extra staff had been recruited. Lights were being strung through the trees. On the beach, an enormous bonfire had been constructed, and bars set up. The American Restaurant had been cleared for dancing, and an army of women was arranging cornucopias of flowers on the walls, which were covered with yellow and white striped silk. The ceiling had been canopied with greenery. Extra tables were being set around the pool, a dais had been built on the lawn and 'Uno . . . dos . . . tres . . .' was ringing out as the microphones were tested.

'What's the celebration?' he said.

'It's for you, darling! Your eighteenth birthday, and because you left school and Max is going to announce that he's taking you into partnership.'

'*What*?'

'Isn't it exciting? I sent out invitations weeks ago and guests are flying in from all over. People who've known you since you were a baby, and we've asked those friends of yours, the Hayes. Max is paying their fares. Alan didn't tell you, did he?'

He shook his head speechlessly.

'I wanted it to be a surprise. We've hired three bands, one to play on the beach, and a guitarist, and there'll be lashings of champagne. Zimmy's coming, of course, and Dan's here already . . .'

As she stopped for breath, he interrupted. 'I don't *want* to be Max's partner! I'm going back to England. Alan and I are starting our own business.'

She looked as though he had struck her. 'Oh, no! You can't! Max needs you.'

He gritted his teeth. 'I've told him for years that I didn't want to stay here, but he's never taken any notice.'

'He's had a partnership contract drawn up. You can't let him down!'

'Loretta, I have my own life to live! And I *hate* what he's done to San Felipe. He's turned it into a concrete builder's yard.'

'But your party . . .'

'There's no reason why the party should be affected. The only change will be that he won't be able to make any speeches about a partnership.'

'Who's going to tell him?'

'I am. You're not to worry about it.' He kissed her. 'Everything will be fine, and it's going to be a super party.'

'I don't think so, not when he hears.' She squared her shoulders. 'But we'll do our best. Oh, Paul, I *have* enjoyed being useful for a change. Everything's so well organised here that there isn't much for me to do. And when Max doesn't come home . . .' She cut the sentence off, and started again. 'Do you think . . . I mean, how would you feel about not telling him until the party's over?'

'And let him make his announcement?'

'Well, yes.'

'All the fuss, and then he'd have to tell everyone it wasn't true? He'd be even more furious.'

'I suppose so.'

'Where is he?'

'In his office. He wants you to join him for lunch.'

'Then I'll go and get it over.'

'Shall I come with you?'

'No, thanks. You can pick up the pieces later.'

For a moment, there was unguarded pleasure on Max's face. He came from behind the desk and put an arm around Paul's shoulders in an uncharacteristic embrace. 'I never get used to the fact that you're as tall as I am. Good to see you home. What d'you think of all the excitement?'

'Everything looks great.' His voice was stiff, and Max raised an eyebrow.

'Loretta has enjoyed it. The whole thing was her idea. Sit down. Let's talk for a while. Drink?'

'Gin and tonic, please.'

He sat in a chair by the coffee-table, and waited while his father fetched drinks.

'So. How's it feel to be a free man?'

'Pretty good. I won't miss school too much.'

'We're going to keep you busy. You won't have time to miss anything. Did Loretta tell you our plans?'

He drained his gin so quickly that he nearly choked, hoping it would produce some Dutch courage. 'She told me *your* plans, yes.'

'And?'

'And . . . and I'm very sorry, but they're not my plans, Dad.' He caught himself, realising that it was the first time he had used the patronymic for years. His father had become Max to him soon after Véronique's death, and had accepted the change without comment.

'I'm not sure what you mean by that.' The warmth had gone.

'You should be. I've always told you that I didn't want to join Raven Enterprises. Alan Hayes and I are setting up our own company in London.'

Max regarded him expressionlessly. 'To do what?'

'Restore old houses.'

'I told you once before that you can build houses here.'

'I don't want to put up new houses. I want to – oh, hell, I can't help it if this sounds sentimental! I want to rescue old places that have been neglected. Places that were built to harmonise with the landscape. Not these gravestones . . .' He flung out his hand in a wide gesture.

'These gravestones have kept you in supreme comfort all your life, and given you an education.'

'I appreciate that. But it's not what I want to do.' He leant forward. 'I need five thousand pounds to get started. Alan and I have the chance of a job already. The parents of a chap we know have bought a Victorian farm-house in Wiltshire, and they might let us do it up. Only we need capital.'

Max stood up. 'Sorry. I'm maintaining enough charities already.'

'I'm not asking for charity. You'd be investing the money.'

'When I invest, I expect a return. I see no future for this scheme of yours.'

'Why not?'

'You've had no proper training, and no experience. You know nothing about cash flow. You'll be broke within a year.

I'm not about to flush five thousand pounds down the drain.'

They were facing each other across the coffee-table when Loretta came in. With an attempt at lightness, she said, 'Well, at least there don't seem to be any pieces to pick up.'

Keeping a tight rein on his temper, Paul said briefly. 'I'm flying back to England tomorrow. I won't be here for the party.'

'Oh, Paulie, you can't!'

He looked back at Max. 'You won't even try to understand! Sorry to put it like this, but I don't want any part of what you're doing to this coast!'

He swung around, but Loretta was standing between him and the door. Tears were pouring down her cheeks and for once she was allowing her face to pucker unattractively.

'Oh, Christ!' he said. 'I'm sorry, Loretta.'

She gulped. 'It's all right. It's just that I'd so hoped you two . . . but you must do what you want to.'

'Your party . . .' He had a sudden painful memory of the collapse of the water-festival after his mother's death. His desertion was no great tragedy, as that had been, but it would cause unhappiness. Loretta had always been his ally, and even in her disappointment, he realised, she was not pressing for him to stay.

He was about to tell her that he would put off his departure for a couple of days, when his father forestalled him. Later, he wondered if their thoughts had been running on parallel lines.

'I'll offer you a compromise,' Max said abruptly. 'Loretta's worked bloody hard on this fiesta. Stay until it's over. Then I'll write you a cheque for five thousand pounds, with one proviso: you'll undertake to repay the full amount within twelve months, otherwise you'll come back and work here.'

If I had any pride, I'd tell him to go to hell, and make my own way, Paul thought. Instead, 'You'll get your money,' he said. 'Plus a year's interest. Ten per cent. Okay?'

Max smiled grimly. 'Okay. And I won't even make you sign a contract. Your word's enough.'

He thinks he's won, Paul told himself bitterly. He's sure I'll be back, so he can afford to be generous, and wait for a year.

Later that day, he said to Loretta: 'Do you think we might invite Elena Ansaldo to the party? I mean, she's nearly grown-up. Maybe . . .'

'I sent an invitation to the whole family. They didn't even reply.'

'I'll try to get in touch with her. I'm sure her father won't let her come, but I want her to be asked.'

'You like her a lot, don't you?'

'Yes, I do.' Then he heard himself saying, 'I'm going to marry her one day.'

She showed no surprise. 'We thought you might.'

'You did?'

'Max and I have talked about it. You meet on the Campo Negro, don't you?'

'You know that?'

'Darling, I think everyone knows, except Rafael Ansaldo. She's a beautiful girl. Max talks to her occasionally.'

'Does he? He's never mentioned it to me.'

'He's tactful. He knows you've been trying to keep your friendship a secret. He thinks she's charming.'

Paul was not entirely sure that he liked the idea of his father becoming friendly with Elena. Max was exceptionally attractive to women . . . but after all, he was middle-aged, and he was married to Loretta. It was absurd even to consider that your father might be a rival. He put it out of his mind, and it was to be more than ten years before it would resurface.

'Do you know whether she's home?'

'She's been here for some time. Zimmy told me they've had an American wine-grower named Alex Bellini staying with them, and Max saw him walking with Elena in the village the other day. There are rumours tht he's going to put some money into Rafael's vineyards.'

'What's he like?'

'I've only seen him in the distance. Fortyish. Short. Grey-haired.'

Forty. Grey-haired. Nothing to worry about there.

He wrote her a note and later when he went to the wall, it had gone, and another had been left in its place. 'I can't get to the cave during the day. We have someone staying with us whom I have to look after. Thank you for the invitation, but of course, it's impossible for me to accept. Could we meet at night some time?'

The note worried him. It lacked the warmth with which she normally wrote, especially after what had been an unusually long separation. A year ago, she had moved on to a finishing school near Lucerne where, as far as he could gather from her letters, she spent most of her time with a tape, measuring the correct distance between knives and forks, learning how to set a perfectly symmetrical dinner-table.

'It's such a waste of time,' she had written. 'I put up with it because next year, when you've left school, it might be possible for us to meet if you're working in London. My great-aunt Emilia lives there. She's very old, but Papa allows me to stay with her sometimes.'

He had hoped to see her over Easter, but instead she had written to say that Rafael was taking her to California, where he was to tour vineyards in the Napa Valley. He'd had only one brief letter since her return which, now he came to think of it, had also been unusually stilted. It had simply said that she had enjoyed herself, that parts of California had reminded her of Spain and that the Americans were very hospitable.

Involved in his final examinations, he hadn't had time to analyse it but now, as he studied the note, he remembered how it had struck him at the time.

He wrote to her: 'Meet me in the cave at midnight tomorrow. We'll have our own party.'

The festive atmosphere built throughout Saturday, ready to explode in the evening. People Paul hadn't seen for years flew in and greeted him like an old friend: film-stars, European aristocrats claiming titles a yard long, Texan ranchers, a former British Prime Minister.

Alan Hayes and his parents were frankly bemused by the company in which they found themselves, and the lavishness of the hospitality.

'You never let on you lived like this,' Alan said. 'That step-mother of yours is gorgeous, and I've never seen so many terrific women in one place. It's like a movie set. My parents can't understand how you can even think of giving it all up.'

'Very easily,' Paul said grimly. 'It isn't always like this. Loretta's organised the party and I don't even remember half the people who are here. They're Max's friends and they're only making a fuss of me because of him.'

By eight o'clock, the party was under way. Women dressed by Dior, Hartnell, Pucci and Fath, bejewelled by Asprey's and Tiffany's, styled by Parisian hair-dressers who had been flown in for the occasion, fluttered like exotic parakeets against the black and white of the men's dinner-jackets. There was a table of *tapas* on the lawn, a seemingly endless supply of champagne. At ten o'clock, a buffet supper was served, with fine French wines.

Paul enjoyed himself more than he had expected to, but always in the back of his mind was the anticipation of midnight.

During a moment of peace, away from the crowd, he saw Loretta. She was looking spectacular. Her cream satin dress fell from shoe-string straps in a narrow tube which outlined her perfect body. In contrast with the elaborately-coiffured hair of many of the other women, hers hung straight and shining to her shoulders, and her only jewellery was a pair of pearl drop ear-rings. When Paul told her admiringly that she made everyone else look over-dressed, she had winked and said, 'Don't imagine it isn't intentional.'

Now she was teetering unsteadily over the lawn to a bar. Before he reached her, she had downed a full glass of champagne and a waiter had poured her another.

When she saw him, she said, ''Nother surprise coming up, darling! Ready for it?'

'What sort of a surprise?'

'Never mind. Secret. Soon.' She swayed, and he caught her arm. 'Sorry, Paulie. High heels on soft grass.'

'Wouldn't you like to sit down? Where's Max?'

'Max? You asking *me* where Max is? Ask the little Contessa. She's the only one who can keep tabs on him these days.' She laughed without humour. 'Le's see: so far this year there's been the lady chairman of a London estate agency, then a Bunny girl from Vegas – she didn't last long – and now there's the Contessa, who needs comfort because her husband has left her. Max is providing it.'

Uncomfortably, he said, 'He isn't serious about any of them, though.'

'No. Amusing himself. That's what everyone says. I think I'm going to have to start amusing myself, too.' She swallowed her drink and looked around for another.

'Come on inside and sit down for a bit,' he said.

'What's the time?'

'Just after half-past eleven.' He would soon have to go.

She took a firm grip on his arm. 'Stay with me, Paulie. I don't want to lose you now. There's the surprise, remember.'

Determined not to be trapped, he looked around, and saw Max.

An attractive, dark-haired woman was holding his hand, but he detached himself and came towards them.

'Nearly time?' he said to Loretta.

'Why not? Party needs a lift.'

He looked more closely at her. 'You all right?'

'Never better, darling. You? Enjoying yourself, I hope?' She seemed to have sobered, and was smiling at him as though she hadn't a care in the world.

He took Paul's other arm and, between them, he was led towards the dais on the lawn. Max sent some waiters to gather the guests.

He realised that a ceremony was imminent, and looked at his watch again. Fifteen minutes. 'What is all this?' he said suspiciously.

'Up you come.' Max pulled him onto the dais and installed himself behind the microphone. Loretta joined them. Embarrassed, apprehensive, he looked for a way out, but he was the centre of attention, surrounded by a solid wall of smiling faces. Zimmy, wearing a dress of scarlet taffeta, with a flower in her hair, was standing just below him, with Dan Bredon.

'Everyone here?' Max leant forward, and his voice boomed over the crowd. 'Right! You'll be pleased to know that I'm not going to make a speech, except to tell you all how delighted we are that you're here. Thanks for coming, and helping us to celebrate my son's eighteenth birthday.' Handsome, at ease, he raised his glass to Paul. 'Many happy returns, and good luck!' There was applause, a few cheers, and everyone drank.

'Your turn.' Max pushed the microphone towards him.

'Oh, shit! Must I?' He had forgotten the amplification and there was a roar of laughter.

Trying to emulate Max's ease, he said, 'No speech from me, either. It's great to see everyone, and thank you all. I hope you're enjoying yourselves.'

Assuming that now he could go, he stepped back, but again Loretta held him. She took over the microphone: 'Listen, everyone! It's just on midnight, when Paul is officially eighteen. We have a little present for him.'

Midnight. He was practically dancing with impatience, but he saw the crowd in front of the dais parting like the waters of the Red Sea. Instead of a procession of Israelites, a sports car came slowly towards him, driven by a smiling José. An Alfa Romeo. He had admired one in a car-dealer's window in Malaga months ago, when he had been shopping with Loretta.

It stopped below him and José jumped out. Loretta said, 'Happy birthday, darling! It's from your father and me, and we hope you like it.'

A cheer went up as he stammered his thanks. 'It's fantastic . . .'

'In you get, Paul! Take her for a drive,' Dan shouted.

'I can't! Not now.'

'Of course you can. Give Loretta a spin around the village.'

There was no escape. Several laughing men forced him into the driving-seat. Max lifted Loretta in beside him.

The car was a magnificent present. He loved driving, but the last thing he wanted now was to take it out.

He visualised Elena, sitting alone in the cave, waiting for him.

But he could not hurt Loretta, so he started the engine, then accelerated through the gates onto the road.

'Let's go up to the point beyond the war memorial,' she said.

Trying to calculate how long it would take, he put his foot down and drove recklessly fast around the narrow curves that led into the village, then circled the plaza. A few hard-core drinkers, still sitting under the trees, turned to look at them.

He made for the promontory, on the far side of which pinpoints of light twinkled from windows of the apartments. Their hard lines invisible in the darkness, they took on a new beauty. It was a still, warm night, with a sliver of moon, and stars scattered thickly above them, but he was only interested in getting the drive over as quickly as possible.

The dirt road out to the point was rough, with a turning circle at the end. When they reached it, Loretta said, 'Stop a minute, and let's look at the sea.'

'We must get back. They'll be wondering where we are.'

'They know where we are. And if you're worrying about Max, the Contessa will keep him amused. Let's enjoy ourselves, darling.'

She was running her fingers through his hair, and had moved as close to him as possible. He began to ease the steering wheel around.

'We'll come out some other time. I'm heading back now.'

She giggled, and grasped the wheel. He realised that the fresh air had intensified the effect of the champagne.

'Stop that!' he said, but she took no notice. She leant over him, pulling the wheel. Her hair blew back into his face so that he was momentarily blinded. The car lurched and the left-hand wheels sank into a sandy ditch which bordered the hard surface. She fell into his lap, still laughing, as the wheels spun and the engine stalled.

'Are we stuck? Good!' Her body was across his, her arms snaked around his neck, and she kissed him on the mouth. When she released him, she said, 'I've been wanting to do that for ages. You know what I said about amusing myself? You and I . . . why not? We wouldn't hurt anyone . . .'

As he extricated himself he said, 'You're drunk. We're going back to the Club.' He started the engine, but the wheels only embedded themselves more deeply into the sand.

His irritation settled into a cold fury. He got out and saw that the car would have to be towed back onto level ground.

'I'm going to walk back,' he snapped. 'If you want to stay here, I'll send someone to fetch you.'

Suddenly cowed, she said, 'No, no! I'm coming!'

She stumbled after him in her high heels, then stopped and took off her shoes. He strode on, not caring whether she was following, or not. He heard her call. The fluorescent hands of his watch told him that it was after twelve-thirty. Despairingly, he realised it was too much to hope that Elena would still be waiting.

Loretta caught up with him. 'Paul . . .' she gasped. 'Oh, God, I don't know what happened to me! It's just that – I'm not very happy at the moment.'

He looked down at her. She was dishevelled and, in the moonlight, he could see that her face was running with tears. Mascara had smudged under her eyes so they looked bruised. His anger began to fade. 'It's all right,' he said wearily. 'It doesn't matter now.'

'Sometimes, when I see Max with those other women . . . But I shouldn't have . . . with you.'

'It's okay, Loretta. You've had too much champagne. Forget it.'

'You won't let it spoil things between us?'

'No.' All it had spoiled was the one birthday gift he had really wanted: to be with Elena.

It was after one o'clock when they reached the Club. The party was still in full swing, and nobody had missed them.

Wondering if Elena might have left him a message, he hurried to the cave, but there was no evidence that she had been there.

Miserably, he went home to bed, and heard later that the last guests had not left the party until nearly five o'clock.

He slept heavily, emerged late and went to the wall, but the hole was empty. He left her a brief note, explaining what had happened. When he wandered down to the Club for lunch, the party-debris had been cleared and, apart from a few guests with hang-overs, the place was back to normal. Max was circulating, looking fit and healthy, having had three hours sleep. Loretta joined them, heavy-eyed, but in control. She smiled at Paul and her only reference to the previous night was when, Max's attention being diverted, she whispered: 'Thanks for being such a gentleman, darling.'

During the next three days, his note remained in the wall. It was an echo of the situation after the *feria* when they had been children. Finally, in desperation, he telephoned the Ansaldo's house, disguising his voice. A woman told him, without explanation, that the senorita was not there.

He was on his way back from one of his vain searches for a message when Manolo called him: 'Heard about your girl-friend?'

'Heard what?'

'She's gone to California with her father and the American. Rafael and Bellini are going into partnership.'

'How long will they be there?'

'Word is that they won't be home for months. They left the morning after your party.'

Two days later, he went back to England, a cheque for five thousand pounds in his pocket, a leaden weight in his heart.

4

It was nearly three months since a brass plate proclaiming HAYES & RAVEN, ARCHITECTURAL RESTORATION, had been screwed into the wall outside the tiny office in Fulham. So far, the partners had spent a great deal of their capital, and earned nothing.

They had advertised in glossy architectural and house magazines, and received a few inquiries, but no firm commission.

The owners of the Wiltshire farm-house, on whom they had been depending for their first job, had decided that their investment was too important to entrust to a couple of youngsters. They suspected that other prospects had also been put off by their youth.

Paul had moved into a cheap room in a Maida Vale lodging-house. Alan was still living with his parents, in order to save money.

Without realising it, Paul's way of dealing with his hurt and loneliness when he arrived in England duplicated his father's after Véronique's death: he turned to work. From morning until night, he painted and renovated the office they had rented, trudged around estate agents looking for those with derelict properties to sell, which a buyer might want renovated, wrote letters to everyone he and Alan could think of who might be interested in their project.

A few friends from his schooldays lived in London, and he embarked on an active social life. He sacrificed his virginity with a girl he met at a party, whose surname he never learned. There was no shortage of attractive women, and he sampled most of what was on offer. The love-making was rarely exciting, but it relieved physical tension and stopped him from thinking about Elena.

As he and Alan faced each other over their empty desks, he said: 'Crawling back to my father will be worse than if I'd stayed in Spain.'

'I know. My parents are getting restive about their investment, too. What we really need is publicity. I mean, how are people going to know about us?'

'That's an idea,' Paul said slowly. 'How about we get in touch with that chap who came to school and wrote about the cottages? Maybe he can suggest something.'

'My dear boys, I'd love to help, but you haven't *achieved* anything, have you? The cottages are dead news. Show me some gorgeous old castle you're doing up, and I could write *yards*. But without it . . .' Bright squirrel eyes peered at them inquisitively. He was a small, neat man in his fifties, with a high-pitched voice and a penchant for patting Paul's hand whenever he could reach it. He had a habit of ending his sentences with dots instead of the last few words. 'Are you fearfully broke? If we were *real* friends, now, I could lend . . .'

'No, thanks,' Paul said.

'Then I'm afraid . . .'

'Do you know anyone else we could approach?'

'I suppose you could try Liz Austen. She's the features editor of *Sophisticate*.'

'What's that?'

'It's a new glossy, love. Terribly up-market. She might be interested in you. I really wouldn't know.' He reached out, and Paul hastily withdrew his hand. 'If you'd only let me lend you a little something to tide . . .'

'We don't need it.'

'If that's the way it is . . .'

'That's the way it is. Thanks, anyway.'

When he had gone, Paul said, 'He gives me the creeps.'

'Not prepared to sell your body to save our careers?'

'He's not pretty enough. Let's ring that woman.'

Liz Austen was brisk and middle-aged. She wore large

glasses with tortoiseshell rims and was intimidatingly elegant, but she listened to them with interest.

'How old are you?' she said, when Alan had finished describing what they wanted to do.

'Nearly nineteen.'

'I remember reading about your cottages. Now look, we're planning a feature about attractive young people with ambition. I think you might fit into it. There'd be colour photographs of you both, with a brief story. Would you be willing?'

They tried not to assent too eagerly.

A few weeks later, a reporter and a photographer came to see them at the office. As they left, Paul said, 'When will it be published?'

'In three or four months, probably.'

'Hell, we'll be skint by then!' Alan said after they had gone. 'I thought it'd be next month.'

Two days later, as they were sitting at their desks, which remained unsullied by any evidence of labour, the telephone rang. It was such a rare occurrence that they both jumped. Paul picked up the receiver.

'Hayes and Raven.'

'Good afternoon. This is Bredon and Bredon.'

'Dan!'

'I got your number from Loretta. Can't talk now. Arrived from L.A. a few minutes ago and I'm off to the studios. Come and have dinner with me tonight. The Dorchester. Eight o'clock.'

They had a long, relaxed meal, catching up on news. Paul, who had been subsisting on the cheapest possible fare, ate so heartily that Dan said enviously, 'It's bloody unfair! If I ate half that, I'd blow up like a balloon.'

'You don't normally live on fish fingers.'

'Is that from necessity? How are things going?'

'You don't need to tell Max, but at the moment, they're not going at all. The trouble is, nobody knows about us. We'll get there, though. I'm damned if I'm going back to Spain with my tail between my legs.'

'The studio's giving me a press reception in the River

Room at the Savoy tomorrow,' Dan said. 'Why don't you and Alan come? At least, it will give you a chance to meet a few people.'

The River Room was crowded. Apart from the free drinks, Bredon and his divorces were good copy, and his latest film had been nominated for an Academy Award.

When he saw the boys arrive, he waved, and beckoned.

'Come and meet Will Foster,' he said. 'Best gossip columnist in London. Knows everybody. Will, this is Alan Hayes and his partner, Paul Raven. Paul's father is Max Raven.'

'The San Felipe Club?' Foster was in his early thirties, tall, impeccably-dressed, with a pleasant smile. Paul noticed that he shared Max's ability to fix the person to whom he was talking with a look of intense interest.

'You've heard of the Club?'

'Who hasn't? Nobody's anybody on the international circuit unless they belong. I met your father once. He's quite a guy. The first developer to open up the Costa del Sol, wasn't he? He must be a millionaire by now.'

'Lord, no, nothing like it! He ploughs all the profits back into concrete.'

Dan had turned away to introduce Alan to some other people. Foster said, 'What are you drinking?'

'Nothing yet. What is there?'

'Everything. This studio does us pretty well.' He stopped a passing waiter and Paul took a glass from the tray. 'So what's your father up to now?'

'The usual. More flats. More hotels.'

'You sound as though you don't approve.'

'Well . . . when I was a kid, San Felipe was a quiet little village. Now it's just another overcrowded holiday resort.'

'You in the business with him?'

'No. Alan and I have started our own company.'

'Doing what?'

'Architectural restoration. We'll renovate anything from a cottage to a castle.'

'That's not a bad line. How does your father feel about it?'

'He'd have preferred me to stay in Spain.'

'Family row?'

Paul liked Foster. He was a sympathetic listener and, after all, this was party chat, not an interview. 'He wasn't too pleased when I told him. He knows I don't like what's been done to the coast.'

They went on talking for a few minutes, then a young actress claimed Foster's attention, and Paul drifted away. He was introduced to several other people, but had little chance to arouse interest in the ambitions of Hayes and Raven.

It had been a pleasant evening, he thought later, but unproductive.

The next morning, the office telephone rang as he and Alan, for want of other occupation, were settling down to *The Times* cross-word.

Bredon's voice was sharp. 'Paul, what the hell did you say to Will Foster last night?'

'Hardly anything. We only talked for about ten minutes.'

'Seen the paper this morning?'

'Which one?'

'Foster's. Buy it, then ring me back.'

The headline over the lead story on the gossip page read: FRICTION IN EUROPE'S JET-SET CLUB, and there was a half-column picture of Max, taken some years ago. Paul went cold as he read the words that went with it:

> New man-about-London is handsome Paul Raven, who is escaping from what he describes as the 'destruction' his father has wrought in a once-charming Spanish village.
>
> With his film-star good looks, property-millionaire Max Raven, owner of the San Felipe Club, is among the best-known English expats in Spain.
>
> But, according to Paul, he has turned San Felipe del Mar into 'an overcrowded holidy resort' by throwing up block after block of ugly apartments.
>
> After a bitter family row, Paul has left Spain for good, and has chosen a career as far removed as possible from cheap property development. With a partner, he plans to

renovate old buildings in Britain – anything from a cottage to a castle.

Paul dialled the Dorchester. 'I had no idea he was going to write anything! We were just chatting.'

'The first lesson you need to learn is that you never just chat with a journalist,' Bredon said grimly.

'But he seemed such a nice chap, and he didn't take any notes.'

'He was on duty. His answer would be that if you're too naive to realise that anything he picks up is likely to go into the column, it's not his fault. *Did* you say all that?'

'I suppose so. More or less. But it didn't sound as bad as it looks.'

'Second lesson: nothing you say ever sounds as bad as it looks in print. The worst thing these characters can do to you is quote you verbatim.'

'I never said there'd been a bitter row. He made that up.'

'An educated guess, based on what you did say.'

'What should I do? Max is sure to see it.'

'Ring him and apologise. I feel responsible, so I'll call him later and back you up. I should have guessed what might happen.'

Loretta answered the telephone.

'It's me,' he said. 'Is Max there?'

Her voice was cold. 'No, and you'd better be grateful he isn't.'

'Is he annoyed?'

'Furious.'

'Oh, Christ!' Stumblingly, he explained what had happened. When he finished, she said, 'I suppose I understand. God knows, I suffered enough from the press. I'll tell Max what you've said, and Dan's call might help.'

'Should I ring again?'

'No. Write to him. He's as much hurt as angry. He thinks you did it deliberately to smear him.'

'He should know better than that! Hell, he's never tried to understand me, has he?'

She said briskly, 'Stop feeling sorry for yourself, Paulie, and try to understand *him* for a change.'

Two days later, as a direct consequence of the paragraph, their first client appeared in the office. Alan had gone out, and Paul was alone.

She was a thin young woman with lank brown hair hanging to her shoulders and wide, pale eyes. She had plucked out her eye-brows and redrawn them into surprised arches. Her face and lips were colourless. She wore huge brass hoop ear-rings, jeans and a creased shirt, topped by a blanket-like shawl.

'Are you Paul Raven?'

'Yes.' His heart had fallen. She looked as though she didn't have enough money to spend on shampoo, let alone a house.

The pale eyes were fixed on him. 'I'm Jan Thomas. I read about you. I've got a place that needs doing up. Interested?'

'Well, yes,' he said cautiously. 'Where is it?'

'Pimlico. Want to come and see it?'

'Now?'

'Why not?' She looked at the neat desk, *The Times* open at the cross-word puzzle. 'Unless you're too busy.'

A dusty, dented Mini stood outside the office, parked carelessly with one wheel on the pavement. She drove badly, crashed the gears, jumped orange lights, and a few minutes later pulled up outside a three-storey house in a run-down Pimlico terrace.

As she pushed open the front door, he heard rock music.

'Some friends staying,' she said casually. 'I'll kick them out when you start work.'

The house was empty of furniture and smelled of damp. There was graffiti on the interior walls, on which peeling plaster had left scabrous blotches. The floor-boards were rotten; doors hung off their hinges. Cardboard was propped over broken windows, others were open, and pigeon-droppings covered the sills. But it was a house which had once been beautiful. The rooms were well-proportioned, with high ceilings and decorative cornices.

She led him through it from the top floor down. She scarcely spoke, but he was too busy trying to estimate the amount of work to notice. It would be a more complicated job than anything he and Alan had anticipated, but he had no intention of rejecting it.

They went down a narrow staircase to the basement, and the music roared out at them. In semi-darkness, half-a-dozen people were lying about on mattresses covered with dirty ticking. They looked up at Paul without interest. Smoke rose from a joint that was being passed from hand to hand.

She leant against the wall, and her intent stare made him shift uncomfortably.

'So what d'you think? Can you do it?'

'What can you afford to spend?'

'Much as you need. My grandfather died a few months ago and left me some money. Could you start soon?'

'I don't see why not. I'll have to talk it over with my partner, prepare estimates . . .'

'Just let me know when you're ready.' Her husky voice was indifferent, as though detail did not interest her. 'Would you like some coffee?'

'Here?' He tried to conceal his distaste.

'I've got a pad in Westminster. We'll go there.'

When they reached a tall block behind Victoria Street, he no longer doubted her ability to pay whatever was required to renovate the house. Her penthouse flat looked over the gardens of Buckingham Palace and a London panorama, with the dome of St. Paul's rising in the distance. It was furnished like an Oriental potentate's seraglio, with a ceiling tented in purple silk, rugs hung on the walls, piles of cushions and a few low tables on the polished wood-block floor.

She disappeared through an archway and he heard the bubbling of a coffee-machine. He lowered himself into the cushions. In a few moments, she was back, carrying two cracked mugs with nursery pictures on them.

She sat cross-legged on the floor. 'Now you can tell me about yourself. I know your name and that your father runs that club for rich layabouts on the Costa del Sol . . .' It was a scarcely-concealed sneer. 'What about you? Why aren't you there?'

Having learnt his lesson about frankness, he said, 'I wanted to do something different. Alan Hayes and I had planned for years to set up on our own.'

'But you had a row with your father before you left.'

'That was a fiction dreamed up by the gossip-columnist. In fact, he's backed me financially.'

She raised one of the pencilled eye-brows. 'Not very generously, judging by your office.'

'He gave me what I needed,' he said stiffly. 'Look, Miss Thomas . . .'

'Jan.'

'Jan. My father isn't involved in our business. Alan and I will be responsible for doing up your house, if you want us to.'

She smiled, with sudden, unexpected charm. 'I'm sorry about the catechism. It was sort of a short cut to getting to know you.'

Disarmed, he relaxed, and gestured around the room. 'This is a terrific pad.'

'Glad you think so. My grandfather was a bastard, but I liked him a lot better when he died. He had a row with my parents years ago, so he left everything to me. More coffee?'

'I'll get it. You, too?'

He took the mugs into the kitchen. It was fitted with German-made units and expensive electrical appliances, but there was a faint smell of old grease. The work-surfaces were stained with spill-rings and covered with a layer of dust. Jan Thomas and her environment were a mass of contradictions.

When he gave her the coffee, she said, 'Go on about yourself. My house will be your first job, won't it?'

He made a wry face. 'How'd you guess?'

'*The Times* cross-word. You really need the work, then?'

'Yes,' he said, honestly. 'It'll be our first professional job, but we've had experience, and I promise you, we won't let you down. We'll get first-class men to do the work that we don't handle ourselves and we'll be over-seeing it all the way.'

'That's okay. The job's yours. And look, I'm having a party here tonight. Why don't you come?'

'Oh . . . well, thanks very much.' He drained his coffee and stood up. 'I'd like to take Alan to see the house within the next few days.'

'The front door doesn't lock. Go in whenever you like.'

'Will your friends mind?'

'They're usually too stoned to mind anything. Take no notice of them. See you tonight, then? Any time after eight.'

'It's a strange way of doing business,' Alan said doubtfully. 'Did you like her?'

'She's weird. Didn't seem to be interested in costs, nor our experience, nor how long it would take . . .'

'Let's not anticipate problems. The first thing will be to get a cheque out of her. If she comes across, we'll know she's okay, then we can get a surveyor, order materials, hire some help. Hey, you realise we've actually got a job!'

To celebrate, they split a bottle of champagne over lunch, and spent the rest of the day making plans. They told each other they were on the way at last.

At six o'clock, Paul went back to Maida Vale to shower and change for the party. As usual, he flicked through the pile of lodgers' letters that were lying on a table just inside the front door. There was one for him from Loretta. He picked it up and took it to his room, but when he slit it open, it contained another envelope, bearing a United States stamp.

His hand shook as he took out the single sheet of paper it contained. Maybe she was coming to England . . .

It opened without salutation: 'I couldn't bear to write before, but I have to tell you: by the time this reaches you, I'll be married to Alex Bellini. He has put money into my father's winery. If I hadn't agreed to marry him, he wouldn't have done it. He said that without me there was no future for him as Papa's partner, because it would be too painful to keep seeing me after I'd turned him down. He really loves me. My father was bankrupt. Everything except the vineyard has had to go. Before we left Spain, he told me he had considered killing himself. I so wanted to talk to you that night. I kept wondering if we could think of something . . . even asking your father to help, but I suppose that would have been foolish. I waited for you in the cave for an hour.

'I don't love Alex, but he's a good man. I expect you and I have grown away from each other, anyway. If we hadn't, you'd have made an effort to tear yourself away from your party and meet me, wouldn't you?'

All the exhilaration of the day drained away, and as he went to Westminster, he was unhappier than he had ever been in his life. He realised he had always assumed that one day she would belong to him. It had never occurred to him that she would marry someone else. His own loneliness had led him to rationalise out of existence their joint promise that when they made love for the first time, it would be to each other, but the knowledge that now she was spending her nights with another man was almost unbearable.

There were about a dozen people in Jan Thomas's flat, some standing at the windows, staring at the view, others draped over the cushions. Most held glasses, a few were smoking, and the sweet smell of grass pervaded the room. A Rolling Stones album was on a record-player, the bass turned up so it was like a huge heart beating. There did not appear to be any food.

Jan was wearing the same clothes she had been in earlier. Her eyes looked unfocused and her voice was slurred, he could not tell whether from drink or drugs. Without asking what he wanted, she gave him a glass of harsh red wine, then paraded him around the room, introducing him as 'my architect'. Most of the guests looked at him speculatively, few bothered to speak. It was altogether a curiously silent gathering.

The words of Elena's letter were still drumming in his head like the Stones' bass. He had decided before he arrived that tonight he needed to get drunk, so he swallowed his wine quickly, and someone refilled the glass. Jan drew him into a circle of men and women of all ages who were sitting on the floor-cushions. As he finished his second drink, she handed him a joint. Once, at school, he had experimented with cannabis, and the only effect it had was to make him fall down the stairs. Now he took a deep drag and held it.

The evening took on a dreamlike quality. He had no idea how the minutes or hours were passing. He drank, and smoked. A pleasant haze enveloped him, and nothing seemed to matter. The letter faded from his mind. If there was conversation, it did not impinge on him. He was scarcely even aware that Jan was embracing him, and when she pulled him to his feet, he floated after her like a moth following a candle.

She led him into a bedroom, in which the only furniture was a huge four-poster. She pulled him down onto it and lay beside him. They kissed, and he felt her hands caressing him. He fumbled at the buttons of her shirt.

And then he began to feel sick. He clapped his hand to his mouth, was dimly conscious of being steered into a bathroom, and the door slamming behind him as he leant over the lavatory pan.

When he emerged, shaking, but somewhat sobered, she was still lying on the bed, naked to the waist. She held out her arms, but he backed away.

'I'm going home,' he said.

His revulsion was unmistakable, and after a moment, a look of pure malice crossed her face. She said softly, 'What's the matter, darling? Don't you want to make love to your big sister?'

He stared at her, not understanding.

'You're Paul Raven, and I'm Jennifer Raven,' she said. 'What a pity you got sick. I'd been looking forward to this.'

'What are you talking about?' He heard himself stammering.

'I've always wondered about incest. And I've always wondered about the Ravens. You're very good-looking, Paul . . . it might have been fun. On second thoughts, though, it's just as much fun telling you, and seeing your face.'

Wondering whether his legs were going to give way, he clutched one of the bed-posts for support, looking down at her, hating her.

She lay back, hands clasped behind her head. 'I read about you in the paper. I wanted to see you. Then I thought what fun to do something to you that would pay back what your father did to me.'

'But your mother left *him*.'

'Only because of the way he behaved. He neglected her and went with other women. I don't blame him, mind you. She's pretty awful. What I mind is what happened to *me*.' She sat up. In the dim light of a bedside lamp, her pale face looked like a wax mask which had started to melt, with its badly-defined features and the invisible lashes around light eyes. 'I've read about the San Felipe Club, and the people who go there, and the luxury. After the divorce, my mother married Harry Thomas, who was my grandfather's accountant, until he was fired for cooking the books. Then she and my grandfather had a terrible row. She said he'd spoiled everything for her, and he said he'd maintained her through one stupid marriage and he wasn't going to do it again. So we moved into a semi-detached in Ealing and Harry is the most boring man in the world, and all my mother can talk about is how Max Raven ruined her life. She even made me take Harry's name. I've grown up hating my father.'

'It was nothing to do with me!'

'You've had all the things I should have had.'

'So that house . . .'

'Was only an excuse. It doesn't even belong to me. It's a squat. When I couldn't stand Ealing any longer, I lived there until my grandfather died. There's no job for you. Never was. Never will be.' She began to dress.

He turned and stumbled out of the apartment.

The next day, with a raging hangover, he broke the news to Alan that there had been a misunderstanding. The Pimlico project had been cancelled.

The one person he told about the sleazy incident was Dan Bredon, and that only a year later, after he read a report that the police had been called to a Westminster apartment where the body of a woman named Jan Thomas had been found. She had died from a massive drugs overdose.

5

He was always to think of the weeks after his meeting with his half-sister, and the letter from Elena, and no prospect of work, as the low point of his life.

It was Dan who finally came to the rescue, by putting him in contact with James Fenton, a young British actor who had just had a major success in a film in Hollywood. Although he had moved to Los Angeles, Fenton wanted to keep a foothold in England, and would be returning for a few weeks to buy a country house. If Paul and Alan would seek out some prospects, there was a possibility that he would ask them to arrange the purchase and do any necessary renovations.

That was the start of their entrepreneurial careers: Fenton bought one of the houses they found. Only a few years older than themselves, he liked their enthusiasm, and hired them to organise its renovation. Becaue of his fame, it was subsequently featured in several magazines. This, together with the *Sophisticate* article, put their names before the public, and commissions began to flow in. They built up a reputation for original ideas and using only first-class material and craftsmen.

Within twelve months, Paul had paid back the loan – somewhat to Max's chagrin, according to Loretta – bought a mews house in Bayswater to do up for himself, and had thrown himself heart and soul into building up the business. He drove around the various sites in his Alfa, which he'd shipped over to England.

He kept away from San Felipe, due to an irrational fear that if he went back, his father would find some way of making him stay. Max came to London occasionally, and rarely missed an opportunity to point out how much better off, financially, he would be in Spain. Looking at Paul's northern pallor, he usually added, 'And you'd be a hell of a lot healthier, too.' All of which irritated Paul to the point where he avoided more than one brief meeting during each of Max's visits.

He more or less succeeded in putting Elena out of his mind, but her image would surface every now and then, and a wave of depression would sweep over him as he thought of what might have been. Zimmy wrote that her husband was a frequent visitor to San Felipe, but she had only accompanied him twice. Bellini had put an efficient manager into the vineyards, and Rafael had virtually retired from active participation, although he was said to be paid generously by his son-in-law as a 'consultant'.

'He rides his horses on the beach every day, pays long visits to Madrid and goes to stay with Elena each year,' Zimmy said. 'He is still dominated by Doña Maria and still behaves like the little lord of the manor. He doesn't speak to Max, of course, and, I undestand, never gives up trying to prevent Victoria from going to the Club. She is a problem. Her drinking increases and she is a discontented, lonely woman, who doesn't have the courage to break away. Doña Maria is more severe than ever and is still in mourning for Don Luis. She spends a great deal of her time praying and rarely talks to anyone outside the house, apart from the priest.

'The village becomes more crowded with tourists every year, and the apartments are always full. A lot of money is being made, but even I have begun to wonder whether the development has not gone too far. There is so little left of the old San Felipe we loved. But Max, as you know, has more energy than he knows how to use up, and needs the constant stimulation of new projects.'

By the time the partners were twenty-five, the firm of Hayes and Raven was well-established. Photographs of their work were published in England, Europe and America, and its originality, high quality and historical accuracy were widely praised.

Paul was poring over plans for a barn-conversion in Hampshire one day when his telephone rang.

The Spanish speech was strange to his ears, as was the name: 'This is Elena Bellini.'

He gasped. 'Elena? Elena *Ansaldo*?'

'Yes. How are you, Paul?'

'I'm – fine. Are you in London?'

'I am staying at Brown's Hotel.'

'Is your husband with you?'

'He has gone to San Felipe for a week, to see my father. I wondered if it has been long enough, now, for us to meet.'

'Long enough?'

'For us to have stopped being angry with each other.' He heard the smile in her voice.

'I wasn't aware that I had been angry.'

'If you hadn't been, you might have written to me. And I *was* angry when you did not meet me that night.'

'Oh, God, Elena . . .' The years telescoped. Her unselfconscious honesty was one of the things he had loved about her. She had never tried to disguise her feelings, whether of affection or irritation.

'Let's have lunch together,' he said.

She was waiting for him in the hotel: slimmer than she had been as a teenager, more elegant and, he thought, more beautiful. Yet his reaction, as she held out both hands, was that he should not be here. He had come to terms with the fact that she could never belong to him. Now his emotions were likely to be thrown into disorder all over again.

But as they walked to an Italian restaurant near Berkeley Square his reservations faded. Sitting opposite her at the table, he could not take his eyes off her, examining the features he'd known so well: the dark, slightly slanted eyes, the fine olive-tinted skin, the full lips that turned up at the corners when she smiled – as she was smiling now. 'My grandmother always says it is rude to stare, but we have a long time of not looking to fill in.'

He laughed. 'You've changed . . .'

'Do you realise you always say that to me when we meet?

And I always say, so have you. We grow older, Paul.'

'And you grow better-looking.'

'Thank you. Before we catch up on our lives, I must ask you a question: Why didn't you come to the cave? For years, it has worried me.'

When he had told her, she sat in silence for a few seconds, then said, 'I am glad to know it was not because you didn't like me any more. But even if you had come, it wouldn't have made any difference. I was going to California with my father. It was already arranged.'

'You might not have married Bellini.'

'I had to.'

With difficulty, he said, 'Are you happy?'

'Yes. Mostly. Alex is a kind man, and he loves me very much. He looks after Papa.'

'Have you any children?'

'No. Now tell me about you. I read about you even in America.'

So he told her about his work, becoming more fluent as she showed genuine interest and asked intelligent questions.

When they had finished lunch, it was as though they had never been parted. They went out into the autumn sunshine and he hailed a taxi.

'Where are we going?' she said.

'I want to show you my house. We'll have tea.'

'How English you are! We have just had lunch, and you think of tea.'

She exclaimed with pleasure when she reached the top of the stairs that led into his sitting-room. He had removed all the interior walls and it covered the whole first floor. 'It's so sunny and open! I have thought that most houses in London were like my Great Aunt Emilia's . . . all brown and heavy. This could be a Spanish villa, with your tiled floor, the cane furniture and trees in pots. And so many books!'

'I haven't been able to discard my heritage altogether. Is your Aunt Emilia still alive?'

'Only just. That's why I've come to London. She's fading away, and I wanted to see her.'

'Have you often been here?'

'Several times.' Seeing his frown, she added quietly, 'Always with Alex, and I couldn't get in touch with you. I should not have done so now, but I couldn't resist it.'

'Will you tell your husband?'

'I've always been honest with him.'

They were standing together at the window, looking down into the mews, where a few of the original stables survived. A couple of girls were grooming two horses after a gallop in Hyde Park, and some bantams pecked among the cobblestones. She said, 'It could be a hundred years ago. I do love this city.'

He took her in his arms, and they kissed. She did not resist when, some minutes later, he led her into his bedroom.

That was the beginning of the kind of week of which he had sometimes dreamed. She would not move into the house with him, in case Alex should want to get in touch with her, but he picked her up at the hotel every morning. He informed Alan that he was taking time off, and told his cleaning-woman that she would not be required.

They separated only when Elena went to see her great-aunt. The visits were necessarily brief, because the old lady had little strength. When she returned, they would make love, and talk, and make love again. She told him about her life in California and, although she did not say so, he felt that she was aware of being out of place there. She did not talk much about her husband, but he gained the impression of a man much older than herself, ruthless in business, but unfailingly gentle and indulgent with her. They clearly lived a quiet life, and most of their friends were Alex's age rather than hers.

One day she asked him if he did not have a girl-friend.

He shrugged. 'Several, but no one who is important to me. They pass the time.'

Sometimes they would cook themselves a snack in his tiny kitchen, other nights they would go out for dinner, then return to the house, until he took her back to the hotel around midnight. When the telephone rang, he disposed briskly of the callers. On Sunday, when London was at its quietest, they wandered hand-in-hand through the West End, looking in shop-windows.

It was an idyll, and he was determined that it should not end. But every time he tried to bring up the subject of her husband, she stopped him, saying, 'We mustn't spoil this. Later, I'll have to deal with my guilt. Now it must be just us.'

The day before she was due to leave London, when they were lying side by side on his bed, he said abruptly, 'We have to talk about the future.'

'No! I don't want to talk about it.' She drew his towelling robe around her, as though for protection.

'Darling, it's *our* future!'

She swung her legs off the bed and went to the window. With her back to him, she said, 'I thought you understood that we have no future.'

'Of course we have! For Christ's sake, you can't go back to Bellini now.'

'I must.'

'Why? We love each other.'

'Yes. But I won't leave Alex. It would be shattering for him. He's never done anything bad to me, Paul . . .'

'He blackmailed you into marrying him.'

'It wasn't like that. It was my own decision. He's been faithful to me, and he saved Papa. There's another reason. He and I are both Catholics, we could never get a divorce.'

'You used to say your religion didn't mean much to you.'

'It doesn't, but there are some things . . . anyway, it's not only me. Alex obeys the Church. He wouldn't even consider divorce.'

'Then come and live with me. I don't care about marriage.'

'I do. I've looked at people in America. There's something missing in a relationship without marriage. And if I came to you, there'd always be guilt. About what I'd done to Alex, about being unable to marry. It would be second-best, and I don't want that for us.'

'I'd rather have second-best than nothing.'

'It would be easier for you. You wouldn't be destroying another person at the same time.' She paused, then said, 'I think now I must go. I'll phone for a taxi. We won't meet again.'

'You really mean this, don't you.'

'Yes. There's nothing you can say that would make me change my mind.'

Suddenly, he wanted to hurt her. 'My God, I don't understand you people! A bad marriage can't be ended because your Church forbids it, but screwing around's all right. I suppose now all you have to do is confess and be forgiven.'

She was pulling her dress over her head. When her face reappeared, it was stiff and angry, but she said nothing. She left the room and he heard her calling a radio-cab.

He went to the door. 'Elena, I'm sorry.'

'Don't go on! When I think about what you have said, it is easier to leave you. I will wait outside for my taxi.'

He could not bear to stand at the window, watching her, and only looked out when he heard a taxi stop. She climbed in, and he willed her to look up, but she didn't.

He did not see her again until she was lying in the San Felipe hospital, guarded by her father.

Part 9

The Present

The morning after his precipitate exit from Elena's bedroom, Paul woke early, in a dark mood.

It wasn't only because of her, he decided. He was simply saturated with luxury, sick of the Club's hothouse atmosphere, the guests' relentless pursuit of amusement, their extravagant spending of apparently limitless wealth, of women like Caroline Jarvis, superficial, selfish, aggressively sexual.

He was longing for London, for his own house, for grilled cheese on toast instead of quails' eggs and caviare, for ordinary people who had to worry about their mortgages and bought their clothes at Marks & Spencer.

He put on shorts, draped a towel around his shoulders and went down to the hard sand at the edge of the sea. It was six o'clock on a clear, sparkling morning. He ran from one end of the beach to the other, and back again. Then he jogged more slowly to the rocks that divided the Club property from the village. It was years since he had scrambled over them. They were dry and warm from the sun, with tiny pools in the depressions.

When he reached the neighbouring beach, he threw down his towel and dived into the sea. Powerful strokes carried him beyond his depth, where he turned onto his back and floated. He had always believed in the therapeutic value of salt water, and its instant availability was one of the few things he missed in London. Now, as his hands finned lazily, his problems, both emotional and practical, seemed to be less demanding. He could even try to convince himself that, since he had managed his life reasonably satisfactorily without Elena for the past five years, he would be able to dismiss her from his mind again.

Back on the beach, he towelled himself, and walked up onto the promenade which had been another of Max's gifts to the village. When he was a child, the narrow lanes from the plaza had meandered down to the sand, and stopped. Now they led to a balustraded walk studded with palm-trees.

He strolled in the direction of the Club and had almost reached the end of the promenade when he saw a man bringing chairs from a bar and opening sun-umbrellas.

He looked towards Paul, and a smile spread over his face. '*Hola*, Paul! *Bienvenido*!' He was compactly-built, with a brown skin and small, neat features. There was a touch of grey at his temples, but his shy smile was still that of a boy.

'*Hola*, José!' They shook hands. 'I've missed you at the Club. You working here now?'

'I own it.' He gestured proudly at the spotless tables and chairs, the red and white striped umbrellas, the potted plants that edged his patch of the walkway.

'How long have you had it?'

'For two years. How about a coffee? Can you spare a few minutes? I've been hoping to see you.' The smile had left his face and Paul looked at him curiously. His emphasis indicated that something more than social chat was proposed.

'I'd like that. It's too nice a morning to rush back to work.' He sat at a table, stretched out his long legs and relaxed in the sun.

José brought mugs of sweet, milky coffee. 'I hear your father is improving.'

'He should be back in harness before too long. Tell me about the bar. Didn't you like working at the Club?'

'Well enough, but Senor Max knew I'd always wanted my own place. When this one came on the market he offered me a no-interest loan. I've nearly paid it off already.'

'You must be doing well.'

'San Felipe is prosperous, thanks to your father.'

'The changes haven't worried you? I mean, you remember it as it was, the same way I do.'

'One must be practical. I'm a few years older than you. My father lost a leg in the Civil War, and for years he had to beg to keep himself from starving. When the Club was built, there was work for anyone who wanted it. But . . .'

'But?'

'You've been away a long time,' he said slowly. 'Not everyone these days feels as grateful as I do. There are problems.'

'Are you thinking about the Campo Negro development? Jesús Azano came to see me. He said no one in the village would work on it and now they're angry because they've heard that Machado is hiring out-of-town labour.'

'Is it true?'

'I don't know. I haven't seen him for days.'

'Even the rumour could cause trouble. Paul, I'd decided I'd have to talk to Senor Max, but then he was attacked and it wasn't possible. Maybe you . . .?'

'I'm only here temporarily. I'm leaving as soon as my father is better.'

'Nevertheless, there are things you should know.'

Paul sighed. 'As long as you understand that if it's anything that affects Raven Enterprises, it'll probably have to wait for Max.'

'That'll be up to you. At least you'll have been warned.'

'Go ahead.'

'In my bar, I listen to people talking . . .'

'About what in particular?'

'You've heard about the tragedy when the balcony of an apartment collapsed?'

'And Jesús's brothers were killed. Yes, I heard.'

'It started then. He and the rest of his family blame your father. Over the past couple of years, they've got together a group, mostly of young men, who say that a foreigner has no right to be making such profits on Spanish soil, that we're all being exploited and that they don't want San Felipe over-run by strangers. They're mostly boys who are unwilling to work, or have been dismissed from jobs for laziness or inefficiency, but that's unimportant: they're aggressive, and they're giving the village a bad name. It's nearly all directed against your father. There have been thefts from the holiday apartments, and people have been mugged. They either fight with the young tourists, or they pretend to make friends, for what they can get out of them. They hang around the plaza and pick up single girls . . .'

'I've seen them. There've been reports in England that parts of Spain are becoming unsafe for travellers. It never occurred to me that they might include San Felipe.'

José smiled wryly. 'I'm part of the tourist industry now. If people are afraid to come here, I lose my investment. Something must be done to stop this.'

'The police . . .'

'They do what they can, but they can't get the evidence that would lead to arrests. The village simply closes ranks when a local man is involved. It's always been like that.'

'What could we do?'

'You could start by cancelling the Campo Negro project. It's caused some of the older people to side with the Azanos, and it's built up the resentment against your father. They regard the Campo as sacred ground.'

'There's a possibility that my father has already changed his mind,' Paul said carefully. 'But will that be enough to stop the Azanos' activities?

'No. The only thing that might do that is for them to be convinced that *El Hidalgo* had nothing to do with the accident that killed Jesús's brothers. They're a big family and they're very bitter. Also . . .' He hesitated. 'There is the question of Manolo Machado.'

'What question?'

'He is increasingly disliked.' He leant forward, and although only a few early risers had emerged onto the promenade, he lowered his voice. 'The Azanos are telling people that *El Hidalgo* is involved in his corruption. Machado takes bribes when there are contracts to be awarded. Jesús claims that they are shared with Senor Max.'

'That's ridiculous!'

'No one who knows your father takes it seriously. But those who are not making a profit out of what he has brought to San Felipe, or are jealous of the rich visitors, are ready to believe Jesús. Another thing – and this I know from my own observation when I was at the Club – any young girl who works there is likely to catch Machado's eye. If she rejects him, she loses her job. The Azanos say that he takes his cue from your father.'

'Max never has affairs with the staff!'

'But he amuses himself with the women guests, who are more than willing. The staff pass on stories about him that need only a little exaggeration, and he appears as a corrupter of young girls.'

The sun was hot on Paul's back, but his euphoria had disappeared. Half to himself, he said, 'I wonder how much of this Max realises?'

'He probably wouldn't take any notice if he did. He doesn't give a damn about other people's opinions.' He smiled briefly. 'There's more. You know that the contractor León was found dead a few weeks after the accident that killed the Azano brothers?'

'Yes. He committed suicide. Drove his car off the cliff, didn't he?'

'His son, Ernesto, is a friend of mine. He believes there was more behind the death than León's distress over the tragedy.'

'Like what?'

José's eyes slid away. 'I've heard it suggested that he was killed to keep him quiet.'

'For God's sake! Killed by whom? To keep quiet about what?'

'Who was really responsible for the price-cutting that caused the collapse of the balcony.'

'Who are they thinking of?'

'I wouldn't know. It's nothing to do with me.'

'They *couldn't* be saying my father was implicated?'

'He and Machado are close. Machado hired León.'

'I don't believe this!'

José continued relentlessly: 'Ernesto's step-mother, a woman many years younger than her husband, whom he was said to have picked up in a bar in Malaga, suddenly had the money to buy a house in Ronda after he was killed.'

'Presumably she inherited the profits he'd made out of cheating his employers.'

'According to Ernesto, his father had been doing very badly. He hadn't had a job for months when Machado gave him the contract for the apartments. And why was she in such a hurry to get away from San Felipe after her husband's body was found? She left almost immediately.'

'Can't Ernesto ask her?'

'She's cut herself off from the León family. She won't talk to them.'

'This is all so vague. Rumours. Hearsay. Guesses. You're suggesting that Machado was involved in the deaths of the Azanos *and* León – and that people think that Max was, too?'

'Of course I know your father had nothing to do with it, but Machado is another kettle of fish – which has been simmering away for a long time. It's just possible that the Campo Negro project could bring the hostility into the open, especially if he has really hired outside labour. Most of us are prepared to put up with tourists because they bring money, but they come and go. We don't like outsiders – even Spanish outsiders – who threaten our livelihoods. If there are fights, more violence, it would be very bad for San Felipe. And for your father.'

A pale-skinned English couple seated themselves under a sun-umbrella and he rose abruptly. 'I must go. It's been a relief to talk to you, Paul. Maybe you can do something. Many of us owe Senor Max a great deal.'

As he jogged back across the sand, where a few families were already spreading their towels, Paul tried to make sense out of what he had heard. He told himself that José had surely exaggerated the influence of Jesús and his followers. But was there any reason why the disaffected youth in Spain should be different from young people in other countries: unemployed, easily led, searching for excitement, sometimes even for a cause? His father was a ready-made target.

Damn it, this has nothing to do with me, he thought. Max will deal with it.

On the other hand, Max was being threatened by the emotional currents that were flowing beneath San Felipe's peaceful surface at a time when he could do little about it. And if

José was right, the problems seemed to be accelerating to a confrontation. He listed them in his mind: the future of the Campo Negro; the Azanos' hostility; the rumours of corruption and even homicide in which Manolo was involved.

Despite his personal dislike of Manolo, and Zimmy's doubts, Paul had assumed him to be reasonably loyal to Max. And yet, he remembered, more than twenty years ago Manolo had secretly organised a smuggling ring without caring that it could cause trouble for Raven Enterprises.

Years ago, he had heard Max tell Véronique that Manolo's hunger for money was an understandable effect of his deprived childhood. There was always, in the back of his mind, a fear that good fortune would not last, and that he would end up destitute, back in a cave in the hills. His only extravagance was gambling, otherwise he squirreled his money away. He spent almost nothing on himself, had free accommodation and food in the Club, appeared to wear the same crumpled, lightweight grey suit, with a tieless shirt, year after year. And, according to José, he didn't have to pay for women's services. Yet he never missed an opportunity to add to his hoard. Max had always believed that it was only himself whom Manolo ripped off, and made sure that he didn't go too far. Now, it appeared, he had extended his activities and put Max's reputation on the line.

His alleged connection with León's death was almost too shocking to contemplate, and Paul clung to the conviction that it could not be true.

As he ran up the steps from the beach, he tried to convince himself that he wasn't in San Felipe to become involved in local scandals. His task was simply to carry out his day to day duties as his father's stand-in.

Back at the house, he dressed quickly, then went down to the office. Marian was not there and the only communication was a brief note from Caro, saying that she was unaccustomed to being stood up but if he cared to apologise, she would not be leaving the Club until mid-morning and would be in her suite. He tossed it into the waste-paper basket, but the prospect of running into her and having to make excuses for his defection the previous night helped him to come to a decision.

He needed advice, he knew where to go for it, and it would take him out of her reach for the rest of the morning.

'So what the hell do I do?'

Zimmy was lying in bed, not a grey hair out of place, her shoulders draped in a curious pink knitted garment which, she said, Max's great-uncle Henry had brought from Scotland for her mother, and had assured her was called a 'hug-me tight.'

Pepita had greeted him with the news that the Senora was in bed with an attack of the *reumatismo*. Looking furtively towards Zimmy's room, she had lowered her voice and added: 'She has been bad for two-three days, but she will not give in, the silly woman. This morning, she cannot move, so I say, "I told you so," and she is angry with me. We are not speaking.'

Giving her the lie, a sharp voice called: 'Pepita, who's there?'

'It's me,' Paul said. 'I'm sorry you aren't well. I'll come back tomorrow.'

'No, no! Come in.' He went to the door and she waved him forward. 'I will go mad with that woman fussing over me and no one to talk to all day. There's nothing wrong, just a little stiffness. Pepita, bring coffee!'

He sat by the bed and recounted his conversation with José, ending with the despairing query: 'So what the hell do I do?'

'That man!' she said angrily. 'I've always known . . . but Max would never listen. He remembers the wretched childhood Manolo had, half-starved, his mother a drunken whore, rotting away until she died in his arms. When he was a baby, he learned to thieve because he had to, to stay alive. He has never grown out of the habit. Even when Max was a little boy, he felt guilty because he had so much and Manolo had nothing. That's why he's put up with him all these years.'

'You don't think Max knows about the bribery?'

'How can you even ask the question? I have heard nothing of it, either.' She added thoughtfully, 'I do know many of the men are afraid of Manolo. Keeping in with him can mean the difference between riches and poverty for a family which depends on work with Raven's, and he does the hiring and firing.'

'What about León's death?"

Her mouth tightened. 'If Manolo was involved in that, even Max won't want to cover for him.'

'I'll have to tell him.'

'Not yet,' she said decisively. 'So far you have heard only rumours. There is something you can do yourself before you pass them on to him.'

'And that is?'

'Try to establish some facts. Go to Ronda and see León's widow. Find out what she knows. I must say, I have wondered about it myself. León was not a suicidal type. I saw him at the Azanos' funeral. He was more defiant than upset.'

'Could his death have been an accident?'

'Curiously enough, that was not even suggested. The immediate conclusion was suicide, because he was overwhelmed with guilt.'

'What did Senora León say at the time?'

'Nothing. Presumably she agreed with the general theory. Ernesto León disapproved of his father's second marriage. It could be that he's simply out to make trouble. On the other hand . . .'

'I'll go to Ronda tomorrow.'

Instead of returning to the Club, he turned towards the hospital. As he reached it, Marian was coming out.

'Something wrong with Max?' he said sharply.

Her face was strained, but she shook her head. 'No. He's a lot stronger. He looks almost normal.' She paused. 'Paul, I've had to tell him about Loretta.'

His first reaction was relief. At least that was one blow he wouldn't have to inflict.

She went on, 'He telephoned the house and when there was no answer he called me at the Club, asking where she was. I couldn't think what to say, and he guessed there was something wrong. He said I was to come to the hospital.'

'He must be recovering if he was prepared to allow you to see him.'

'I would never have minded what he looked like,' she said quietly. 'Anyhow, he cross-questioned me. I couldn't bring myself to say she'd left for good. I said she'd been upset about the attack, and his illness, and that she'd gone away for a while, to give him time to recover.'

'That sounds pretty unconvincing. Max is no fool.'

'He didn't say much. You know how he hates showing his feelings.'

'Yes. I hoped we could put off telling him for a while longer.'

'He asked whether she'd left any message. I told him you had a letter and he wants me to bring it to him.'

'It's at the house. I'd better go and see him.'

'No. I think he wants to be alone. He said to tell you not to come today. I'm to give the letter to one of the Sisters.'

'But I must . . .'

'He means it. I heard him giving orders that he wasn't to be disturbed by anyone. Perhaps he needs to get used to the idea that she's gone. Anyhow . . .' Her bitterness was an echo of Paul's own feelings: '. . . he still has Elena.'

'Did he mention her?'

'No. But he wouldn't, to me, would he?' He realised that it was the first time she had indicated her knowledge of the affair.

As he drove back towards the road, he passed the white cottage. The two old men were sitting on their terrace, straw hats shading their faces.

On impulse, he pulled up and went through the gate.

Esteban rose and held out his hand. His wrinkled face was tranquil, all the wildness gone. Gregorio, shorter, broader, with the seamed skin and powerful shoulders of a man accustomed to hard physical work, looked suspiciously at Paul until he recognised him.

Esteban was beaming. 'Max's son! I would have known you anywhere! The colouring is different, but you are very like the little Max I used to know.'

They shook hands, and Gregorio brought out another chair.

'Good to meet a new relation,' Paul said, smiling.

'You know we are related? My sister says she always knew, but I never suspected. She told me when I came back from the mountains.'

'Were you surprised?'

'And delighted. Moira and Andrew were my great friends. So was Max.'

Paul found himself talking as though he had known the old men all his life. Esteban was gentle, cheerful, and he found it difficult to equate him with the potential killer he had seen. Gregorio said little, but his leathery face showed no boredom as Esteban reminisced about the Ravens' early days in San Felipe.

After half an hour, Paul said regretfully, 'I must go. Zimmy told me you often come to the Club. I hope I'll see you there soon, even though Max is in hospital.'

'Thank you. And you need have no fear that I will throw another fit. I am safe for some time, and Gregorio can always tell when one is coming on. He takes precautions – unfortunately, this time he was a little too slow. I should have been locked in my room until it passed off.' He spoke of his illness without embarrassment.

'I'd be happy to see you any time,' Paul said.

By ten o'clock the next morning, he was driving his little Seat up the precipitous road to Ronda. He had not been there since he was a child, and had forgotten how spectacular the mountain scenery was: the great grey rocks, olive plantations which gave way to pines as he wound higher, waterfalls splashing hundreds of feet into chasms. And then the hill-top town, sitting on a kind of land-island, entered over an arched stone bridge that crossed a gorge. He pulled up for a moment and looked down, remembering stories of how, during the Civil War, the Falangists and Republicans had tossed each other over the bridge as fortunes had shifted from one side to the other. His mind's eye saw the bodies bursting like egg-shells as they crashed from rock to rock. Now, golden eagles wheeled below him.

Protected by its inaccessible position, Ronda seemed little touched by tourists, at least this early in the season. He drove around the colonnaded square, parked near the 18th Century bull-ring and walked through the narrow streets where white houses crowded against each other. The Municipal Gardens were pink with peach-blossom.

A couple of telephone calls the previous day, from himself to José, and José to Ernesto, had elicited Senora León's address. He had informed Marian that he was taking the day off, without offering any explanation. A call to the hospital had reassured him that Max's condition was unimpaired by the news about Loretta.

He found the house set back from the cliff-edge, with a spectacular view across the gorge, down into a lush valley studded with a few farm-houses, then up to the mountains.

A few seconds after he had knocked at the door, he heard a call: 'Who is it?'

'Senora León? Could I see you for a minute?'

'I'm busy. What do you want?'

'If you'd open the door, I'll explain.'

A bolt was drawn, and the door was opened on a chain, just enough for a pair of eyes to study him through the crack. Apparently reassured, she released the chain. 'Who are you?'

She was a small woman with black hair built up into a beehive above a white, powdered face, wearing a floral cotton dress, covered by a black apron. One of her cheeks was smudged with dust.

'I'd like to talk to you about your husband,' he said.

Immediately, she pushed against the door, but he reacted automatically, and slid his foot into the gap. Then he gasped: no Hollywood detective had indicated that the crash of solid oak against an instep was extremely painful.

'Senora, I've only come to ask a few questions! I don't mean you any harm.'

Her voice was shrill. 'I don't want to talk to you!'

'Why not? I've come all the way from San Felipe . . .'

'Machado sent you?'

'Of course not! Why should he? And would you please let me get my foot out of this door.'

She stepped back. Over her shoulder he could see a hall,

filled with the evidence of imminent departure: packing-cases, suit-cases, piles of furniture.

Noticing his glance, she came out and closed the door behind her. She was probably in her late thirties, with a pinched, suspicious face. Powder had gathered in the crevices and her narrow mouth had been artificially enlarged by dark red lipstick.

'Who are you?'

'My name is Paul Raven.'

The apprehension returned. 'Are you of *El Hidalgo*'s family?'

'Yes, I'm his son. Senora, there are rumours in San Felipe that my father was involved in the accident that caused the Azano brothers' death and your husband's suicide. Do you know about this?'

After a brief hesitation, she said defiantly, 'Why should I? Don't you believe it?'

'I *know* it isn't true. I'd like you to tell me about your husband.'

For a moment, he thought she was going to retreat, then she said, 'Come and sit down.'

She led the way to a bench that overlooked the gorge,and added, irrelevantly: 'I hate this place. I feel that something keeps pulling me to the edge of the cliff and one day I won't be able to stop myself from walking over it.' She paused briefly: 'I'm going away. He won't be able to find me . . .'

'He?'

'Machado.' He was aware of her eyes, assessing him. After another moment of silence, she said: 'I can tell you things . . . if I do, will you make him pay for what he did to my husband?'

'What Machado did? I'll need to hear what you have to say first.'

She looked away from him, across the valley. After a moment, she began to talk, in a flat voice that was the more convincing for its lack of emotion.

'We had no money. Rodrigo hadn't been able to get work. He'd been slow with his last few jobs and the word had been passed that he was unreliable. Then Machado came to see him. He knew that Rodrigo would agree to anything to get the contract for the new apartments.

'He had to guarantee that costs would be cut to the bone and he would use the cheapest materials. Machado was charging Raven Enterprises for the most expensive, you understand, and putting the difference in his pocket. He said that the more money Rodrigo could save, the more likely it would be that he'd be given work in the future.' She added expressionlessly: 'It seems he overdid the economising. The balcony came away because too much sand had been mixed with the cement, and it crumbled. The Azano brothers were crushed under the rubble. Immediately, Machado announced that Rodrigo was entirely responsible.'

'You say he'd been carrying out Machado's instructions?'

She nodded. 'I said he must go to *El Hidalgo*. Why should Machado get away with it when we were ruined? At first he said that they had been together for a long time, and it was unlikely that *El Hidalgo* would believe Rodrigo León. But eventually I persuaded him. He left home the evening after the Azanos' funeral. Later, one of the builders who had worked with him told me that on the way he'd called in at a bar between our house and the village. He was boasting tht he was going to fix Machado. He had a couple of brandies, but he wasn't drunk. He left, and then he disappeared. It was two weeks before his body was found. The car had come off a section of the cliff road where there was just room for two cars to pass.'

'What do you think happened?'

She said fiercely, 'He didn't commit suicide. Nor was it an accident. Rodrigo was a careful driver and he knew that part of the coast like his own backyard. Some of the men in the bar, who had heard that he was on his way to see *El Hidalgo*, were Machado's friends. I believe one of them got word to him, and he met Rodrigo on that narrow stretch and forced him over the cliff. He was in the outside lane. There are no crash-barriers. A car coming towards him, too far over, dazzling headlights . . . he would have swerved automatically. Machado at once told everyone that he had killed himself. He claimed that he had been suicidally depressed about the Azanos. It was not true! He was optimistic that he could convince *El Hidalgo* of the truth, and that he would be given a new start.'

'You're only guessing all this!'

She smiled without humour. 'You think so? After Rodrigo's body was found, Machado came to me and asked questions. I could see that he wanted to find out how much Rodrigo had told me about their "arrangement." ' Her mouth became a thin line. 'I made a mistake, but I was too upset to think clearly. I said I knew all about it, and that I was suspicious about the way he had died. I said I was going to *El Hidalgo*. He told me that if I made trouble, there might be another little accident. Then he said he would give me some money, on condition that I left San Felipe at once. He hinted that *El Hidalgo* himself wanted the whole business to be hushed up because of the effect it would have on the tourists.'

'You took his money?'

'Why not? I had nothing. My husband was dead. And I was frightened of Machado. I only wanted to get away. The money helped me to buy this house. But I'm lonely in Ronda, and he knows where I am. Sometimes he comes here, to make sure I'm still too afraid of him to talk. If he knew I was telling you . . .' She shivered. 'But in a couple of days, it won't matter. I've sold the house to some foreigners at a profit, and I'm going somewhere he won't be able to find me. You must not tell him you've seen me until then.'

'Would you talk to my father before you go?'

'I won't go near San Felipe ever again!'

'May I know where you'll be, in case I need to contact you?'

'No! I'm not letting *anyone* know where I am. You can pass this on to your father yourself if you want to.' She rose, backed away from the cliff-edge, then ran towards the house.

He called, but she slammed the front door behind her. The chain rattled and the bolt was shot.

He walked back to the car. Once again, it seemed, Zimmy's instinct had been right.

It was nearly two o'clock, he was hungry and he needed to think over what he had discovered. He found a small restaurant and ordered fried chicken and a salad, with a half-carafe of white wine.

Going over their conversation in his mind, he was scarcely aware of what he was eating. He didn't doubt the woman's story of Manolo's deal with her husband, but he still desperately did not want to believe that Manolo had arranged León's death. Nevertheless, the arguments could not be dismissed: Manolo knew that his good life would end if Max were to find out that it was he who had instigated the 'economies' that had caused the original tragedy. It had been easy for him to direct all the blame onto the contractor – Paul remembered Loretta's letter, which had described León as a 'cowboy.' Nor was it illogical that most people had accepted the man's death as suicide, committed after the shock of discovering that he had killed two men and that his own career was in ruins.

He drove slowly down the mountains. The shadows were lengthening as he passed Wayne Bridger's ostentatious villa. He wondered again about Manolo's connection with the bank-robber, and concluded that it could have been the simple attraction of like to like.

By the time he came to the plaza, dusk had fallen and the streets were lively as tourists gathered for their early evening drinks. The inevitable groups of local youths lounged on the street corners, studying the foreigners and choosing their marks. On his first night back he had thought them harmless enough. Now he saw them with new eyes: potentially violent, his father's enemies.

Marian was awaiting him at the Club. Her curiosity was almost palpable, but he ignored the waiting silence, the raised eyebrows. 'Seen Max today?'

'Yes. He wanted to know where you were. I had to say I didn't know.'

He ignored that, too. He did not intend to share his discoveries with anyone before he had talked to Max. 'How is he?'

'He's coming home the day after tomorrow. I spoke to Dr Sanchez. He's amazed at the speed of Max's improvement. If he doesn't overdo it, he should soon be back to normal. Apparently he's been teaching himself to talk again, into a mirror. Sanchez caught him at it yesterday. He can't walk properly, because of the broken ankle, and his left leg's still weak, but he's been exercising that, too.'

'Did he mention Loretta?'

'No. And he didn't seem upset. It's as though she didn't exist.' Although her voice was carefully neutral, he detected an uncharacteristic brightness in her eyes.

He looked at his desk, regarding her neat list of messages without enthusiasm. He could feel the beginnings of a tension-headache at the base of his skull. 'Anything urgent here?'

'No.' She hesitated. 'Paul, have you seen Machado?'

'Isn't he around?'

'Apparently not. You know he handles the property maintenance? A maid reported a blocked drain in one of the villas this morning. Nobody could find him. His room's locked.'

'I expect he's still avoiding me. Probably doesn't want any more discussion about the Campo. What did you do about the drain?'

'What he would have done. Called the plumber.'

Kneading the back of his neck, he said, 'I'm going to the house, Marian. Tomorrow we'll try to get everything straight before Max comes back. I'll have to see Manolo and Victoria, and sort out the Campo sale, among other things.'

The night air was refreshingly cool, with a breeze that brought the smell of salt from the sea, but he found that his mind was swirling around the problem of Manolo, and his head was pounding.

Unwilling immediately to face the empty house and decisions that would have to be made, he drove towards the picnic area at the top of the Campo Negro. The distant lights and the peace made the violence that had put Max and Elena into hospital more than ever obscene.

On an impulse, he left the car and walked past the tables and benches to the stand of umbrella pines under which they had been found. Elena, bruised and almost naked, and Max, unconscious and bleeding. Once again, he had to close his mind to the picture.

There was a full moon and the trees were casting long shadows. He looked at the Campo, stretching ahead of him, a finger of unspoiled land reaching out from the edge of the village.

To his right, he could just make out the bushes which hid the cave where he and Elena used to meet at the edge of the wide, flat shelf planned as the site for Max's supermarket.

As his eyes ranged over the land, they registered an alien shape behind some trees. It was not far from the cave, a slab of black in the moonlight, all angles and straight lines which had nothing to do with nature.

He was on his way towards it when clouds briefly blotted out the moon. Cautiously negotiating the rough ground in darkness, he had reached the trees when the moon reappeared. He found himself staring up at a bull-dozer, squatting there like a monstrous metal dinosaur . . .

Christ! Bloody Manolo again, so sure that nothing would stop the development that he'd already hired the ground-clearing machinery. And somewhere there must be men ready to start work, presumably being paid by Raven Enterprises while they waited.

He decided that getting rid of the men and the machinery was one action he would take without bothering to consult Max.

He was in the office early the next morning. Marian was already there, cool and imperturble in a cream silk dress and high-heeled sandals, glasses pushed up on her head.

'I want to see Manolo right away,' he said. 'Will you get someone to find him?'

After fifteen minutes, she reappeared, breathless. 'He's gone!'

'Gone?'

'I sent Carmen to look for him. He's nowhere about the Club. His room was still locked, so I used the master key. All his clothes have gone. Everything.'

He stared at her. 'Did anyone see him leave?'

'One of the porters saw him go out with a suitcase yesterday. There's another thing: Paco Orlando's disappeared. Two of the guests had booked an early tennis lesson and he didn't turn up. I went to his room . . .' She spread her hands.

'Jesus, at this rate you and I'll soon be the only ones left!'

'It looks as if he's run out on Victoria.'

'Maybe he's eloped with Manolo.' She didn't smile and he went on hastily, 'Orlando was counting on her to back his tennis ranch with the money she'd get for the Campo, and nothing's been finalised yet. I wonder . . .' He stood up. 'That can wait. Manolo's the one I want. I'm going into the village. Maybe someone's seen him. He can't just have evaporated into thin air.'

He did a round of the bars and cafés, then Max's properties. One or two men claimed to have seen him in his car the previous day, but no one had talked to him.

That afternoon, he called in to see Zimmy on his way to the hospital. For once, she had no suggestions, and was as puzzled as he.

Max was up, dressed, and sitting at the window of his room. His broken ankle was still in plaster, but his facial muscles had regained their strength and the blue eyes were once more startling in their intensity; the familiar, ironic smile quirked the corners of his mouth. They shook hands.

'It'll be good to have you back,' Paul said.

'And to be back. Marian says you've been doing a good job. Thanks.'

Paul had already decided against immediately breaking the news about Manolo, hoping that a few more hours would provide at least a clue to his whereabouts. The problems his father would have to face on his return seemed to be multiplying hour by hour.

'How's my car?' Max said. 'Did you have the damage repaired?'

'It should be ready; I'll fetch it when I leave here. And I'll come and pick you up tomorrow. What time?'

'Don't bother. Sanchez said he'll drive me home during the morning. See you around lunch-time. Make sure there's champagne on ice.'

The Porsche had been resprayed, the dents removed. Even Max's eagle eye would not be able to discover where the half-brick had landed.

On his way back to San Felipe, Paul stopped at Wayne Bridger's villa. His momentary hope that Manolo would be there was dashed. The place was closed up. No one answered the door.

He decided to ask once more if anyone had seen him, and pulled up outside the Bar Jiminez. He was about to go in when he heard a shout of 'Fascist bastard!' It came from a group of young men in the square. As he looked around, another spat at the car, and they began to advance. He accelerated away and, for the first time, realised that he was regarded as an alien in the land of his birth.

That evening, he spent a couple of hours playing host in the Club, hoping that Victoria Ansaldo would turn up, but she did not, and no member of the staff had seen her, Machado or Paco Orlando.

At nine o'clock the next morning, he told Marian: 'I'm going to see Victoria. I have a feeling that Orlando's departure must be linked with Machado. If anyone'll know where they are, she will.'

'Rafael won't welcome you.'

'Screw Rafael! I'm sick of this stupid feud.'

As he drove the few hundred yards to the Ansaldo house, he began to wonder how much his decision had been influenced by the possibility of seeing Elena. But if he did, so what? They were finished. Or so he tried to assure himself.

The iron gates were open. He ran up the steps and kept his finger on the bell, hearing its continuous ringing.

Elena opened the door. She was wearing Levis and a loose red shirt. Her hair was tied back with a red ribbon and her face was without make-up. Her skin was like creamy coffee. They stood, looking at each other, then she said quietly, 'Hello, Paul.'

'I haven't come to bother you,' he said. 'I want to see Victoria.'

'She isn't . . .'

Rafael surged through the big, dark hall and brushed her aside.

'Where is she?' he shouted. 'Where's my sister?'

'That's what I came to ask you. I want to see her.'

'She left the house the day before yesterday and she hasn't

come back.' He gripped Paul's shirt. 'Do you know where she's gone?'

He disengaged himself. 'No, I don't, but she's been seeing the Club's tennis professional, Paco Orlando. He's disappeared, too.'

Like an echo, Rafael repeated, 'She's been seeing a tennis professional?'

'I believe they've known each other for some time.'

'A *Spanish* tennis professional?' He asked the question as though it was important.

'Mexican.'

'It's unthinkable! They've gone away together?'

'That would be my guess.'

Rafael seemed to shrink inside his riding clothes. He cleared his throat and whispered, 'She had her car serviced a few days ago. She was planning it . . .' He stopped, as though remembering to whom he was talking. 'I told you never to come near my house! You will leave at once! You and your father . . . if it hadn't been for that Club . . .'

'I'm leaving,' Paul said. 'If Victoria's gone away with Orlando, I'm sorry. For her and for you. But, for Christ's sake, she's a middle-aged woman. She has a right to arrange her own life!'

He had reached the car when he heard Elena call, 'Paul, wait!'

She was trying to pass Rafael, who was barring the door. He went back and, given strength by anger, picked up the smaller man and moved him bodily out of her way.

She ran down the steps, then turned. 'Father, whether you like it or not, I am going with Paul. I have my own life, too. When I come back, you and I will need to come to an understanding.'

She got into the car. 'I want to talk to you in private,' she said, grim-faced. 'We'll go to the Campo.'

Confused, and still irritated by the encounter with Rafael, he said, 'The other night you didn't even want to see me. What's brought about this change?'

'Who said I didn't want to see you? It was my first night home. I'd been in hospital, remember? You burst in with

Victoria, without warning. My father was furious. I asked you to leave because I didn't feel strong enough for a row. I didn't mean you should disappear for ever! Why didn't you get in touch with me again?'

'Can't you guess?'

Before she could answer, he had to pull out into the middle of the road to avoid Titi, who was running in the direction of the Club, gripping his imaginary handle-bars. He had a parcel in a bag slung over his shoulders, and waved.

They rounded a curve and the Campo was ahead of them. Surprisingly, a number of people were standing around, all looking in the same direction, with the self-satisfied air of holiday-makers watching workers. More purposefully, a dozen village women were hurrying towards them.

Then they heard the rumbling of machinery, the scrape of metal on stones. The bull-dozer's great scoop was lifting rocks and earth, leaving brown scars in the land.

Forgetting Elena, Paul jumped out of the car and raced towards it. There was one man in the cab, three others were leaning on shovels, watching.

Before he could reach them, the village women converged, their shrill voices raised in angry protest. He saw them join hands, spread into a line and head straight for the machine.

Either the bull-dozer operator did not realise their intentions or he had his orders. Only feet from them, he lifted another scoop. Dirt and stones showered down. Dirt, stones – and something else. One of the women darted forward. An appalled silence fell as she held up a creamy-yellow skull, with grinning teeth, earth-filled eye-sockets and nostrils.

The operator stopped the scoop in mid-air. The watchers were transfixed. It was as though the world had come to a standstill.

Then the women broke their line. They fell on their knees, scrabbled in the loosened earth and began to extract other bones, and more skulls.

They were old women, some well on in their seventies, but their gnarled, arthritic fingers dug deep as they crawled on hands and knees. Without a word being spoken, one of them moved along the line and collected the bones they turned up.

A hill of skeletons began to rise: rib-cages piled on skulls, shoulder-blades, femurs.

The macabre ritual was interrupted as a group of young men arrived from the village. Paul recognised one as the youth who had spat at his car the previous evening. Another was armed with a shot-gun. They had obviously come with the intention of stopping the bull-dozer, but they stopped when they saw the bizarre pyramid of bones. Then one whispered, '*Mi abuelita*!' and went to an old woman who was brushing earth from a skull, as gently as though it was the head of a baby. Her eyes were blinded with tears as she gestured her grandson away and went on with her digging.

A siren howled, and a *guardia* car swept up.

At that moment, Paul saw a movement in the trees. A familiar, squat figure was hurrying up towards the main road at the top of the Campo.

With the *guardia's* arrival, some of the tension was broken, and the crowd, recovering from its awe, began to mill around the women. Some joined the search, chattering excitedly as they made new finds.

Paul skirted them, and shouted. Manolo heard him, and began to run. He gave chase, but was only in time to see him leap into the passenger seat of a car which had been parked by the picnic area. It accelerated away and disappeared towards the coast. It was the yellow BMW he had last seen at the San Felipe airport, and it belonged to Wayne Bridger.

A few minutes later, he pulled up outside Bridger's villa. Its garage doors were open. The BMW was inside, with Manolo's ancient Ford beside it.

Loud, angry voices were coming from beyond a brick wall, through which an arch led to a rear terrace.

As he reached it, he saw the two blonde girls, wearing only bikini pants, stretched out on loungers. They might have been invisible for all the notice that was being taken of them.

Manolo was backing away from Bridger, whose fist was raised as he shouted, 'Nobody does this to me, understand?'

Sunlight twinkled on beads of sweat on Manolo's forehead and his mouth moved soundlessly, but when he saw Paul he straightened, gathering the remnants of his dignity.

Bridger noticed the direction of his look, and turned. 'Who the hell are you?'

'Paul Raven. I want a word with Machado.'

'Get in the queue! You Max Raven's boy?'

'Yes.'

'Then you can tell your father he's in trouble. Him and this . . . this . . .' His face was purple as he sought for words.

'I don't know what you're talking about,' Paul said. 'What were you doing at the Campo Negro?'

'I bloody bought it, that's what I was doing. He . . . ,' He gestured towards Manolo, '. . . told me a week ago that the Ansaldo woman was going to sell it. He said Raven wanted it, but she'd let it go to the highest bidder. So I outbid him. What nobody told me was that the place is a fucking graveyard. And now she's run out with my money!' His jowls were quivering and Paul could see a distortion of his own face reflected in his mirror sun-glasses. 'It was a put-up job, wasn't it? You lot, Machado and that woman. Fifty thousand bloody quid I paid her. Cash. What was your share?'

'My father and I didn't know anything about it. Why would you want that land?'

'I don't, now. Me and my colleagues were going to build our own Club, right on Raven's doorstep.' He took off his glasses, and rubbed the reddened bridge of his nose. 'You see what they were digging up?'

As much to himself as to Bridger, Paul said, 'Those old women knew what was there. That's why they were so determined the land shouldn't be developed.'

'Nobody told me that!'

Manolo spoke for the first time. 'It's not important! They can bury those bones somewhere else, whoever the hell they belong to. It'll be forgotten when the building starts. There'll be jobs for everyone.'

'Not from me, there won't,' Bridger snapped. 'You saw the cops arrive? I been living here peacefully. I'm not going to get mixed up with the *guardia*.' He glanced at Paul, 'I had a few problems in England . . .'

'I know.'

'I like it here. I don't want any trouble, and that land's trouble. I can smell it. What I *do* want . . .' He loomed over Manolo, '. . . is my money back.'

'I haven't got it. Victoria Ansaldo . . .'

'I don't care who's got it. I want it from *you*. Now.'

'I'll get it! I'll get it! I'll find you more land, too. No need to cancel our plans. We'll just move elsewhere.'

'*We* won't do anything of the kind, mate!' He turned to Paul. 'I offered this sod a job, but you can have him back. I want no part of him.'

This time, it was Manolo who raised a fist, his face enraged. Bridger simply smiled, and pointed to the house. Two men were in the doorway, leaning against the wall, watching them: big men, wearing shorts and vests, with bulging muscles and unfriendly expressions.

Manolo took a deep breath. His aggression shifted to Paul. 'This is all your fault,' he said venomously. 'You interfering young bastard! If you hadn't come back . . . First your mother, then you . . . you've always tried to turn Max against me.'

A cold anger swept over Paul and he forgot everything but his conviction that Manolo must not be allowed to return to the Club. He said softly. 'I've been talking with Senora León.'

The dark skin turned a sickly yellow. 'I don't know what she told you, but that woman's a liar . . .' He stopped.

Both of them had forgotten Bridger, who was watching with interest.

Still without raising his voice, Paul said: 'Maybe we can't prove what caused León to run his car over the cliff, but too many people know how you've been conducting Max's business. Taking back-handers from men needing work. Your instructions to cut costs, that killed two men. And you've tried to cheat him on the Campo deal . . .'

'Which gives Raven and me something in common,' Bridger murmured.

'That was your fault!' Manolo shouted. 'If you hadn't come back and tried to take over . . . then he tells me you're the boss and I'm to take your orders! *Me*! I know him, he'll talk you into staying. It's what he's always wanted. But I'll never work for you!'

'You're right about that! So after forty years, without a word, you walk out on him when he's ill.' His contempt made even Manolo flinch.

'I have to look after myself!'

'I want you out of San Felipe, Machado.' Paul said quietly. 'I'm telling Max everything I've found out about you. Then the *guardia*. You go now, and you might have a chance to get away before they start looking for you. And that pays off anything you might think Max still owes you.'

Looking into his unyielding face, Manolo seemed to shrink inside his ill-fitting suit. 'You can't do this!'

'Try me.'

Bridger interrupted: 'Hang on! He doesn't leave until I've got my money.'

Without pausing to consider, Paul said: 'We'll buy that land from you, for what you paid.' We? Suppose Max didn't want the Campo now?

But it was too late to renege. Bridger held out his hand. 'It's a deal. And don't you worry about Machado. I'll see he goes – and that he doesn't come back. I've got a few friends around here who keep an eye on what's going on. In fact . . .' He looked at the glittering gold watch on his wrist. 'I'll give him just fifteen minutes to get his things together and leave my house. Starting now.'

Manolo stumbled towards the door. As he brushed past the two impassive minders, he turned and looked at Paul. His face was a mask of hatred.

Bridger walked to the car with him. 'Your father's an arrogant bastard, and I don't like him. But he's well rid of Machado. He set up this whole deal. Told me it would make Raven mad as hell if I were to buy the Campo Negro. I'd been waiting for a chance like that . . .' He looked wistful. 'I don't suppose he'd reconsider my membership of the Club?'

'I don't think so. You've just cost him a hell of a lot more than that land is worth,' Paul said grimly.

He was shaking with reaction when he drove away, realising that he had taken far more on himself than was his right. But whatever his father's initial doubts, he must realise that he couldn't protect Manolo any longer.

People were still standing about when he pulled up at the Campo, but the frenetic activity had quietened. The police had cordoned off the area where the bones had been found and a couple of them had taken over the digging from the exhausted old women. Elena was not there, and he guessed that she had walked home.

Although he badly wanted to hear what she had to say to him, he knew that his immediate duty was to his father.

Max was already back at the Club, sitting in a wheel-chair behind his desk, which was covered with papers.

'Welcome home. How do you feel?' Paul said.

'Back to normal, except for the ankle and a leg that lets me down every so often. Hence the wheelchair. I gather Manolo's disappeared.'

'He reappeared. I need to talk to you about him, if you feel up to it . . .'

He left out only his meetings with Elena, and Max listened to his report almost without interruption.

'. . . so Manolo's gone, you're up for fifty thousand and, whether you like it or not, the Campo belongs to you,' he ended.

'You *have* been busy. I don't care about the money, but Manolo . . . Christ! I hadn't realised . . .' He looked unseeingly across the room, then said heavily, 'I can't say I've ever really liked him since we were grown up, but he's part of my past and if it hadn't been for him, I'd never have got the money to build the Club.'

'You paid off any debt long ago. I'm sorry . . . this is a lousy home-coming. I've exceeded my brief. I should have seen you first, but that bastard . . . if I had any doubts that he was responsible for León's death, he removed them.'

'You did absolutely right, and I'm grateful. Not only for your detective work, but for relieving me of having to get rid of him myself. I've thought about it more than once. He's been in trouble before, apart from the smuggling. A woman from the village claimed rape and had to be paid off. He pulled a knife on one of the waiters last year. But I always remembered his awful childhood and I couldn't bring myself to fire him. This time . . . Jesus Christ! Murder! And although I always understood that he'd cheat me when he thought he could get away with it, I didn't know he did it to the men. No wonder the village is up in arms.'

'He really tried to screw things for you with the Campo. If it hadn't been for those bones, you'd have had a rival club almost next door.'

'With a membership of every criminal on the coast. It doesn't bear thinking about.'

'Did you know about the graves?'

'No. Like most other people, I've always assumed it was some village superstition that made the place special. Never thought much about it. I wonder who the hell they were?'

'Zimmy knows.'

'She does? She's never mentioned it to me. We'll have to find out. I used to know everything that went on in San Felipe, or just about. The place isn't what it was.'

'You changed it,' Paul pointed out.

'I *started* it. But it was going to happen anyway.'

Marian opened the door. She glanced from Max to Paul, looking unusually flustered. 'Mrs Bellini's here . . .'

Elena was still wearing jeans and her white shirt. Her face was set and angry, but when she saw Max, she held out both hands. He took them and Paul found their obvious pleasure in each other almost too painful to watch.

Looking up at her, Max said, 'We never did get to have that talk, did we?'

'Sister Magdalena told me you sent roses. My father wouldn't allow me to accept them, but thank you.'

'I also wrote you a note.'

'I didn't get it. He would have guessed it came from you. I suspect he destroyed it.'

'It wasn't important. An apology because I'd let you down.' He looked at Paul, who had moved to the window and was standing with his back to them. He said politely, 'You and my son know each other, I believe.'

'A little while ago he walked out on me at the Campo Negro.'

'I went back for you. You'd gone.'

'I waited for nearly half an hour, then I went home to tell my father what was happening.'

'I'm sorry I left, but something came up. Anyhow, I can't see that we have much to say to each other. I'll leave you with Max.'

He turned towards the door, but she moved in front of him. 'What is the matter with you? You don't come and see me in hospital, you don't even inquire about my health. Surely we can at least be friends? Even if you do have – have other interests.'

'I don't know what you're talking about!'

Max's voice was quietly amused. 'Was that what you wanted to see me about, Elena?'

'Of course it was! How could I have gone to him directly? I had to come to Spain and see to my husband's property, then I was going to London. It seemed to be sensible to see you first . . .'

'To find out how the land lay?'

'Yes. But now I'll ask him myself. Paul, are you married?'

Too astonished to speak, he shook his head.

'Engaged? Living with some lady who is not your wife?'

'No.'

'Then why are you treating me like this?'

His control snapped. 'You want me to spell it out? You and Max. How long has it been going on? All the time you were married? Maybe it had started even before we were together in London.'

He had always known that she had a temper, but he was unprepared for her reaction. Even her hair seemed to crackle. Her eyes narrowed and her voice became a rasp. They had been talking in English, now she switched to Spanish: 'You are accusing me of having an affair with *him*? You must be mad!'

'No need to be quite so emphatic,' Max said.

She ignored him. 'You say that I have been sleeping with your father? How dare you . . .' Scarcely pausing for breath, she battered him with a stream of angry words. When she finally slowed down, she said, in English again, 'My God! You leave me speechless!'

This brought a roar of laughter from Max. They both glared at him, then she, too, began to laugh.

Scarcely daring to analyse the implications of her anger in case he had misunderstood, Paul said, 'Then why . . .? Everyone naturally assumed . . .'

She held up her hand like a policewoman stopping traffic. 'You are insulting me again! There was nothing natural about it! But we will sit down and talk like rational human beings. If you can convince me that there was a reason why you made that ridiculous accusation, I might consider forgiving you.'

She went to a chair by the coffee-table, sat down and folded her hands in her lap, waiting.

'I'd better leave,' Max said.

'Stay! I think you will enjoy finding out what a fool your son has been.'

Paul gathered himself. 'I'm sure he will. But what the hell was I to think? When I arrived here I was told that he'd been attacked when he was with a girl up in the hills. I know him. He's often taken women there.'

'I'd had a letter from Elena, saying she wanted to talk to me,' Max said, patiently. 'I suspected what it was about, and I knew she wouldn't come here, because of Rafael, so I met her at the airport. I hate to disillusion you, but my amorous reputation's exaggerated. I don't screw *every* woman I take for a drive.'

'I'm not the only one who thought . . . Zimmy, Dan Bredon, Loretta. That's why she left.'

Max made no comment, but Elena was stricken. 'It can't be true! Loretta is his wife!'

'She seemed to be prepared to put up with the other women. You were the one she couldn't compete with.'

'Ah, Dios, that's awful! But didn't you explain, Max? How could you let everyone go on thinking that I was another of your – conquests?'

'Nobody asked me. I only guessed how Paul felt the other day. I told him he'd better go after you while I was out of action.' He paused, and added apologetically. 'It was a joke that seems to have misfired.'

She was angry again. 'That was not a nice thing to do! As if I would have . . . you're my father's age!'

'True. Unthinkable, isn't it?'

The telephone rang and he reached for it automatically. Paul hardly registered the conversation. He was looking at Elena like a treasure-seeker who had just discovered there *was* gold at the end of the rainbow. Everything else had become unimportant.

When Max hung up, his voice was brisk. 'Sorry to interrupt this illuminating conversation, but Zimmy wants to come and see us. I told her you'd pick her up in ten minutes.'

'Can't someone else . . .?'

'She said it's urgent. And in the meantime, I'm going to have to call the *guardia* about Machado.'

'I will go, too,' Elena said. 'But I must ask you about the Campo? Who hired that bull-dozer? Was it Victoria?'

'You can tell your father that she sold the land to Wayne Bridger. He'll know the name. Bridger and Machado organised the digging, but it's been stopped. That's all we know at the moment.'

'Those bones . . .?'

'I have a feeling Zimmy wants to tell us about them,' Paul said. 'Why don't I drop you home on my way to fetch her?'

'Come back and have lunch with us. Maybe we'll know a bit more,' Max said.

'Thank you. If I can get away. My father doesn't know I'm here.'

As they left the Club, she looked around and said, 'Do you realise this is the first time I've set foot in here? It's beautiful. From the way my father talks, I had expected a place in which any nice girl would be ashamed to be seen!'

'I'll give you the grand tour this afternoon.'

She put her hand on his arm. 'Could we find a little time for ourselves? We have so much to talk about.'

'I have plans for that.' He pulled up at the entrance to the Ansaldo house. 'In the meantime . . .' He put his arms around her and she clung to him as their mouths met, tongues seeking each other delicately. When he released her, he said. 'There might even be time for other things besides talking.'

* * *

Zimmy waved away his inquiries about her arthritis, and as he drove her back to the Club, she said, 'For the first time in my life, I am very angry with your father. I hope he is well enough to hear what I think of him. There's no excuse for what he has done.'

'The Campo? He had nothing to do with that. He didn't know anything about the land-clearance until I told him.'

Her face crinkled with suspicion. 'Then who . . .?'

'Bridger and Machado.' In abridged form, he repeated what he had told Max.

Her hand was plucking agitatedly at her skirt when he finished, but her voice was calm. 'The village must hear about this. There's so much bitterness, I'm afraid of what might happen.'

'Max is buying the land from Bridger, and there won't be any development. I think the main thing that's worrying him is what Machado has done.'

'Poor Max! He has been so badly let down by that man.'

'Yes. Zimmy, you knew about those skeletons, didn't you? Hell, there must have been half-a-dozen bodies buried there.'

'Seven,' she said. 'Seven men. When I thought the digging had been ordered by your father, I realised that I should have told him about it long ago. He would have understood. San Felipe is his village, too.'

'You'll tell him now?'

'Yes. The time for secrets is over.'

Max had given orders that he was not to be disturbed. From outside came the chatter of guests sunning themselves beside the pool, and Marian's word-processor clicked in her office. But Max and Paul heard only Zimmy's voice as she took them back more than fifty years, to the night the bodies had been buried on the Campo Negro. The night, too, that Andrew and Moira Raven had died.

It was nearly midnight when Andrew arrived at the Bar Jiminez, breathless, to tell Zimmy that her brother was at his house, badly wounded. His little party of Republicans had been ambushed by their enemies and he had been shot while escaping. He needed help to reach the fishing-boat that was to carry him to his pre-arranged meeting with the Republican forces further up the coast.

While she dressed, Andrew led her donkey, Burro, from his stable and they hurried through the silent village, back to the *finca*.

Moira had bound up Esteban's thigh, and given him a glass of brandy, but he was still in considerable pain.

As they helped him onto the donkey, Moira whispered to Zimmy, 'Max . . .?'

'I looked in on him on my way out. He is asleep. I'll be back long before he wakes.' Despite her concern for her brother, she managed to smile, and Moira was reassured. It was the first time Max had spent a night away from home, but he had begged to be allowed to stay with Zimmy, as a special treat, since they were leaving for England in a week.

Supporting Esteban on either side, Zimmy and Andrew set out to take him to the tiny bay where the boat was waiting.

He was taken on board, and they watched it glide away. There was no moon and the sea was quiet. Within a few minutes, its silhouette had merged with the darkness.

Then they trudged back to the Bar. Andrew said good-night, and started on his way home.

Zimmy watched until he turned the corner, thinking how much she was going to miss the Ravens when they left for England. But it was good that they were taking Max away from this war . . .

She felt like an old woman as she climbed the stairs. She paused outside Max's room to listen to his even breathing. A few more days, and he would be gone. She wondered wearily whether she would ever see him – or, indeed, Esteban – again.

She had taken for her own the red room in which the Ravens had spent their first weeks in San Felipe, and, as she did every night, looked up at the painting that hung above the bed-head to bid a silent good night to her mother and Henry Raven. She was so accustomed to their state of undress that she saw nothing incongruous in it.

Knowing sleep would be hard to win, she lay under a single

sheet and, though she was not a religious woman, prayed for Esteban and his friends, for an ending to the Civil War, for Max, Moira and Andrew and their safe journey to England.

The village was quiet and she had no inkling that during her trek to the bay, events had occurred which would have their echo half-a-century later.

The sky had hardly started to lighten when she was awakened from a restless doze by a rapid tapping on her door and Pepita's voice. 'Wake up, Senorita! Something is happening!'

Her head felt too heavy to lift. 'What is it? What's the time?'

'Five o'clock. Come to the window.'

She stumbled across the room. The street was alive with shadowy figures, all hurrying in the same direction: men wearing hastily-donned overalls over vests; some women dressed, others still in their ample Mother Hubbard night-gowns, with shawls around their shoulders. Nobody was talking and, as she threw open the window, all she could hear were their footsteps.

She saw Aquilina's small, round figure, her flesh quivering as she broke into a run.

'Where are you going?' she called.

Aquilina simply pointed in the direction she was moving.

Fully awake, she dressed quickly and, pursued by Pepita, ran into the street.

They caught up with old Maruja, the seamstress, who was hobbling along on two sticks. She looked at them blindly, then stammered: 'Mother of God, Senorita! Such a dreadful thing.'

'What's happened?'

'Calvino the shepherd found them.'

'Who did he find?'

Maruja's head bobbed and grey tendrils of hair floated like spiders' webs as she shivered. 'One is Aquilina's Ricardo . . .'

In the early light the flat ledge of the Campo was like a huge stage, with a backdrop of rocks. More than a dozen men and women were standing, rigid as sculptures, looking down at the ground. Zimmy edged between them, and clapped a hand over her mouth to stifle a scream. Seven bodies were lying there, side by side. She recognised Jaime's big frame, although his face was hidden in the rough grass. Blood had soaked the back of his shirt and dried into a black pool around him. She saw Roberto, a handyman who had sometimes helped her in the Bar, in profile, because his head was twisted at an angle it could never have achieved in life. Gil, the barman, was there, also face down, and bloodied. There were others she could not identify, because the backs of their heads had disintegrated into a soup of blood, grey matter and slivers of white bone. The only man lying on his back was Aquilina's son, Ricardo, and she was sitting beside him, cradling his head in her lap.

Of the group of young Republican guerrillas who should by now have joined their comrades, only Esteban had survived.

Pepita retched and ran for the trees, where she threw up. Zimmy looked around at the people's faces, stunned into immobility. Some had their eyes closed. Two or three women clasped their hands in prayer.

She realised that she was standing next to Calvino, whose youngest son had been among them and was, presumably, one of the unrecognisable bodies. He met her eyes, and whispered: 'They were all shot in the back. This wasn't war, it was murder.'

Zimmy stopped talking. After a moment, Paul asked softly, 'Did you ever find out who did it?'

She blinked and looked momentarily surprised, as though she had forgotten she had an audience.

'We didn't try,' she said, 'My dear, you must understand the bitter political hatreds there were then. On the way to the fishing-boat, Esteban had told us they had been ambushed by about twenty masked men. Someone had betrayed them. We realised that the attackers must have been their friends, or relations. *Our* friends or relations. Two of Aquilina's other sons were Fascists. If they had killed their brother, she didn't want to know it. Gil's uncle, Roberto's father . . . they were on the other side, too, members of the Nationalist group led by Don Luis Ansaldo.

'After a while, people fetched picks and shovels and began

to dig graves. The old priest who had replaced Father Miguel – so old he scarcely understood what was happening – gave them the last rites. By eight o'clock in the morning, it was all over. The ground had been smoothed and grass scattered over the graves. They were not even marked.

'There is no doubt that some of the murderers were among us, men who were shattered when, in the light of day, they realised what they'd done.

'We could only guess that they'd been overtaken by mass hysteria, each man's hatred for his political enemies feeding off the other's. They must have made those young men, whom they'd known all their lives, stand facing the top of the Campo. Then they shot them. It had been a kind of madness and it was only when they saw their mothers and fathers and sisters grieving over the dead that they came to their senses and were ashamed of what they'd done. And so were the rest of us. I think we felt that, in a way, we all shared their guilt, for it had happened in our village.

'We went from the Campo to the church, and there we decided that finding out who had been responsible would achieve nothing. It would destroy families and only create hatreds that could lead to more deaths. Even those who had lost children agreed, because they were afraid to know who had killed them. From the moment we separated and went back to our own homes, the massacre was never mentioned again.

'Don Luis gave permission for the shrine to be built, and every year since then the surviving relations of the dead have made a pilgrimage to the Campo.' There was a deep sadness in her voice. 'You see why there was such opposition to your plan for its development, Max. Nobody who remembered it wanted the tragedy to be resurrected. Over the years, it's come to be accepted that the old people have some silly superstition about the Campo. It would have been better if it had stayed that way.'

'Did you ever discover who betrayed Esteban and his men?' Max asked.

'No. I doubt that we'll ever know.'

'Do you think Don Luis was in on the massacre?' Paul said

'Who can say? He led the local Fascists and he hated all Communists. When the request to build the shrine was made, he asked no questions and he agreed instantly. Even if he wasn't actively involved, he knew what had happened.'

'And what about my parents' death the same night?' Max said. 'Hell, it's hard to believe that was a coincidence. When did you find out about the fire?'

'I was drinking coffee when I got back from the church, trying to get over the shock of what I'd seen. You were still asleep upstairs. I was to take you to the *finca* later in the morning.

'Don Luis arrived. He looked like another dead man. The massacre was not mentioned. In fact, he denied having heard any disturbance during the night. He said that when he got up, he had smelled smoke and a few puffs were rising above the trees between his house and the *finca*. He went to look and found that although the walls of the finca were still standing, almost everything inside had been destroyed. The bodies of Moira and Andrew were lying in the studio.

'By that time, I think I was beyond being affected by any more horrors. My whole life had suddenly become a nightmare. I went there with him. He was in shock, almost incoherent. The police arrived and the bodies were taken away. There was nothing to connect the fire with what had happened on the Campo. As far as I know, nobody suspected that Andrew and I had helped Esteban to escape.'

'It was never investigated?'

'We were in the middle of a Civil War! The only police we had were men too old to fight, only interested in surviving until, they hoped, they would get their pensions from whichever side won. They didn't want to antagonise the Nationalists or the Republicans. They weren't going to create another drama out of what was clearly a tragic accident.'

'Anyhow, my parents were leaving Spain. They were nobody's enemies,' Max said thoughtfully.

'No. Andrew never made any secret of which side he supported, but he'd taken no active part in politics and Moira was determined that they wouldn't get involved.'

'So I suppose we must accept the coincidence.'

She shrugged. 'It was fifty years ago. It's part of history.'

'History seems to be catching up with us. Did Paul tell you that we're buying the Campo from Bridger?'

'That isn't going to improve your reputation with the people, especially now. They'll be wondering what you're going to do with it. Max . . . be careful!'

Despite the morning's events, the luncheon turned into a celebration of Max's return from hospital.

Elena returned, saying that her father had gone riding and her grandmother was staying in her room, so she had not had to explain her departure. Max had invited Zimmy, Marian and Dan Bredon to join them.

Waiters wheeled in a table already laid, and Max opened two bottles of Tattinger. They ate lobster, followed by tender veal medallions in a creamy sauce spiked with brandy, and they discussed, compulsively, the happenings of the past couple of days, and Zimmy's story of the origin of the Campo graveyard, which she repeated, in an edited version, for those who hadn't heard it.

Paul took little part in the conversation, because he could not take his eyes off Elena. She had changed out of her jeans into white cotton trousers and a white silk shirt etched with a swirling black pattern, like outlines of indecipherable writing. Her hair was loose, her eyes enlarged with a touch of green shadow and black eye-liner, her lips were barely coloured with coral. She was exotic and elegant, and heads had turned to watch her as they walked through the lobby.

Max played host expertly, his charm reaching out to embrace them all. Paul and Zimmy were, perhaps, the only ones to understand why a shadow occasionally crossed his face and his mind seemed elsewhere. During her account of that night so long ago, his parents had been very close to them, but now they had gone again.

A Chateau d'Yquem was served with feather-light almond mousse and *tuilles*. For coffee, they moved from the table which was instantly wheeled away, to the deep sofas and armchairs. Max heaved himself out of his wheel-chair and, leaning on a stick, limped carefully to the bar to pour brandies.

'I didn't realise you were able to walk,' Dan said.

'I've been practising with the stick, but it's too damn slow, and my leg occasionally collapses.'

Paul remembered that walking at anything less than a brisk stride had always irritated him. Véronique had protested at being forced to trot to keep up even when they went for what he called a leisurely stroll.

When everyone had a brandy, he raised his glass to Elena, 'To your first visit to the Club. May there be many more, now the ice has been broken.'

Zimmy added, 'Perhaps one day we might even persuade your father to join us.'

Elena looked down at her glass, then said quietly, 'I hope so. But it is hard for him to change.'

'How did he react to Victoria's departure?' Max said.

'He was very angry, but he seemed to be even more upset by what happened on the Campo this morning. And I thought my grandmother was going to collapse.'

'But she must have known about it. Your grandfather certainly did,' Zimmy said.

'She didn't say so. In fact, she hardly said anything. I haven't seen her since. She has been resting all morning.'

'Rough on an old woman to be reminded of a thing like that after all these years,' Paul said.

'I suppose so.' Her face lightened. 'I'm afraid it will be another shock when I break the news that I have ventured into this den of iniquity.'

Max said, 'I hope you can convince Rafael that we won't corrupt you.' He turned to Paul. 'By the way, it's more convenient for me to stay down here at the Club until I'm a bit more mobile. The house is yours.'

Paul flicked a glance at Elena. The corners of her mouth turned up, and he knew she understood the kind of plans he had made for the rest of the afternoon.

Casually, he said, 'I promised I'd give you the grand tour. How about a stroll?'

The house made her gasp with pleasure. 'Even in California our friends did not live in such luxury! Does anyone use that pool?'

'Certainly. Max swims all year, indoors and out. Shall we try it?'

'I have no swim-suit . . .' She saw his raised eyebrows, and laughed. 'I have got out of the habit of being unself-conscious with you.'

'You never were in London.'

'And won't be now.'

Watching each other with hungry eyes, they undressed, then he ran his hand over her smooth skin: shoulders, breasts, waist, down over her stomach, lightly touching the dark triangle of hair, to her thighs.

'Not yet!' she said. 'Swim first.'

Evading his reach, she dived into the water. The glass partition that cut off the outside end of the pool in cold weather was open, and she swam to the far end with strong, even strokes.

'I'm glad you look good when you swim,' he said. 'I hate women who are clumsy in the water. D'you realise that this is the first time we've swum together?'

'As your father might have said, perhaps this is the first of many.'

'He and my mother used to swim naked. They usually locked the doors from the house, but one day they forgot and I saw them. I was only a kid, but I thought then that it looked like fun.'

They played in the pool for fifteen minutes, touching each other, separating, coming together again. Finally, impelled by a single impulse, they emerged and he led her, dripping, into the room which had been his since childhood. Careless of damp sheets, they fell onto the bed and reached for each other.

Feeling the soft flesh of her breast under his cheek, he remembered Loretta's hard, uninviting body, and thought of other women, brief affairs, one-night stands in London. All had been attempts to fulfil a physical need: screwing. With Elena, he made love. There was a vast difference.

At last, her hold loosened and he lay beside her. 'When can we get married?' he said.

'As soon as possible!'

'No doubts now? No guilts?'

'No guilts. There have been doubts, but they were nothing to do with you, and you've cured them.'

'What were they?'

'I have been feeling so dirty. In hospital, I couldn't bear the thought of a man touching me again. I made the Sisters wash me all over two or three times a day.'

'I've never been able to contemplate killing another human being,' he said, 'but I'd make an exception for those three, if I could get my hands on them.'

'Four, not three.'

'Max said three.'

'There was a fourth. A Spaniard.'

'Did you tell the police about him?'

'I didn't see the police. Sister Magdalena told me that Max had given them all the details and he had insisted that I shouldn't be questioned.'

'How was it that he thought there were only three of them?'

'He probably didn't see the fourth. He was only a shadow, standing back under the trees. But he came out and kicked Max and I saw his feet. He was wearing *alpagatas* and I have an impression of someone saying, in bad English, "Not her! Not the lady. Only him." But, of course, they took no notice.'

'We must pass this on to the *guardia*.'

'No, Paul! I couldn't go through it all again. Please! It's over. I could never identify him. Let's change the subject.'

'One moment: those doubts? Not wanting to be touched by a man?'

'Couldn't you tell? Now it's as though the other was just a nightmare. You and I are real.'

They went up to the balcony, where padded loungers were set facing the sea. They stood for a moment, looking at the view.

'For years Max wouldn't come out here.' he said. 'This is where we watched the accident that killed my mother. It changed things between us. But I've a feeling that after all these years, they're beginning to change back. I've been learning a good deal about him since I've been here. And about myself.'

'I think you and I have a lot to learn about each other, too.'

She stretched out on a lounger. He pushed another beside it so he could hold her hand.

'I hope you understand now why I got in touch with your father before you,' she said.

'If I had been attached to another woman, what would you have done?'

'Gone back to California, and concentrated on running the wine-business.'

'I'd forgotten you were an heiress. It doesn't mean that you'll have to live in America, does it? I mean . . . hell, I'll even go there with you if I have to, but . . .'

She interrupted. 'I worked all this out before I left. I've had offers for the vineyards. I decided that if you were still free, and still wanted me, I would sell up and come to you in England.'

He kissed her. 'How's your father going to react?'

'It won't be easy for him to accept. The only thing that might influence him is realising that if he doesn't, he is going to lose me altogether.'

The next morning the telephone rang when he was in the office with Max, going over accounts, filling in the briefer reports he had made in the hospital.

Max handed him the receiver. 'Elena.'

He had not asked questions about the progress of their relationship and Paul's only reference to it had been the previous evening, when he had apologised for his misinterpretation of the facts. Max had laughed, and said, 'Forget it. It's bloody flattering when a man of sixty finds he's regarded as a rival by his son, especially with a woman as gorgeous as Elena Ansaldo.'

Now, as Paul took the telephone, he tactfully wheeled himself out of the room.

Her voice was scarcely more than a whisper. 'Oh, darling, it's going to be harder than I thought! I told him last night, and he said he would rather die than allow Max Raven's son into our family.'

'Let me come and see him.'

'No! Not yet. I must give him time to get used to the idea

Paul, he said that all the bad luck he has ever had was caused by your father.'

'For God's sake! If it hadn't been for Max in Berlin at the end of the war, he might not have got back to Spain for years.'

'I don't know that story, but it doesn't matter now. I can't even let them know I'm calling you. He actually threatened to lock me in my room.'

'Can we meet today?'

'I've told him that I'm not a naughty child and I intend to see you as often as possible.'

He hung up. Uneasily, he remembered that Rafael had blackmailed her into marrying Alex Bellini by threatening suicide. Was it conceivable that this time he could prevent her from marrying by the same means?'

Later in the morning, he drove Max along the coast to the current building site, where an apartment block was almost completed. There, Max announced to the work-force that anyone who could prove he had been forced to pay Machado in order to get a job, would be recompensed.

In his office again, he called London and arranged to bring out an independent architect and a surveyor to inspect every property. If there was even a hint that inferior materials had been used, repairs were to be made instantly.

'What are you going to do about the Campo?' Paul said. 'Zimmy thinks you should announce pretty soon that you're not going to develop it or the Azanos are likely to cause trouble. Will you tell them about Machado and León?'

'I must. I hope I can persuade them that I knew nothing about it. There are a few things I need to think about first, but I'll call a meeting with some of the villagers here next week, and we'll try to thrash out the whole business.'

By lunch-time, he was looking tired, but his energy was unimpaired.

'If this is what you're like when you're just out of hospital, I'd hate to be around when you're fit,' Paul remarked.

'I'm doing what I enjoy most.' He wheeled his chair around the desk. 'Let's have a drink on the terrace.'

Hearing the movement, Marian came in. 'Max, you'll wear yourself out!'

'Nonsense! I need to catch up with who's staying. Come and join us.'

'I'll be with you in a few moments.' She sighed and said to Paul. 'I've been working for him for six years. I haven't won an argument yet.'

When she had gone, Paul looked after her and said, 'Have you ever thought . . .?'

'An occasional passing fancy. But she's the best secretary I've ever had, and I'm not going to upset that apple-cart.'

They made a royal progress to his table on the swimming-pool terrace. Within seconds, they were surrounded. Handsome, smiling, he embraced the women, shook hands with the men. Many of them pulled up chairs and the circle expanded. Without being asked, the waiters, who seemed equally pleased to see him, brought trays of drinks which would not appear on anyone's tab.

But even his strength was giving out after half an hour amid the crowd, and Marian, seeing the tired lines deepening in his face, announced firmly that it was time for lunch.

As they returned to the suite, she said, 'This afternoon you're going to rest for at least two hours.'

He looked at her affectionately. 'I couldn't do without you, you know.'

She turned away and only Paul saw her normal controlled expression replaced by naked longing. Alas, poor Marian. But he wondered whether, when Max had lived alone for a while, he might not change his mind about the advantages of an efficient secretary over a wife. He hadn't mentioned Loretta and to all appearances, she might never have existed. Poor Loretta, too.

For lunch, Marian had ordered a pot of Beluga caviare and slices of thin toast. She left them together, saying she had work to do, and Max insisted on opening another bottle of champagne.

'Time I left,' Paul said, spooning about twenty pounds sterling worth of greyish eggs onto his toast. 'I could start getting used to the good life.'

To his surprise, his father said, 'Yes, we've kept you too long. You need to get back to your own work.'

'What's this? No more arguments?'

'When you're lying in a hospital bed, there isn't a lot to do, so you think. And bloody uncomfortable it can be. Your past mistakes rise up to clout you.'

'Hey, you're not going soft on me?'

'Not at all. I'm not apologising for the mistakes, either. They're past. But you've made a name for yourself in England. I have to admit, I'm bloody proud of you.'

Paul felt an uncomfortable lump rise in his throat. 'Shit, you'll have me in tears. Thanks, anyway. But Alan's managing pretty well, I needn't go for a while yet.'

'Make it a holiday then. I'm feeling fine. Sanchez says that if I take things easy, I'll last indefinitely.'

'If this morning's your way of taking things easy, indefinitely isn't likely to be too long.'

'Special occasion.'

'We've celebrated your home-coming already.'

'This is because I've decided to sell off the hotels and apartments.'

Paul stared at him. 'That *is* a surprise! Who to?'

'Dan wants them. He's had enough of Hollywood. He plans to retire here – I wouldn't be surprised if Zimmy was one of the attractions – but he says he'd go crazy without something to do. We'd talked casually before about a partnership, but now he's offered to buy Raven Enterprises outright. We discussed it late last night.'

'Does he know anything about running a property business?'

'He's a quick learner, and I'll be on hand if he needs help.'

'What about the Club?'

'I'm keeping that. It'll be like the early days, before we expanded.' He hesitated. 'I've realised that without Machado it wouldn't be easy to run the rest of the business. He was one of my mistakes, but he was efficient and over the years I've left more and more of the donkey-work to him. I'm not sure I could manage it by myself and I don't want to import anyone else.'

'You won't mind losing what you've built up?'

'Hell, no. I've *done* it. Even without the Club, I've made enough money to last for the rest of my life and have something over. Now you know that you're not going to be pressured to stay, will you come back for the occasional holiday?'

Paul looked at him with an affection he had not felt since he was a child. 'Of course I . . .' He corrected himself. 'Of course we will.'

He took Max at his word, and he and Elena spent blissful days together, driving in the hills, making love, swimming, or simply lying in contented silence on the balcony of the house, looking out to sea. Their happiness was only marred by Rafael's continued hostility. She reported that he and Doña Maria avoided speaking to her unless it was absolutely necessary, and he spent as much time as possible out of the house, riding, or undertaking unnecessary errands in Malaga.

When he was home, she found the silent meals under their accusing eyes difficult to endure.

Paul argued that she should move in with him altogether, but she refused. 'I couldn't do that to him,' she said. 'As it is, at least he can pretend that I remain a virtuous widow, even if I'm engaged to the son of his enemy.'

Max sent messengers into the village to invite a representative few to whom he wanted to talk: his former gardener, Eduardo Azano, and his nephew, Jesús, who must be told where the blame for his brothers' deaths lay; two or three members of the older generation whom Zimmy had named as surviving family of boys who had died on the Campo; Zimmy herself, and José, the bar-owner, as an efficient disseminator of news throughout the village.

A few days before the meeting, he asked Paul to go to the airport, as his representative, and pick up a guest who was arriving on the shuttle.

'Sure. Must be someone special to get this personal treatment. Who is it?'

'A friend. You'll be recognised.'

Paul's heart sank. It had to be a woman: Max, unrepentent

about the trouble his reputation had just caused, up to his old tricks.

But it was Loretta. Slim and chic, her shining hair folded into a French roll at the back of her head, her make-up perfect, her pale pink, pleated skirt without a crease, she greeted Paul with a kiss.

Dazed, he said, 'I thought you'd gone for good.'

She laughed. 'I changed my mind after he wrote to me.'

'He wrote? My God, he's a secretive bastard! How did he know where you were?'

'In the note I left, I said I'd stay in Paris for a few weeks. I thought . . . just in case he might want me back. He knew I'd be at the Georges Cinq.'

He opened the car door for her. 'When did he write?'

'After he'd realised what we all thought about him and Elena. He actually had the nerve to say he was ashamed of me for having imagined he'd have an affair with her.'

'Elena said the same thing, about him.'

'So we have to believe them, don't we? Oh, Paulie, it's good to be back.'

'What about Palm Beach and the superannuated millionaires?'

'The other old ladies can have them.'

'Don't expect him to have changed, Retta.'

'I don't. But I've decided I don't care. He wanted me back enough to make an effort. He needn't have bothered, and he'd have been free. So it's back to square one: I'll go on hating his other women, and he'll go on being irritated with me because I fuss about my looks and I'm always late. But maybe we'd both rather have it that way than live apart.'

The only person who did not seem wholly happy to see her back was Marian, and Paul watched with sympathy and admiration the way she managed to hide her despair at the final dashing of her hopes.

The next couple of days became a holiday for four, with Max and Loretta enjoying a second honeymoon. She said privately to Paul, 'It mightn't last for ever, but it was worth going away for.' She took her place at his side in the Club, helped him with the exercises he was doing to strengthen his leg, took over from Marian as watch-dog to make sure he did not tire himself, limiting his visitors, of whom one of the first was Esteban.

She stayed with him in the suite at the Club and Paul was grateful for the opportunity to be alone at the house with Elena, who reported no relief from the silent hostility of her father and grandmother. 'They speak to me occasionally now,' she said, 'But I don't dare to mention you. The last time I did, my father left the room.'

'Have you told them we're leaving for England soon?'

'Yes. It was as though they were deaf. They didn't say a word. My father spends hours out riding every day. I'm sure it's just to get away from the house while I'm there.'

'I should go to him . . .'

'It wouldn't do any good. He wouldn't see you. Oh, Paul, he is such an unhappy man. All his life, things have gone wrong for him, and the worst thing is that, although he says your father was responsible for many of them, he really knows he has only himself to blame.'

'You're not going to let this affect us, are you?' It was a question which had been nagging at him.

'No! I married Alex because of him. I'm dreadfully sorry for him, but I'm not going to allow him to spoil this. We leave as we planned.'

There was no uncertainty in her expression. The last shadows lifted from his mind.

For all the *guardia* could discover, Manolo Machado might have disappeared from the face of the earth. They reported to Max that his description had been circulated throughout Andalusia, as wanted for questioning about his part in the deaths of the Azano brothers and Rodrigo León, but he had not been sighted.

'He's got money. He's probably in Tangiers by now,' Max told Paul. 'In a way, I'm not sorry. We came a long way together and I've more than one reason to be grateful to him.' He paused. 'You know I had a daughter by my first wife?'

'Yes.'

'There was a time when we thought she'd been kidnapped by gypsies. A few of them had been around the village. We found them – they didn't have the child – but an odd thing happened. With almost no provocation, Manolo attacked one old man. Much later, he told me how he'd never got over what the gypsies had done to his mother, deserting her in San Felipe when she was about to give birth. The old chap, we'd been told, had been here before and it occurred to Manolo – it did to me, too, in fact – that he might have been one of the group. Maybe even his father. He said he would have killed him if the police hadn't dragged him off.' He stopped, then added reflectively, 'Manolo found Jennifer with Titi. Haven't heard of her for years. I often wonder what happened to her. She'd be in her thirties now. Christ, I might even be a grandfather!'

At five o'clock on the day Max had scheduled the meeting, Eduardo and Jesús Azano arrived first, followed by an elderly man and a woman, whom Paul recognised as having been at the Campo when the skeletons were found. They were clearly antagonistic. Eduardo was nervous and ill-at-ease, Jesús sullen. None of them offered to shake hands. Zimmy arrived with José a few minutes later.

Max had rested during the afternoon and was sitting behind his desk, in his wheelchair. Apart from a slight twist to the left side of his mouth and a dark patch where his face had been bruised, there was no other sign of his disability. The strength of his personality was undimmed.

Listening to his flawless, unaccented Spanish, laced with colloquialisms as he greeted the visitors, Paul realised that his own use of the language had become over-careful and pedantic through disuse. Although he had been born in Spain, Max was more a part of the country than he would ever be.

He leant against the wall, watching as everyone settled. Zimmy was the only one wholly at ease, her bright eyes observing every movement.

Max had just begun to speak when there was an unexpected interruption.

They all turned to the French windows, where Titi was

tapping eagerly. Paul opened them and he darted in, gripping his imaginary handle-bars, carrying his inevitable package.

He went straight to Max and they embraced. There were tears in the little man's eyes. 'Gone away,' he stammered. The smooth skin, which Paul had thought unchanged when they had first met in the Campo, had fallen into lines of distress, and it was as though a layer had been stripped off, revealing the sixty-year-old face that lay beneath it.

Max patted his arm. 'It's okay, I'm back now. You all right?'

Titi nodded, and, oblivious of anyone else, uttered a brief, muddled stream of words to the effect that the weather had been nice and a lady had bought him a little grey burro-doll with a straw hat on its head, and the Senorita Pepita had made him a cake.

He stopped talking as suddenly as he had begun, and Max said, 'Off you go, now. And see that you get something to eat. We'll talk some more later.'

Titi nodded, and settled his package. His face lifted as he beamed at everyone impartially, and he ran off.

Max began again. 'I've asked you to come here because there are a few things I want to get straight. Let's start with the matter of the Campo Negro. It belongs to me now, but as soon as it can be arranged, I propose to hand it over to the village. I suggest that you, Eduardo, and perhaps your friends here, should form a committee to decide what to do with it. I will also underwrite the cost of a memorial to the men whose bodies were found there.'

Paul enjoyed the looks on their faces. José was nodding triumphantly, with a smug, I-told-you-so expression. Eduardo and the elderly couple appeared to be utterly confounded. Only Jesús remained implacably hostile.

Max gave them no time to recover. Looking directly at Jesús, he said, 'I understand there are some people who are encouraging others to believe that I was responsible for the accident that caused your brothers' deaths. In the sense that I employed and trusted Manolo Machado, I was. But the order that caused León to save money by skimping on building materials did not come from me. I knew nothing about it, nor about Machado's other activities. He has now left San Felipe . . .'

At that moment, they heard – and felt – the explosion.

Afterwards, Paul had the impression that it had been followed by a few seconds of total silence, before the roaring of the fire, and the screams.

He raced into the lobby. People were shouting and pushing in an effort to escape billowing clouds of smoke that were issuing from the direction of the kitchens. Gas cylinders were exploding like bombs. He fought his way through the panic-stricken crowd, and reached the entrance to the American restaurant. It was ablaze. A waiter, his white jacket on fire, fell through the service door, screaming. Paul drenched him with the contents of a bottle of mineral water, then dragged him towards the lobby where waiting hands supported him. He glanced up. The hands belonged to Jesús Azano.

He turned back. It was clear that no one else from the kitchens was going to get through the flames. Suddenly the fire leapt towards him, driven by a sudden rush of air. His shirt caught alight. He ran towards the door, into a jet of water from a hose, and the flame was doused.

The fire had started to burn through the inside wall that separated Max's suite from the public rooms. He looked in. The office was empty.

The Club's guests had gathered near the pool. Several women were hysterical. A party of men, including Dan, José and members of the staff, had turned garden hoses onto the building.

'Where's Max?' he shouted to Dan.

'Last I saw, he was going towards the kitchens.'

A small rear courtyard, which was surrounded by the kitchens and a series of utility-rooms, was an inferno of reflected heat.

Paul paused to soak his head under a garden tap. The kitchens were a solid sheet of flame and he heard crashes as ceilings collapsed.

His eyes caught a movement beyond the open door of a large store-room. Feeling the heat searing his eye-balls, he took a deep breath, held it, and went in.

The room was used to store furniture. A pile of small gilt chairs in one corner was burning, shelves around the walls had collapsed. An old table was smouldering, its varnish sending out clouds of smoke.

At the back of the room, he saw the wheelchair on its side and, on the floor beside it, Max and Titi. Max was trying to reach the chair, but he was hampered by Titi, whose arms were wrapped around his neck.

Paul dived through the flames. Sparks fell on his face, burnt the hairs on the back of his hands. He tried to pull Titi away, but his arms only tightened. It was as though he and Max had been vulcanised together by the heat.

Max had managed to reach a kneeling position. Paul righted the chair, grasped him under the arms, heaved the two of them into it and set it in line with the door, over which a curtain of flames now stretched. He gave it a violent shove. It crashed through the fire and he flung himself after it.

Max was gasping, his skin like paper. Titi had released him, slipped to the ground and was sitting up. He was rigid with terror, making small mewing sounds like an injured kitten.

Dan ran towards them. 'Christ, where was he?'

As Paul nodded towards the store-room, its door-frame collapsed, bringing down a shower of plaster and wooden beams which blocked the entrance.

Dan grasped the wheelchair, but before he could move it, Max said, 'Where's Titi?'

Titi had gone.

Paul said, 'From what I could see, he wasn't hurt, just frightened.'

When they reached open ground, they stopped to gulp in fresh air. He looked down at his father. Great blisters were rising on his palms. His thick dark hair, its silver streaks blackened by soot, was singed. There were rents in his shirt where it had been burned through, showing reddened patches of skin.

'What the hell were you doing in there?' Dan said.

'Wondered whether anyone might be trapped in the kitchens.' His voice was hoarse from the smoke. 'The store room door was open and I saw Titi huddled on the floor

Flames all round him. I shouted, but he wouldn't move. I had to go in and fetch him. Tried to walk, but my bloody leg gave way. The ramps we use for heavy deliveries were outside, so I got in on the wheelchair. Poor little sod . . . when he saw me, he jumped at me and put his arms around my neck like a baby. That made the chair tip over and I couldn't get up because he was strangling me.' He looked up at Paul. 'And then, thank God, you arrived.'

It was nearly midnight when they gathered in the house. The fire was out, but coals still glowed in the Club's devastated wing.

Max had requested the villa tenants to allow their extra rooms to be taken over for those whose suites in the main block had been soaked with foam and water. Some had lost all their belongings and he had given them *carte blanche* to choose whatever they needed from the boutiques, at his expense.

By the time he, Paul and Dan had returned to the terrace, San Felipe's two fire-engines had arrived and the blaze had been contained. The full extent of the disaster was not realised for some hours, when the bodies of four members of the kitchen staff were found among the ruins. Paul was reminded of the atmosphere after his mother's death as those who had escaped silently watched them being removed.

Realising that occupation was the required anodyne, he ordered the staff to take over the kitchen in the house, organise fresh supplies from the village and prepare an evening meal for the guests.

Dr Sanchez and a team of nurses were summoned from the hospital to treat burns and cases of shock. When everyone else had been dealt with, he examined Max, shook his head in amazement and remarked: 'You have the constitution of a Miura bull. That little stroke must have crept up on you unawares.'

With this encouragement, Max refused to go to bed and insisted on being driven into the village to comfort the families of the dead men. On the way home he said, with the first trace of weariness he had shown, that the experience had been worse than being trapped in the store-room.

'What was Titi doing in there?' Paul said.

'He's always used it as his private dining-room. He won't eat when there are people around, so when they give him anything in the kitchen, he takes it there. I guess that saved his life.'

They found Dan, Marian, Zimmy and Elena awaiting them at the house. Elena had arrived soon after the explosion, had searched frantically for Paul and been in tears when he reappeared.

From the balcony, they could see winking torches, the shadows of men moving among the ruins. The Club was swarming with police who had been drafted in from Malaga to confirm the origin of the fire, which they were almost certain had been a bomb placed in the kitchens.

'Has anyone seen Titi?' Max said. Nobody had. He shrugged. 'He went off under his own steam, so there can't be much physically wrong.'

Paul was pouring night-caps for everyone when they heard the police sirens.

A waiter came to tell Max there were two *guardia* waiting to see him.

They were standing stiffly at the top of the stairs, their shiny black hats tucked under their arms, but relaxed when he handed them each a drink.

When he returned, he said bleakly: 'It was what we've been afraid of. The *guardia* had a telephone call from ETA claiming responsibility for a bomb. They said it was a warning to tourists that until the Basque Separatists achieve independence, Spain will be no place for foreigners. Shit! Four men dead and I'll lay you a bet that the bastards who killed them will never be identified.'

'Who could have set the bomb?' Paul said. 'It isn't easy for strangers to get into this place, and certainly not into the kitchens without being seen.'

'They've interviewed the staff. No one knows a damn thing.'

A pervading exhaustion seemed to overtake everyone at the same time, as they each tried to come to terms with the tragedy. There seemed to be nothing more to say.

After a moment, Dan stood up and said he would drive Zimmy and Elena home. They nodded silently.

Paul and Elena went downstairs ahead of the rest. 'See you tomorrow?' he said.

'Of course. And perhaps by then Papa will be calmer. He was very angry when I came out after we heard the explosion. He said it was nothing to do with us. Paul, will this change our plans?'

'Maybe I'll have to stay here a little longer. I suppose it'll depend on how Max is tomorrow, after the adrenalin's stopped flowing, and what he wants to do about the Club.' He drew her into a dark corner and kissed her.

'Another few days, and there'll be no more good-byes,' she murmured.

Max and Loretta were still on the balcony. When Paul joined them, Max said: 'Are you thinking the same as I am?'

'Titi?'

'Had to be. He had a parcel. He's happy to carry anything for anybody. The terrorists simply handed it to him and told him to deliver it. He left it on a table in the kitchen. There are dozens of deliveries during the day and nobody bothered to check the package.'

'What do we do now?'

'Hope that nobody else thinks the same as we do. Christ, can you imagine what effect it would have on Titi if he were arrested? And for something he knew nothing about! It'd kill him.'

The next morning, Paul found him sitting on the balcony holding a mug of coffee and looking over the devastation of the Club. Joining him, he said, 'God, what a mess!'

'It's not as bad as it appears. Only one wing's gone. I'm going to close up for six months and rebuild.'

Paul looked at him in amazed admiration. 'You don't seem too affected by what happened. I think you thrive on trouble.'

'I'm upset that four men died, and angry with the unthinking, selfish shits who caused their deaths. But for the rest of us, life goes on. Nearly a hundred people depend on me for their livelihoods. If I sit around weeping it won't do them any good.'

A phrase Paul had heard when he was a child surfaced in his memory: 'Don't let the bastards grind you down?'

'Right.' Max levered himself out of the chair and tested his weaker leg. 'Damn, it still feels like rubber. I'm sick of that chair. Let's get moving. I want you to check on Titi. Bring him back here . . .' He stopped. 'No. He won't come to the house. Take him to the Club. I have to go down there, anyway. Sanchez said he'd be up to see me during the morning, and I'd like him to have a look at Titi as well.'

Titi's cupboard-in-the-wall was empty, the door closed, so Paul followed the route he had taken when he had searched for Manolo, driving through the streets and the plaza, along the promenade, asking in shops and bars. He questioned Zimmy, searched the beaches, and the Campo Negro, where the bulldozer scars were already being filled in. No one had seen him.

The Club was like a bee-hive when he got back. A number of guests were leaving, and their luggage was being packed into a van. The fleet of Cadillacs was drawn up outside the entrance. Hardier souls, who had decided to brave the inconvenience and stay on, were wandering around the devastated wing, congratulating each other on their escapes. Several couples were making their way purposefully to the arcade of shops to replenish their wardrobes. There was still a police presence and the Club's guards were on hand to make sure no-one went too close to the ruins.

Max was moving rapidly in his chair, directing an army of workers. Marian was at his side, note-book in hand. Some rooms were to be transformed into temporary kitchens and dining-rooms, and already a van-load of new equipment had arrived from Malaga.

When Paul reported that he had been unable to trace Titi, he looked worried. 'I wish we'd gone after him last night, but there was so much else to do. He's got to be found.'

'I didn't know where else to look. Nobody seems to have seen him after he disappeared from here. I'll go out again, if you like.'

'I'll come with you. I've had an idea . . .' He stopped as yet another police car pulled up beside them.

One of the *guardia* who had broken the news about ETA saluted, and said: 'We have further news for you, Senor. It seems that our call last night was a hoax.'

Max's eyebrows shot up. 'A hoax?'

'Did you see the stop-press paragraph in today's *Sur*?'

'I've had no time to read the papers.'

The *guardia* handed him a cutting, and he read it aloud. ' "ETA terrorists tonight claimed responsibility for placing a bomb which partly destroyed the exclusive San Felipe Club, and killed four members of the staff." ' He looked up. 'So?'

'We have had a report from Malaga of another telephone call. It was from a person claiming to be the leader of ETA in Andalusia. Our colleagues said he was very angry, and denied that ETA had been involved.'

'You believe that?'

'*Si*. The terrorists are always ready to claim genuine responsibility, but they have been lying low since the public outcry after the Barcelona incident.'

'I remember. A dozen or more innocent people killed,' Max said grimly.

'And as a result, the ETA cell there virtually wiped out by a series of *guardia* raids.' He shrugged. 'Of course this is no more than a temporary halt in their activities, but it seems we will have to look elsewhere for *your* bomber.'

When he had gone, promising that investigations would proceed with vigour, Max and Paul looked at each other.

'Who the hell could it have been?' Paul said.

'Have you any ideas?'

'Jesús Azano? He's made most of the trouble over the past few months.'

'He'd hardly set a bomb at a time when he'd be here himself. Try again.'

Paul took a deep breath. 'Manolo.'

'It could have been. He knows the routine here. He knows Titi.'

'Will you tell the *guardia*?'

'I want to make sure first. Then I will. I'm finished being sorry for Manolo. Come on, let's find Titi.'

* * *

Fifteen minutes later, they were bumping over a rough track that wound into the hills.

'What makes you think he'd come out here?' Paul said, as he spun the wheel to avoid a rut.

'There's an old hut – or there was, it's probably fallen down by now – where he went after his father was killed. He's just had another bad shock, so it occurred to me that he might have run there instinctively.'

They reached the brow of a hill and looked down into an overgrown valley, studded with big grey rocks. All that remained of the hut was a pile of collapsed timbers. The umbrella-pine against which it had leant had been uprooted by wind and its naked branches lay over the mound, forming a kind of canopy.

'Want me to drive down?' Paul said dubiously.

'The car might frighten him. We'll walk.'

'You can't . . .'

But Max was already on his way, leaning on his stick, calling softly, 'Titi! *Hola,* Titi! It's me!' Nothing stirred. Paul caught up with him and took his arm. 'I feel as though I've gone back half a century,' he muttered. 'Last time he was hiding by that big rock.'

They went towards it, but he was not there, and they were turning away when Paul saw a small grey object lying in the undergrowth. He picked it up. It was a toy donkey with long grey ears sticking up through a tiny straw hat decorated with flowers.

'He's been here,' Max said. 'He said yesterday that some woman had given him a burro-doll.'

'Think he's hiding from us?'

'He's gone. I'm sure he'd have answered when he saw me.'

'So where do we go now?'

'Zimmy's. She knows his haunts.'

She was on her doorstep. When she saw the car, she beckoned urgently.

'I saw him a few minutes ago, making for the beach,' she called. 'Look among those big rocks at the far end, below the headland. He likes to sit there and watch the waves.'

Paul drove onto the low headland. He left Max sitting in the car and walked to the top of a rough flight of steps which led to the beach. He had a panoramic view over the sea, and down onto rocks, which stood like houses in a petrified village, with narrow streets of sand running between them. This was the wilder part of the beach, unsafe for bathing because sharp, submerged rocks ran out into the sea. The sun-worshippers and swimmers were at the other end, where the sand sloped gently into calm water.

Rafael Ansaldo was riding at the water's edge. On horseback, he looked a different man, Paul thought. No longer the bitter, envious, petty dictator, but a free spirit, sitting his saddle easily. The horse's mane and tail were flying back as it pounded towards the headland.

Then he saw Titi, squatting in a narrow defile between the rocks, watching Rafael.

'He's there!' he told Max. 'I'll go down.'

'Take it easy. Don't frighten him.'

The horse was only a few feet from the rocks when Rafael, in a superb display of horsemanship, put it into a tight turn, like a polo-pony, easily maintaining his balance as he guided it into a zig-zag, using the rocks as an obstacle course.

Paul was on his way down the slope when Titi darted out of his shelter, straight under the horse's head, and grasped one of Rafael's stirrups. Startled, the animal reared and pawed the air. Rafael was caught unawares. He slipped sideways, clawed at the saddle, then fell. His left foot slid through the stirrup and was caught fast. His head crashed against a rock. The horse, thoroughly frightened, turned and raced in a wide circle, hauling him beside it.

It had taken no more than seconds, but later, with every detail etched on his mind's eye, Paul felt as though he had seen it in slow motion. He leaped down onto the sand. The horse, desperately trying to rid itself of the weight that was like a dragging anchor, galloped towards him. Seeing the possibility of help, it slowed and stood still, trembling. He grabbed the bridle and moved to where Rafael was lying. The foot was still caught and his body, with its spread legs and the trunk flat on the sand, was like a Y that had fallen on its side.

Paul looked at the blood that had turned his face into a scarlet mask, and the angle of his head to the spine, and had no doubt that he was dead.

People ran towards them.

A young English tourist was the first to arrive. 'I saw it!' he gasped. 'Jesus, he didn't have a chance!'

As he was releasing Rafael's foot from the stirrup, he heard other voices: 'Bloody horses! Like temperamental women . . . you never know what'll upset them.'

'Anything could have frightened it . . .'

The chorus was taken up: 'A scuttling crab . . .' 'A wave breaking too close . . .' 'A stray dog . . .' 'A child . . .'

The first arrival said importantly, 'There were no kids about. I saw everything. Just happened, out of the blue.'

José had run from his bar and was pushing through the crowd. In Spanish, Paul called, 'Telephone the hospital for an ambulance! Senor Rafael's been injured!'

A middle-aged woman wearing the British tourist's uniform of floral cotton dress and flat white sandals, a cardigan over her arm, came to his side. 'I'm a nurse . . . if there's anything I can do?'

'I think it's too late.'

She knelt on the sand. After a moment, she nodded.

He stood up and looked around. The crowd had fallen silent, and one or two people had turned away, sickened.

Titi was nowhere to be seen.

'But why did he do it?' Max said. 'Titi's always avoided Rafael. I don't think they've spoken for years. Even when we were kids, he kept out of his way.'

He was in bed, having been ordered there to rest, despite his vigorous protests, by Dr Sanchez, who had come to the house after he had pronounced Rafael dead on arrival at the hospital.

Paul was sitting beside the bed, having broken the news to Elena. He had driven her to the hospital, then taken her home, weeping. She had asked him to leave, saying she would prefer to be alone when she told Doña Maria.

'I didn't get the impression that he was aggressive,' he said.

'It was more as though he wanted to talk to Rafael. Did you see where he went?'

Max shook his head. 'He didn't pass the car. You're sure no one else saw him?'

'Someone would have said something. The horse was behind one of the rocks when it happened. He was probably hidden. Oh, Christ, is this another secret we have to keep?'

'It was an accident. I want to talk to him before we make up our minds what to do. There's still the question of Machado.'

'D'you think you'll get any sense out of him?'

'I can sometimes. You have to know how to sort out his ramblings. We'll wait until he turns up. Poor, bloody Rafael. Riding was the one thing he was good at. Ironic, isn't it?'

Paul said, 'It crossed my mind when I was watching him that it was the first time I'd ever seen him enjoying himself.'

Feeling that he was being forced to see too much of the *guardia*, Paul made a statement about his view of what had happened. Several of the people who had been on the beach also did so and there was no suggestion that it had been anything but an unfortunate accident, caused by a temperamental horse.

He spent the rest of the day helping Marian at the Club. Elena telephoned during the afternoon, to say that she did not want to leave Doña Maria, who had taken the news with unexpected courage, and had insisted on making the funeral arrangements herself.

Later, when her grandmother had gone to bed, she slipped out and they had a scratch meal together in the Club's temporary restaurant, talking little.

It was late when he went back to the house. As he began to let down after the day's tensions, he realised that he was exhausted, but at the same time too restless to sleep. He poured himself a Scotch and wandered outside. The garden was moonlit and silent, and his mind went back over the past hectic days, from the surfacing of a fifty-year-old tragedy, to the bombing of the Club and Rafael's equally tragic death. He could pretend no real sorrow, because he had never liked the man, but his heart ached for Elena, who had genuinely loved her father, despite his shortcomings.

He strolled over the route he had taken on his first night, up towards the *finca*. A warm breeze set up a susurration in the trees and as he reached the vine-covered walls he saw the leaves stirring and heard a faint rustling that could have been a small animal. It stopped, started again, closer to him, and then came an unmistakably human sigh. For a moment, he stood still, then he moved towards what had once been the *finca's* doorway. Tendrils of vine brushed his face and hair like searching fingers. It was pitch dark and if anything moved, he could not see it.

His heart almost stopped as he felt a hand clasp his own.

He took a step backwards, spilling his drink. Titi was looking up at him, and he heard him whisper, 'Max?'

'No. It's Paul. You frightened the life out of me! What are you doing here?'

'Looking for . . .' He stopped.

'For what?'

'Looking for Max and the Senor and Senora.'

'What Senor and Senora? Max is down at the house.' He took the little man's hand. 'Come with me. He wants to see you.'

'See Max.'

Paul left him in the sitting-room, where he sat on a sofa, hands clasped in his lap, his feet not reaching the floor.

Max insisted on getting up, despite Loretta's protests.

As he helped him down the stairs, Paul said, 'He was in the *finca*.'

'Christ, he hasn't been there since his father died! He's terrified of the place.'

'He said he was looking for you and the Senor and Senora.'

'My father and mother! He was looking for *them*?'

Titi hadn't moved, and Max sat on the sofa beside him.

'Why did you want to see the Senor and Senora?' he said gently.

Titi looked at Paul, and said nothing.

'You'd better go,' Max said. 'He'll talk if we're by ourselves.'

* * *

It was an hour before Paul heard him call.

There were traces of tears in Titi's eyes, which still retained the innocence of a little boy.

Max was looking as though he had received a severe shock, but he said quietly, 'Take him to the back bedroom. He'll sleep here tonight.'

In the room, Titi took off his canvas shoes, lay on the bed and closed his eyes like an obedient child.

When Paul returned, his father said, 'I can hardly believe this! His mind's gone back in time. He's nine years old again! The shock of the explosion and the fire must have caused it. He's been telling me about the night my parents died, as though it was yesterday. They weren't killed in the fire. They were shot!' The frown lines deepened between his eyes. 'He was rambling, and it took me a while to realise that he wasn't talking about *now*, but fifty years ago.'

'Could you make sense out of it?'

'I'm trying. You know that he'd been with his father, Jaime, and the Republican guerillas in the hills. While they were in hiding, he'd often acted as their messenger, taking letters to their families or collecting supplies. He says that on the evening they were due to leave San Felipe, Esteban had given him a note to take to Zimmy, asking her to look after him until Jaime came back.

'I already knew, because Zimmy and Esteban told me once when we were discussing his escape, that she never received it. They've always assumed that he must have lost it.

'But it seems that on the way to her house he met Rafael, on horse-back. Don Luis was a fanatic anti-Republican and Rafael obviously knew that Titi's father was one of the group his own father hated. Titi had been warned not to talk to anyone, so he tried to run away, but Rafael rode him down, and took his letter away from him.' He was talking slowly, trying to put the story into a logical sequence.

'Titi didn't want to go to Zimmy without the letter, thinking she'd be angry with him for having lost it, and he knew he couldn't go back to the hills, because Jaime had told him he was going away. So he hid in some bushes, and eventually went to sleep.

'In the meantime – I'm guessing this part – Don Luis must have read the letter and realised that Esteban's group was planning to leave that night. His men simply waited for them to come down from the hills. There were only a couple of paths, which were easily covered. We know what happened then.'

'How about Titi?'

'When he woke up, he was confused. Then he heard shots on the Campo. He reached there just in time to see his father and the rest of his friends – apart from Esteban, of course – being murdered. The Nationalists left the bodies where they were and went away. Titi sat beside Jaime, trying to talk to him. He couldn't understand why he wouldn't answer. Eventually, he decided to go to my parents, whom he loved. He found them lying "asleep" on the floor.' A look of pain crossed his face. 'There was blood, and they had "holes" in them.'

'But there was no fire?'

'That started after he got there. He said there was another big bang; the oil-lamp, which was alight, jumped off the table – I remember that there were wood-shavings all over the place – and fire broke out. It sounds as though someone had shot through the window. He managed to get away, but it seems clear that the shocks he'd had caused his mind to shut down, burying the memories, until yesterday. Hearing the explosions, being caught in the fire, must have unlocked the protective mechanism.' He added sadly, 'It would have been better for him if it had stayed locked. He's very upset. I've been trying to tell him it all happened a long time ago, but he thinks it was last night.'

'Were you able to ask him about Manolo, and the bomb?'

'I tried. He knew who Manolo was, of course, because they've both lived here all their lives. But when I asked him about the package he'd delivered, he simply didn't understand what I meant.'

Paul thought for a moment. 'How does all this tie in with what happened on the beach today?'

'You might find this hard to believe: he wanted to ask Rafael to give him back his letter.'

* * *

The day after Rafael's funeral, Max received word that Manolo had been arrested in Algeciras, as he was preparing to board a ship bound for North Africa, on a tip-off from ETA that he had been responsible for the bomb that had been set in the Club.

Infuriated at being blamed for a crime they had not committed, the Basque organisation's local members had conducted their own investigations and had turned up, in a Malaga bar frequented by the underworld, a former terrorist who had been approached by Manolo, and had agreed to provide him with an explosive device.

For once working on the side of the police, ETA had passed on the information, and Manolo had been recognised in Algeciras.

Questioned, his defiance had rapidly collapsed. The charges against him would range from fraud to murder.

After Paul had heard the story from Max, he said, 'Titi?'

'Oh, Manolo tried to implicate him, but it didn't work. I had a word with the police, and his name won't be mentioned.'

'How much did that cost you?'

'You won't see the cops running around in Porsches, but one or two of them might manage a new bicycle.'

Two days later, announcing that he was tired of being a cripple, Max discarded his wheelchair. With a secret smile, Paul watched Marian and Loretta vying with each other to give him support whenever he would permit it.

Work was started on a memorial to the men who had died on the Campo, in the centre of the flat ground that had once been the projected site for a supermarket.

One afternoon, Jesús Azano arrived at the Club unexpectedly, asking to see Max. Neither Paul nor Marian was present at their meeting, but Jesús emerged after half an hour, and they watched the two men shake hands.

When Max joined them in Marian's office, he said, 'We've identified the fourth man.'

She looked blank, and Paul explained the discrepancy between what Elena and Max had seen the night they were attacked.

Max said, 'It was Jesús's son, Carlos. Aged fourteen. He

knew how his family felt about Raven Enterprises. He'd picked up those English louts and they were wandering about the Campo when they saw the Porsche, then Elena and me. Carlos told them who I was and said something to the effect, "Let's get the bastard." Then things got out of hand. The others were more interested in Elena and I became a side-issue. Apparently Carlos kicked me, but then he was so appalled at what was happening to her, that he ran away.

'After the meeting the other day, Jesús decided that maybe there was more virtue in Raven Enterprises than he'd suspected. He disbanded his little group of thugs and he's actually turned vigilante to make sure there's no more violence.

'Last night, it seems that Carlos's conscience got the better of him and he told his father what he'd done. Jesús came to apologise.'

'I hope he's going to be punished!' Marian said.

Max shrugged. 'He was wearing *alpagatas*. The kick probably didn't even leave a bruise. And he didn't go near Elena. I think we can leave it to his father to deal with him.'

Elena was inclined to occasional overflows of tears, and turned to Paul for the comfort he had been longing to give. She had reminded Doña Maria that she would shortly be leaving for England, where she intended to marry. The old woman, her round, yellow face masklike, simply nodded, and refused a suggestion that she might meet her future grandson-in-law.

She announced that she had decided to move as soon as possible from San Felipe to the house on the vineyards near Jerez. Elena told Max and Paul, 'I've given it to her. It's smaller, she won't need so many servants, and she says she only came to San Felipe in the first place because it was her husband's family home. I think she will be happy there.'

'What will you do with the house here?' Max said.

'Sell it. I have no sentimental feelings for it. I hated my childhood there.' She smiled at him. 'I hope that when we come out from England, you will have room for us in your home.'

'I can manage you two and about six kids. Any more might be a crush.'

Paul said, 'Don't put ideas into her head. Two or three will be enough. How will you like being a grandfather?'

'Might be fun.' He glanced at Loretta, who was lying on a sun-bed, as sleek and groomed as a Siamese cat. 'Not sure about being married to a grandmother, though.'

The day before they were due to leave for England, Elena telephoned Paul. Her voice was hesitant: 'A curious thing has happened. My grandmother wants to see you and Max this evening.'

'What for?'

'She won't tell me. She simply said, tell them to be here at seven o'clock. Will Max come?'

'Hang on. I'll ask him.'

Max raised his eyebrows, then nodded. 'Summons from Her Majesty? Certainly I'll go. For no other reason than curiosity. It'll be the first time I've been in that house since just after I arrived here from England after the war.'

Elena met them at the door.

Doña Maria was sitting in the gloomy drawing-room, in a stiff, thronelike chair. She was clad in even deeper black than usual, with black lace over her hair. She had lost weight, Max thought, and the plump face was wizened, but the button eyes were still sharp, and no more friendly than they had been at their original meeting. She didn't ask them to sit down, but after a moment Elena gestured towards chairs.

As he looked around at the heavy furnishings, the dark family portraits on the walls, the crucifixes and religious icons, the maroon velvet hangings, Paul could understand her dislike of the place. It was hard to imagine that laughter was ever heard here.

The old woman's voice was hard, the Spanish consonants lisping through her tongue. Without preamble, she said to Max: 'Before my husband died, he asked me to tell you something when the time was right. I am carrying out his wishes. I have never, myself, felt it was necessary, but now that my son is dead, there is no reason why you should not know. It has to do with the death of your parents . . .'

That night again, Paul thought. The Raven family's dead past, it seemed, was reluctant to bury its dead.

'I already know that they were shot before the fire,' Max's voice was hard.

'Do you? I wonder how . . .? But it doesn't matter. I will go on. I would be a hypocrite if I pretended that I had any fondness for your mother and father. My husband spent too much time with them.

'You will also know that on that same night, the Communists whose bones have now been exhumed from the Campo Negro were captured and executed. Rightly, I believe.'

Paul saw his father's mouth tighten as he watched the implacable old face.

'A little before midnight, my son, who was unable to sleep, heard noises on the other side of the wall. When he looked out of his window, he saw a man standing at the door of the *finca*. It was opened and in the light, he recognised Esteban Jiminez. He knew Luis and his men were hunting the Republicans so he went out to tell them. I was asleep so I knew nothing of this.

'But Luis had gone into the hills to search for Jiminez, the only member of the party who had escaped, and it took Rafael a long time to find him. The men wanted to go to the *finca*, but Luis said that Jiminez would have gone. He ordered them to disband and he came back here.

'He did not know until the next day that two of them had disobeyed him, believing there was a chance that Jiminez might still be at the *finca*. Later, we heard that your mother and father had attempted to stop them from entering. There was a struggle and they were both shot. Luis's men searched the *finca*, and then left.' She stopped and, for the first time, showed signs of tension, as the fat, wrinkled hands clenched in her lap.

Max leant forward and said softly, 'Who were they?'

She brushed the question aside. 'It doesn't matter. They were patriots, and later they were killed in the war.'

'Who started the fire?'

She closed her eyes briefly. 'Rafael stayed on watch at his window after his father had gone to bed. He was . . . excited by what was going on. He told us later that he wanted to be sure Esteban Jiminez did not come back. He heard the shots, and saw our men leave. Then, a little later, he saw someone else go into the *finca*. He fetched his shot-gun, and fired through a window. He must have hit an oil-lamp, because he saw flames. He was too frightened to wake his father. By the next morning the *finca* had been burned.'

'That's what Don Luis wanted you to tell me? To assuage his own conscience?' Max said.

'He was distraught when he discovered your mother and father were dead, but after Rafael told us what he had done, I persuaded him that there was no point in making an issue of it. Rafael hadn't killed them, and the village had decided that the incident on the Campo must be forgotten. Everyone accepted that your parents had died accidentally.'

'It was Titi who went into the *finca*.' Max said. 'Unmistakably a little boy. I wonder who Rafael thought it was?'

She looked at him steadily. 'My son is dead, Senor. There is no point in speculation. My husband spent the rest of his life trying to make it up to you. But he loved our son. Just before he died, he said "If there is ever a day when it cannot affect Rafael, I'd like you to tell Max Raven the truth." '

Nobody spoke, and after a moment, she said bitterly, 'In the end, you have won, haven't you? Rafael and I always resented you, because Luis tried to give you what should have been his. And now your son has Rafael's daughter – and the vineyards.'

'So you did . . .' He stopped.

'I couldn't allow you to deprive Rafael of his rightful inheritance. I'm sure you can understand that.'

Max didn't answer. He stood up, bowed formally, and left the room. Paul and Elena followed.

The airport was crowded with tourists coming and going, but Elena and Paul, with Max, Zimmy, Loretta and Marian were ushered into the V.I.P. lounge, where champagne and canapés were awaiting them.

Just before their flight was called, Paul and his father strolled to the windows. As they looked out at the runway, Max said: 'You're a lucky man. Elena sometimes reminds me of Véronique – and I can give no higher praise.'

'Do you still miss her?'

'Sometimes. But I've been pretty lucky, too, with Retta. That was something I realised in hospital, when I thought I might have lost her.' He raised an eyebrow and smiled ironically. 'Another discovery I made: Age may not wither, but custom eventually does stale the infinite variety. I think I'll try monogamy for a change.'

Wondering whether the visit he had received from Caroline Jarvis after his stroke had influenced his thought, Paul said lightly, 'I hope it won't be too much of a shock to your system.'

'Not mine. It might surprise Loretta, though.'

A few minutes later, he and Elena were aboard their aircraft. As it taxied onto the runway, he looked out of the window and saw, on the viewing roof of the terminal, Max, waving his Cordoban hat, white teeth gleaming, his dark hair ruffled by the breeze, surrounded by three women who adored him.

THE END